The Ghosting of Anne Armstrong

Part of the Goldsmiths Press Practice as Research series

The Goldsmiths Press Practice as Research series celebrates and explores the multiplicity of practice research and the ways in which it is published. The series is committed to pushing the boundaries of doing and disseminating research.

The Ghosting of Anne Armstrong

A Novel

Michael Cawood Green

Goldsmiths
Press

© 2019 Goldsmiths Press
Published in 2019 by Goldsmiths Press
Goldsmiths, University of London, New Cross
London SE14 6NW

Printed and bound by TJ International, UK
Distribution by the MIT Press
Cambridge, Massachusetts, and London, England

A CIP record for this book is available from the British Library

ISBN 978-1-906897-95-6 (hbk)
ISBN 978-1-906897-97-0 (ebk)

www.gold.ac.uk/goldsmiths-press

Goldsmiths
UNIVERSITY OF LONDON

For Cas

One of the most extraordinary cases of witchcraft that has ever been printed. I know of nothing that surpasses it in interest, save the great Lancashire case, which has been re-published by the Chetliam Society, and illustrated with an admirable preface by its learned President, Mr. Crossley.

We are here introduced to a witch-finder ... who tells us her experiences, which are of the most peculiar description. The reader must test her depositions with his own critical acumen. He must draw his own conclusions as to the accuracy of a tale that would run like wildfire through Durham and Northumberland. I know nothing of the result of the affair. I need not say that all the accused persons deny their guilt.

James Raine, ed. 1861. CLXXXVIII. Anne Baites and Others. For Witchcraft. *Depositions in the Castle of York Relating to Offences Committed in the Northern Counties in the Seventeenth Century*, Surtees Society Volume XL: 191 (fn).

When you look at her strange life, you wonder what kind of language you can use to talk about her – through which discipline will you approach her?

Hilary Mantel. 2004. Some girls want out. *London Review of Books* 26 (5) (March): 14–18.

Figure 1 Map of Northumberland, 1672.

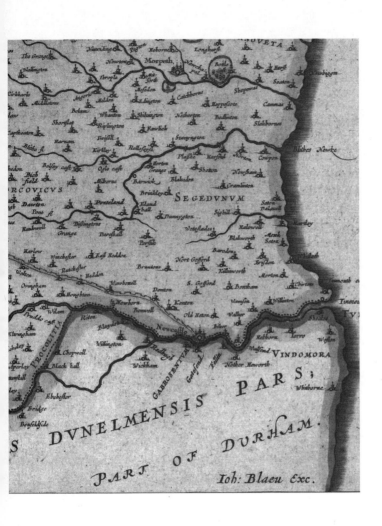

Northumberland: 1673

It had to end this way.

No one came to fetch her, in any form, on this late summer's day, the air hanging heavy in a grey haze after months of rain and wind. But she knows they will all be waiting for her at Thomas Errington's house, the Riding House.

Much as she hates the winters, she fears the summers more. In the summer the green closes in, thick, dark, suffocating. As the track tunnels its way through the woods, she can hardly breathe for the press of trees. The mud pulls at her feet so badly that often she has to sidestep the deeply scored ruts, in dread of the dense traps of undergrowth creeping up to the edge of the road, lying in wait.

At least when the trees are bare, your eyes can dart about between the stark columns of wet bark, catch glimpses of the things that flit through the play of light and shadow. Shifting into one shape, then another, disappearing and reappearing where you least expect them. Now, in this dank, sodden summer, you can only hear their whispering, flinch from shadowy hands darting out of the rank foliage.

She walks faster and faster, cold sweat rolling down her skin under her shift. She has reached the part of the track where it sinks deep into the dirt. The banks on either side are nearly her height, left bare by those who have worn this route down over a longer time than she can imagine. Alone, she joins the ranks of the dead, like her forever tramping towards an end they dare not think about. Roots of the overhanging trees protrude from the walls of earth, twisted bodies and ghastly contorted faces gurning savagely at her. Underfoot there is as much dung as mud, churned so deep and thick she is forced to clamber out on to one of the side paths.

Slipping where the rain has washed the trail into a wet sheen, blocking her ears from the rattle of the leaves as she brushes by, she weeps for the switch of rowan left lying on her cot in Burtree House. Only her haste in getting away without being stopped by her mistress could account for her forgetting it. Mable Fouler is still furious at the disgrace brought upon her home by her servant, but Anne is driven by something far greater than fear of her mistress.

The call of some bird, mournful, malevolent, carries through the trees. Her feet, caked and clumsy with the sludge of the road, kick into huge hills of matted needles, black ants swarming out and stinging her. Nettles whip her legs, burn her arms and hands. Clouds of midges and gnats swirl up around her, blinding her, clogging her nostrils, getting into her mouth, until she pulls her apron over her head, running half blind and not daring to stop, knowing they are waiting.

The track opens out into a flare of field just before Broomley. She is a quivering white thing exposed to the sun after the rock it has crawled under is kicked away. She knows a path that cuts behind the village and heads as fast as she can towards it, even though this carries her back into the depths of the trees. By now she has walked over half of the three miles she has to cover, but the woods have yet to play their worst trick.

As the trunks and leaves and undergrowth close in on her, she senses the wood gathering itself. The air around her becomes as still as death, each leaf, stem, blade and branch utterly motionless. Her body crashing on feels huge and clumsy in a world devoid of any other movement. And then she feels it approaching: only a suspicion at first, then an intimation, and then the rush of air pouring through the trees in one vast exhalation, a single breath straight from the mouth of God, the great sweep of a disappointed sigh washing over her, enveloping her in a flood of swaying, surging green.

She falls upon her knees in the muck of the path, pressing her face into her apron as it rolls over her. Then it passes beyond, leaving her in the choking stillness of its wake as she huddles on the ground. She knows of nowhere else but here, in this valley gouged out by the Tyne running grey and swollen not far below her, where the air behaves in this way. As long as she can remember it has reminded her to fear God. But now, since last April, when the wind comes the only thing she can think of is Jane Baites, walking up to the door of her father's house in Corbridge.

The memory looms up, threatening to overwhelm her. And then she starts running, tearing her way through a blur of green and brown and black that can hold no horror worse than that breath.

And so, panting with fear like a small beast, she bursts out of the wood and into the clearing carved out of the trees for a mill, the Riding Mill.

She freezes on the edge of the open space. There is one more terror between her and the Riding House. Before her is the pack bridge, with the burn racing beneath it. She forces her feet on to the stone of the bridge, its low walls only wide enough for a single person. She keeps her eyes on them, congregated at the door of the Riding House, waiting. There they stand, good neighbours all, of whom no one would speak ill: Anne Forster of Stocksfield, Anne Dryden of Prudhoe, Lucy Thompson of Mickley, Margaret and Michael Aynsley of Riding, Mary and Anthony Hunter of Birkenside, Dorothy Green of Edmondbyers, Anne Usher of Fairlymay, Elizabeth Pickering of Whittingeslaw, Jane Makepeace of New Ridley, John and Anne Whitfield of Edmondbyers, Christopher and Alice Dixon of Mugglesworth Park, Catherine Elliott of Ebchester, Elisabeth Atchinson of Ebchester, Isabel

Andrew of Crooked Oake, Isabell Thompson of Slaley, Thomasine Watson of Slaley, Anne Parteis of Hollisfield, Isabell Johnson of Allendale. And Anne Baites from Morpeth, and many others from Morpeth and from Berwick too, whose faces she knows but not their names.

And Jane Baites of Corbridge, of course, in the front of this crowd, smiling, like all of them, she with a feline smile.

Chapter 1

Feb. 5, 1672–3. Newcastle-on-Tyne, before Ralph Jenison.
Anne Armstrong, of Birks-nooke.

Eggs. Why it had to be the eggs, I do not know.

I have seen things of much less value provoke a charge of bewitching – a mumbled threat when a poor woman is denied a cup of ale at the kitchen door is enough. And it is never the solid householder who has turned her away that is charged, but the woman who has asked for alms. It is a woman nearly always, an old woman, usually a widow outside any husbandly control or protection, living alone in some tumbledown cottage beyond the village, a woman bent, aged and poor, with only an ill word to remind the world that she is here upon this earth, that the poor too have a place under Church and manor. An ill word, and then a cow sickens soon after, or a child, and there she is, standing before the rich and powerful, in gaol or hanging by the neck thereafter, and all for a cup of ale.

But for me, it was the eggs. No begging of course, what with my being a servant to Dame Mable Fouler of Burtree House, no less, who sent me those two miles or more to Stocksfield-on-Tyne to get eggs from Anne Forster, and get them at a good price. And when my mistress says a good price, you may be sure I did not beg but bargained, and bargained hard, for a good price, knowing no matter how much she said she thought of her servants as family, I would not be spared the punishment due for paying too much for eggs.

Ah, but Anne Forster could bargain too, and between us we bargained so well that we bargained ourselves out of any trans-action. She stayed pleasant enough throughout, though I may have been a bit sharp, my mistress being very much in my mind as I haggled, and when it was clear we could not agree on the price, Anne Forster asked me, in as kind a way as you could wish, if I would sit down, so that she could look at my head.

I thought it might be the yellow crust in the roots of my hair, the scald Dame Fouler was treating with warm poultices of linseed meal and mashed carrot. I hoped Anne Forster had not seen me scratching, for I tried hard not to, no matter how bad the itch. My mistress had told me about the insects breeding under the crusts, and I knew for myself the fetid odour the scabs let off.

Anne Forster gently removed the linen cap Dame Fouler insisted that I wear, as much to protect my head from my fingers as from the ill effects of the air, and smoothed back my hair with no sign of disgust. I was in hope then that my skin was returning to its healthy state. As she lifted the hair from my scalp and let the thin strands fall, I remembered that there were those who could use their cunning to read the head like the books I have seen Dame Fouler take up of an evening, squinting in the candlelight, her lips moving over the shapes her fingers followed on the paper. I had heard that when they ran their fingertips and palms over your skull, as Anne Forster's hands were now running over mine, they could see there the shape of your character, your temperament and disposition, as well as they told me a physician could from blood and phlegm and bile.

The feel of her hands moving through my hair and across my scalp was restful, and she looked at my head without a word, emitting a low hum all the while, not so much a song as a soothing sound. And then she lifted up my face and half-smiled, and I knew she was done, and I stood and turned to walk away. I looked back once to where she stood, still with that half-smile and no word, and then I walked home, or I should say, to Burtree House. The house in Birches Nooke where I grew up was nearer to Stocksfield, but I hardly ever saw what remained of my family there since my mother died and my father moved away. Anyway, my work awaited me, as did reporting back upon what I had almost forgotten, the eggs.

I tried to tell him that I did not know what she might have read from the shape of my skull. Maybe, in not buying the eggs too dear, she saw that I served my mistress well, too well, showing what a good servant I could be for darker, more dangerous things. But he was a busy man, and a man of business, who moved me along in my story with a wave of his hand, wanting me to get on past the business of bargaining for eggs to what happened next.

Hurrying me through the story that I had walked twenty bitter miles to tell, as he well knew. 'Northumberland,' he had directed a man with a quill to write on his piece of paper when I said where I was from: 'The Information of Anne Armstrong of Birks-nooke in the County aforesaid taken upon Oath the 5th Day of February 1672.'

'Informant saith that ...' Oh, so easy to put that down on paper, but not a word there about what it cost me to come here to say this.

We had thought, after a December colder than anyone could recall, that the mildness of January – by which I mean only that the water, and the air itself, were no longer frozen – signalled the end of the ice and storms. But the weather was deceptive. February thrust us back into the deepest cold, and a winter that felt as if it would never end.

So to be here on the first Wednesday of the month, the day when I had been told the Justice of the Peace in Newcastle summoned people to his grand house to hear complaints, I had trudged through icy mud that cut as much as it clung, the dung on the road following the river to the town thick but faintly warm, no cart driver giving me a lift, no one to keep me company so that I talked to myself like a mad woman, rehearsing for my ears alone the story I had to tell, stepping all the while between ruts dug deep into ground so wet it could absorb no more water, feeling for the parts pressed down enough by wheels for my feet not to slip and slide, the edges of my dress mud-caked and my sleeves too from several falls, only the story I had to tell driving me on, on until I passed through the West Gate of the town walls, and then on and on over hard, slick cobbles, enduring rough retorts to my asking after the house of the Justice of the Peace, some kindness too and finally some directions that brought me to Trinity House in the Broad Chare, where a line of people stood, slowly working its way into the house.

A constable hovered by the door to constrain any who became violent in their accusations or defence. A cautious man, this Justice, this Mr Jenison as I was told. This was not actually his house – well, not the place where he lived, I learned from the low talk in the queue, the constable calling out for silence every now and then, and not above poking at us with his cudgel. Oh no, too careful to hold court where he lived, Mr Ralph Jenison, Esquire, merchant and coal-owner, a prominent and wealthy citizen of Newcastle-upon-Tyne.

The person who gave me directions had called Trinity House the House of the Mariners. It was a pretty building, built around a handsome square surrounded by many rooms. Most of these, someone else near me was saying, housed such of the Fellowship of Masters and Mariners who had fallen into poverty or were not able to sustain themselves. A good place then for Mr Jenison, who owned the building, to set aside somewhere to hold his Sessions for the likes of us.

Once in the house, the line slowly snaked its way past a pair of great doors, open so that we could see into a magnificent hall with a chapel off the side. Further along we came to the Justice's chamber, large enough in its way, with plenty of room between Mr Jenison and those seeking his judgements. He was raised up on a chair placed on a podium, a large desk before him, a man they called the clerk presiding over a considerable pile of paper at a desk one level lower, and another man standing between them and us as we came before the Justice, each in turn directed to a place on the floor directly in front of him.

By the time I stood there, he seemed distracted, half-listening. He signalled that I should start, and the quill of the man hunched over his papers scratched away from the instant I began to speak.

'About three days after,' I said, 'seeking the cows in the pasture a little after daybreak, I met an old man with ragged clothes, who asked me where I was on the Friday last. I told him I was seeking eggs at Stocksfield.'

'*Informant saith.*' But how could I tell him about the stain of the dawn, the sky hanging heavy and dark over the low ridges about me, the thin, clutching branches of the trees, the mist still lurking among their boles along the edges of the pasture, seeping out across the rough grass like tendrils seeking me out? And even this would leave out how hungry I was, up with no breakfast hours and hours before my employer would think to rise from her bed.

For I was a house servant, the only live-in servant that Dame Fouler could afford. As such, I was her claim to respectability, living proof that she could afford to pay for my upkeep. Not with wages, of course; a place in a corner to sleep, and some food, less than my father could give me in his house at Corbridge, but the promise of something when I left her household, though the chance of my leaving grew slimmer with every year I served her. For this could only be through marriage, and how could I hope to meet a man who would take me as wife and give me a home of my own when Dame Fouler gave me no time of my own, no oppor-tunities to go out?

My time was her property, she said, while I was living under her roof. As a maid of all work I was kept busy the whole day long and much of the night, cleaning and cooking and mending indoors, working with the animals outdoors. And not only as a dairymaid; I had to help with the husbandry too, working with livestock as much as any man, which is what I was doing that morning, the dew soaking the hem of my dress while I looked for and called and cursed those cows.

If I was sent to run errands – looking for eggs, say – she made sure I would meet as few other people as possible. Socialising, she said, provided opportunities for servants to spread gossip about the families they worked for, and led to maidservants with bellies swelling out of wedlock. For these reasons she refused to give me any time off, and you can be sure – this I would not be saying to Mr Jenison – that I would make as much use of my time away from the house as I could, on the paths and in the pastures.

When it was not so early, and so cold, and I was not so hungry. My dame reminded me constantly that a servant's use of her employer's food was an unlawful act, so I dared not take so much as a crust before having to go out while she was still asleep, though my belly clawed at me. Shivering and shaking as I was in the dank half-light of the morning, I nearly fainted clean away when the man appeared out of a swirl of the mist. But then I saw that he was old, and scrawnier even than me, or at least so he looked at first, with his clothes falling and flapping about him in rags, thin arms and legs protruding, his hair awry and his eyes rheumy, his beard long and unkempt.

But his voice: oh, now that was a different thing. Thin maybe, but sure of itself, as he told me of what was to come.

The Justice, however, was far from sure of what I was reporting, and stopped me after I had told him faithfully what the old man had said. Read this back to the informant, he said to the clerk, and ask her if what you have down is correct.

'He told her that the same woman that looked at her head,' the clerk read out to me from his piece of paper, 'should be the first that made a horse of her spirit, and who should be the next that would ride her; and into what shape and likenesses she should be changed, if she would turn to their god.

'And withal told this informer how they would use any means they could to allure her: first, by their tricks, by riding in the house in empty wood dishes that had never been wet, and also in eggshells; and how to obtain whatever they desired by swinging in a rope; and with several dishes of meat and drink. But, if she eat not of their meat, they could not harm her.

'And, at last, told her how it should be divulged by eating a piece of cheese, which should be laid by her when she laid down in a field with her apron cast over her head, and so left her.'

These were not my words, not all of them, and not in the way I spoke them. Perhaps I agreed too easily that they were, they being close enough to what I had said. I would learn that the words, as caught by the quill and inked on to paper, would now be my words, far more so than those my mouth shaped into the air where they could change shape or float away. I would learn how important it was to correct them as they were read back to me, when I could take them back as my own, these orphans of the air, and make of them what would suit me best. Something I could stand by, and not try to change or alter in any way on another occasion. For this the Justices would not allow, with any departure in the future from what they had on the page to be proof only of my lying, then or now or all the time.

But on that first day I nodded my head, said yes, these were my words, and then, when the Justice said to me, well, what next, I went on, wondering now in what ways my voice was disappearing into the scritch-scritch-scratching of the quill.

After he was gone, I said, I fell suddenly down dead. And I lay dead upon the ground until somewhere near six that morning.

'How –' began the Justice, and I said, the bells; as I began to return to myself I heard the sound of the six o'clock bells drifting through the mist from Bywell, summoning me to say the Lord's Prayer as they do three times a day. Our Father, which art in heaven, I pray as they ring at six in the morning, at noon, and at six in the evening, knowing that there is magic in the bells, and that their sound drives off evil spirits and demons.

The clerk had stopped writing, but now returned to his paper. The Justice looked at the line of people behind me, each complainant restless to come forward for their turn before him. 'Leave it as "somewhere near six that morning,'" he said to the clerk, then turned back to me.

And when I arose, I said – leaving out how difficult it was to get back to my feet, how stiff and sore I was from the cold, damp ground, and my terror, befuddled as I was, at not being able to find the words to pray, as if I were the one accused of witchcraft and required to recite the Lord's Prayer without error, or stumbling, or stammering – I went home, I said, but kept these things secret.

I did not even tell Dame Fouler when she said hard words about my not being able to find the cows, and sent me out again directly to look for them without giving me my breakfast. But what would you care for that, Mr Justice? For all your lean looks you appear well fed enough, so this too I will keep to myself, and the fear I felt when the darkness would claim me again and again, never knowing when I would fall down dead.

But I did tell him that ever since that time, almost every day and sometimes two or three times a day, these fits would take me, and I would lie dead – 'as dead' they read back to me, but no, dead, dead I said, although I do not think they changed it on the paper – often from evening till cockcrow.

How could I tell them, there in that big, echoing room, the crush of people behind me, the stern face in front, the never-ending scratching of the pen every time I breathed a word, how could I tell them what it was to die, to die again and again. To describe, in a hurry, people waiting, wanting you to get to the point, what it is like to lose yourself, to fade, to fall away, feel your very self slipping through every attempt to hold it, keep it, like the frantic grasp of fingers at the air. Could he, that powerful, imposing man barely listening to me, know the terror of losing his sense of who he is, the impending doom that gathers when you know you are about to disappear.

The fits, I wanted to tell him, began with a whirl of images in my poor brain. A moan would be the last thing I knew of my self in the flesh, and then I would be lost, first in a rush of memories, confused, contorted, but mine at least, and then a storm of terrifying visions in which every sense of what was me or mine would be torn to tatters and swirled away, and then – this is important, very important to everything else I had to tell him – suddenly I would be in a still, dark place of clarity, perfect clarity. The fits did not leave me confused; with my self gone, everything would be clear, sharp, distinct, as if especially designed to increase the horror.

But all you want to know is what happened, and so I will tell you what happened.

When I was lying dead – or 'as dead,' or 'in that condition' as your clerk will write – which had come upon me one night before Christmas, I was on the floor, paralysed, unable to move, or lift myself, to do anything as myself, unable even to be myself, when at the door the darkness began to gather itself together, to thicken into a shape. I lay there, suddenly all too aware of myself, a self helpless, naked (despite the modesty of my shift), exposed, open to anything anyone chose to do. But my every sense was quivering, the more alert through not serving me, seeing, hearing, touching, tasting and smelling even, reaching out into the blackness of the night – it was, I remember, shall never forget, about the change of the moon – desperate to know something of what was moving about now in the murk of the room.

And then that drifting concentration of the dark took on a form, a human form, the form of a woman, and there, kneeling down towards me, a hand reached out to smooth my hair, another followed to join it in holding my head, turning it, looking at it – yes, looking at it, as the outlines of a countenance now became visible, eyes a faint glow, the mouth a terrible smile forming, and then a full face came into focus; the face of Anne Forster.

Yes, it was Anne Forster who now lifted my head, gently at first, and then suddenly so firmly that I, for the first time since falling into the fit, felt a sensation, a physical sensation – and it was pain.

The pain of the rough leather of a headpiece being pulled over my head, catching at my thin hair as it was tugged behind my ears;

the scratch of the cheekpieces along either side of my face, the cold of the bit rings against the edges of my mouth. Then came the strangle of the throatlatch as it was yanked underneath my jaw, the tightening of the browband across my forehead. And I was not to be spared the noseband, suffocating me as it was pulled under my nostrils and forced my mouth closed. Then, of course, the bit: my strapped mouth forced open, the metal bar pushed in between my teeth until it pressed up against whatever made up the inside corners of my mouth, gum or flesh or muscle, I had never thought to think which, knowing now only how easily hurt this hidden place is, how much an animal must do whatever the force applied there tells it to do.

And then I was pulled up to my feet, a beast entirely at the mercy of that leather and steel.

Anne Forster sprang to my back, turning my head first this way and then that with the reins. She had need of those reins, because she could not use her legs to press into me, or hammer me with her heels; no, a dame, a lady was Anne Forster as she sat upon me cross-legged, and rode me out into the night.

I could do no more than snuffle and roll my eyes as the crownpiece rubbed against my ears, the browband being too short, the cheekpieces too, so that the bit pulled the corners of my mouth and banged against my teeth. The throatlatch was not adjusted properly either, interfering with my breathing as I flexed. Even I, a maid of all work, knew that the width of three or four fingers should be able to fit between a throatlatch and a horse's cheek.

But all my pain and discomfort did was ensure that my rider's wishes were clear, the more clear for the ill-fitting bridle.

So we moved through the dark, with hardly any sense of touching the ground.

"'Rid upon this informant cross-legged,'" said Justice Jenison, his voice rising in disbelief. 'You mean you became this animal, this horse, and she rode upon your back? Come now, girl, come now.'

When you are ridden, I wanted to say, you are a horse.

But all I said was what happened: she rode upon me cross-legged until we came to a clearing deep in the woods. There I could hear the rush of water, which I knew we could not cross. But my rider did not hesitate, and pulled my head to guide me to a narrow stone pack bridge over a burn.

Once we had crossed, she lit off my back. Here are my companions, she said, and this is where we meet, here at the Riding bridge-end. Then, none too gently, she pulled the bridle off my head – over the poll, I nearly said, my head still being in the likeness of a horse. But when the bridle was taken off, I stood up in my own shape.

Stood up, embarrassed at having been on my hands and knees, and looked around, and saw Anne Forster standing with Anne Dryden of Prudhoe and Lucy Thompson of Mickley, and ten more who I did not know, looking at me and smiling in the dark, their moist lips glistening around the yellow of their teeth, their eyes a dull shine.

But worse still, behind them, silhouetted against the sheen of a whitewashed building – was that Mr Errington's house, the Riding House, which I knew well by daylight, but hesitated to think of as even the same building as it glimmered in the dark, the white of its walls seeming to have a light of its own? – mounted on a bay horse, was a tall man all in black, or a black man, I should say, his darkness going deeper than his clothes. And that horse, who knew from what human form divine it had been transformed. The steam from its nostrils floated out into the night air as it pawed and pranced.

'Bay, you say,' interrupted the Justice, 'bay? How could you see the horse's colour in the dark?'

But I was not to be stopped by such a detail. 'Bay, as I thought,' I said. 'I thought from its stout build, its small, flat head, its wide, deep chest, that this was a Galloway. Galloways are usually of that colour, reddish-brown or dark, with black points, and the legs too, usually black.'

'She knows her horses, her work horses at least,' said the Justice, as much to himself as the clerk, who looked uncertain what to write. Seeing no guidance from the Justice, he put down, as he would later read back to me: 'And a long black man riding on a bay Galloway, as she thought.' This, he decided, was quite enough, and looked up.

'Which they called their protector,' I said, speaking directly to the man writing my words down. He looked confused, so I added: 'the sable man on the bay Galloway, which they called their protector.'

'Their protector?' The Justice looked at me sharply. 'Do you mean by this the Lord Protector of the Commonwealth?'

I shook my head. 'Which they called their protector,' I repeated.

'Remember, girl, His Majesty is back upon his throne,' he said. 'Their "protector," then; go on, what did these people do, with their "protector" on his bay Galloway?'

I regretted the details now, what they had called him, the colour and breed of the horse, but I could not stop myself. I had to tell what I saw, how I saw it.

I moved on, as quickly as I could, it becoming clear now that I was exhausting what little attention I had gained. And when they had hanked their horses they stood upon a bare spot of ground, and asked me to sing.

Oh, but to say it like that, 'bid this informer sing,' as they would read it back to me, and not to be able to talk about the churning of the darkness with shapes forming and shifting, turning in a circle around me, faces breathing out a hiss of words and hands pointing and prodding, feeling my hair, touching my face, pulling at my shift and saying all the time, sing, sing us the song, the sssss's drawn out thin and cutting into the air.

And then lifting my voice in a cracked keen:

O, I shall go into a hare
With sorrow and sighing and mickle care,

And I shall go in the Devil's name
Aye, till I be fetchèd hame.

Yes, yes, the sibilance filling my ears, that is the song: go on, go on.

And I went on, not knowing where the words came from, or such tune as I could manage, my throat stretched to clear itself of the press of the throatlatch, the corners of my mouth sore where the bit had cut against them. And as I did so, the circle around me broke up, spread out over the bare ground of the bridge-end, the figures each swirling out into a dance of their own.

Hare, take heed of a bitch greyhound
Will harry thee all these fells around,
For here I come in Our Protector's name
All but for to fetch thee hame.

And now the chorus, come, the chorus, they called, clapping, gyring, floating back towards me with their faces in mine, muggy warm breath on my cold, sore cheeks, the chorus they said, joining in on words I had never known I knew:

Cunning and art she did not lack
But aye his whistle would fetch her back.

And without choice the next verse, rushing out of my mouth, half the twirling forms singing with me,

Yet I shall go into a trout
With sorrow and sighing and mickle doubt,
And show thee many a merry game
Ere that I be fetchèd hame.

And now, I swear, the dancing shapes smudged and smeared, black against black, blurring into other shapes, many shapes while I sang: first, a hare, then human again, male or female one could not tell, and then a hound, later a cat, sometimes a mouse, and other shapes I could not tell or now remember. And all the time, my voice, crying and straining for the notes, now with the other half of the dancers singing with me,

Trout, take heed of an otter lank
Will harry thee close from bank to bank,
For here I come in Our Protector's name
All but for to fetch thee hame.

I hardly knew what I was singing, although I felt the terror of trying to escape, of changing shape from one form of prey to another only to find my pursuer changing too, changing each time into my natural predator.

My audience, dancing and singing in this dark place where I could see they often met, were laughing when each twist and turn of the quarry was more than matched by the transformations of the hunter, they too swirling through the shapes, pouncing on each other, squirming away or tearing at each other, depending upon which shape they were in.

Cunning and art she did not lack
But aye his whistle would fetch her back,

they chanted, again and again, turning each time to the tall, dark man, still mounted, but still, so still, except for giving every now and then a nod of his head in acknowledgement,

Cunning and art she did not lack
But aye his whistle would fetch her back.

Wilder and wilder it became, the spinning and swirling and singing and shouting, and then, as my voice began to give way entirely, the last harsh croaks of verse and chorus cutting at my throat like broken glass, the shapes began to settle, first into the various animals, and then, as their dancing slowed, into human forms, although forms I would shudder to meet again, even those I could now see as Anne Forster, Anne Dryden and Lucy Thompson.

I bowed my head as the singing stopped, jerking it up as Anne Forster approached me, bridle in hand. But by then I was too tired, too sore, too scared to do more than accept the bridle and the bit, stand mute and motionless as all was tugged into place, and I was mounted.

I took my place then in the dreadful cavalcade of humans and horses, and who was to say which was which, with the dark man on his Galloway at the head of the procession as he led it over the pack bridge, the tumble of water from the mill race now loud again in the silence following on the end of our ceremony, the sweat and steam rising off us into the cold, the trees swallowing us up into their denser blackness. And then, one by one, beasts and riders broke away, each in their own direction, Anne Forster and myself too as she rode me back to Burtree House, where she left me crumpled and weeping on the floor in my own shape, sore and soaked and shivering.

You see, she said, I have fetched thee hame.

Chapter 2

Silence had fallen as I told this, the Justice sitting motionless, the clerk too, having only managed to get certain words down, surely not all I had to say, even the people pressing in behind me for their turn having fallen quiet, listening to my words.

Encouraged, I went on, told how for six or seven nights together this was repeated. Different people mounted me and rode me to the Riding bridge-end, but it was always the same procedure: the bridling, the mounting, the riding, the singing, the dancing, the shape changing and the hunt, presided over by the silent, dark, mounted man.

On the last night, however, we did not go to the bare ground at the bridge-end. A man I did not know was on my back, and why, I do not know, he unbridled me at the door of the house called the Riding House, hidden away in the clearing and squatting just over from the mill and its cottage.

I had walked this way before, but never been inside. Now I was hurried in, to find the air in the front room thick with candle smoke and laughter, and many of the company there, welcoming me by pulling at my arms and clothes, and treating me as one of their own. But there was more in the air than smoke and noise; to my amazement, those I had come to know by sight well enough now, even as they danced and changed their shapes, were flying through the fug of the room in wooden dishes and eggshells, swooping and climbing like swallows, and calling me to join them. Choose a dish that has never been wet, they told me, using every means to allure me. Despite my amazement I could see this for the cheap trick it was, a child's game and no more, and I was relieved when they tumbled to the ground as a voice, not loud but clearly not to be disobeyed, ordered us through to a back room.

There I saw Forster, and Dryden, and Thompson, and the rest, and their protector too, who now they were brazen enough to be calling their god.

A large table nearly filled the room, and he was sitting at the head of it in what looked to me to be a chair of gold. Black, and dark, and silent as he was when on his horse, he sat straight-backed, his arms lying on the gold rests on either side of the chair. As the last of us was herded into the room, he raised one hand and pointed above, to the heavy beams, and there we saw a rope hanging.

My nerves failed at this, but one of the women reached out and touched the rope, as it seemed he desired us to do. This was to no effect. Lucy Thompson pushed her aside, and touched it several times, and then Anne Dryden, who touched it three times. Instantly, some fine food – I could not see what, being held back by the crush around the table, but Anne Dryden said it was exactly what she desired – appeared upon the table, and she fell upon it, eating without regard to manners, tearing and pushing food in her mouth, pulling back her head and laughing in triumph, grease and juices running down her chin.

The dark man tapped a cane smartly against the floor, and the dozen people in the room came to some kind of order, taking their turns to touch the rope three times, and finding upon the table whatever food it was they wanted.

My sore mouth ran with saliva as I saw over their shoulders many kinds of different meat and drink, not clearly, for I hung back though they made space for me. I was hungry, hungry as I almost always was in Dame Fouler's house, as I always had been as long as I could remember, and the glimpses I had of the fare appearing at each touching of the rope gnawed at me, the delicious smells taunting me.

There was so much food, more even than this ravenous company could consume, and I could not take my eye off the remains; but when the last mouthful that could be managed was eaten, she who had touched the rope last drew everything left upon the table towards her, bundling it into her apron and parcelling it up to take away with her. No word was said about this and I gathered it was their usual custom, the reversions going to the one who had had the least time to eat.

It was the food that brought me back to myself. I had not forgotten the old man I met while searching for the cows; so much of what he told me that early morning had come about in the darkness of my fits, from the woman that looked at my head being the first to make a horse of my spirit, to who should be the next that would ride me, and into what shape and likenesses I should be changed, if I would turn to their god.

As I have reported, he told me they would use any means they could to allure me, and on this night this is what they had done; first, by their tricks, flying in the house in empty wooden dishes and eggshells, but more compelling yet, teaching me how I could obtain whatever food I desired by swinging on a rope.

But, if I ate not of their meat, he had said, they could not harm me. So I had not touched the rope, or looked too long at the table, and went home as hungry as when I had come.

And after this, I decided to avoid their company. It had become too easy to accept the bridle, which was put on ever more kindly, and the ride also was made more comfortable. There were times I enjoyed the strength of the animal I became, flexing my powerful body through the dark, hardly touching the ground into which I normally sunk with each heavy step as I trudged along in my own likeness.

On occasion while singing, I had begun to wonder what it would be like to whirl away into another shape, hare, greyhound, cat, or bee, whatever, but even thinking of this scared me more than watching those others do such things.

So I found ways to avoid being drawn into their gatherings; sitting up in Dame Fouler's room as she slept, finding reasons to go to my father's of an evening. But then they came to me in their own shapes at different times of the day, meeting me on the roads when I was sent out, or coming by Burtree House on one pretence or another. And they threatened me, saying if I would not turn to their god, the last shift should be the worst.

But I stayed firm, and from that time they have not troubled me.

Is this the end of your evidence, said the Justice; is this everything you have come to tell me?

I could not tell in what mood he said this, or how it was meant, but as the clerk sat back and lifted his pen from the paper, I said, 'On St John day last – St John the Evangelist, that is, as we are taught in church, being the 27th day of December – I was in the field, seeking Dame Fouler's sheep ...'

The clerk was writing again, and I found myself taking comfort from his dipping the quill and inking what I said on to the paper.

'... and I lay down, being weary, and cast my apron over my head, as I so often did to block out the world. And when I took the apron from my face, I found a piece of cheese lying next to my head. I got up, smoothing the apron down over my skirt, and stood in awe, remembering that this was exactly as the old man had said it would be.

'Then I picked up the piece of cheese and took it home. I hid it from Dame Fouler, who was angry again that I had not found the sheep, and sent me out once more. When I got back in, quite late, I sat and looked at the cheese, and wondered if divulging what I knew of the gatherings at the bridge-end would be for good or ill.'

I had to be careful now: for that one week I had, after all, been part of the group, that group of – what? But I had been forced to join, and taken no part in magic other than that which was used upon me, and I was hungry, so very hungry, hungry before what supper I was given, hungry after too, always hungry.

'But suddenly,' I said, 'I lifted up the cheese, and bit into it, and finished it like one famished, as I was, and then waited for the time I could get away, to come before Your Worship, and tell everything that happened to me there, there at the Riding bridge-end, and in the Riding House.'

And that was it: I had told all I came to tell, or at least what I felt able to tell.

Before my voice had quite fallen silent, while my last words were hanging in the air, the Justice said to the clerk, read it back to her, let her confirm what she has said. The clerk too was still finishing, his quill sweeping over the paper, but when he was done, he lifted up the pages and read back to me my story – or a version of my story that I hardly recognised at times.

Oh, most of the information was there, the who, the where, the what, but where was I? In my place now was this other woman, this 'she', this 'her', this 'informer' and 'informant'. Someone else who was saying what I said, so that I wanted to call out, no, no, that is not what happened to me. But it was, when it came to the facts of what happened; it was not how it felt, what I felt, to sweat with fear, to hurt in those places, to stare into the dark and not know what would happen next, to see and not to understand ... No, I could hear two voices speaking now, as the clerk read what I had said back to me. His voice, and somewhere in it the ghost of my voice, buried in the tangle of words they liked to use for the law. Words thin, starved of everything that made what happened real, true, what happened as it really did happen.

So I listened to their 'bridled this informer' and 'the last night this informer was with them' and their 'further this informer saith that' and waited for the clerk to reach 'and did eat of it, and since that time hath disclosed all which she formerly kept secret'.

There was nothing to change, and yet everything had been changed. The force of it leached out, the story now as pale as the paper he brought over to me while I nodded my head dumbly. And then he proffered the quill, the one that had been so busy with my words of late, and he said, Make your mark, here, tapping the paper below where the swirls of ink ended.

My mark? I had heard of this, knew of the practice, but had not thought to prepare myself for it today, being so busy with the story, going over and over what I should say, and how, my mouth overflowing with what I remembered, my tongue wrapping itself around the words I wanted to form.

So to have something pressed into my hand, a thing so unfamiliar to its grasp, caught me unawares, unsure. I knew quills well enough, could pull them out of a just-dead fowl without thinking, the warmth yet in its body, the kick and scratch hardly gone from its legs, the flex of the wing giving slightly as I tugged. But this cold thing, long and thin and pale, stripped almost completely of its barbs and cut square at the tip, was a foreign thing to me, strange for me to use.

And what mark to make? What mark would be my mark? I could not think, and let my hand tell me what to do, let it put upon the page who I was, and how I felt, those things taken away from my story.

I saw my hand stab a dot at the paper, press and make it round, black, firm. Here I am, it said, and then my hand lifted for a moment and came back down to enclose that dot in a ring, draw a circle to protect me. It slipped a little as I concentrated hard to help it close the loop, and a splash of ink spread out; but this was outside the circle, and I was clear and safe and solid inside, protected by the round line.

I gave the clerk back his pinion feather, taken from a goose I would guess, and he seemed to be relieved, as if I had given him back a prized possession that he was glad I had not broken. Then, in front of me, he wrote a word to the left of my mark, another to the right, and a last word beneath it.

'This,' he said, 'is your name, here, "Anne", there "Armstrong's", and below, "Mark".'

These were letters I did know how to recognise, but it was good of him to tell me, especially as the Justice was calling for the papers now. There were two pieces of paper, one with writing on both sides, the other with writing on one side only. My mark was on the back of the second piece of paper, where there were only a few lines of writing. Should I have gone on, I wondered, so that I filled all their space, wasted none of their paper? But the clerk was taking them back, writing something to the side on the first piece of paper as he did so.

'Come, bring those here,' said Mr Jenison, while the clerk, flustered, said, 'I have Anne Forster's name down in the margin, Sir, but not yet –'

'No need, Clerk, no need, Forster is enough for now.'

A careful man, a cautious man, as I saw from the first. How careful, how cautious, I was still to learn. Would only learn in the spring, when I would have to walk again, walk in the pouring rain to Morpeth, no word ever having come back to me after all I had said, all they had written down in the Justice's house, Trinity House, in Newcastle.

'The Latin, and then let me sign,' said Mr Jenison, holding out his hand for the papers.

The Justice made his mark and then gave the pages back to the clerk, who folded them so that the writing was neatly parcelled inside. Then he wrote something on the outside and held up the package of my words.

'For the Assizes, Your Worship?'

The National Archives

I leaned back, looked around the Map and Large Document Reading Room on the second floor. Quiet, industrious heads were bent over whatever they'd ordered up from the Archives' acres of secure storage, each absorbed in the private mystery they hoped it would help solve. The obligatory silence was really a low hum, a white noise of scuffling, page-turning, pencil-scribbling (soft leaded only, pens strictly forbidden), suppressed coughs, the padded footfall of researchers carrying material to and from the seats they had chosen, the rub of clothing against desk edges and chairs, the occasional murmur of help being provided by a staff member.

I returned to the first page of the deposition, feeling over three hundred years of grime rub against my fingertips, work its way into their lines and swirls as I studied the pages.

The edges of the paper were worn, uneven, ragged in some sections. At times the writing almost overran the right-hand side, although there was always a comfortable margin on the left. Space for capturing the next stage in the legal process, the names of those to be investigated further. How much horror was there in the squeak of the quill in that space, the name trailing behind the progress of its sharp-cut point?

Only the one name in this deposition, 'Anne Forster', squeezed into the margin roughly in line with the first appearance of that name in the body of the text. And yet at least two other names had been given. Why did they not join Anne Forster in the margin?

I focused as closely as I could: 'Informeing saith' – yes, 'Informeing,' *sic erat scriptum* – 'that being servant to one Mable Fouler of Burtree House. In August last her dame sent her to seek Eggs of one Anne Forster of Stocksfield in ...' what was that next, some kind of y followed by two letters with a line over them, what were they, ah yes, 'sd' so, 'said' ... 'said County ...'; I looked up to the top left-hand corner and there it was, 'Northumberland.'

This was it, the nearest I was going to get to Anne's voice: inked on to paper by another hand, the writing a constant balancing act between the legal demands for precise language and faithfulness to the deponent's language, littered with the required Latin formulations, saturated with the language of the law, infiltrated by the brevigraphs, extensions, sub- and superscript, contractions, and whatever other resources the scribal practices of the time relied upon to get the information down as someone spoke, at the mercy of the vagaries of spelling at the time, whatever personal writerly habits survived clerical training in conventional orthography, the smudging of the quill, the crossings out and corrections.

The Justice's signature at the end of the testimony was firm, clear, easy to make out – R. A. Jenison – and the line he'd drawn under his name on the left of the page was, I thought, confident enough, a strong and heavy sweep of the quill thickening as it progressed from left to right.

Anne Armstrong's mark, parallel on the page to the right, was more of a mystery. Her attempt at a circle with a heavily inked-in dot in the centre looked like a mixture of assertion and retreat, an affirmation of who she was combined with a need to be protected, hidden.

After Jenison had signed and Anne had made her mark, the pages had been folded, once along their length and twice across their width. This formed an oblong on the outside of the folded up pages, into which had been written:

The Examination of
Anne Armstrong
Contre
Foster Dryden and
Thompson

I had to turn the page sideways to read this. The document had been opened up and smoothed flat when it was archived, making the space marked off by the creases of the folds perpendicular to the body of the deposition. The information on the makeshift cover of the deposition was in the same anonymous hand that had taken down Anne's testimony – a clerk or scribe, I assumed, the roles probably rolled into one for the relatively informal process of a Petty Session.

Whoever it was had underlined the names of those accused with a single, emphatic line. Was this to make up for all three not being written in the margins, a sign of his determination to get them registered here at least? The force with which he'd underscored their names had caused the line to blot towards its end.

But where did these pages holding Anne's voice, or the echo or reverberation of her voice, perhaps merely an approximation of her voice, go, after being so neatly processed and packaged?

The Assizes, surely.

It certainly looked as if this is where Anne's words had been forwarded. After all, I had found the deposition taken on 5 February 1672 (ah, the Julian Calendar, of course, the English seeing Pope Gregory's calendar as a plot to return them to the Catholic fold) in The National Archives' online catalogue under ASSI, the government department reference for the Records of Justices of Assize, Gaol Delivery, Oyer and Terminer, and Nisi Prius.

Wherever it had gone, the matter had not ended there. This deposition was filed along with a number of others, each begging the same question, none of them, even on the most cursory first reading, giving the sense of an ending. Whatever else I would come to know about this voice I had stumbled across, it was a voice, insistent, compelling, increasingly desperate, that refused to be silenced.

And yet here it lay on the page, lost to history as it apparently was to the courts at the time, making my work clear – to conjure it up, hear her again.

I looked at the cardboard box holding the depositions retrieved from the bowels of the secure storage area. On its lid was an oval stamp with a crown in the centre that stated the material inside was 'Supplied for the Public Service'. I couldn't help but wonder which public my work would serve. Anne Armstrong had about her the feel of a very private obsession.

Chapter 3

Humphrey Mitford, Esq., slumped into the seat of his coach, did not look well, and far older than his forty-one years. The heavy winter storms of 1672 showed no signs of abating on this early April morning. High winds and a driving rain battered the vehicle as it pulled out from the park surrounding the Manor House. He was concerned about the bridge that would carry them over the Wanney and on to the road to Morpeth; unable to communicate with his driver in the general tumult, it was with some relief that he heard the wheels clatter on to the stonework. The expensive French plate glass of his window – to his irritation, English glass could not withstand the rough usage which coaches suffered from the wretched roads, although he had heard the Duke of Buckingham was encouraging the manufacture of plate glass in Vauxhall – was a grey smudge through which he could barely make out the torrent, nothing like the picturesque river that usually danced over its bed of sandstone downstream from the bridge.

Hopefully the villagers were being more careful than the vicar of Mitford, who drowned at the stepping stones in December, and the Purdy sisters, caught and swept away a few weeks later while they were washing vegetables on the banks at Bowie's Green. News of shipwrecks off the coast was constant, and reports of damage to the scattering of houses making up the village made him feel more acutely than usual the peculiar sense of helplessness that always settled upon him as he passed beneath the ruins of the family castle, lurking on its mound which the river girdled like a moat. It too was barely visible in the downpour, which only made its glowering presence more oppressive.

The castle had been the home of the Barons of Mitford since the 1100s – until, that is, Bertram de Mitford rebelled against

Henry III and it was given to the Earls of Pembroke and Athole. This injustice had only been righted twelve years ago when the majority of the lands which had belonged to the family were returned to Humphrey's father, an enthusiastic royalist, upon Charles II's Restoration to the throne.

Robert Mitford then succeeded in doing what his ancestors over the preceding three centuries had struggled to do, reclaiming the family's rightful properties. This was a glory Humphrey could never hope to match. He had followed his father into law, but never with anything like Robert Mitford's success as a barrister. Nor did he serve as a Member of Parliament as his father had done, or even as High Sheriff of Northumberland, an office attained by both his father and grandfather. Humphrey's appointment as one of the Justices presiding over the local Sessions of the Peace – the duty carrying him over the torrent of the Wanney on this storm-tossed Easter morning – was, he knew, something of a formality hanging over from the family's manorial responsibilities rather than any distinction he himself had earned. The few years he had spent at the Inns of Court allowed him to quote a little Bracton when required, or draw upon some of Coke's erudition to impress criminals and spectators alike with his superficial smattering of the law. But he did not have much more than this with which to impose the dignity of his position upon the occasion.

Not that the occasion demanded that much dignity: four times a year he was required to join the other Justices of the Peace for the County of Northumberland to try criminal cases and deal with routine administrative tasks. A hundred years ago they would have tried everything from murder to the failure of a tradesman to display his name on the side of a cart, but these days the Quarter Sessions were restricted to misdemeanours and petty crime. Any more serious wrongdoings that might come their way – be they murder or treason, perjury, forgery, witchcraft, bigamy or abduction – had to be referred to the Courts of Assize, held twice a year when the Judges of the King's Bench Division of the High Court of Justice were sent out from London to travel across the rural circuits.

Humphrey and his fellow Justices could thus look forward to days of Hair Powder Tax Certificates or Woolwinders' Oaths, possibly a Gamekeeper's Deputation Game Certificate, the regulation of a troublesome alehouse, no doubt a slew of bastardy orders, maintenance and settlement documents, presentments and punishments of dissenters for not attending the services of the parish churches, the registering of Roman Catholics and other subversives or foreign people such as Jesuits, Jews and the French, not to mention the usual robbery, disorderly singing, bankruptcy, buggery and the theft of anything from grain to saucepans, sheep, cattle, poultry and horses. Given the current weather they would, of course, have to attend to an extra load of repairs to roads and bridges.

He turned his attention to the road as the coach swung into the valley which it followed along the Wansbeck into Morpeth. The steep-sided course of the river often praised for its loveliness was now a dark tunnel through a surging wall of trees, swathes of rain curtaining off the beautiful perspectives normally afforded by the curves in the road. Several more bridges had to be negotiated over the river run wild, each one an uncertainty although they became increasingly substantial as they approached Morpeth. Road and river swung to the right when they entered the town, skirting the outlying buildings as they made their way around to Morpeth Castle, high on its plateau above the sturdy and, it must be said, pretty arrangement of buildings cupped in the bowl below it. Today this, like the charming scenery of the lower hills surrounding and beyond the town, was erased by sheets of rain.

The coach made its way up the muddy sweep of the driveway encircling the prominence upon which the castle stood. Or rather, what was left of the castle after the Parliamentary army demolished the bulk of it. It pulled up in front of the only remaining solid structure, a still-impressive gatehouse with two turrets, and Humphrey clambered out. Water streamed off his hat and cape in an instant, and despite his driver's best efforts he was soaked by the time he reached the large double doors.

Shaking himself off and passing his outer clothes to a servant, Humphrey Mitford, Esq., hurried towards the second, and much grander, of the two doors that opened off the entrance. His haste, short of unseemly, was not only driven by the weather but the need to reach the garderobe on the far side of the large single chamber making up the first floor of the gatehouse. Of late he had found himself plagued by the urge to piss much more frequently than had been his habit, and often at the most awkward moments. Arriving at a destination after even the shortest travel was one of these, at the moment when he was required to display the greatest dignity. The length of this morning's journey had him hurrying across the room that served as the courtroom, ignoring the aumbrey directly across from the door in which the seals and paraphernalia of justice were displayed, a small spurt of urine discharging itself before he could undo his breeches.

He managed to disentangle himself from his drawers in time, and aim the full stream into the fug emerging through the hole in the stone seat. For all the pressure to piss, the stream was noticeably thinner; not many years before he would have emptied his bladder in a quarter of the time. He rearranged his dress and dabbed at the travel grime on his face from the slop-stone set into the small sill of the window. The water was cold enough not to open the pores of the skin and make him more vulnerable to disease, but he still splashed lightly and hastily, unable to shake the feeling that the staff awaiting him were taking note of how long he was in the privy.

The smell did not entirely dissipate when he emerged. Between sittings the gatehouse served as lodging for the constable, the cooking – and other – odours from its upper floor where he lived with his household penetrating through to the courtroom.

Back under the eyes of his staff, Humphrey Mitford walked with great deliberation towards the large blaze in the intricately moulded fireplace, allowing himself to enjoy the heat in a lei-surely fashion. The fire's effectiveness was marginally improved by a free-standing screen which divided the first floor of the gatehouse and kept out some of the wind. The lesser of the two doors opening off the entrance passage led into the section so cut off, a stark space reduced to its bare wooden floor, oak-boarded ceiling and limewashed walls. Here the plaintiffs, prisoners, and guards waited until they were called through for the handing out of justice.

Not that the area demarcated as the courtroom was much grander. It too was remarkably unadorned, the cabinet full of legal trappings aside, and relied for its effect on a raised bench where the judges positioned themselves centrally, with county magnates and honorary commissioners ranked on either side in descending order of importance or else reduced to the low bench in front. Facing the bench was an even lower table for the sheriff, under-sheriff, and court clerks, and behind this a rudimentary jury box and prisoner's dock, as near as possible to the grand door through which the Justices entered and, more importantly, whatever air was able to infiltrate this stuffy space. Anything that reduced the risk of those prisoners suffering from gaol fever infecting others in court was not to be undervalued. It was particularly appreciated by Humphrey given the current state of his health.

On both sides of the room there were partitioned spaces for jurors and privileged observers, but this morning the room echoed emptily to the sound of a few court officials arranging them-selves and their materials at their table with a steady clopping of heels, ostentatious shuffling of paper, and sibilant whispers – the whispering in honour of the proceedings to come. The full court would convene in the following week, the first week of Easter, when the Justices were required to hold their General Quarter Sessions of the Peace. Then, upwards of a hundred people would squeeze into the makeshift courtroom. Today Humphrey had the space to himself and a small team of clerks.

It was their work to clear up the last of the preliminary hearings before the trials proper began. A solitary Justice of the Peace was empowered to conduct the pre-trial examinations, and this Easter it was Humphrey's turn to weed out weak cases before indictments were drawn up. The court did not initiate prosecutions; it was the responsibility of those who believed themselves to have suffered some wrongdoing to report the crime and identify the culprits. In Humphrey's experience the accusations were like a lance into the boil of daily life, releasing its suppurating puss of petty meanness, malice and hatred. Life, as he experienced it on the bench, was a stewing mess of ill will, anger and recrimination.

The diligent Justice – and Humphrey was a diligent Justice – had then to spend his time wading through a flood of complaints, investigating what could be investigated, calling witnesses and binding them over to appear at trial, examining accused persons and committing them to gaol or releasing them on bail. He made a point of doing everything he could to ensure that those cases that went before the court were worth its time. As far as he was concerned, the trial itself was simply a pageant that confirmed the real work of the pre-trial investigations.

As always, there were a large number of complainants gathering on the other side of the screen. Today, with the rain drumming insistently against the massive walls of the gatehouse, this was a sodden knot of people who had pressed forward into the shelter of the entrance before being shaped into something like an orderly line by the rough handling of the bailiff and his men processing them through the lesser of the two doorways. Humphrey settled on his bench and awaited the list being finalised by the Clerk of the Peace. As far as he knew, this clerk was honest enough, although God knows he'd worked with some who weren't. Many a Justice's clerk managed to make as much of a profit out of his fees for the Sessions as an Assize Court Judge, some even without attracting undue complaints of extortion. The current clerk, however, a lean, neat and trim man, seemed content with the modest gentility and social opportunities conferred by his office. He ran the Sessions in a decidedly professional and efficient manner.

He also discharged his duty by ensuring that the procedures were adhered to and that the Bench was properly directed as to the law and its powers with some tact, never presuming when a district judge was presiding that he was in need of the kind of advice a lay magistrate found necessary. Nevertheless, Humphrey did find the clerk's thorough legal training and sound practical knowledge of the law intimidating. He made sure not to reveal this, doing his best to grasp the clerk's sense of things ahead of any pronouncement or decision he needed to make. He had watched all too many of his less self-conscious colleagues bluster and pontificate their way through the complexities of a case before giving way, inevitably, to the Clerk of the Peace's firm hand.

Morpeth's Clerk of the Peace was adept at ensuring through the subtlest means that his guidance prevailed, and in such a way as not to seem to exert any influence upon the Bench. The advice he provided was always to do with some point of law, and nothing more. Admirably neutral it might be, but it carried considerable weight when it came to the outcome of the case. These contributions to the legal process were managed with self-effacing ease while the clerk appeared to be entirely preoccupied with the administrative business that was his prime concern – the drafting of documents, returning of accounts, drawing up of indictments, arraigning prisoners, entering judgements, awarding their process, and, above all, making up and keeping accurate records of the proceedings that came before the assembled Justices.

Ultimately, the smooth running of the Quarter Sessions depended on the clerk, even if he delegated most of the clerical work to a staff of associate and junior clerks he had gathered about himself. In his hands, this was a compact and proficient administrative department, a team of anonymous, shadowy figures who moved about the courtroom with the mechanical efficiency and near silence of the inner workings of a clock, ticking away in the background. The cryer was the peacock of this small, dun group, eager to carry out his proclamatory function once the court was in session, but at the moment chafing within the routine clerical services to which he was largely restricted while there were so few to call.

These included carrying over to the Justice the roll of complaints. Humphrey barely looked at the list as the usual parade, each complainant still outraged at the offences they believed had been committed against them, passed before him. He submitted himself to the torrent of accusations from the aggrieved parties, cutting these short as soon as he had the gist – speed being the main concern of Justices in a severely overloaded system – and, only if he thought it worth his while, hearing out a witness or two or examining the accused. Quickly, he bound over one accused of threatening behaviour, another of disturbing the peace, another of verbal abuse; he fined three accused of assault, ordered the bailiff to convey to gaol to await trial three accused of fornication, five of burglary, and one of seditious speech in a case that promised for a moment to be interesting but looked likely, as the accuser went on, to be dismissed by the grand jury. Trying to establish if there was enough evidence for the accusations in the steady stream of rancour spilled before him was far from easy. He dismissed out of hand several allegations of assault, one of wood theft and two of poaching. With increasing haste, he settled an apprenticeship dispute between master and servant, bound over for trial several recusants and a soldier accused of selling his arms, ordered the seizure of the goods of a group of gypsies and the search of a wax manufacturer for illicitly made candles.

Dealing with a woman 'charged for the felonious taking away of a cheese, the goods of her Master' was bringing him, with no small relief, to the end of the list, when his eye fell on the last allegation. He looked over to the Clerk of the Peace, who glanced up from his paperwork and gave a short cough behind the fist he raised to his mouth.

'Anne Baites and others; for witchcraft,' called out the cryer.

Chapter 4

Apr. 2, 1673. Before Humphrey Mitford, Esq.
  Ann Armstrong, of Birchen-nooke, spinster.

The drab bundle of damp grey being ushered towards the dock did not seem capable of carrying an accusation of such weight.

It was not unknown for capital offences to come before a Justice of the Peace, but when they did, the duty of a Justice was clear – cases carrying the death penalty must be referred to the judges of the Assize. Part of that duty, however, was to establish whether the offence did merit capital punishment. Many felonies were punishable by death, but the Justice had to decide – as in the case of the stolen cheese Humphrey had just dealt with – on their nature and severity.

Did the theft of the cheese constitute grand or petty larceny, for example? Only in the former case would it carry the death penalty. Offences against property and persons limited to theft and assault were rarely, in these more enlightened times, treated as capital offences, and therefore they need only be referred to the Quarter Sessions. It was for him to decide whether the cases of assault that came before him today were capital felonies – as they would be if, say, they had involved the slitting or cutting off of the nose – requiring him to forward them to the Assizes. Simple battery called only for the handing down of a fine or imprisonment. Then again, assaults so slight as to constitute a misdemeanour allowed Humphrey, as he had done this morning with so many of the accusations, to exercise his extensive powers of summary conviction, trying the case himself without referring it to any trial by jury. He was happy to let the woman who had stolen the cheese live, for example, although the fine he imposed was met with anything but gratitude.

A charge of witchcraft permitted him no such latitude. Along with all other cases involving a felony – murder, manslaughter, infanticide, treason, perjury, corruption, arson, rape, clipping of coins – he was obliged only to conduct a preliminary examination. Not that this was a trivial process. The examination had to be put in writing accurately, suspects committed to prison, prosecutors and witnesses bound over to appear at court. The depositions as taken down before him would serve as the basis for the court's case, so the written transcripts of any examination he carried out had to be treated with especial care in felony cases. Any lapses would reflect directly on him.

Humphrey eyed the approaching accuser in this case more closely than any of the sorry cast he had processed. Immediately, her appearance grated. She did not seem especially dirty as she drew herself up before him. If anything, now that he looked at her more closely, her clothing was less dishevelled than most of the crowd she had been a part of through the morning, huddling in the soaking rain for some time before his arrival – but, unaccountably, he felt there was something shifty about her. Not necessarily dishonest or deceitful, although an air of this hung about her hunched posture, her downcast eyes, the exaggerated demonstrations of humility, but shifting in a more literal sense, as if her actual shape was indistinct, uncertain. The standard grey with splashes of dull white in which she was dressed had a peculiarly colourless quality about it that went beyond the general hue of her clothing. It was as if her very substance had leached itself from the late morning murk of the courtroom. He found himself having to look twice to catch some idea of her overall appearance, something he became aware of doing again and again as the examination went through its prescribed procedures.

The girl – for she was surely no older than this – raised her eyes to Humphrey when she reached the desk, more directly than was normally the case between ranks as disparate as theirs, her mouth already an open O.

Before she could utter a syllable, the cryer called out, 'Anne Armstrong, of Birches Nooke, spinster.'

The girl pressed her lips together as her name was called and turned her head towards where the clerks were gathered, focusing on the exact point where a hand hovered above paper, a white flare between a black sleeve and the dark wood of the table, poised to catch her words. The thought crossed Humphrey's mind that a moment of silent communion followed, not between two people, but between the gape of the girl's mouth and that disembodied hand; he had to restrain himself from actually shaking his head in an attempt to clear it of the impression.

While the Clerk of the Peace put the girl under oath, Humphrey became conscious of a shift in his sense of what was taking place in the courtroom, a heightened yet strangely distorted awareness of certain details, insignificant details at that. This disturbed him, and then he remembered he was not well. Clearly his condition was worsening with the effort he had to expend for the day's work. Through the course of the morning he'd been finding it increasingly painful to swallow, even saliva; his eyes had been growing hotter, and now burned within their sockets, and his brow felt both papery and moist when he passed his hand over it – a clammy hand at that, which made it difficult to tell if his forehead were hot or cold. He wished his wife were here, with her soothing hands and low, comforting voice.

He was trying to dredge up one of the standard questions used to open the deposition process when the girl began to speak. It took an act of will to concentrate on the words that tumbled out of her mouth. The difficulty he had in making sense of them lay not only in his own condition. From the first, the court was thrown midstream into the torrent of a story to do with a Morpeth woman who had been associating with witches. At first, there were scattered references to what he was after, specific accusations, with names, places, witnesses, verifiable dates, but these were soon reduced to swirling flotsam in the flood of words. The odd name and place rushed by, but as for what followed, Humphrey had not heard so much arrant nonsense in a long while: devils and dancing, animals and flying, some sort of blasphemous ceremony ...

The strange thing was the effect of the tirade on the speaker herself. While she poured out this balderdash, it was as if she began to change, grow, her very person reforming itself in the air about her. The more nonsense she spoke, the more confident her voice became, and with this she seemed to be increasing in size, becoming firmer, more definite, more grown-up even, a woman youngish still but in her prime. Enough, however, was enough, and what he'd heard was quite enough.

From the instant the informant began to speak, the scribe's hand had flown over the paper in a feathery scrawl, an insistent scratching accompanying each word, underscoring the flood of words riding her breath into the courtroom. Both ceased at the same instant as Humphrey called out, more loudly than he intended: 'Stop.'

He turned to the Clerk of the Peace, and asked him to read back the record. The scribe passed this to him, and in a voice as dry and steady as his appearance, the clerk recited from the page: 'Northumberland. Information Ann Armstrong of Birchen,' – the clerk looked over to the scribe with a slight frown – '*Birches* Nooke, *Capt Coram* Humphrey Mitford –'

Humphrey waved him past the Latin, choosing to ignore the clerk's evident disapproval. After the slightest beat, the clerk read on:

'The said informant saith upon her oath that Ann, wife of Thomas Baites, of Morpeth, tanner, hath been several times in the company of the rest of the witches, both at Barwick, Barrasford, and at Riding bridge-end, and once at the house of Mr Francis Pye, in Morpeth, in the cellar there.

'And the informant further saith that the said Ann Baites hath several times danced with the devil at the places aforesaid, calling him, sometimes, her protector, and, other sometimes, her blessed saviour.

'And the informant further saith that the said Ann Armstrong hath seen the said Ann Baites several times at the places aforesaid riding upon wooden dishes and eggshells, both in the Riding House and in the close adjoining.

'And the informant further saith that the said Ann hath been several times in the shape of a cat and a hare, and in the shape of a greyhound and a bee, letting the devil (who she calls her protector) see how many several shapes or likenesses she could turn herself into – and further this informant saith not.'

Keeping his eyed firmly on the clerk, Humphrey asked, 'And does the deponent really have nothing further to add?'

'That is where you stopped the informant, Your Worship.'

'Well, it is enough. Does the deponent agree this is a true record?' Humphrey asked, steadily ignoring the girl. 'If so, let her sign.'

The clerk handed the paper to one of his associate clerks, who passed it to an assistant who placed it in front of the girl. She looked at it and shook her head.

At first the clerk thought the girl was going to complain about being cut short. The scribe, however, read the situation correctly. He leaned over to her, and wrote 'Ann' under the script – script with which he was rightfully pleased. Despite the speed with which the girl had spoken, he had taken her information down without recourse to shorthand. Oh, he was comfortable enough with the technique, having studied a number of the shorthand manuals available, but he prided himself with producing a full text, neat and free enough from corrections – Birches Nooke aside, on this occasion, and the spelling of the girl's Christian name – not to require copying out for the records. Most scribes barely managed to get the substance of what was spoken down, having to produce fair copies afterwards from rough drafts, but his hand was fast and steady, his knowledge of the legal formulae sound, and his own ability to turn a phrase more than enough to give the necessary form and structure to a deposition. What he put before Anne was, as far as the requirements of the legal system were concerned, a faithful report of the words she had spoken, a good enough account of her accusation and her evidence to be read out aloud during the trial, where she and the witnesses would be called upon to answer any follow-up questions.

Only her signature was required to make the deposition official. Passing the pen to the girl, he pointed to the place where he had written her first name: 'Ann –'. She pressed the quill to the page after the dash, moving its point in what appeared to be an attempt at a circle. Her evident unfamiliarity with the instrument resulted in something short of this, with a thickened smudge of the line at the start and two attempts at making the beginning and end of the line meet in a satisfactory closure. This done, she stabbed a small dot into its centre, slipping slightly so that it appeared to be more of a light stroke than a point. Her efforts were unnecessary as any mark would have done, with the scribe writing carefully after it, 'Armstrong her mark', and then dashing down the *Capt Coram me* that had to precede the Justice's signature.

Before passing it back to be handed to the Justice, however, he scanned the names of the accused with a view to noting the people he would need to call for trial. As usual, he began listing them next to the information he had taken down. He had only begun to write 'Anne Baites', was still writing, the 's' in fact, when the Justice called irritably for the deposition. The assistant clerk took the paper so swiftly in his haste to obey that it slipped away from under the scribe's pen, resulting in a short streak of ink running away from the letter.

Marred now in the scribe's eyes, although perfect in every other respect, the document was placed in front of Humphrey, who added his name heavily, the quill splitting under the pressure, and announced to the court: '*Ignoramus*'.

The Clerk of the Peace was looking down as Humphrey spoke, shuffling through some paperwork. He did not look up, but stopped what he was doing and placed the papers on the desk.

'Your Worship?'

'*Ignoramus*,' repeated Humphrey, 'not found; the accusation is rejected and the case is not approved as a true bill.'

The clerk, stung by this spelling out of the legal expression, nevertheless stepped from behind his table and approached Humphrey with his composure intact. Leaning in as closely as he could, he said, evenly, quietly, 'I believe that the acts of 1554 and 1555 stipulate that accusations of a capital felony *must*' – the stress was slight, but could not be missed – 'be forwarded for trial. We' – the pronoun gently opened up responsibility for this beyond the presiding Justice – 'are required only to direct it to the appropriate court, as I am sure Your Worship is aware.'

The clerk was close enough to Humphrey to point at the one name the scribe had been able to write in the margin of the deposition. 'And those accused of a felony – I believe we need to add Mr Francis Pye, and ask further about the Baites woman's husband, never mind "the rest of the witches" – have to be examined by at least one Justice and imprisoned pending trial or released on bail. Release, of course, requires the presence of two Justices, one of whom should be of the *Quorom*.'

The slightest of inflections on 'two' was enough to bring to mind the limitations of Humphrey's role here as a single Justice of the Peace; a Justice of the Peace, what is more, not included, as the clerk's less subtle reminder of this point of law made plain, in the *Quorom*, that group of Justices specifically chosen for their specialised knowledge of the laws of the land.

'Well, I do not intend to imprison anyone, or release anyone on bail. I do not believe we are dealing with a felony here, only the spreading of false rumours, which it is well within the powers of a Justice to suppress. There is no need to call in those accused. The evidence given is simply not sufficient to warrant a trial, and neither is the crime. Who is the victim here, where is the harm?'

Humphrey stabbed the indictment with his finger with each question, keeping his eyes down. He found himself reluctant to look at the clerk as he held his ground, but he was also aware, somewhere in the margins of his vision, of the girl's eyes, locked in on him in a steady, unwavering stare. He had no idea how much of the exchange she was able to hear or understand, but he especially did not want to engage that grey, watery look, as strong as the deluge outside beating on insistently. He wondered vaguely if she were mentally deficient; surely the confidence he could feel across the space between them was born of its own lack of comprehension.

'If I may, Your Worship,' said the clerk, his voice coming from a place Humphrey could no longer recognise, 'it is, surely, for the grand jury to assess the indictment and decide whether the case should come before a trial jury.'

'I say again, *no bill*. The case is to be dropped, and is not to appear in the Proceedings of the Sessions.'

Despite his outer composure, the clerk was at a loss: Humphrey Mitford was normally the most compliant of Justices. He had some experience with the increasing tendency of certain magistrates to deal summarily with an ever-widening range of matters. But Mitford, if anything, was generally reluctant to take authority into his own hands. The law, the clerk had always thought, provided a refuge for Humphrey Mitford, a way of disappearing into formality, blending himself into the thickets of due process. Armstrong's accusations appeared to have driven him from cover, forced him to show his hand.

For his part, Humphrey was loath to explain his decision. He knew that to do so would weaken his authority. And yet he was already regretting snapping at the clerk, for whom he held a real respect. He himself couldn't understand his outburst. He only knew that something about this woman's testimony annoyed him intensely.

At one level, the source of his irritation was clear: the woman's evidence was simply fantastic. Humphrey did not think, as many people did these days, that witches only existed in the minds of poor infatuated people, but he had no time for old crones flying through the night, humans changing shape, men and women making pacts with the devil or having intercourse with demons or taking part in orgiastic rites. These were the sort of prurient fantasies the imagination might engender in popish countries, demonological inventions in the Continental or, it must be said (with due deference to His Majesty, more especially His Majesty's father), in the *Scottish* style. The English, thank God, were more down to earth, having the good sense to prosecute their neighbours only if they had done some actual harm to them, or to their families or their animals. In Humphrey's experience, his countrymen were hard-headed enough to know that afflictions caused by a witch's malice – death through a wasting disease, lamed legs, paralysis of one side of the body, the killing of cattle, horses, sheep and pigs, the burning of barns and goods, the bewitching of beer being brewed – provided some possibility of proof, and therefore successful prosecution. Any other claptrap, such as this woman's accusations of dancing with the devil, flying on dishes and eggshells, changing into cats or dogs or bees or whatever else, had no place in an English courtroom. And it was certainly unlikely to find its way into the terse prose of a good, solid indictment.

But his response to her testimony, his speaking to his clerk so sharply, was driven by more than that. For a moment, a brief moment, Humphrey allowed himself to wonder what she actually thought when she made these absurd accusations. Was this sheer invention, or was it based on some kind of hearsay? Was this woman's head really full of visions of her neighbours shrunk to a size that fitted into dishes and eggshells? Or had those vehicles of flight grown to a size that could accommodate her neighbours, and the animals and insects whose shapes they adopted, taken on a human scale? His mind could not hold the pictures she had called up, and his passing attempt at trying to imagine what she said she saw blurred into a weaving, buzzing, whirling parade of phantasms skimming around the walls of this – he looked at the deposition – Riding House.

Humphrey pressed his fingers to the bridge of his nose, squeezed his eyes shut and then opened them to look again at the deponent's name: Armstrong. Enough of them about down here now, but her people would have come from the Middle Marches, way up in the wild, hilly country of the Cheviots and North Pennines. Is that where this Scottish nonsense came from, that borderland where total lawlessness once prevailed? Where the Armstrongs had been among the most powerful of the Reiver clans raiding and marauding and feuding, giving themselves free rein to ride through the passes and mosses and over the fells on raids against anyone on either side of the border, since Reivers were never fussy which side they stole from or murdered.

'May I suggest,' the Clerk of the Peace spoke softly, 'Your Worship, that we put this matter before another Justice, one from the *Quorom*, to confirm your judgement? It so happens that Sir Richard Stote is sitting tomorrow, and I am sure he will be ...'

Humphrey Mitford's head was hurting badly, his hands moist and shaking, and every bone and joint ached with the effort of taking a stand against the foreign foolishness this Armstrong woman was trying to put before his court.

His court? He, a pale, faltering figure of justice, severely distracted now, his mind filled with strange thoughts. Chief among them, beating at him like the rain against the gatehouse, the odd idea that wherever Anne Armstrong came from, it was some kind of borderland, a borderland where no laws that he could command applied.

Riding Mill

When they first noticed the girl sitting on the bench, none of them were sure how long she'd been there.

A small grey thing, she was huddled into the heavy, dark wood. But she was watching them over her arms, folded around her knees, which were drawn up tightly against her chest.

The slats must have been wet. The rain had only just eased off enough for them to convince their parents they should be allowed to go to the play park until it started again. All three stopped as they caught her stare: Peter at the top of the slide, knuckles white against its metal edges, Victoria suspended halfway up the mesh of the climbing frame, and Sarah leaning forward against the chains of a swing, feet thrust against the protective covering beneath.

For a moment they were locked into the silence. The tumble of the burn beyond the safety fence, much heavier than usual because of the weeks and weeks of rain, ran on through the quiet. The hills rising away on three sides up to the woods and fields and the moors beyond were still, a hand cupping the heart of the village motionless between beats.

And then Victoria pulled her eyes away and called out something to her friends as she went back to her climbing. Peter threw himself on to the slide and careened down in a tangle of elbows and knees, and Sarah kicked into the protective surfacing to push herself high into the air. As she flew up the parish hall slid beneath her view, along with her parents' house across the road. Swooping backwards, she glanced at the bench and its dull little bundle, which had not moved at all.

The girl did not get up or try to join them as they played on, swapping equipment, fighting over turns, jostling each other, yelling full-voiced, moving in and out of games which were only half-formed before being discarded or shifting into something else. Red faces, bright eyes, warm breath hanging in the cold air, blurs of movement, they played on into the gathering dark, thick and green as it concentrated within and then spread out from the dense mat of trees and foliage which cradled the village.

The inevitable rain came ghosting in with it, along with Peter's elder brother, waterproofed and put out at having been dispatched to call them in. The shouting followed the children as they ran up the path, echoes hanging in the air and then slowly subsiding, leaving the park to its quiet. Peter's brother hung behind, old enough not to want to be part of that scrabble of noise disappearing around the parish hall. He felt the silence falling around him, reclaiming the park as the mist formed in the air. He breathed in the smell of recently cut lawn and the fertilised fields beyond the fringe of trees. Then he saw the girl in her thin, damp, ankle-length dress, looking steadily at the deserted equipment. The empty swing was still moving, squeaking softly as the rain pattered on to the play equipment.

Anyone looking down on the park could have seen them; he walking towards the bench, she, sitting up now. From the road, it seemed as if they were talking, although Peter's brother would say nothing about this when he came in for tea, withdrawn as always into his mid-teen surliness.

Play Park Vandalised in Riding Mill

The Journal, 14 November 2011

AXE-WIELDING vandals have run amok in a small Tyne Valley village, causing severe damage to equipment in the play park behind the Parish Hall.

A climbing frame, swings, and a slide were gouged and had pieces hacked from them. The trail of devastation continued to a wooden bench at the Weir on the nearby March Burn.

'It would appear some youngsters got hold of an axe and went round attacking things,' a police spokesman said. 'Huge splinters were left everywhere which need to be cleared up, so it could be a while before the park is fully reopened.

'This has clearly been a mindless act of vandalism which we are treating seriously. Nowhere is completely crime free, but this is very unusual for Riding Mill.'

Chairman of the parish council, Councillor Harry Blenkins, said: 'It is sad because the bench that was damaged was donated in memory of someone who died.

'You don't expect this in a place like Riding Mill. There is a strong community spirit here which can sometimes be lacking in other areas. This spirit, which demonstrates all that is good about living in a traditional village setting, was clear to see at some recent events such as the garden walkabout and scarecrow competition – both of which were well-supported by local residents.

'In addition to this, Riding Mill has friendly, thoughtful residents who make newcomers to the village feel welcome. But unfortunately this sort of vandalism happens all over the place these days. What people would like to do to those responsible is not printable.'

It is believed a number of people were involved in the attack and some teenagers from Prudhoe are being questioned.

It has also been reported that a bicycle was recently stolen from outside the Wellington Inn and a warning has been placed in the Parish News asking people to be vigilant.

Chapter 5

The clerk to the Clerk of the Peace takes the freshly drafted deposition from the scribe – a new deposition, in a different hand from the hand of the day before, the ink still wet – and hands it to the Clerk of the Peace. The Clerk of the Peace waits for the shuffling and whispering to die down, looks at Sir Richard Stote, who gives the slightest nod, and then the clerk reads out to the courtroom:

'Northumberland. The Information of Anne Armstrong, spinster, taken upon oath 4th April 1673, in the twenty third – *fifth,*' he makes a mental note to remind the scribe that he should write out more neatly the number of years since the execution of Charles I – 'year of the reign of Charles II. Before Sir Richard Stote, one of the justiciary: Who saith that since this informant gave information against several persons who rid this informant to several places where they had conversation with the devil –'

'Whom they call their protector or blessed saviour,' calls out the deponent, surprising the court with her interjection.

The clerk pauses to write this into the deposition, squeezing it in between the more usefully spaced lines of the scribe assigned to the Quarter Sessions today. This scribe's handwriting is larger, too, making it easier to read in the gloom of another day of rain lashing the gatehouse. Larger, yes, but to the clerk's annoyance, far less tidy, creating the potential for inaccuracies that could be embarrassing, if the messy enumeration of the years by which the present king's reign is measured is anything to go by. He resumes, with a careful eye on the freshly inked words:

'This informant saith she hath been several times lately ridden by Anne Dryden and Anne Forster, and was *last night ...*' – the stress is accompanied by a faint pause and a questioning look at Anne, who nods firmly, '... ridden by them to the Riding House in the –'

'Close upon, not in,' says Anne, and the clerk carefully squeezes this in above the line and reads out the correction,

'– *close upon* the common where the said –' he goes through the names that follow slowly, writing each one in the left-hand margin as he does so, correcting the scribe's spelling where necessary, '– Anne Forster, Anne Dryden, Lucy Thompson, John Crawforth, William Wright, Elizabeth Pickering, Anne Usher, Michael Aynsley and Margaret his wife, and one Margaret, whose Christian name –' he draws a line through the obvious error, shaking his head as he inserts the correction above it, '– *surname* she knows not but she said to the protector she came from Corbridge, and three more, whose names she knows not –' he frowns at the next word, which the scribe has scribbled out, '– were all present with their protector and had all sorts of meats and drinks they named siltt upon the table by pulling a rope, and they took the bridle of this informant and made her sing to them –'

'While they danced,' interjects the deponent, which the clerk reads out as he inserts it into the text,

'– and all of them who had done harm gave an account thereof to their protector who made most of them that did most harm, and beat those who had done no harm, and Mary –' the clerk turns the page over, '– Hunter said she had killed George Taylor's filly, and had power over his mare –' another frown at a smudge, '– and that she had power of the far hinder leg of John Marche –' he peers more closely at the page, '– John *Marche's* ox.'

The deponent has a satisfied look about her as the clerk writes *Capt & Jurat coram me* in the space below the information on the left before passing the document to Sir Richard.

'And further this informant saith not?' Sir Richard inquired, without looking up.

Anne nods.

'And further this informant saith not,' says the clerk, impassive.

'Well, put that in, write it on the page below the information as given so that we know it cannot be tampered with. Anything added after this will not be seen as coming from the deponent.'

The clerk reached out for the piece of paper. Nothing in his demeanour indicated the irritation he might have been expected to feel at his professional practice scrutinised and corrected, let alone the lecture in due process appended to it.

'But hold off there, for the moment.' Sir Richard pulled back the deposition, incomplete as it was, and the clerk let his hand drop.

Richard Stote – Sir Richard Stote of London, Knight Bachelor but, more importantly, if rumours in legal circles were correct, about to be promoted to Serjeant-at-Law. Once so elevated, he would join this order of barristers in having precedence over other lawyers, with exclusive jurisdiction over the Court of Common Pleas and rights of audience in the Court of King's Bench and Exchequer of Pleas. He could soon be travelling up north in a markedly different capacity to the relatively humble role he was now playing in his home county; Serjeants-at-Law, and only Serjeants-at-Law, could become judges of these courts. Doubtless this fact helped the clerk maintain his customary restraint, despite Sir Richard's unintended provocations. Possibly the clerk reminded himself too that Sir Richard was currently Reader of Lincoln's Inn, a post that required him to give lectures to the law students there. This was no small achievement: Stote was from a wealthy family, but their prosperity stemmed from their mercantile interests in Newcastle; rather than enter trade, he had pursued a legal career both successful and lucrative.

Surely a man of such eminence, and on the brink of much more, could direct the information provided by this Armstrong woman to the proper court, in the process binding over the witnesses and committing the accused to custody to await trial at the next Assizes?

Sir Richard Stote, Knight, of Lincoln's Inn and Jesmond Hall, a Justice of the Peace for that County, stared at the deposition for some minutes. Then he leaned forward to the clerk and asked, 'What is this "siltt" of which she speaks? "Had all sorts of meats and drinks they named siltt upon the table," she says. What is it exactly that they eat?'

Despite himself, a flicker passed over the clerk's face. Then, perfectly contained again, he turned to the deponent. From her face he could see that she understood the question, but had no idea of how to expand upon the term.

'I believe, Your Worship, that this is a variation on, perhaps simply a wrong transcription by the scribe –' he gave the scribe a half glance '– of the Northumbrian word "sile", derived from the expression to flow, possibly also to strain, as in to purify milk through a straining dish. This would indicate that the drinks in question had been produced by this process.'

'Ah, not the meat, then?'

'I expect not, Your Worship.'

Sir Richard turned back to the deposition. Then he turned to the deposition taken by Humphrey Mitford, Esq., which the clerk had included in his paperwork for the day's proceedings.

'So this Morpeth woman, Anne –' scanning the document, looking for the word, '– Baites, wife of Thomas Baites, of Morpeth, is what brings this case before us at these Sessions?'

'Yes, Your Worship, although you will see that the accusations made by the deponent, Anne Armstrong, range over large portions of Northumberland, from Morpeth to Berwick and Barrasford –'

'Yes, but always coming back to this Riding – bridge-end, house: where is this?'

'The Riding in question is, I believe, in south Northumberland, on the banks of the River Tyne.'

'But the deponent confirms that she was there "last night". And yet she was giving her information to Mitford on Wednesday, when would that have been, just before lunch?'

'Yes, Your Worship. We had hoped to complete the preliminary examinations in the morning – which we did in all cases, excepting this.'

'And she is back here in Morpeth this morning. But the distance must be – what, twenty, thirty miles from that place to here?'

'I cannot confirm that, Your Worship – indeed, I am not sure it is my place to do so. But the deponent does say –' he turned and looked at Anne '– she was ridden there. By witches.'

Anne nodded, but Sir Richard ignored her.

'Well, unquestionably she did not come by coach. It takes me eight and a half hours – by coach – to get from Newcastle to Carlisle, on the best road in the region; which is not, of course, saying much as roads here go. That is sixty-odd miles, so how are we to believe that she can get back here by breakfast from this Riding ... Riding House, twenty or thirty miles from where we are gathered today? Unless, that is, we give credence to her story of being ridden by these witches, Anne Dryden and Anne Forster.

'A regular occurrence, it would appear. Often involving many other witches, if this list of names is anything to go by. To whom we must add Baites, of course, if we take Mitford's investigation, such as it is, into account as well.

'Now look at this –' Sir Richard appeared to be speaking out loud to himself, but the clerk leaned forward with a polite look of attention '– she tells Mitford that Baites is often in the company of "the rest of the witches". What other witches? And she tells me that "... since she gave information against several persons who rid her to several places where they had conversation with the devil ..." But when was it that she gave this information? I see nothing of it in Wednesday's deposition.'

The clerk sifted through the papers on his desk with the air of one who knew this was not necessary. 'Nothing else was appended to the papers I put before you, Your Worship,' he said.

Justice and clerk looked at the girl. She remained silent for a moment, as if considering something. Then she said, 'The others were Anne Forster of Stocksfield, Anne Dryden of Prudhoe, Lucy Thompson of Mickley, and more whose names I did not know then, but several of which I have given to you now. I spoke of them to the Justice at his house in Newcastle. In February.'

'Newcastle? February?' Sir Richard turned to the clerk.

'That will be Ralph Jenison, then, at one of his Petty Sessions,' said the clerk. 'Are you sure, girl, Mr Jenison in Newcastle?'

'Mr Jenison,' she said, 'in Trinity House, Newcastle.'

Justice and clerk withdrew into separate silences, each absorbing this new turn in their own way.

Sir Richard was the first to speak. 'Mr Jenison will have handled this by the book. There's a man who always plays it safe, as well he should, what with an uncle who was an infamous Puritan vicar and a cousin who is a Jesuit priest. Why then have we not heard of this prior deposition?'

The clerk shuffled his papers again, staring down at his desk.

'Jenison is, if I'm not mistaken, on the benches of both Newcastle and Northumberland Counties,' said Sir Richard.

The clerk affirmed this with a nod.

'So even if this –' he looked at the deposition before him '– Stocksfield, and the other places she talks about, are in Northumberland County, he would have been able to deal with the case.'

'He is too, on the Morpeth panel for gaol deliveries,' said the clerk.

'So he could easily have had the accused held here instead of Newcastle, and passed the case on to these Quarter Sessions. But he hasn't. And then this woman comes before Mitford going on about this Anne Baites, wife of Thomas Baites of Morpeth, and strange doings in a cellar in Morpeth. And two days later she comes before me, and doesn't mention Morpeth, or Mr Francis Pye of that town.

'It seems to me she's gone to a lot of trouble to make sure her case comes before us here in Morpeth, although that is what it should have done in the first place. Some kind of ruse, I would say.'

The clerk had managed to look politely interested in Sir Richard Stote's ruminations thus far, but he took the Justice's pause for thought to raise the simple observation that cut right through them.

'Mr Ralph Jenison would, as you say, have been careful to follow the proper procedures. He would, as is required of any accusation involving a felony, have passed it on to the Judges of the King's Bench Division when they arrive in Newcastle for the Assizes.'

Adept as he was, the clerk allowed no hint of the frustration he so often felt – and had been feeling more strongly than usual over the last few days – to colour his voice when trying to guide Justices of the Peace. 'This was the point I wished to impress upon Mr Mitford.'

'Well, why is the matter back before us, then?' demanded Sir Richard.

'I do not know, Your Worship. The Assize judges in commission for this year are Sir William Ellis – he has recently replaced Justice Archer who, I believe, was not in support of the king's suspension of the Declaration of Indulgence – and Sir William Wylde. And I am sure they are being particularly scrupulous of late, given the concern of the king and his advisors over the willingness of the judges to support the king against opposition from the Commons. I would not, under the circumstances, expect them to be complaining that they have more work than they can deal with and delegating felony cases to the Quarter Sessions.'

'Whatever transpired,' said Sir Richard, turning his attention back to the informant, 'the fact that this woman is standing here makes it clear that she did not receive a satisfactory outcome from the information she gave to Jenison.'

'If you wish, Your Worship, I can send a message to the Clerk of the Assizes for the Northern Circuit in York enquiring after the deposition taken by Mr Jenison.'

The girl looked steadily at each speaker in turn as they spoke. Even if she was not following what they said, there was something about her demeanour that stuck Sir Richard as compelling, as if her composure carried a mute but insistent appeal. He had been struck by her calm, detailed corrections to her accusations as read back to her by the clerk. This stood in marked contrast to the nature of the information she had given, as if she were aware of how outlandish it must sound and wanted to corroborate it with the precision of her details.

'Well, the matter is before us now, and to refer it to the Assizes will make us look weak, as if we can't sort the wheat from the chaff in our own territory.'

'The point, if I may say so,' said the clerk, 'is that this is an accusation concerning the invoking of evil spirits and communing with familiar spirits. Under the Acts of Elizabeth and James these are felonies –'

'You are not, I hope, implying that I am unfamiliar with the Act Against Conjuration, Witchcraft and Dealing with Evil and Wicked Spirits?'

The sharpness of his question caused the clerk to step back and stand almost, but not quite, to attention. The pose he adopted seemed to Sir Richard to be just short, only just short, of a reminder – could that be a sardonic reminder? – of the formalities of his position.

This brought to mind the advice an outgoing Justice had given Sir Richard many years ago, a warning really, he realised today, that it was wise to accommodate his clerk in all things. A venison pasty, the outgoing Justice suggested, and a pottle of wine maybe, served to the clerk during the Sessions, and always, always the prompt payment of his appropriate fees – his fee for the gaol calendar, for example, otherwise the magistrate may well find himself sending his undersheriff trotting to the remotest places in the county in search of it, and without the calendar he would be powerless to execute judgement upon the prisoners condemned at the Sessions.

Then again, he doubted this particular clerk would be so petty. His very proper sense of procedure would not allow it, the same proper sense of procedure that lay behind the silence drawing the Justice inevitably towards the conclusion he knew, and the clerk knew, he would have to reach.

'Indeed, Your Worship,' said the clerk, breaking his silence after he was sure it had had its intended effect. He reached for the depositions taken today and yesterday from Anne Armstrong, but this was a move too far for Sir Richard. The certainty with which the clerk assumed that he had been brought around to the view that the indictment had to be referred to the grand jury of the Assizes stuck in the Justice's craw.

'Have you any idea how many witch trials end in acquittal?' he asked the clerk, sure that he did, to the exact number, but he could not help himself. 'Over half the witchcraft cases are dismissed for lack of evidence, and barely one in five end with a conviction. So let me tell you that I don't want to be the one making some grand jury at the Assizes squirm as it tries to find a way to reject a bill rather than risk the life of someone sent to trial for the most dubious of felony charges.'

The clerk had stepped back again, dropping his hands, but it was the girl's eyes that Sir Richard Stote became aware of, those dark, translucent eyes fixed on his face, almost hungrily, as he spoke. Had she been staring at him this way throughout his speeches?

'And yet,' he went on, shaking himself free of that stare, speaking again more to himself than the ostensible audience he had in the clerk; 'and yet, we have full names, what is it, seven, eight of them –'

'Nine, I believe you'll find, Your Worship,' said the clerk, feeling he was breaking into a private rumination; 'and one Margaret, whose surname she says she does not know, as well as three more women, I think it is, whose names she also does not know.'

Sir Richard was tapping the depositions again. 'Names, and there's harm – "all of them who had donne harme gave an account thereof to their protector, who made most of them that did most harme, and beate those who had donne no harme." Mitford, as I understand it, would not find this a true bill because there was no *maleficium*, no harm done and no victims.

'But here we have –' Sir Richard turned in his chair, and for the first time since he had asked the question or two which had provoked the girl's outpourings, he looked at her, ruminatively, not really focusing on the face hanging white in the dank gloom of the courtroom being hammered by the rain '– both harm done, and the names of those to whom it has been done. George Taylor's filly, she tells us, was killed by one Mary Hunter, who also has power over his mare. And the "farre hinder leg" of John Marche's ox.

'So, now we must think of more than the king and the courts, and the learned demonological writers. I am with Mitford this far: this woman can go on about dancing with the devil and changing shape and eating and drinking their siltt – a good word, that, I must remember it – but harming someone's live-stock by occult means, now that is serious. We know the cost to these men of losing a filly or a mare, and an ox that cannot do its work.

'Let's leave this Baites woman out of it for the moment,' he said, suddenly dashing his signature on to the deposition and then holding the page out to the clerk, 'with her riding on wooden dishes and eggshells and changing into cats and hares and greyhounds and bees; it's Hunter we should be after, Mary Hunter.'

The clerk took the deposition from the Justice and passed it to the scribe, who placed it in front of Anne.

'Mary Hunter of Birkenside,' she said.

'Of Birkenside,' repeated the clerk, beginning to turn to his assistants.

Before he could pose the question, the girl added, 'And another.'

'Another? What other?'

The girl looked steadily at Sir Richard, and raised her shoulders and her hands, palms outward.

'And another,' Sir Richard said to the clerk, 'she not knowing her name. No need to add "and further this informant saith not"; clearly this deponent has a lot more to add, and we're going to be re-examining her thoroughly. Where is it that this Hunter woman has been crippling and killing those animals? And who is this other that has been causing harm? We need more evidence, some real evidence, if we're going to let this case go any further. I need to talk to Taylor and March, hear what they have to say.'

It wasn't clear if the girl was following this sudden shift in the proceedings. She simply followed the scribe's finger to the place above his hurried addition of 'Anne Armstrong's mark' below the Justice's signature.

Again, she concentrated hard on drawing a circle – too hard, the point of the quill digging into the paper and then pulling away to the left before she arched it back around, the line ending in a smudge without joining up, the dot she aimed at what should have been the centre landing instead in the space where beginning and ending had failed to meet.

She looked at her efforts critically, and then said, 'Edgebrigg.'

The word dropped into the hall like a stone into a pool, a still, black pool, sending ripples across the murmuring surface of Sir Richard's voice to the surrounding banks of the clerk's silence.

The Justice of the Peace looked up in surprise, glancing first at the girl, and then focusing on the clerk. The clerk caught his gaze for a moment, and then turned to his assistants. A low, sibilant exchange followed, and then the clerk stood up from the huddled consultation to announce, 'Eddysbridge.'

'John March and George Taylor of Edgebrigg,' the girl confirmed, with several emphatic nods of her head.

'Eddysbridge,' said the clerk. 'A hotbed of the Anabaptists, high up in the wilds between Durham and Northumberland.'

'How far, man – how far from here?'

More consultation among the clerks followed. 'It is in the Derwent Valley, on the banks of the river itself. About thirty, thirty-five miles, we would say, from Morpeth, twenty or so from Newcastle. You cross over the bridge there on the way to the village of Edmundbyers in County Durham.'

'Edenbyers,' said the girl; 'Mary Hunter of Birkenside, and the other, whose name I do not know, is from Edenbyers.'

The clerk looked thoughtfully at the girl. 'Edenbyers. Yes, I have heard this Edmundbyers called by that name, though it is not an appropriate way of saying it – or an appropriate name at all for such a place. *Edmund*byers is famous for its witches, as is the surrounding area – which includes, one of my assistants tells me now, this Birkenside, or Birkside, a wood, he believes. In the past many local women and men in the Derwent Vale have been brought before the courts for witchcraft and proven guilty. The area is, then,' he said slowly, 'well chosen, for a case of this type.'

'And there's barely any difference,' one of the more junior clerks muttered, 'between Anabaptism and heretical witchcraft. They say the devil himself has visited Edmundbyers.'

A ripple of laughter ran through the junior clerks, quickly shushed by the Clerk of the Peace, but not before another burst out, 'And Catholics. Catholics, Baptists, and witches!'

Sir Richard raised his hand, eyes closed, and held this pose for a minute or more.

'Protector,' he said eventually, slowly. He looked down at the deposition: "'... were all present with their *protector*," she says, several times. Not Lord Protector, I'll give you, but could there be any political significance in this?'

He gave a hard stare at the girl.

'I think not; then again ...'

He appeared lost in his ruminations for a few moments more, and then spoke again, brisk and businesslike.

'What I want you to do, Clerk, is to find out what happened to the deposition made before Mr Jenison. Whatever we discover there, it is my view that we have a new set of accusations before us, accusations I wish to examine further before deciding that they should be referred to the Justices of the Assize.

'I shall, in the meantime, visit this Edmundbyers or Edenbyers, passing though Birkenside and Eddysbridge on the way. It sounds like this area is at the heart of all sorts of trouble. And I'll take this –' he waved a hand at the woman in the dock '– girl with me. I want her to identify the other woman whose name she does not know, and tell her what she's told us. Then I want to see what she has to say in reply. Let's see if we can find this Hunter woman and March and Taylor too.

'I shall return to Jesmond tonight, and leave for these villages tomorrow. Tell the bailiff to get ready to accompany me, with some of his men. And one of your assistant clerks.' Sir Richard looked up at the lead-coloured, water-streaked panes of glass set in the walls of the gatehouse, where the ghost of the sun was now glimmering in a faint corona. 'Weather allowing, I shall be back in time for the opening of the Sessions of the Peace on Monday.

'And send a message to Sir James Clavering at Axwell Park, asking him if he'll be so good as to join me. I'll need a Durham man with me while I'm investigating in the Palatinate; I've had trouble before with their special jurisdiction.

'And do not forget,' he said, with a flourish that took in all his court officials and set the yards of ribbon loops on the shoulders of his coat in colourful motion, 'that when I get back, I expect to have that deposition taken by Jenison on my desk.'

The National Archives

Dust. Careful as I was, a small puff of dust rose from each of the first three depositions – 2 April, 4 April and the confusing 5 February – as I placed them on the desk.

Every page I lifted from the acid-free cardboard box came away with a similar exhalation of the tiny particles of detritus accumulated over several centuries. How much survived from the courtroom in Morpeth? How much of the paper fibre, ink specks, textile filaments, human hair, animal hair, plant pollen, minerals from the soil, human skin cells, minuscule creatures, volcanic ash and burnt meteorite particles as well, for all I knew, along with other microscopic elements I could hardly guess at, had Anne herself breathed in and out in the courtroom, or carried in from Birches Nooke, Stocksfield, Edmundbyers, Muggleswick, Eddysbridge, Corbridge, the picturesque villages encircling my home in Riding Mill that I was learning to see in a different light as they swum up to me out of their past, leaving their powdery trail?

The pages were stored flat and face down, so they fell naturally face-up as I turned them out of the box in which they'd been stored. On the lower right-hand corner of each page a number had been typed with an old-fashioned manual typewriter, numbering the sequence of the depositions. This must have been done when the documents were transferred from York to the Public Records Office, but this number now corresponded with the final numbers in The National Archives' online cataloguing. So, ASSI 45/10/3/34 on the computer was here simply 34, the number typed on each page of the first deposition.

The Information of Anne Armstrong etc. etc. *taken upon the 5th Day of February 1672*, number 34 – the first deposition?

Not, apparently, according to the *Depositions in the Castle of York Relating to Offences Committed in the Northern Counties in the Seventeenth Century*. Along with all the other depositions from the region in this period, Anne's evidence had been transcribed in Volume XL of this substantial series. Published in 1861 by the Surtees Society, 'dedicated to the publication of manuscripts illustrative of the history of the ancient kingdom of Northumbria,' this volume was edited by the society's secretary, James Raine. It was here that I found the first historically documented listing of Anne Armstrong's name, in the chronologically arranged succession of depositions under the heading, *CLXXXVIII. Anne Baites and Others. For Witchcraft*.

The heading was taken from the name of the first woman Anne accused if – and here was the mystery – one assumed that the first deposition in the series was the one in which she accused Anne Baites, on 2 April 1673. 'Ann, wife of Thomas Baites, of Morpeth, tanner,' did not appear often afterwards in the testimony Anne gave to the Justices over the next few months and, in any event, if the series of depositions had been strictly chronological, the section numbered *CLXXXVIII* in the published transcripts should have begun on 5 January and been entitled *Foster, Dryden, Thompson and Others. For Witchcraft*. Or something along those lines.

'One of the most extraordinary cases of witchcraft that has ever been printed,' wrote the editor of the volume in a footnote, adding only, 'I know nothing of the result of the affair.'

For the moment I was less interested in the results of 'the affair' than where it began. And somehow these transcriptions did not feel as if they would lead me there. The anonymity of the standardised print font, the blank, uniform margins around the text, the footnotes, index, even the steady, regular march of the page numbering, seemed to cut the words off in some way, excise them from the world that had produced them. For all the information they provided, the transcribed pages felt strangely empty, dead to the touch, haunted around the edges in ways they wouldn't allow me to access.

There was no clue here as to why, in The Publications of the Surtees Society, deposition number 34, the deposition given before Ralph Jenison that set off the whole sequence, came *after* the depositions numbered 35 and 36, those given before Humphrey Mitford and Sir Richard Stote on 2 and 4 April 1673 respectively.

This was too obvious an error for James Raine, editor, not to have noticed and corrected. Apparently those archiving the material in 1911, when the depositions were moved from York to the Public Records Office, had noticed the irregularity, and rearranged the running order so that it followed chronologically – 5 February, 2 April, 4 April, 9 April, and so on.

But what if one gave James Raine, secretary after all of a society dedicated to 'the transcription, editing, translating and publication of original historical documents', his due; what if one worked on the assumption that he had carefully preserved the original running order of the depositions, the running order instituted by the Clerk of the Quarter Sessions in Morpeth as an accurate record of the legal process and maintained as such by the Clerk of the Assizes in York?

I had read and re-read the much briefer depositions of 2 and 4 April, the transcriptions and the originals. Nothing in the records of what Anne had said to Mitford and Stote gave any indication that they knew of a prior document recording accusations she was now expanding upon; Anne's information could be read as referring to earlier accusations – 'the rest of the witches', 'since she gave information against severall persons who ridd her to severall places' – but if a good Justice of the Peace picked this up, it would only have been while she was speaking. As far as one could tell from the transcriptions and the originals, I thought, checking them against each other, she was not asked to expand upon these allusions as she was giving her testimony.

Which begged the question, did Mitford or Stote know of an earlier deposition, and – either way – what was its place in the story that was beginning to emerge from the gathering pages? Did it, I wondered, tell us something of just how careful a man Ralph Jenison, Esq., was?

I picked up the deposition for 5 February again, running a fingertip lightly over its tacky surface, tracing the ink. These were the only tracks that Anne had left in the dust of the records, all that was left of her as a once-living, breathing being.

Gingerly, I touched the slight smear of the circle she had drawn around the heavily inked-in dot at the centre of her mark, trying to guess as I did so where the heel of her hand would have rested on the document. Could the contact she had made with the page still contain something of her, something that would communicate with the graze of my fingertips over the paper?

This was, after all, the way she had chosen to identify herself on paper, a medium foreign to her, but one she was determined to master, to use to make her story known: a circle around a dot, the mark saying this is me, this is who I am among the eleven million historical documents covering a thousand years of history filed away in The National Archives.

Can you not find me?

Chapter 6

Sir James Clavering was not a happy man as he was carried down the lovely arc of the drive at Axwell House in Sir Richard's coach. He was too aware of the girl perched on the seat on the back of the coach, squeezed next to a junior clerk and a servant who did his best to make it plain that the presence of neither was welcome in a place usually reserved for him alone. She seemed at home in the light drizzle which set in after the heavy rains, while he was all too glad of the quarter lights between himself and the grey-green of the lush woodland which swam by them as the coach juddered its way down to the River Derwent in the early morning murk.

It was not only in his reflection that his aquiline features blurred: on days like this, troubled as he was, he had to admit to himself that the celebrated lines of his nose and jaw, once sharp and strong in the tumble of dark and curly hair still all his own, were beginning to give way, loosening and running as his portrait would if left out in the damp haze he was passing through.

Something about that girl, riding up there exposed to the elements, and apparently happy to be so, bothered him. Bothered him in a way that could not be assuaged by the knowledge of the strong and healthy pack of the bailiff's men on horseback following in the wake of the coach.

When Sir Richard's servant turned up at Axwell, he'd not been surprised. The Claverings were an illustrious family, and he'd served as both High Sheriff of Durham and Mayor of Newcastle. In this last capacity, however, just on ten years ago, he had been embroiled in events that made him regret having to have anything to do with the girl.

Newly installed as mayor at the time, Sir James had taken down a complaint made by one Jane, wife of William Milburne, of Newcastle. She claimed that a woman she had failed to invite to her wedding supper had threatened her life, attacking her several times 'in the perfect similitude and shape of a cat' and on other occasions in 'her own perfect form', usually late at night when she was in her chamber.

Despite the highly fanciful nature of what she reported, the information Jane Milburne had given was full, vivid, consistent and ultimately compelling. He had been taken with the precision with which she remembered events, and her descriptions of the cat leaping at her face, biting into her arms, bearing her down to the ground were so intensely recreated that he had instinctively almost begun to raise his hands to protect his own face, and actually felt the suffocating effect of being pressed to the floor for over quarter of an hour by a furry, clawed creature.

He was amazed then when the grand jury had thrown the case out, calling it the evidence of a weak deluded woman who only imagined that she was bewitched. 'It is strange that any magistrate should write down such ridiculous evidence,' they recorded when they rejected the bill as '*Ignoramus*' and the case was dropped from the proceedings.

'Not found' Sir James could accept, but the impugning of his professional judgement was more difficult to swallow. Worse still, it made him question his judgement, leaving him unsure as to how to deal with similar cases in future.

Six months later, a respectable baker and brewer in the city came before him saying that his wife had become ill after buying a pound of cherries from a huckster who then accused her of taking twopence-worth more than she should have. She was, he said, suffering fits so 'sad and lamentable' they had astonished all who saw her. Sir James had been quick to dismiss the case, although privately he had been taken with the sincerity of the baker's account. He was not about to follow up on information that included the baker's wife crying out that the spirit of the huckster was trying to carry her away, a spirit that the baker himself said he saw when she pulled aside the bed curtain at three in the morning.

Barely a month after that he'd dismissed the case of a father saying that his seventeen-year-old daughter was in danger of her life because an apparition that only she could see was torturing her, even though the deponent was a solid yeoman he'd once come across doing jury duty. Since then he'd avoided charges of this type whenever he could, but here he was being carried towards exactly such a case in a coach crashing through thick underbrush as the driver tried to avoid the worst of the road.

Sir James did not come this way often, but he recognised Shotley Bridge as they passed though the village without stopping, even though the horses must have been tired by the pull up Burnmill Bank. Cresting a ridge, their path followed a gradual descent that became steeper as they closed in on the first of their destinations.

The coach turned off the road onto a boggy track that didn't dry out much as it followed the swell of an increasingly steep slope covered in birch. The heavy run-off continued in wide sheets of water as the track disappeared into the trees, the roof and sides of the coach scratching against branches as they followed the darkening tunnel. Sir James wondered how those seated atop the coach were doing, but Sir Richard seemed confident that all was well. The mud flying up from the wheels and spattering against the glass subsided as the driver drew to a halt; he was asking directions of someone walking along the track, someone who answered slowly, taking some time to sort out the distinction between Cronkley Wood and Birkenside. Eventually the coach dragged itself out of the marshy soil, and continued for perhaps a half mile before pulling up between several run-down stone buildings. The bailiff and his men, having fallen behind to avoid the worst of the mud flung up the coach, now pulled up alongside. Sir Richard opened his window and asked if they were at last at Birkenside.

'Well, look about then,' he said when told they were; 'find me this Hunter woman – Mary Hunter of Birkenside.'

The men scrabbled about, but it took only a few minutes to establish that the buildings were empty, the small clearing they formed in the wood deserted. Irritably, Sir Richard told the driver to move on to Eddysbridge. This involved turning the coach, no easy task in the limited space of the clearing with its dilapidated houses, and returning along the passageway through the birches. Once this was cleared, they rejoined the road and soon came to the Derwent River. As they approached it they could see, cutting through a tangle of forest growing up along the rushing water, a bridge that looked surprisingly substantial given its remote location.

On the right of the road there was a small jumble of houses gathered up against the bridge, with a few more buildings on the opposite bridge-end. Beyond the thick growth along the banks of the river ran small stretches of cultivated land, but they could see no one moving about.

Sir Richard tapped the roof of the coach with his cane. When it stopped he leant out and called to the bailiff, who had drawn his mounted men close in upon the rear of the coach. The bailiff appeared at the window and Sir Richard gestured at the houses. As the bailiff and his men spread out into them a profound silence settled, underscored by the occasional snuffling of the horses and the low sound of the water sweeping under the bridge. The woman on the back of the coach stayed quiet too, and so each member of the small group gathered on the coach sat wrapped in their own thoughts.

The bailiff came back, shaking his head.

'Across the bridge, then,' Sir Richard snapped, tapping the roof and telling the driver to follow the bailiff.

The coach eased forward reluctantly and rattled over the stone. Beneath them, the Derwent, not that big a river, but strong-flowing, surged against the constraints of its banks.

The bailiff disappeared into a small collection of farm buildings set amid a fair acreage of well-worked land. He came back, shaking his head again, hands open in a gesture of emptiness.

'Well,' said Sir Richard, banging the roof and leaning partially out the window of the coach so that he could address the girl. 'George Taylor, John March, of Eddysbridge? Where are they? And for that matter, Mary Hunter of Birkenside?'

The girl was looking at Muggleswick Moor which rose up before them, but she pointed west. 'Edmundbyers,' she said.

'Fair enough, I suppose,' said Sir Richard, pulling his head back in. 'Edmundbyers seems to be the centre of all things in this part of the world, so take us there, driver.'

It was only as he gave the direction that he realised the girl had used the proper form of the village's name. No more Edenbyers, it would seem.

The road began to climb steeply, rising up above the tree line and bringing them to the foot of the high moors. Here they found themselves exposed to a strong wind blowing in from the west, as it clearly did much of the time if the scrawny trees with their ragged tangles of branches were anything to go by, twisted and bent to the east.

Bypassing the village of Muggleswick, the road ran along the foot of the moor towards Edmundbyers. As they turned into the wind it whistled its way into every fissure of the creaking coach. Sir James wondered again about those sitting outside, the girl especially. It was not so much concern he felt as a quiet dread of the resilience of her presence; dogged, imperturbable and, for reasons he could not explain, oppressive.

After a quarter of an hour or so the driver knocked on the side with his whip, and Sir Richard leant over Sir James to look out of the window. There, on the other side of the valley carved out by the Derwent, were a number of thatched cottages huddled around a small green. Perched precariously on the slope of a hill falling away to the river, bisected by a fast-running beck, the houses crowded in on each other as if looking for some kind of defence against the wind. From their vantage on the south side of the valley, Sir Richard and Sir James had a clear view of Edmundbyers, remote, isolated, exposed, as they circled around the village along the lower reaches of the moor. The track then curved down below the level of the village, crossed a bridge, and climbed back up towards it.

Before they reached the first houses, the outline of a church appeared above them on the bank. It quickly became apparent that it consisted of walls, and walls alone; the building had fallen into ruin, as a number of country churches had during the Commonwealth of the Puritans.

They drove on past the remains and through a narrow gap between the tightly clustered houses. From close up they could see the thatched cottages were humble affairs, not much better than huts. A triangular common given a little shelter from the wind by the buildings opened up before them, and the driver brought the coach to a halt.

Sir Richard and Sir James looked out to see a small gathering of people – several different gatherings, when one looked closer, clearly formed into factions, each group leaning into itself as if seeking shelter from more than the wind.

The bailiff dismounted, his men doing the same and spreading out behind him as he began calling the villagers to some kind of order. The clerk climbed down from the coach and began scrabbling about trying to set up his small portable writing desk as the bailiff opened the formalities of the proceedings in a way that made it clear why men of his rank were so often unpopular. The term bum-bailiff was heard often enough in the Morpeth Sessions, and Sir Richard cringed at the language this bailiff was using. He clearly went about his business with little regard for the niceties of the law, but his methods were effective. By the time it was appropriate for Sir Richard and Sir James to emerge from the coach, the villagers of Edmundbyers were ranged before them in an acceptable enough way.

The Armstrong woman had climbed down from the back of the coach, and was hovering half-hidden between the rear wheels.

As the bailiff was getting into his stride, an old man appeared from the direction of the ruined church.

'Mr Dury,' he said as he approached, 'John Dury, Your Worships, rector of this ...' he gestured at the ragged assembly on the common, 'parish, since 1629. Dispossessed,' he went on in a voice firm beneath the quaver of age, 'in those evil days when king and archbishop were sent to the scaffold, and when those clergymen who refused to acknowledge Parliament were turned out of their churches and left to find whatever living they could in the wide, cold world.'

He extended his arm in a wide sweep that took in the desolation all around, as if this in itself clearly demonstrated how hard done by he had been.

'My place was filled by an impious intruder, a preacher imposed by the Commonwealth. But after the Restoration he was sent packing and I was given back my church and my parish. Not to find things as I had left them, oh no, oh no,' he said, with a flourish taking in the whole village; 'come, let me show you, come this way ...' The rector was pulling on Sir Richard's cuff, and in deference to his age and urgency the representatives of the court allowed themselves to be ushered towards the church, shepherded along while the clerk trailed behind struggling to get his writing desk back into portable mode.

'You may see,' Mr Dury said, wrinkled face gurning with passion, Adam's apple bobbling in his thin neck, wisps of white hair flying about his head, 'the extent to which dilapidation has proceeded during the melancholy interval of Puritan ascendancy.' This was plain: the north and east walls were bulging dangerously outwards from the chancel, despite some rough attempts at repair.

'These,' said the rector with some pride, 'were at one time fallen down almost altogether, and I have rebuilt them from the stones on the ground. Granted,' he went on, catching the glances exchanged between Sir Richard and Sir James, 'I set them with mud instead of mortar of lime. Please do not wonder at this; wishful, on my return, to rebuild my church, I found myself with scant funds to do so. It is, I am sorry to say, still far from being in decent enough condition for the celebration of the Divine Mysteries.'

By now the clerk had set up his desk again, but as he began opening its lid to get out his quill and ink, Sir Richard gave him a quick glance and shook his head.

'It goes without saying that the communion vessels have disappeared, and of course the two church bells. But, as you can see, the building has gone through more than a period of passive neglect; there has been, on the part of my parishioners, a good degree of intentional dismantlement ...' Mr Dury again, with a general wave, allowed the building to speak for itself.

His audience could see that the church had at one time been roofed with lead, a few fragments of which reflected dully in the debris of ruined masonry heaped up to a height of two or three feet outside what remained of the north wall. The south wall of the chancel had not suffered as badly, with the masonry looking sound and supporting two narrow round-headed windows, each with a deep splay, in perfect condition.

'Whatever I have done by the way of repair,' Mr Dury said, wringing his hands, 'I have done as my bounden duty as rector; the chancel is, as tradition will have it, my responsibility, but as Your Worships will know, the nave is the responsibility of the parishioners and they have steadfastly refused to do any work on that part of the church. Indeed, I have watched it grow ever more dilapidated while I have laboured alone these eleven long years with my own hands to rebuild the chancel.'

'The principal roof timbers look intact,' said Sir Richard, as much out of a wish to show some official support for the old man as any interest in the building. He was beginning to feel they were reaching the limits of whatever proper and dutiful attention they owed the old rector. 'We must return to the common, Mr Dury,' he said, 'and get on with our business. Would you care to lead the way?'

The rector's face, uncharacteristically for one of his profession worn and brown from outdoor labour, fell. 'But if I may, Your Worship,' he said as the group turned and began moving away from the church, 'it was as far back as 1661 that I petitioned the dean and chapter to hold a court at Edmundbyers for the correction of abuses: non-attendance of divine service neglected for private meetings and conventicles,' he counted off the list on his fingers as he went on with some urgency; 'ill observance of boundaries and commons; the restoration of a road which late belonged to the parsonage-house; sheep grazing in the churchyard and the close adjoining it ...'

'It's clearly an ungodly lot you have here, Mr Dury, but that's Durham business and I'm sure the ecclesiastical court there will get to you in good time. We're here on Northumberland affairs, although it may be that what we have to deal with will have some effect on the abuses you have been suffering in this parish.'

Old John Dury the rector dropped back, deflated, and trailed behind the group as it moved on.

Out of the corner of his eye, Sir Richard caught the scuttle of someone disappearing through the cottages as they approached them. A particularly ragged example of the village's population, the way he scurried out of sight had something furtive about it.

He was about to ask the rector who this was and why he appeared to be avoiding the assembly on the green when he saw Anne walking towards them from the cottages. The odd impression struck him that she had been engaged in some way with the shabby figure, but when she saw him looking at her, she stopped short, waiting. This may have been purely out of deference, but before he could call out to her he was distracted by Sir James clearing his throat.

'Did you notice,' he said quietly, 'the smell of wild garlic filling the air in the churchyard? And see how many rowan trees are planted at the doors of these houses – both protection against witches. That stable too, do you see: horseshoes nailed to its doors, to stop witches getting in and harming or stealing the horses.'

They'd reached the cottages, and when Sir Richard looked again, Anne had tucked herself into the tail end of their small procession. The voice of the bailiff washed over them as they passed through the buildings, calling the assembly on the common to order. His preferred way of doing this was to distribute insults as widely as possible. He knew, he told the cheerless company, all about their running to wise women and charmers whenever they had ailments to be cured. The people gathered on the sparse, worn grass of the common shuffled and looked down, avoiding eye contact.

He wouldn't be fooled, the bailiff went on, and neither would these important men be; it was well known that a wise traveller in these parts always grips his thumb in the palm of his hand or carries a silver sixpence to ward off evil, so they should answer honestly when questioned, or – and here he shook his heavy cudgel at them – they'd be carried away to gaol to await the Sessions.

He levelled a long, steady glare at the group when he was done, then stepped back and turned to the Justices with a self-satisfied air.

'I think you'll find them ready now, Your Worships,' he said, ushering Sir Richard and Sir James forward with an obsequious sweep of the hand.

The wind off the moor moaned through the houses. The clerk, relieved to finally have the opportunity to set up his desk and get out his writing materials, sat with his quill poised, a blank page before him.

It was the rector who spoke first, from the place he had taken to the side of the gathering. 'You will know, Your Worships, that at least one case of witchcraft was recorded in this village. The year before my place was taken from me and filled by an interloper, Margaret Hooper became possessed and showed signs of derangement after a visit to a farm at Hunstanworth. I examined her, and she was unable to say the Lord's Prayer, and began to foam at the mouth.

'This is all I can report, but others here,' Mr Dury said, turning to his parishioners, 'claimed to see a black beast, which struck her feet and dragged her on to the floor before throwing her into another room. Those present smelled a terrible stench and flames and smoke issued from this monster, is this not what you reported? And when her household knelt to pray, invoking the Almighty to save Margaret Hooper, a divine presence like a child with a shining face was seen, after which, they say –' he looked at the group accusingly '– she began to recover.'

'This without the help of the Church, I must say, Your Worships,' said the rector, moving away from his parishioners to stand nearer to the Justices.

'Well, what have you to say,' said Sir Richard, 'to this or more recent matters?'

Quiet and wind reasserted themselves, and then one woman spoke, looking around at her neighbours from under her downcast brow as she did so. 'Jane Frizzle,' she said, 'of Crooked Oak.'

Sir Richard leaned in towards the rector, who said, 'A few shabby houses thrown upon themselves, in Shotley Low Quarter, a few miles from here.'

'She is a notorious witch,' said the woman, 'flying at night and casting spells on men, and cattle.'

'They try to distract you, Your Worship,' said the rector. 'Jane Frizzle is said to be a witch, but her crime is to be old and live in a remote spot. The houses of Crooked Oak are lost in the woods, at the end of the roughest of tracks which dies out just before the Derwent gorge. Nothing is really known about her among those gathered here, it would appear,' he said, glaring around at the assembled villagers, 'not even that she died some time ago, and lies buried in a lonely field at Greenhaugh, near Carterway Heads.

'I confess, however, that I myself would not go out to Crooked Oak again by choice; it is a strange place, apart from the fact that if one is caught there in the dark, one could easily wander over the edge of the gorge, and crash down on to the rocks of the Derwent. But Anne, wife of Thomas Richardson, has lost the use of her limbs and I must render what assistance I can. Not that she or her husband welcome this. They swear someone has power over her, and has asked the devil's assistance to take away her life.'

'Someone? Who then? Enough of this,' Sir Richard shouted. 'I want names, names. Mary Hunter, of Birkenside, are you here? Well, are you?'

The quiet grew oppressive as he waited for a response. None came.

'We have heard enough stories about this place,' said Sir Richard, voice still raised. 'Now we are here for real evidence, actual witnesses. George Taylor and John March, of Eddysbridge, are you present? We know you are not at your farms, so step forward, this instant.'

'George Taylor and John March, of Eddysbridge, yeomen, step forward,' echoed the bailiff, smacking his cudgel into the palm of his hands several times. 'George Taylor and John March, of ...'

A man stepped out of those gathered on the common, reluctantly. His dress was a cut above most of the villagers, and Sir Richard assumed John March, as he now announced himself, owned the land he worked. A solid witness at last, he thought, an impression reinforced by the bluff, unfanciful way of speaking. He nodded at the clerk, who began writing as March's voice lifted into the silence of Edmundbyers.

'About a month since, Your Worship, I went to a place called Birkside nook –'

'Birkside nook,' interrupted Sir Richard. 'Do you mean by this Birkenside, down the valley here?'

John March looked confused. 'No, Your Worship,' he said, looking about at his neighbours. 'No, I mean Birkside nook, near Stocksfield-upon-Tyne.'

One of the small throng of villagers whispered something to him. 'That would be, Your Worship, Birches Nooke, as they say it there, where this woman –' he pointed at Anne, who had stepped forward '– hearing me named began to speak to me, and asked me if I had not an ox that had the power of one of his limbs taken from him. Telling her I had, and enquiring of her how she came to know, she told me that she heard Mary Hunter and another, at a meeting among diverse witches, confess to the devil that they had taken the power of that beast.'

'Mary Hunter,' interjected Sir Richard. 'This is now Mary Hunter of Birkenside of whom we speak?'

John March nodded.

'Mary Hunter, who is not present here?'

John March looked at the ground and nodded again.

'Mary Hunter and another. Which other?' said Sir Richard, with some force. 'Come on now, which other?'

John March raised his head slightly, his eyes moving from side to side in a guarded way. 'She –' he nodded towards the girl, who was looking at him intently '–not knowing her name, said only that –'

Sir Richard turned on the girl. 'I have thought it proper to carry you here, Anne Armstrong, to this place you named, this Edmundbyers, for you to cause the woman to come to you, that you may charge her and she challenge what you charge. Who is she, where is she?'

He moved in close on her as he spoke, and Sir James moved forward with him. The girl met his gaze for an instant, and then gave an unearthly sound, a wail. Her hand was raised, and pointing over Sir James's shoulder. Sir Richard turned on his heel, followed the eyes of those assembled on the common as they focused on a lone woman making her away across the edge of the village, small against the moor looming behind her.

The woman froze, clearly feeling the concentrated attention of the village, but not looking up.

'Well?' said Sir Richard, as Anne stood, one hand over her mouth, the other still pointing, quivering.

Sir Richard was about to order the bailiff to bring the woman over when she turned, pulled herself fully upright, and walked steadily towards them.

'Who is this?' asked Sir Richard of the rector.

'Dorothy Green, a widow,' he replied, and before he could add anything further the girl dropped her arm, stood firm and said, 'I challenge her. She is the person that joined with Mary Hunter in the bewitching of the ox.'

Sir Richard turned to John March.

'The ox now continues lame,' said the yeoman, 'and has no use of his far hinder leg, but pines away, and is likely to die. And Anne Armstrong told me that Mary Hunter and –' he looked briefly at Dorothy Green, then back at the Justice '– this woman confessed before the devil that they bewitched a grey mare of mine too.'

March squared himself before both Justices, and went on in a steady voice with the scratching of the clerk's pen underlining his words.

'Further, about a fortnight before Michaelmas last, me and my wife were riding home from Bywell on a Sunday at night upon the same mare about sunset; and a swallow came, Your Worships, which flew through under the mare's belly above forty times and more, and crossed her way before her breast. And I struck at it with my rod above twenty times, and could by no means hinder it, until of its own action it went away.

'And the mare went very well home, but within four days died. And, before she died, she was two days so mad that she was past holding, and was struck blind for four and twenty hours before she died.'

Another man shouldered his way through the gathering. 'George Taylor, of Edgebridge, yeoman,' he declared.

'At last. Well, speak man, speak, what do you have to say about this?' asked Sir Richard, waving his hand between the Armstrong girl and Dorothy Green.

'Your Worships, I went to Birches Nooke, between Stocksfield and the Riding, to speak with –' he pointed at the girl '– Anne Armstrong, who had oftentimes formerly desired to see me. She being asleep upon a bed, her sister awakened her and raised her. Being asked if she knew me, or could name me, she answered that if I were the man that had a foal lately dead, and if I lived at Edgebrigg, my name was George Taylor.

'Upon my demanding of her how she came to know this, she told me that she heard Mary Hunter of Birkenside confess before the devil at meetings that she and another had gotten the power and the life of my foal.

'The foal began not to be well about Michaelmas last, Your Worships, and died about a month after. It had no natural disease to my knowledge, but often swelled in several parts of the body. Its head and lips were sorely swollen, and no matter how often I endeavoured to bleed it, thinking thereby to prevent its death, I could never get any blood in any part of its body.

'When it was dead, I opened it to see if there were any blood or not, and I think that a quart pot would have held all that it had, drawn around the animal's heart. And Anne Armstrong told me that she had heard Mary Hunter and another – this woman here, as I am now told, Dorothy Green – confess to the devil that they had the power of my oxen and kyne, my horses and mares too –'

'And now, at this precise moment,' said Anne, her interjection taking them by surprise, 'he has a grey mare, the dam of the foal, pining away, and in the same condition that the foal was in.'

She stood back, folding her arms in triumph without bothering to have this new information verified.

George Taylor kept looking directly at the Justices. 'What I will say, Your Worships, is that my goods do not thrive, nor are they like my neighbours' goods –' here, a quick glance at John

March, '– notwithstanding I feed them as well as I can, they are like anatomyes.'

Sir Richard Stote looked at Sir James Clavering. Any attempt at coming to a conclusion was interrupted by the rector pushing his way back in front of them. 'You see, Your Worships, in Edmundbyers superstition survives and comes to light in unexpected quarters.

'But if you ask me, it is the Presbyterians and Baptists of the Derwent that are the real danger. It is no secret that they hold seditious meetings in which they plot to rise up and murder bishops, deans and chapters and ministers of the Church. I heard myself of their plans to destroy the Common Prayer Books and to pull down all churches; no wonder then, that I cannot get help here to rebuild mine.'

Seeing he was losing the attention of the Justices with this return to his building travails, the rector moved on hurriedly to the other threats he believed to be lurking in and around his village: 'And, further, to kill the gentry that will not join with them –'

'For goodness' sake, man,' Sir Richard interrupted. 'None of this is necessary for the record, Clerk,' he said, before turning back to the rector.

'This "Muggleswick Park Conspiracy" was a lot of nonsense, a comic affair hardly short of a farce. I am well aware that no more than two hundred men gathered at Farnley Wood, and having thrown up a few earthworks they dispersed the next day. The Westmoreland men never even got here.'

'But the Anabaptists –'

'Please, Mr Dury,' said Sir Richard, raising a hand. 'Let us avoid mixing up the Baptists, Independents, Tremulatores, Millenary, Presbyterians and any others you'd care to accuse with the heretical witchcraft that brings us here today.'

He turned away from the rector, whose face fell as he found himself presented with Sir Richard's broad back.

'Sir James, are we agreed that we have heard enough to bind these men over to appear at the Sessions? And any others who wish to present evidence for the accusations. No, no,' he said as one member of the sullen collection of villagers indicated a wish to speak, 'no defendants at this time, or witnesses for the defence.'

Sir James raised his mouth to Sir Richard's ear, speaking quietly and earnestly; when he was done, Sir Richard looked at the villagers again.

'As yet,' he said, 'no one is to be charged. But, Clerk, issue a warrant to this Dorothy Green to appear before the magistrates at the Quarter Sessions for a proper examination. Put out word that Mary Hunter is ordered to appear as well, and will otherwise be hunted down and found out and brought to court. And bind over Taylor and March; they too must present themselves at the Quarter Sessions next week. Bailiff, make sure they understand, and will comply – I am sure you have ways of making sure they do.

'And anyone else who wishes to prosecute in this case, against Green, or Hunter, or any other person they believe they have –' he stressed the next word heavily '– *evidence* against them.

'They – you,' he said, addressing the assembled villagers sternly, 'must know I want none of your silly women's nonsense in my court.'

He turned back to his fellow Justice. 'You see then what I am prepared to do, Sir James, well within the letter of the law, following proper criminal procedure. I want a full bench of the Justices to be convened to consider this matter. I want Sir Thomas Horsley there, Howard, Salkeld, and Mitford, of course, I don't care how sick he is.

'And Jenison too, especially Jenison: he'll have some explaining to do, when it comes to that missing deposition.

'How soon can this be done, eh, Clerk?'

The assistant clerk, aware of his junior status and trying to think what the Clerk of the Peace would say, stalled as long as he could. 'A full bench, Your Worship?' he said. 'Well, obviously the Justices will be at hand during the General Quarter Sessions, although they will find it unusual to be called to a pre-trial investigation at this point in the Sessions –'

Sir Richard Stote harrumphed. 'Sir James, we should be able to get them together by mid-week, do you think?'

Sir James nodded, almost overwhelmed by the relief of not hearing his name being included in the list of Justices to be called.

'So, the ninth of April then, Clerk.' Sir Richard then turned to the bailiff. 'Tell those that are bound over and those that have accusations to make that they must appear at the Quarter Sessions next Wednesday, in Morpeth, first thing.'

The National Archives

Dust, dust again, blackening the palms and getting under the fingernails, irritating eye and nostril, obscuring the already painfully difficult-to-read handwriting. But it was the dust that gave a special aura to archival research, the sensation, yes, the physical sensation that one was somehow closing in on the subject of one's research, only a film of dirt between you and a hand you could reach for, a body, a whole person who could be summoned up through the surface of the document.

Dust was also the guarantee that these documents had lain undisturbed, undiscovered by scholarly rivals, and so were in some way one's personal intellectual property. I put my hand into the box and lifted the first page of the next deposition. Feeling carefully, I confirmed the suspicion that gathered as I studied the pages on the desk: the dust betrayed the presence of others, the trace of their having passed through before me. The coating on the depositions had that slightly greasy quality documents take on when they've been handled comparatively recently. Mingled in with the fine particles was the moisture of the fingers, breath, body of other readers, absorbed by the humidity-free atmosphere of the storage facilities but leaving its after-effects on the page.

My first impulse was to resent whoever it was had also been following Anne's trail. I knew how foolish this was, knew full well I wasn't the first to stalk her through the thickets of history; I knew too, how jealous the most proper of researchers could become about their particular quarry, filled as they were with the vain hope that they would be the first to track down the elusive prey, finding it quivering, palpitating, trapped finally in its secret lair.

The problem was that there was so much missing from the evidence to hand.

I was, I knew, lucky to have anything at all. But I needed more. What did this collection of pre-trial depositions amount to? On their own, they were a combination of compelling detail and tantalising openness, a way into a story that had gripped me but had no clear plot or outline, a confusing beginning and nothing like a conclusion.

I'd searched ASSI 45, the Criminal Depositions and Case Papers from 1559–1971 for the Northern and North-Eastern Circuits, several times by now, finding no more than I had already on the Assizes. I'd also tried ASSI 44, the Indictment Files for the Assizes of Northern and North-Eastern Circuits. These included the precepts to the sheriff of the county to prepare for the session, lists of Justices of the Peace, and of jurors, recognisances, gaol calendars, and coroners' inquisitions, but I found nothing there to do with Anne Armstrong's accusations. Now I tried, as something of a long shot, ASSI 47, the Miscellanea for the Northern and North-Eastern Circuit. Maybe there was something among the 'miscellaneous correspondence of the Clerk of Assize, coroner's inquisitions, jury lists, and returns in criminal cases and pleadings arising from civil actions heard at nisi prius'.

The catalogue description wasn't encouraging: 'The series is still largely unsorted except by date,' I read; it 'contains a significant numbers of items from the seventeenth century, which have clearly become detached from the files or bundles to which they originally belonged. Until it proves possible to undertake substantial editorial and conservation work on them, only a rough indication of the contents of each piece can be given in the list. Physical description: 74 bundle(s).'

I added it to my online order form in any event, and then was surprised to see that it was not currently available. Someone else was using ASSI 47, and I was told to check on the current status of this order on the display terminals in the reading room.

There were terminals in the restaurant on the ground floor as well, so I went downstairs to have another coffee while I waited.

ASSI 47 had not yet flashed up as available when an idea struck me. Leaving my coffee, I took the stairs as quickly as possible back up to the second floor. I didn't go to my desk, but went straight to the section of the room separated off for collections. Waiting to the side, I watched as people collected documents too large for delivery to the locker linked to their desk or – as was the case for all my orders – dating from before 1688.

Looking as unobtrusive as possible and smiling disarmingly at the staff with their inquiring looks, I stood for an uncomfortable fifteen or twenty minutes until a large man, bearded with longish grey hair straggling away from a bald patch, steered his girth up towards the collection desk and presented one of the familiar-looking brown cardboard boxes. The staff member checking it in tapped something onto his keyboard, and the display terminal mounted above the desk told me that ASSI 47 was now available.

Instead of picking it up, I approached the man who had handed in the box, catching him before his low waddle had got him out of the collection area. Talking was acceptable in this section, and I spoke as quickly as possible to placate the widening eyes turned on me.

'The Assizes? North-Eastern Circuit 1673? No, no,' the large man said, in a tone used to being authoritative and, it soon became apparent, regularly correcting others, 'before 1876 it would be the *Northern* Circuit.'

I mumbled something apologetic but this was ignored.

'Anne Baites? That's the Armstrong depositions, of course. Yes, I've worked on those. Not much more here than in the transcriptions, although God knows those are incomplete, and inaccurate. Watch out for them, I only use them for ease of referencing.'

I said I would, and then tried to give some indication of who I was and what my interests were. Clearly my name didn't register as anyone important in the field of Early Modern witchcraft, which I assumed the large man was. And clearly he wasn't going to introduce himself to anyone who didn't recognise him, his self-importance extending to the shabby look cultivated by certain senior academics determined to hold themselves above the corporate takeover of the universities.

'Among the most remarkable texts in the history of English witchcraft,' he said, with an air that made it plain that if anyone knew, he did, 'but I've moved away from it. A colleague of mine was conducting a major study of the Armstrong case some years ago; had some success developing the folkloric elements of the case, but found it difficult to establish any background information to give it a more straightforward historical context.

'A pity, as I think she –' as opposed to you, was the implication I found impossible to ignore '– would have developed some interesting thoughts on it.'

I thanked him for bringing the box back, only to be told it was unlikely I would find it useful in any way. 'Your Latin better be good, and your knowledge of the courts of the period, as well as the script. Even then, it's totally disorganised, lots of bundles wrapped in packets and tubes, dusty as all hell. I –' even I, that was '– couldn't make much of anything in there.'

The man turned away, carrying his considerable bulk across the reading room with all the dignity he believed it deserved. I took the box to my desk and found everything he had said was true. The few documents I tried to open and look at were simply impenetrable, faded, poorly written, thick with grime and dense with scrawled, abbreviated, legalistic Latin. If there were references to the Armstrong trial at the Assizes in this box, they were well and truly beyond my abilities to find. Well, that was history for you, as much about the evidence that happened to survive as what actually happened in the past.

Chapter 7

Anne Armstrong begged off returning with the Justices. It was, she said, easy enough for her to walk back to Birches Nooke, which was far from the route the coach would take. Bound over sternly – 'she has every reason to attend the Sessions,' Sir Richard argued: 'there is too much at stake for her now not to have her accusations heard in the court' – she was left to make her own way home.

Young but strong enough by the look of her wiry frame, Anne strode off on the Stanhope road, taking a path running sharp left immediately after crossing the bridge. Anyone watching from the village – and some sharp, hard eyes were following her – would see her retracing the route the coach had taken. Her small figure moved surprisingly swiftly up the rise of Muggleswick Moor, settling into a steady pace as the path levelled out.

No one said anything to the modest cavalcade of Justices and staff rumbling out soon after Anne, and passing her quickly on the moorland track. No word or glance passed between the officials and the girl, she walking steadily, eyes fixed on the path directly ahead of her.

The coach had long passed the intersection where the track turned north to Eddysbridge or south to Muggleswick village, which was just as well, or someone in the entourage may have thought it odd that without any hesitation Anne turned south. She'd heard the clatter of the coach crossing the bridge below, the sound of its disappearance comforting, given her intentions.

I took a path that passed behind Muggleswick, screened from the village by a thick patch of trees as I walked straight on. I'd been walking for over an hour and the day was showing the first signs of fading. The drizzle had eased off, but now the colour began to drain from the sky. I shivered as I drew level with Snape Wood, the shadows thick among its heavy trees.

In its depths, the Derwent twisted like a snake with a forked stick on its neck, digging itself ever deeper into the dark gorge ahead.

If I had wings, or the art of those who came to ride me off into the night, I would have taken to the air and soared to my destination. Instead, I had to walk on, listening to the river spill and crash among the rocks below me until I came to a path dropping away into the gorge. I took this, careful of my steps as I descended into an ever-thickening wood of oak. Bulbous cankers yawed out at me from the ancient trunks, faces tortured into silent, frozen screams. Branches rattled at me, determined to catch me up into the thick, darkening green.

I had to slither down the last yards, holding on to whatever was to hand as the path delivered me to the ford. I took off my clogs to feel my way across the deceptively smooth rush of the water.

I collapsed into the grass, drained by the constant fear. My head began to fill with tales of old Jane Frizzle, hanged for bewitching farmers. Some said she was still alive, grown older and older, older than any person who had lived before, and travelling the night with a broomstick for her palfrey, practising strange spells on maidens alone in the dark. And somewhere in the gorge, the Muggleswick Giant, whose limbs were so enormous his favourite female hound had littered in one of his shoes; dead now, yes, for He had shown me the mighty hunter's grave in Muggleswick churchyard – but who was to say, I thought, looking out from under my arm, that the giant stayed underground at night, beneath the tombstone on which He had spelled out the name 'Edward Ward' to me.

Oh yes, the worst stories I knew, those that clung to me now in the pitch black, were the ones that He had told me, stories not all to do with the dead, or those who should be dead. He had taken me to visit Anne Thomas in the farmhouse not far ahead, her husband neglecting his work and sitting next to her each day weeping over her useless limbs, wiping the drool from her mouth with a rag when he wasn't blowing his nose with it, crying out again and again that it was the witches who had power over her, and cursing the rector from Edmundbyers when he came by to offer comfort. As if there were any assistance the rector could offer to someone whose life had been given over by others to the devil.

I crossed the small meadow the river had carved out of the bank and began climbing the path. This was the route joining Crooked Oak to the river, so it was more heavily used and worn into the ground than the one I had followed down to the river. I was able to keep a steady pace, rising up quickly out of the depths as if carried by my own dread.

I felt some relief when I reached the first of the stone farm buildings lurking in the dark. At least I did not have to pass the cottages beyond the farmhouse. Usually, coming from Birches Nooke, I'd enter the village from the far side, trying to avoid looking into the filthy dark of their windows, knowing that in one Isabelle Andrew was lying, stuffed again from one of the witches' feasts in the Riding.

My hands finally found the beginning of a dry stone wall, telling me that the farmhouse was near. Feeling my way, I could sense rather than see the building looming ahead. I knew it well from other visits, its stone walls and slate roof, the front door in its pretty surround. It was much older and more strongly built than Mr Errington's house, but neither house had brought its owner much luck. Through the windows I could hear the broken heart of Thomas Richardson, crying faintly and steadily as he rocked over the slack body of his wife.

Ten yards or so before the door there was an outshut, a small, low extension to the farmhouse that must have been built as a byre, but was too run down now for cows. I stood for a few minutes, to catch my breath – or so I told herself, but this was only to deny the fear that clawed at me now that I was here. Fear yes, but reverence too, and not unmixed with fondness when I was in His presence.

For it was He who had found me, given me my gift. And if since then it was me who had sought Him out, this was only when the burden was too great, when I needed to add his knowledge to the abilities he had given me.

There was a light at the opening which served as a window for the outshut, as there always was at night. For all the fineness of the farmhouse, I had seen shielings better built, less run to ruin than this outbuilding; whether this was because Thomas Richardson was too concerned about his wife to care, or too mean to offer Him anything better to live in, I did not know. I pushed against the planks that served as a door and saw Him reading, as I knew he would be, as long and as late as his rheumy old eyes would allow in the smoky glow of the tallow dip.

I pushed harder and entered; he did not lift his eyes from the page as I put a hand on his shoulder and fed more of the burning cloth into its saucer of grease. 'Don't waste, girl,' he mumbled as the small flame flared up. 'So, what is it to be?'

I fell on to the dirt floor, the exhaustion of my limbs not reaching my mouth as I gabbled out what had happened in the courtroom and the village.

He sat silent as I talked, his eyes fixed on the book before him, turning a page as my account went on.

'Wednesday,' he said, lifting a face worn by years of exposure to the elements. 'That doesn't give us much time. And no trial yet, all still preliminary? Well, we shall have to make sure you are ready. Half of those watching won't know the difference between a court of law and a show in a playhouse, those places of idle inter-course, vanity, and unlawfulness.'

The few teeth he had left showed dirty white in the darkness of his mouth as he spoke, but his voice had the same authority I'd heard when first we'd met, the same confidence with which he'd asked me where I'd been on the Friday past. There in the early dawn – that flat, grey daybreak hardly worth the little light and even less warmth it brought, my thoughts consumed by my empty stomach, my damp feet, the missing cows – I'd thought he was merely an old man in ragged clothes. It was his voice that told me that he was more, much more than that, the voice that caught me in his grip before I took in anything he actually said. The voice that made me trust him although the words he spoke confused me, mystified me. How did he know about the woman looking at my head, when all I'd said was that I was looking for eggs in Stocksfield that Friday?

This first mystery was nothing, of course, to what followed, the foretelling of my being ridden to the witches' gatherings, the shape changing and dancing, the flying, the swinging on the rope and feasting. And their efforts to tempt me, powerless unless I ate their food, and then the cheese, the cheese that made me tell everything I had kept secret, those things that happened when I was in my fits, those fits that started the instant he turned away, disappeared into the haze still clinging to the edges of the field as I fell down, thinking as I fell that I was dying.

'But will they come to watch me, hear what I have to say about them?'

He put a large grimy hand upon my own. 'They will come. Do you think I do not know them? Those that burst into my church to protest that I was an "Intruder", a trespasser on the incumbency of John Dury? They came to the Sessions then, when I charged them with disrupting my service. Thirteen years, they said to the Justice, Mr Dury had been their rector in Edmundbyers, aye, and Muggleswick too. That's as may be, I said, but he is one of the clergy who are thought inadequate, and so driven from the parishes of the Commonwealth. They were found guilty and fined, those three men, and I was confirmed in my place.

'Yes,' he said, his voice losing its strength for a moment, suddenly querulous; 'John Dury was dispossessed during the rule of the Puritans, and is now returned with the Restoration. And I, Thomas Boyer, am driven from my parish and deprived of my living by the Royalists.'

The strength returned to his voice as the taper guttered and flared. It was as if I were no longer there, or there in the form of some other kind of audience altogether, a congregation into which I had been transformed. He raised himself in his chair, then half-stood, leaning on the ruin of a table before him as if leaning forward in a pulpit.

'But if he thought the Restoration of the monarchy would bring a triumphal return to his living, I am sure he has often wondered about the wisdom of coming back! The parishioners reject him and all his ways – as you saw today,' he said to me, briefly registering my presence, 'when you were there with the Justices. And why? Does he ever stop to find out why they will not help him?'

I had heard this all before, each time that I came here, in fact. I took comfort now in the familiarity of the story, having learned to follow, if not fully understand, its twists and turns, as tortuous as the river streaming down from Eddysbridge through Snape Wood, the Gorge, Muggleswick Wood, Narrow Comb Wood, Windybank Wood, and on through Bog Wood, where Mary Hunter, Dorothy Green and the other witches materialised out of the blank dark to make me sing while they danced with their devils.

I knew what came next, how the parishioners of Edmundbyers and Muggleswick, after objecting so strongly to the intruder, began to fall under the spell of his preaching – 'Yes, my *preaching*,' he would say, thumping the table so hard I feared it would collapse before him – and then, after his twenty years there, would not let him be sent away.

They wrote a petition, he would tell me again, a petition to the Mayor of Sunderland, to be sent up to the House of Commons – see, see, they had it printed up, and I have a copy here, he would say, scrabbling through the papers piled about him. A petition, a list of grievances drawn up and signed by sixty-two persons, including women and children, all indicted by John Dury for absenting themselves from Holy Communion.

He half-bent again tonight, down towards the flickering tallow, holding the well-worn document in its smoky light, and read:

To all Christian people, know that our parish has been destitute of a preaching Minister, to our soul's great griefe and dreadful hazard of destruction ...

'A preaching minister, that is what they called me,' he said, '"such a one as our soules longed after"; and listen to what they have to say of Mr Dury.'

With all our soules we besought that we might be exempted of that John Duery, because we know him to be no preacher, and his life and conversation scandalous, and that he had two places at present, Edmundbyers and Muggleswikk; and also that he publicly confessed in a pulpit before an open assembly, that he could not preach ...

'And how did they reply, those prebends of Durham?'

That once they had authorised him, wee neither could nor should depose him, and also told us in plaine terms, that if he could read the prayer booke and an homily, it was nothing to us what kind of man he was.

'And they wonder now, those senior members of the clergy, at the people's unwillingness to rebuild his church, or anything else he undertakes in his "Perpetual Curacy" of Edmundbyers and Muggleswick. Hear what else the people say of him.'

This simple, yea (dare we say) sinful minister, who is ignorant of the very principles of religion, one of the most debased among the sonnes of men, for he will neither preach himself nor permit others to preach.

'You see then why I wouldn't leave, why my parishioners cling to me, begged me to stay after I was ejected on Black Bartholomew's Day ...'

My favourite bit came next, the bit I could see in my mind as he talked, the bit where he would recount what Mr Dury had done on his first Sabbath back in Muggleswick.

I knew the place; the church in the village had not suffered nearly as much from the neglect that had brought the one at Edmundbyers to ruin, and Mr Dury was not going to have the separatists invading his church here as they had become used to doing. So he took the lock from the door and fastened on one of his own.

This was in the dead of winter, and when Mr Dury's disloyal parishioners began to turn up, they were forced to mill around the locked door in the biting frost and snow. And when the old man arrived, my Mr Boyer, not so old then and much loved, he gathered them together and began to discharge his divine duties among the snow-tipped graves in the churchyard, 'to the infinite dishonour of the Almighty and great grief of their minds, and the dreadful endangering of themselves in that stormy time of the year,' as he would thunder each time he repeated the story.

The next Sabbath day Mr Dury found that the parishioners – being, as he would report them, as devious as they were disloyal – managed to procure a key and had gathered together in the church well before the time he normally arrived. They had even begun their service, so he stormed up the aisle while the preacher was in the full flight of his exhortation, and then stood beside him, reading from the Book of Common Prayer at the top of his not inconsiderable voice.

Unable still to drown out the sound of the intruder, he began pulling at his coat while he was in the pulpit – an indecorous sight for any religious ceremony, but one that always amused me and, I was sure, only made Mr Dury appear the more absurd.

When this too failed to silence Thomas Boyer's sermon, he ran back down the aisle to the entrance where the rope for the bell hung, and began pulling on it. He rang the bell as loudly as he could for as long as he could, but then the parishioners burst into a hymn, and then another and another, until his pealing began to lose its strength. He gave up and stamped out of the church, exuding tears of fury.

It was out of malice, the parishioners of Muggleswick would report in their petition, that he called a communion for the next Sabbath, and entered upon the sacred action, without any preparation sermon before the day, leaving them open to being listed in the courts as recusants. Which they were, Durham refusing them and their petition, the petition that would never reach the House of Commons.

'That was the last of me,' the old man said, 'at Muggleswick and Edmundbyers too. Monarchy and episcopacy were restored all over England in a profligate flood of joy.'

I could see him, stepping out of the church at Muggleswick, knowing for all the bravado of his congregation that he would never preach there again.

'But John Dury's church only grows ever more dilapidated,' the old man said, taking what comfort he could; 'and I think even the room I use upstairs in the inn at Allensford is more fit as a place of worship.

'For you see, Anne, my dear,' he said, bringing himself back to me, 'I spent my time in their prisons under the Clarendon Code, and I am careful now. Here where I live, I obey the Five Mile Act, forbidden from living within that many miles of the parish from which I have been banned.' He took my hand and stroked it, as if I were the one that needed pacifying.

And then he dropped it and pointed at someone apparently standing in the darkest corner of the hovel: 'For I will not swear the oath never to resist the king, or attempt to alter the government of Church or State. I trust no Royal Declaration of Indulgence!'

His bleary eyes focused on me again.

'And our influence continues, dear Anne, it continues: and that is why this work on which we have embarked is so important, and why we cannot give up now. For John Dury, that arrogant, sad, lost soul, is it any wonder he is a stranger to his parishioners? Does he not see this is a dark and fearful world in which we live exposed and vulnerable to evil, the more so up here in this untamed and lawless part of the world?

'He and his kind draw their lines, saying this is religion, that superstition, and we do not deal in superstition; we have no "magical" assistance to offer for misfortunes brought upon people by Providence or their own sinful nature.

'So how else are they to understand the evil that lies in wait in the heather, the stones, the river, the wind, the sky, that kills their children and injures their animals, that gives them unbearable pain, in their teeth, their limbs, their minds. The very earth is pregnant with malevolence, and if the Church cannot help or protect them against it, to whom else must they go but the cunning folk, those who claim to know ways of controlling a world that is otherwise deaf to their pleas, ignores their hardest efforts, scorns their most dear sacrifices, yea, the very prayers they make in church!

'And if those same cunning folk then themselves do evil, do them harm, to whom must they turn? To the clergy who hide behind their theology, saying "the age of miracles is past" and "to believe in the power of Satan is to belie the majesty and sovereignty of God"!'

I had never had the opportunity to hear one of Thomas Boyer's sermons to his congregation, but in my visits I had grown accustomed to his holding forth to an invisible audience many times the size of his hovel, his cracked voice straining away into the empty dark. At times too he would break into the singing of a psalm, as if supported by a throng of raised voices. I wondered if I should join my voice with his, but then the thought of singing as the darkness twisted itself about me, taking on shapes human, animal, fiend and devil, silenced any thought of this. I would wait instead until he began preaching again, surrendering to his words and allowing myself to fade back into the ghostly crowd with which his voice filled the room, watching only for the moments when he would become aware of my presence.

Blank now to me, lost maybe to any audience, he went on. 'And so now the Jesuits are left free to argue that it is they and not the clergy of the Church of England who are Satan's true opponents, describing the rituals at which the devil is worshipped and claiming to exorcise demons from the bodies of recusants.

'But we have had hotter Protestants,' he said, shaking a finger at the low roof that sloped down above his head, 'who understand the sinfulness of humankind and warfare against the devil, eager to destroy the witch who has broken her baptismal covenant with God and thus become both an affront and a threat to the well-ordered godly Commonwealth. The judges and Justices of this land have but to read the great English demonological tracts by our Puritan intellectuals and learned Protestant demonologists and there they will see that Scripture itself tells us that God has permitted the power of Satan to work with weak and wicked women and men to chastise a sinful mankind ...'

My attention drifted, but I was jerked alert at the sound of my name.

'Ah, but Anne, be warned,' the old man was saying, focused now entirely on me. 'I have told you the story of Grace Sowerbutts in Lancashire, fourteen years old like yourself when she accused three women in her parish of using devilish and wicked arts. They were able to transform themselves into dogs, she said, and haunted and vexed her for years. They transported her to the top of a hayrick by her hair, and tried to persuade her to drown herself. They sucked the blood of a baby, causing it to die, then dug up the body and cooked and ate some of it at one of their meetings, using the rest to make an ointment that enabled them to change themselves into other shapes. They transported her to their secret meetings where they met,' he said, turning to the book on his table and squinting in the poor light of the taper, 'with "four black things, going upright, and yet not like men in the face", with whom they feasted, and danced, and fornicated.

'And after hearing her evidence many of those in court were persuaded of the guilt of the women she accused.

'But then – now listen, Anne, for this is important – the accused fell weeping upon their knees and asked the judge to examine their accuser. And then – listen, Anne, listen to what Thomas Potts writes – "the countenance of this Grace Sowerbutts changed."

'And when the judge took on the task of examining Grace Sowerbutts, she could not, writes Mr Potts, "for her life give any direct answers, but strangely amazed, told him she was put to a master to learn …"'

Thomas Boyer slammed his hand upon the page, causing me to jolt upright. 'After which those in court then stated that Grace Sowerbutts –' he turned again to the page, his face lit luridly from below by the small flame on the table – '"had gone to learn with one Thompson, a seminary priest, who had instructed and taught her this accusation against them."

'And what was the judgement of the court?'

It was as if he expected an answer from me, when all I could do was wring my hands and shrink away from him.

'"Thus were these poor innocent creatures," Mr Potts says, "by the great care and pains of this honourable judge, delivered from the danger of this conspiracy; this bloody practice of the priest laid open."'

He sat back, eyes fixed on me. 'They are going to ask how it is that a servant girl is able to make such detailed accusations about the witches at their unholy gatherings. They will wonder how it is you know of such things, Anne, but you are to say nothing more of me, of the ragged man.

'For I am no papist priest, and you can give direct answers now, Anne, saying what you have seen and done, seen and done since I first found you in the early morning, in the field, hungry and cold and looking for cows. You can tell them those things that have come to pass as I said they would, those things and more, those things you now tell me ...'

His eyes stared blindly into the darkness closing in on both of us as the taper first flared, then shrank back into only the faintest glow.

'So take your corner there, my little Anne, and sleep. And on Wednesday go and tell them that there are indeed devils and witches, for you have seen them, and danced with them, and sung for them.'

Anne was tired, bone-weary, and the fug of the old man's cramped space, warm with his smells and the heat of his talking, lulled her and had her dropping off even as his last words floated about her, wove their visions into her exhausted thoughts. But as the darkness behind her closing eyelids ate away at his words, she felt the comfort of knowing that she did not need his words any more, his stories, his Graces and priests and Mr Potts. Yes, all those things he had predicted at daybreak on that grey morning when he had first appeared to her *had* happened, but now it was she who had seen these things, the flying wooden dishes carrying her neighbours, others in eggshells, their swinging too on a rope and their feasting on what fell to the table, their changing shape and dancing.

And more, yes, as he had had to admit tonight, so much more than he had foreseen; for what the old man had seen, she had done, and more, yes, so much more.

She gave herself over to sleep then, knowing that this other world, this other world he had led her to but she had entered, she now knew better than him. Better than his books and papers, because she had felt its truth, truths that her eyes could see and her hands could touch.

And it was to this world that she would bend her voice on Wednesday, make real for the Justices in Morpeth, as real as it was to her.

Riding Mill

Thieves smash church window

BBC News, Tyne & Wear, 22 May 2012

CHURCH burglars hurled a rock through a £5,000 stained glass window to steal just £2 from the collection box.

The raiders struck in the early hours at St Cuthbert's Church in Riding Mill, Northumberland.

They climbed through the gaping window and hacked a wall-mounted collection box from the stonework. They then ransacked the vestry, leaving a trail of chaos.

Last night a police chief branded the break-in 'disgusting and cowardly. There is no place in our communities for anyone who behaves in this way,' he said.

Church vicar, the Rev Canon Patrick Massey, said: 'The damaged window was dedicated to the Venerable Bede and is one of seven in the church depicting the Northern saints. It dates back to the early 19th century and is irreplaceable.'

The window is on the north side of the church, concealed from public view, and that is where the thieves gained entry. The lower half of the window was shattered.

'We have collected absolutely every shard of glass, but we don't know whether it can be put together again,' said Rev Massey.

'The church is normally such a peaceful place. This whole ordeal has been very upsetting for everyone. The people responsible for this have not only hurt the building, they have hurt the community.'

St Cuthbert's Church, which stands in the heart of the quiet village, was built in 1858 as a Chapel of Ease to the parish of Bywell St Andrews, to enable parishioners to attend services more easily.

It became the parish church of Riding Mill in 1962 and is described as 'a beautiful example of Victorian gothic village church architecture.'

The colourful memorial windows lend a sense of calm and serenity to this well-loved church, which is usually open between 9am and 5pm each day.

County councillor Joan Hill bemoaned the attack, saying: 'It is sad that this type of incident has occurred. The church is much loved by the residents of this desirable place to live, and I hope that the police manage to find the culprits as soon as possible. Their actions have caused thousands of pounds of damage to the church all for the sake of a couple of pounds.'

Northumbria Police ask anyone with information to contact them on 101.

He nearly bumped right into her as he came out of the side entrance of the Wellington Inn.

Bloody small doors – bloody small people back in 1660, he thought, looking up at the date carved into the lintel he'd banged his head on, not for the first time – hardly enough room for a man to squeeze through these days.

Sorry, he said to her, trying to regain his balance. Probably thinks I'm drunk, as if I've got enough money for that. In his defence, he rubbed his gammy leg.

She looked damp, cold in that thin dress. The yellow of the streetlights washed over her, but he didn't think she was much older than him. Her face was a bit of a blur in the drizzle.

He had to lean in towards her, bend his head down to catch that thin wisp of a voice. Afterwards, he couldn't remember hearing her say anything specific, but the next thing he knew he was crossing the road with her, she not even looking left or right and him just following on without his usual planning for an unsteady dash of sorts. Oddly, his balance felt a bit better than usual, and he was only a little behind her by the time they reached the pavement on the other side. Then she disappeared into the shadows of the driveway next to the old mill.

When he lost sight of her he felt his balance go again, having to search for her side to side in the shadows not helping. Then there she was, just ahead of him, walking slowly enough for him to catch up, arms wrapped around herself, her head down as she mumbled or hummed something to herself. As he neared her she sped up again, walking straight on to the old stone pack bridge. When he caught up with her she was standing at the foot of the bridge, looking into the low rush of the March Burn that filled the quiet. Then she darted on to the bridge, almost dashing across it into the darkness of the path leading on between some houses and a high stone wall, trees hanging thick above. He followed quickly, the grey of her dress glimmering faintly ahead.

The path began to steepen, rising against the wall on the right. He could see her head clearly as it rose above the coping stones. She was looking over the wall into the grounds of St Cuthbert's. She turned briefly to look back at him, her eyes with the faintest shine, the rest of her greyness almost one with the stone. Then she moved on quickly to where the path opened out into St Cuthbert's Lane, turned right and then right again through the gates of the churchyard.

By the time he reached the gate, her pale figure was passing through the old cemetery, the graves huddling up against the church. He followed as she disappeared into the deeper dark behind the church, with no clear idea why he was traipsing after this grey girl. Then again, he wasn't above being led into a dark corner by a girl, even if he wasn't sure what she had in mind. It was more than that, though: some compulsion much stronger than any hopes he might have had was running through him, blurring his thoughts and running through every muscle.

The air was an earthy, musty fug as he followed her through the old tombstones, many at odd angles where the ground had subsided, one or two fallen completely flat. She picked her way between the dead of the village, rounding the church. He found her staring up at one of the stained glass windows. She turned her face to him, calmly, steadily, before pointing up to it.

Then he watched her bend down, finding at her feet, as if this had been carefully planned, a broken corner of one of the oldest, most weathered headstones. He didn't know why he did what he did next, or even how, given his leg, but he too bent down and put his hands on the stone. Suddenly he felt stronger than he had in years, his feet steady on the ground, his head clear, his stomach not heaving, his nerves not jangling; then he grasped the triangular piece of stone firmly in both hands, stood up, drew back his arms, and threw.

The shattering of glass was not nearly as loud as he thought it would be, the soft lead holding the pieces in place giving easily, the bottom of the window crumpling rather than shattering, the top staying in place. The wash of the burn helped to swallow up what noise there was, and then the silence wrapped itself around them again.

She did not look at him as she placed her foot on the sloping wooden doors set into a long-disused coal bunker angled into the ground. So this was why she'd picked this window. With no apparent effort she lifted herself through the cleared lower half of the frame, and disappeared inside the church. Instantly, panic at the thought of being alone in the dark gripped him and he clambered up after her, amazed at how easily he was able to do this.

He dropped on to the wooden pew beneath the window and then slid sideways to the aisle. The church was suffused with a soft glow, some low light left on up near the altar gleaming dully on the brass of the communion rail and the gold mosaic set into the backing of the altar table. The sickly sodium sheen from the streetlights on St Cuthbert's Lane gave a faint luminosity to the stained glass, the figures filling each of the windows looking down at him in silent, accusing horror. For some reason this made him feel braver, stronger; how long had it been since anyone looked at him with anything but distaste or pity.

She was heading towards the entrance and he followed, running his hand along the hymnals and pamphlets neatly arranged near the heavy, locked door. She reached up and touched the bell rope hanging down from the rising emptiness of the squat insides of the steeple, watching it swing lightly. Then she bent down and began scrabbling at a metal plate with a slot in the middle set into the stone work; he could just make out a sign above it that read, 'Please put your offering in the box below. Thank you.'

He was overwhelmed with the need to break open that small box, even though he knew there could be little of value in it. She pulled back and looked at him. He peered about in the gloom, saw the dim gleam of the candle holders on the altar, and ran up the aisle. He came back clutching a heavy brass candlestick, at least a foot and a half long with a solid brass base. He swung it again and again at the stone around the metal plate of the collection box, chips flying into the shadows. The candlestick bent and buckled, but gave him a lever to force into the gap that he had hacked into the stone. He could not remember the last time he had felt the elation that flooded through him as the plate came away, even when it revealed only a tiny pile of small change inside. He clawed at it, dropping as many coins as those he offered to her; when she simply smiled, he stuffed them into his pockets, dropping even more in the process.

She was already floating through the dark, up towards a door on the left leading into the vestry. He followed her into the room, where he found her tearing out the ceremonial vestments for the clergy and the choir hanging in some cupboards, flinging them into the air, her mouth open in silent laughter as they drifted and floated down around her. He joined in, sweeping a row of wooden filing boxes off a shelf, kicking them as they fell to the floor so that their carefully organised contents exploded into the room. Then he opened the door of another built-in cupboard to find it full of papers, books and some liturgical objects. He pulled them out, tossing the papers up into the air, pitching the icons at the wall, and skidding the books across the floor. Between them they grabbed at everything they could get their hands on, not even pretending to look for anything as crass as money any more, but simply dancing in sheer delight, swirling about in the shower of robes which they caught in the air, tossing them up again and again. He was infused with the joy of not feeling scared or off-balance, the floor solid beneath him and not dipping and weaving like a deck at sea.

And then she ran out into the nave; mid-laugh he threw an armful of vestments to the floor and hurried after her. Already he was bumping into pews, tripping over the low step in the aisle. He could see her dark shape clambering back up to the broken window, and he followed as fast as he could. Only now, in the sickly glimmering of the streetlight through the windows opposite, did he see that the stained glass he had knocked through was the bottom half of the Bede, the venerable bloody Bede, now only intact from the waist up but still holding his quill at the ready, staring at a book and utterly unaware his legs had gone.

He bundled himself clumsily through the space he had made, and felt with his feet for the slick tiles of the coal bunker; he slipped and half fell, slithering down the bunker and rolling on to the wet grass. He looked around, but she was nowhere to be seen. He tried to scrabble to his feet, the graveyard shifting under his unsteady legs. He clung on to headstone after headstone as he did his best to run through them, looking about wildly for her. Stumbling, falling, half rising as the memorials to the dead begin to spin about him, the ground swaying now, tilting, faster and faster until the earth beneath him was one long oceanic swirl. Panic choked him as he gagged on the rising vomit, and he fell on his back as his ears were flooded with an endless crashing peal that deafened him to the long, sustained wail drawn out from the deepest part of him.

Chapter 8

Ralph Jenison hoped, sincerely hoped, that the Armstrong business was behind him. He was therefore rather unnerved when a letter was delivered to his rooms at Trinity House in the Broad Chare informing him that his presence would be required at the Quarter Sessions, specifically to participate in a pre-trial investigation of the girl's accusations of witchcraft.

There was no reference in the message to his having had previous dealings with her, but he would be surprised if the deposition he had taken some three months ago didn't drift back up to the surface once those murky waters were stirred again.

Those eggs, why did she have to come to me about those eggs, and that old man, a false prophet if ever there was one – if he existed at all, wasn't another of her inventions. And, of course, her being transformed into a horse, and then the ropes, and the food, the tugging down of the feast. Well, he knew where such ideas had begun, the source of her fantastical 'evidence'; but where, he wondered, fingering the paper telling him he was required in Morpeth, at the castle, for the Sessions, would it end.

Ralph Jenison could see them still, their shifts soiled below as they swung, dead weight heavy in the air, the ropes creaking with their burden of dead meat, no banquet here, blood not wine; tug on this only to put an end to the struggling and strangled cries, the helpless, dancing fingers of the bound hands, the breathless gurgling, not to draw down a feast.

Not again, if he could help it.

He was barely twenty when he made his first trip to London. His father was one of the Hostmen of Newcastle-upon-Tyne, so it was easy enough for him to arrange for his partners in London to provide Ralph with accommodation and introductions. Any trader who wanted to deal in coal from the River Tyne had to go through the cartel, and so William Jenison could be sure that they would go out of their way to look after his son and heir, already making his own way in the same business.

The younger men of the London company with which his father was currently negotiating were determined that this neophyte from the north experience the best the capital had to offer, and chief among the entertainments to hand when he arrived was the play of the season. You're lucky, they said to Ralph, you're here in time to catch its third – third! – performance. Plays normally change daily, but this one has run for three consecutive days. It is performed by the King's Men at the Globe Theatre – come, you must have heard of them! They are widely recognised as the best company in the land.

And always in trouble with the Master of the Revels too, so you can be sure their plays are entertaining. Only last April Sir Henry forbad the performance of John Fletcher's new play, although it is nothing less than a sequel to Mr Shakespeare's *Shrew*. 'Foul and offensive,' he said, full of oaths, profaneness, and public ribaldry. Well, we can live in hope for this one then, for it is based on such a shocking affair. 'The Late Lancashire Witches'!

One of the young men declared himself bored with the never-ending public fascination with witchcraft. Ah, but this is a play of real events, said another, a further scandal up north, where witches are still rife. *The Witch of Edmonton* too, his companion responded, was a true story, well known, and I hope they've made as good an amusement of it. Better, better, he was told, they have used the actual court documents for their script! And so topical I hear the matter is not yet resolved!

Ralph Jenison remained quiet, not wishing to appear unsophisticated, though he wasn't immediately overawed by this gaggle of young men who appeared to speak constantly in exclamations. His own town was by no means short on public entertainments and he felt he would have no trouble impressing these scions of London business when it was their turn to travel in pursuit of profit. His silence had less to do with going to the theatre than the subject of the play he was being given no choice in going to see.

From as early as he could remember he'd found the topic of witches and witchcraft distasteful: not for any religious, political or even superstitious reason – he simply disliked the kind of immoderate and unwholesome interest it provoked, the prurient fantasising that replaced any sober attempt at judging it or dealing with it. An evening's entertainment taken up with such distasteful – yes, that was it, that was the word he kept returning to whenever he was forced to think about witchcraft – such *distasteful* practices didn't strike him as worthy of his first night in the cultivated city of London. But the theatre, open to the sky, three-storied, packed with what must have been three thousand people, was impressive enough. He was glad of the seats his new companions were able to afford on the second level, with a good view over the action on the stage extending out into a pit packed with people. 'Groundlings', his companions called them, with a dismissive snort.

Ralph was surprised to see so many of the gentry, including gentlewomen, on the level he and his companions occupied, given that this was the vacation. Although the courts were not in session in London, the conversation around him was humming with the news that the characters they were about to see played by actors on stage were actually present in the city – in prison, for the most part. Certainly the four found guilty of being witches by their local Justices were here, and their accusers too, having been brought down from Lancashire to be re-examined by the Privy Council and the king himself. Originally there were seven, someone near him was saying, but three of them died while imprisoned in Lancaster Castle. The dramatists were working so close to the events that they did not as yet have a conclusion for their story, but the crowd were more than happy with the gruesome details.

Once the play was underway, Ralph found he was almost as caught up in the bizarre events portrayed as his companions. This had nothing to do with the action, which was a muddle of sleights and tricks, twists and turns, interruptions and digressions interspersed with bouts of combat, flirtatious conversations, and amorous relations. It was the spectacular effects, oddly enough, that were most convincing, and Ralph Jenison found his senses overwhelmed with the scenes of transportation and transformation, the visions, enchanted objects, festivities, and demons summoned up on stage, culminating in the cutting off of a cat's paw which turned out to be a woman's hand.

On this hand there was a wedding ring, recognised by the woman's husband, which was in some way crucial to the resolution of the plot. Thinking back now, he recalled part of the story: something about an upright and hospitable gentleman discovering that his wife has a secret nocturnal life as the leader of a group of witches. Mistress Generous, if he remembered correctly – he'd never liked such obvious naming devices – was forever challenging the authority of her husband, and there was a complicated subplot involving a family in which the proper order of things was more radically subverted, with a father cowed by his son, the mother by her daughter, and the children by the servants. By the conclusion, the family's butler who was determined to lord it over his employers was rendered impotent on his wedding night by a bewitched codpiece, and a miller had wounded Mistress Generous with his sword while she was in the shape of a cat, leading to the discovery of her central role in the gathering together of the witches. Order was restored with their prosecution and conviction, but if Ralph Jenison were to be honest, it was the pails of milk that walked on their own, the pies filled with living birds and young cats, the jokes, the songs, the dances, that stayed with him long after his evening at the theatre.

Unquestionably there was no poetical genius that impressed him, no art, or language, or greater understanding of witchcraft; instead, like the rest of the crowd, he'd given in to the ribaldry and fopperies, and did not argue with his companions when they were swept out by the throng into the busy Bankside night, declaring it 'a merry and excellent new play'. It was only later that he thought to take some umbrage at the assumption that believers in witchcraft are not only suitable subjects for comedy, but rustic northerners, a breed apart from the sophisticated audiences of the south.

Time had erased his resentment along with most of his recollection of the play. He would hardly have remembered it at all so many years later if it were not for Anne Armstrong. As she spoke, a scene from the theatre came back to him: in it, one of Mistress Generous's servants refuses to get her horse, and she bridles him instead and rides him to the witches. 'Horse, horse, see thou be, and where I point thee, carry me,' she said, or words to that effect, and Robin, the boy servant, was most convincingly changed into a horse, snorting, shaking his head, pawing the ground and chewing the imaginary bridle; he then knelt down to become the horse's head, facing the cheering crowd and dancing his forelegs impatiently as the witch leapt up behind, from the torso straight up as the rider, with her lower quarters extended out backwards, forming a most comic horse's ass-end. And so they galloped off the stage, the witch cackling and the boy neighing 'Help! Help!' loudly over the shouts and laughter of the groundlings.

He wondered if Anne Armstrong's transformation was anything like as effective. What was he meant to have seen in his mind's eye when she told him that she had been bridled and ridden upon, cross-legged, 'in the likeness of a horse'?

But there was another scene too, that was called back by the girl's evidence. The boy is ridden to one of the witches' nightly meetings where he spies on their festivities, on this occasion a 'wedding feast'. What was it Anne Armstrong had said? There was a rope hanging over the room, which each witch touched and then whatever food they wanted came down upon the table? This is exactly what the boy Robin sees in the play, the witches calling for meat and drink, and pulling on ropes which make the food appear. He could see again the boy's head, raised up and poked through a curtain of some kind, peeking out as the witches banqueted, tugging on the ropes for roast beef, bottles of wine, poultry, fowl, fish, butter, milk, whey, curds and cheese, even the bride's posset. He remembered getting hungry himself as the witches called out, "Tis come, 'tis come,' each time they pulled on the ropes and the food materialised.

This was a long time before the Armstrong girl was born, but it was striking that in the years in between there were, to his knowledge, no other claims of the bewitched being turned into horses and feats where food and wine fell from the rafters.

He'd set his clerk to follow up on the matter. If, as he'd been told at the time, the dramatists had made extensive use of court documents, records must be available. And so they were: manuscript versions of the boy's testimony were circulating widely and his clerk had found transcripts of the deposition that were, he must warn the Justice, of varying degrees of accuracy. Those by Harleian and Dodsworth were, he said, handing copies of these over, most to be recommended, the one by Rawlinson being extremely rough and full of omissions.

And so Ralph Jenison had before him not only the memories of a night out so many years ago, but reliable copies of 'The Examination of Edmund Robinson, son of Edmund Robinson of Pendle Forest, eleven years of age, taken at Padiham before Richard Shuttleworth and John Starkey, Esquires, two of His Majesty's Justices of the Peace within the county of Lancaster, the 10th day of February, 1633.'

He turned to these, Anne Armstrong's deposition next to them on his desk, and read on, read on too through the trial of the 'Graund Witches of the Forrest of Pendle' and 'the Witches of Salmesbury', read on into the night.

And when he was done he sat back, and said out loud to the empty dark beyond the candle his clerk must have lit for him before leaving: 'I have you now, Anne Armstrong, I have you, chapter and verse; wherever you got this from I have you, chapter and verse.'

The National Archives

I lifted the next deposition in the sequence carefully out of the cardboard box.

Halfway through my time at the Archives, and I had only reached the fourth deposition in a substantial series of documents. This was the one James Raine had dated 9 April 1673. I could see nothing confirming Raine's dating in the way the deposition had been archived. The original had a much longer and more complex case heading than had been reproduced in the transcript where it had been, as in the published versions, reduced to the date, place, and the names of the Justices.

I hadn't needed the encounter with the renowned historian to alert me to the fact that the transcriptions could at times differ markedly from the originals. If anything, along with finding out for myself the ways in which the transcriptions were sometimes incomplete and inaccurate, I was also learning something of the logic behind their gaps and alterations.

No doubt Raine was following the editorial conventions of the Surtees Society. Possibly he had developed a few of his own when working through so many documents. He used modern capitalisation and punctuation and often expanded abbreviations, especially when it came to the names of places and people, although he tended to follow the archaic spelling. There were, I supposed, endless features of the original that an editor could choose to change or leave out. Raine seemed to have hacked away at the tangle of tight script pushed up against the right-hand margin of this deposition with particular efficiency.

In the original, the case heading looked a lot more formal, if the more liberal use of Latin was anything to go by. The combination of my weak grasp of the language along with script that was both smaller and closer to some kind of conventional court hand-writing made my eyes and head hurt.

At least it appeared as if the deposition had been drawn up by the same hand that had drawn up the depositions of 2 and 4 April. I was no expert, but the minor variations in the common secretary hand of the period looked similar enough – minims often becoming a line, 'o' and 'e' virtually indistinguishable, set habits in the often bewildering array of possible spellings of the same word across different documents, a similar sweep to the strong line drawn under the name of the county in the top left-hand corner.

This was reassuring in its way, giving at least a hint of the presence of the invisible, shadowy figure behind the hand guiding the quill. The depositions themselves contained no clues to his identity, no signature or colophon, no statement of his rank or social status, no suggestions as to his education or his relationship with his superiors and subordinates. His role in the drawing up of the documents was, after all, meant to be simply that of mediator, putting down on paper what the witness said. But I was beginning to understand how much the character of the scribe informed the information given. What was recorded was not always, possibly rarely, the exact words as spoken by the deponent. By convention framed in the historic present, the oral testimony no doubt given in the first person was recorded as a third person narrative in the past tense; slipping between direct and indirect speech, summary and verbatim report, third and first person, punctuated with stock words and phrases, the recorded account was as much the work of the scribe as the deponent.

The main clue to this scribe's character was his handwriting – the first thing to disappear in the published transcription. Having waded through a good number of depositions in the box to get to those to do with Anne, I gained the impression that this scribe's comparatively neat hand showed an exemplary commitment to the business of taking down Anne's evidence, given that this was never meant to be a document for display, merely a functional record for purely practical purposes. He had a good ear for pungent detail too, capturing a word here, a turn of phrase there that seemed to carry a whiff of her voice, Anne in the dock pouring out her story.

Before I could get to what she said in this deposition I had to get through the morass of the case heading, without even a paraphrase in the transcription to help me. I had no idea why Raine had chosen to give such a minimal account of the heading, and settled down to work my way through it.

The opening words made the entire journey down to Kew worthwhile: the first word was unclear – was that 'At'? – but the next two could be made out, if with some difficulty, given that the second was abbreviated: 'general c~ sess^m'; 'general session', surely. Some difficult script followed, possibly a heavily abbreviated reference to the reign of the king, and then *Comita Northumbri* something something *Morpeth Comitat* something *nono* or was that *novo die* ... what was it, April? The ninth day of April? So, buried in the Latin and squeezed, italicised script, 'At a general session, county of Northumberland, Morpeth, 9th April ...'

That confirmed Raine's date, but at a 'general *session*'? That would be the Quarter Sessions, surely.

But what about ASSI 45, then, the fact that the deposition was filed under the Criminal Depositions and Case Papers of the Northern and North-Eastern Circuits of the *Assizes*? This is where it had been archived all along, first in York, then at the Public Records Office, and now The National Archives. The natural assumption then was that Anne's accusations had been heard, as they should have been, given the nature of her charges, at the Assizes.

I looked at the date again: 9 April.

The Assizes were held twice a year, in the Lent and Trinity vacations. The Lent vacation would have been in late February or March, Trinity in July or early August.

April? The Quarter Sessions were held four times a year, in the week after the annual feasts of Epiphany, Easter, Midsummer, and Michaelmas.

I couldn't think why I hadn't checked the dates before. 9 April would be the Wednesday of the first full week in April, the week after Easter.

Anne's evidence was given at the Quarter Sessions, unquestionably.

I logged back on to the search page of The National Archives. In theory the records of the Quarter Sessions were meant to have been kept from the fourteenth century onwards, I was told. In reality the earliest surviving record was the *Vetera Indictamenta* of 1580–1630, a single volume of indictments for that period, with no other records surviving until those of 1680, after which there was a complete series of order books running until 1971.

1630 to 1680: fifty years of missing records, with the Quarter Sessions records for Morpeth in 1673 lost somewhere in the extended silence of that void.

If the case had been confined to the Quarter Sessions, whatever decisions had been taken there were lost to the archive.

But why were Anne's accusations being heard at the Quarter Sessions? Why was a felony being tried – and this now clearly was a trial of some sort, something at any rate beyond the pre-trial proceedings of 2 and 4 April, 5 February too, for that matter – at the Quarter Sessions and not the Assizes?

For that matter, why had Anne not come before a grand jury? As I understood it, this was the next step in the legal process, where her accusations would be assessed to decide whether there was sufficient evidence to try the case before a trial jury.

I couldn't help it. Was this what Anne was trying to guide me towards? I stared hard again at Anne's mark at the end of the testimony she gave on 9 April, willing it to speak. The same circle with a point at its centre, but drawn so forcefully it had torn into the paper, deep enough for my fingers to read it like braille.

I turned back to the first page, the second half of the case heading. This was comparatively easy to work through, made up as it was of the list of names of the men before – *Coram* – whom Anne appeared. The names were in their Latin form, but manageable: Horsley and Stote were listed as *Milite* (Knight, I presumed) and Mitford 'Humphido Mitford' and Jenison 'Radulpho Genison', joined by 'Jacobo Howard' and 'J ...' was that 'Joannes? Salkeld?' as *Armigeri* (Esquire, that must be).

I could fake my way through the rest, I was sure: *Justitiariis* or whatever it was must be Justices, of the Peace, perhaps? I was on safer ground with what came next, something like, 'the Information of Anne Armstrong of Birches Nook in the aforesaid County ... Spinster ... something ... court of justice...' Close enough, I had the idea: if Anne had not been called before a grand jury, she had appeared before a full bench of Justices.

But that was not the last of the evidence lost in the transcription that the original deposition had to offer up. The first line of the next paragraph, the first in the body of Anne's evidence, had been entirely omitted in Raine's transcript. This was an omission it was hard to justify; for in it, it slowly dawned on me as I painstakingly tried to make it out, was nothing less than the clue to the sequencing of the depositions.

'... the information by her given to Sir Richard Stote, Knight, of aforesaid county the 4 April and further information by her given to Ralph Jenison Esq another' – Justice of the Peace, that must be – 'of aforesaid country on 5 day of February in the year of the King 25th is likewise true.'

'... and further information by her given ...'; Raine had left this out entirely, only transcribing 'Anne Armstrong of Birches Nooke, Spinster, saith, that the information she hath already given is truth'; this contraction, this summary of what actually appeared in the original document, skimmed over the fact that this was the occasion on which the deposition of 5 February was first introduced to the court.

This gave a different weight, surely, to the clerk's formulaic 'She now further saith…'; what Anne had to say on this occasion was in addition to, a development of, what she had said to Ralph Jenison on 5 February. It would have all the weight missing from what she had told Humphrey Mitford and Sir Richard Stote.

She was ready now, ready for her big performance. Ready to tell everything that had been building, growing, expanding in her gut until she felt she would choke, her throat filled with the rising bile of what she had to tell: 'She now further saith,' I read, my finger blackening with the dust coating Anne's words as I ran it along under each sentence as taken down by that neat, busy hand I was coming to know almost as well,

that Lucy Thompson of Mickley, widdow, upon Thursday in the evening, being the 3rd of Aprill, att the house of John Newton off the Riding, swinging upon a rope which went crosse the balkes, she, the said Lucy, wished that a boyl'd capon with silver scrues might come down to her and the rest, which were five coveys consisting of thirteen person in every covey…

Chapter 9

Apr. 9, 1673. At the Sessions at Morpeth before Sir Thomas Horsley
and Sir Richard Stote, knights, James Howard, Humphrey Mitford,
Ralph Jenison, and John Salkeld, Esqrs.

They were impressive enough, country Justices though they were, when ranged at the long table on the raised section at the heart of the courtroom. It was still cold, too cold for April, and they appreciated the fire in the hearth behind them. There was little enough by way of any other comfort, so the grandeur of the regalia in which the Justices had adorned themselves was as much a protection against the dank grey of the third day of the Easter Quarter Sessions as an attempt to awe criminals and spectators alike with the circumstance and dignity of their position.

Sir Richard Stote, chairman for the day's proceedings, looked out over the plain wooden floor and limewashed walls, the low desk before him with its bustle of clerks and assistants, the bailiffs puffed out and standing expectantly next to the jury box and prisoner's dock, the jostle of faces and body parts appearing and disappearing through the opening between the court and the section of the room packed with plaintiffs and prisoners waiting their turn for justice. He looked forward to the days to come, not too distant now, when he would be above all this, joining those more august dispensers of the law at the Assizes. Then he would enter York, Lancaster, Appleby, Newcastle but twice a year and in a fashion resembling the progresses of royalty, sheriffs escorting them with a gallant train of gentlemen, cavalcades of horsemen issuing forth to meet them as they entered the county, he and his fellow judge received everywhere with hospitality and respect and welcomed with ceremony and state.

Reminding himself of this strengthened his hand for the business of the day. Soon the partitioned spaces at the sides of the room would fill with jurors, but for now it was the officers of the court beginning to fill their places at the lower benches with exaggerated officiousness. And steady, silent, but clearly more than ready, the Clerk of the Peace had already taken his place at a desk immediately below the bench. He looked at Sir Richard and then nodded to the bailiff, who walked to the screen, called out a name, and then brought Anne Armstrong into the courtroom. Small, grey, nondescript, she was positioned in the dock and he stood aside, arms folded over his large chest and resting on his larger stomach.

Only then, with the stage set, as it were, did Sir Richard signal to the clerk that the people crowding up against the doors to the court could enter. The bailiff's men saw to this, pushing and shoving the throng into some sort of order as it spilled on to the broad stone-flagged floor of the gatehouse. The bustle that attended their entry began to die down as they found their places, the spectacle providing awe enough to impose silence as they tip-toed and peered over and through the press of their neighbours.

When he was sure the people were suitably focused upon those ranged above them, Sir Richard turned to meet the expectant, enquiring gazes of Sir Thomas Horsley, James Howard, Humphrey Mitford, John Salkeld and Ralph Jenison.

'I have just returned from Axwell House where I have been the guest of Sir James Clavering. Sir James accompanied me on Friday last into some of the more troubled areas of the Derwent Valley. There we carried out investigations into the accusations brought before these Sessions.

'These accusations, as some of you understand all too well already, involve the offence of witchcraft –' a ripple ran through those gathered on the court room floor '– and should be passed on directly to the Assizes.'

Anne Armstrong's downcast eyes flickered up briefly and then settled again on the rim of the wooden dock.

'However, I think it best we consider this case ourselves before forwarding it to the judges of the Assize. We do not wish – do we? – to appear incompetent, foolish even before the King's Bench. So it is best that we apply our collective mind to the facts of these accusations made by one Anne Armstrong– ' he gestured towards the girl '– of Birches Nooke, a place, I am told, some twenty miles up the valley of the Tyne.

'We have before us this morning the evidence given to me last week, evidence that was in part given to Mitford here some days before, which he took upon himself in his individual capacity to label as *Ignoramus*, "no bill".

Humphrey Mitford held his stare on the rough wooden surface of the desk, his dejection eloquently expressed in the slump of his shoulders.

Sir Richard waited a moment to see if he had anything to add, but Mitford remained silent.

'Well, there was hardly anything there – some dancing and singing and what-not with the devil here in Morpeth – and so we may leave that deposition aside for the moment. When she came before me, however, the Armstrong girl made further accusations, specific accusations including names and places and involving actual harm committed by magic.

'The places concerned, on the borders between Northumberland and Durham, have a reputation for deviances of all kinds, political and religious as well as supernatural. For this reason I went out there, taking Sir James with me in case of any legal sensitivities with the palatine.

'I have bound over the accuser and several witnesses to appear before us with a view to establishing the basis of a case against the accused, who are many and various. They, no doubt, wish also to be heard. I remind them that the accused are not expected to come before us, as we have not yet decided if there is a case against them to be answered. These are preliminary proceedings in which we are engaged and I am sure in any event that the list will be added to today if the deponent, Anne Armstrong, continues as she has done thus far.

'I have also found – my thanks here to the Clerk of the Peace –' Sir Richard inclined his head towards the clerks' desk '– a document that has caused me some concern.

'Clerk, if you will. You will see,' said Sir Richard as the pieces of paper were passed to the bench, 'that this is a deposition made before Mr Jenison on the fifth of February, at his offices in Newcastle – in Trinity House in the Broad Chare, I believe?'

Ralph Jenison nodded, a small, reluctant nod.

'And you can confirm that the title written on the cover of this deposition is an accurate summary of its contents?'

He pointed to the document the Justices were passing among themselves; they turned it over to see, in the oblong formed by the folding of the pages, written in the same hand that had taken down the testimony, the names of those accused, Foster, Dryden, Thompson, underlined with a single, emphatic line.

Sir Richard did not wait for any confirmation before asking if that were indeed his signature at the end of the information given. Sir Thomas found the place and tapped on the signature, firm, clear, easy to make out – 'R. A. Jenison' – the line drawn under the name, a strong and heavy sweep of the quill, thickening as it progressed from left to right.

'And that is Anne Armstrong's mark?' Sir Thomas asked, moving his finger to the right.

Ralph Jenison focused on the circle with its heavily inked-in dot in the centre, and nodded again.

'This is the deposition which was, I am told by Mr Jenison's clerk, taken down with all due procedure and referred, quite properly, to the Court of the Assize, concerning as it does an offence carrying the death penalty.

'How it did not find its way there is something of a mystery, but as far as our business is concerned, this may prove fortuitous.

'As you will see, the accusations made in this deposition are of, shall we call them, the Scottish or Continental style, God save His Majesty – read, read, you'll see what I mean – changing shapes and flying, taking part in unholy rites, obtaining food by magical means, and so on, bizarre accusations not often heard in our English courts. This makes them all the more remarkable, given that such things would be much harder for a girl like this –' Anne's eyes flashed up again '– to invent.

'But they also make it plain that the purposes of these meetings – meetings which have direct bearing on those since reported to us here in Morpeth – extend to *maleficium*, in this case injury to livestock and persons. It is of concern to me, therefore, that these earlier charges were somehow lost or mislaid.'

Sir Richard fixed his eyes on Ralph Jenison, the other Justices lifting their eyes from the document to stare as well. If Jenison had looked up, he would have seen too that Anne Armstrong was looking at him, icily.

Chapter 10

He could feel them, though, those eyes, the cold, grey eyes of the deponent, fixed on him; seeing him not so much now, shrinking into his place at the bench, but as he picked his way through the February-black night along the river before turning the key and easing the latch on the heavy door of the archway leading into the courtyard of Trinity House. Avoiding the gatekeeper, passing quietly behind the back of the banqueting hall, through the low yard with its almshouses and into the corridor in which his chambers were situated.

Ralph Jenison breathed more easily when he had the door closed behind him. Lighting a small candle, he made his way to his clerk's desk, peering at the tidy bundles of well-ordered papers set about on its surface. The efficiency of the man made it easy to find what he wanted in a pile of documents to the right, each neatly folded once along its length and twice across its width. He removed one and inserted it deep into the middle of another pile on the left.

He was patting this down so it did not appear disturbed when he jerked around, certain someone was watching him. The flame of his candle flared and then died before his hurried breath. He stood dead still in the darkness of his chambers, waiting for the night to swallow him up again, turn him invisible as he drew himself into the weight of his overcoat.

Slipping away, a shade among the shadows, he passed back through the low yard, his eyes firmly averted from the almshouses. It was easy during the day to ignore the rumours, and occasional quaking witness, of the ghost of a woman who had hanged herself in one of these buildings, but tonight it felt only too possible that she could put in an appearance.

Hat lower, collar higher, Justice Jenison hurried into the next courtyard, trying to remind himself that he had every right to be there, more than any other in fact, being the owner. He had bought the property only recently, and let it to the Masters and Mariners of this Town for the peppercorn rent of half a gallon to be paid each year on the vigil of Saint Peter and Saint Paul.

The prestige this earned him was small comfort as he exited through the archway and turned into the Broad Chare. Directly ahead of him on a hill across the river he saw the silhouette of All Saints Church, and this made him walk all the faster down to the quayside. The route he was taking was not the quickest way to his house but it was the quietest at this hour. When he came to Stony Hill Square halfway down the Chare, he turned into Spicer Lane, only then beginning to feel he was in the clear.

But he could not shake the feeling, as he passed to the Justice next along from him on the bench the document headed 'Northumberland, 5th Day of February 1672', a document bearing his signature, a document his clerk would swear had been sent on to the Assize Court, that the eyes he'd felt upon him in his chambers were the same eyes that settled upon him now, unwavering in the grey morning light.

Ralph Jenison did not like to think of himself as a squeamish man. Publicly he displayed as few qualms as the next Justice when it came to imposing the death penalty. There weren't many alternatives: prison was not intended as punishment, only a place to hold the accused while they awaited trial. What else was there to do with someone who had set fire to a heap of hay, or broken down the head of a fish pond so that the fish could escape, or stolen a shoulder of mutton? Hanging offences these had to be, and the number of offences for which one had to hang seemed to be rising inexorably.

Ralph Jenison would use what other options he had. The pillorying of offenders in a public place at noon on market day, that seemed appropriate for cheating at cards, selling defective goods, uttering seditious words. He'd used this too for more repugnant offences, although he'd grown more cautious since a pilloried man he'd convicted of 'a fowle and great trespass in attempting an Act of Uncleanness with a girl about eight years old' was stoned to death by the crowd. The stocks, parading offenders through the streets in a cart, whipping, these he could only use for vagrancy and theft of goods worth less than a shilling.

Witchcraft was, without a doubt, an offence that led to the gallows, but Ralph Jenison found he did not have the stomach to repeat one of the first duties he'd had to discharge when he was elected Sheriff of Newcastle.

It was a long time ago now, hard on the triumphal entry of Oliver Cromwell into the town. He would rather not have been as prominent as he had been in the festivities and feasting – it was just the sort of thing that staunch Royalists were never likely to let him forget – but the arrival of the victorious leader of the Parliamentary army had occurred barely two weeks after his election to the office. It had fallen to him then to organise the ringing of bells and firing of guns, the blazing tar barrels and music being played on the bridges, the lavish food and the entertainment in the house of the mayor.

So Ralph Jenison was taken aback when, shortly after the heady events of welcoming Mr Cromwell, clad still in his leather and steel, as stern in the face of the festivities accorded him as he had been in the retaking of Berwick, he discovered that the next major duty pertaining to that year's shrievalty was not nearly so agreeable.

Twenty-one prisoners recently tried at the Assizes had been left for execution in Newcastle. Ralph Jenison had no knowledge of the crimes for which they were convicted prior to his assuming office, but that they were to be hanged was certain and neither Sir Arthur Hazlerigg, the military governor of the town, or his deputy, Lieutenant-Colonel Paul Hobson, who would normally have superintended the execution, were available. There was nothing else for it then but that the unpleasant duty must be discharged by Sheriff Jenison.

The hanging at the West Gate attracted a large and blood-thirsty crowd, gathering in a carnival atmosphere to observe the gruesome display. Cheers drowned out a few lost wails of grief when the carts hoved into view with their cargo of the condemned, white linen shirts over their clothes and caps on their heads, tied two together with their backs to the horses' tails. The carts were surrounded by constables on horseback, each armed with a pike, for which Ralph Jenison was glad as he stood next to the gibbet dressed for the occasion in his ceremonial robes.

Some of the criminals went to their death seemingly uncon-cerned; others were drunk and mocking those making a great dis-play of their repentance. Once they reached the long, low scaffold, they were pushed and prodded and forced in batches of seven to mount a wide cart made expressly for the purpose of their death. A cord was passed around the neck of each and the end fastened to the gibbet while the chaplain who accompanied the condemned made a show of praying and singing a few verses of the Psalms. Relatives were permitted to mount the cart and make their farewells, but when the time was up – Ralph Jenison gave each group about a quarter of an hour – the chaplain and family members were ordered off. The executioner covered the eyes and faces of the prisoners with their caps and then stepped off the cart himself. He waited a moment, looking at the sheriff only for the sake of the occasion. He knew precisely how long to give the condemned to anticipate their end. More importantly, Ralph Jenison could not help but feel, the pause was judged by building the crowd to the exact pitch they felt was their due, and only when this was reached did the executioner lash at the horses spanned in to the death cart.

Ralph Jenison lowered his eyes – in prayer, he hoped those watching would assume. He glanced up after some moments, the sounds alone being almost too much to bear. Or so he thought, until he caught a glimpse of veins bursting, skin turning purple, blue and yellow. One man was in extraordinary pain, the knot, either through lack of skill on the part of the hangman or through a deliberate wish to supply some variety to the macabre show, pulling up directly under his chin, with no hope of dispatching him quickly.

Even for those hanged most efficiently, the strangulation was going to take several minutes, Ralph Jenison knew, anywhere from five to twenty minutes, although hopefully loss of consciousness set in before that. Who knew what the actual experience of the hanging felt like, other than the person being executed? As far as the law was concerned, the longer the better, to serve as a deterrence to other would-be criminals. A 'good hang', Jenison had been told as he tried to prepare himself for this day, was the most gruesome one possible.

He did not turn away quickly enough to miss the 'angel lust' visiting several of the men. This was a source of much humour in the crowd, including the good wives giggling and pointing, some swaying with their babies in their arms. Ralph Jenison was left with the indelible image of the stains of urine and other mucus and fluid on the tent-like projections of the men's breeches, unable to avoid seeing, too, the discharge of blood down the legs of the women.

As soon as they were allowed, friends and relations tugged at the ankles and feet of the hanging men and women so that they would die more quickly and suffer less. He gave this permission when he felt the display of dangling and dancing had done its work, but was surprised to see the relatives of some of those hanging from the gallows being prevented from performing this act of mercy. 'He said to me that if I fight too much you must give me a pull,' a wife of one of the condemned wailed as others in the crowd held her back. He turned to one of his officers, who said, 'Leave it be, Sir. Touching him at the moment of death will allow his spirit to escape, and you wouldn't want that for a witch. That's why they are hanged further apart than usual, Sir, so their bodies won't touch when they swing.'

Ralph Jenison still had to oversee their being cut down and the whole procedure being repeated, twice more on this hanging day. There were unseemly scuffles next to the scaffold as relatives and friends tussled with the executioner's men. The bodies and clothes of the dead belonged to the executioner, so those relatives wishing to claim them had to buy them from him. There were rumours, too, of bodies being sold to surgeons to be dissected, the only explanation for men facing up to each other while standing directly over any bodies unclaimed by relatives. To enter the afterlife, a person's body had to remain whole, and Ralph Jenison was relieved to see some of the dead being pulled away between the feet of those fighting over them and hurriedly removed for burial.

Not all of the dead were buried, of course. There was still the business of dealing with the murderers who, after being hanged on the common scaffold, were taken down and their bodies covered with tallow and other fatty substances. After this a tarred shirt was pulled over them and fastened down with iron bands, and then they were taken away to be hung with chains on a gibbet erected at the spot, or as near as possible to the place, where their crime was committed, there to hang until they fell to dust.

Now if Anne Armstrong had accused one, or only the first three women, Ralph Jenison might not have gone as far as he did in attempting to misdirect and then dismiss her accusations. He did not like or trust the girl, that was certain, but his instinctive reaction to her had also been pervaded with the memory of a phalanx of bodies jerking and swaying outside Newcastle's Gallowgate.

Yet despite his best efforts, his secretive manoeuvrings, here she was called forward to repeat and no doubt expand upon her wild, deadly denunciations. Beneath her steady stare, he felt the revulsion at the pit of his stomach rising up in his throat.

Chapter 11

Apr. 9, 1673. At the Sessions at Morpeth, as aforesaid.
Ann Armstrong, of Birkes-Nuke, spinster.

The clerk administered the oath to Anne Armstrong before reading out slowly, carefully, in a flat voice, the information she had given to Sir Richard a few days previously.

He asked her to confirm that this was true and then he held up the document with the information given to Ralph Jenison in February. He then read through it, after which he asked her if this document 'is likewise true.'

Ignored and left to lie on the clerk's desk, to Humphrey Mitford's relief, was the deposition taken down in his presence: brief, unfinished, of no consequence to what was to follow.

Anne Armstrong began to say that it was shorter than what she had said, but when Sir Richard interrupted, insisting on a simple yes or no, she said, yes, true, the information she had already given was true.

'Now, have you anything to add?'

Anne looked directly at Sir Richard, and began speaking steadily, as if reciting the strange facts she had to report with enough precision would give weight and credence to matters not treated with sufficient seriousness by those who had listened to her before.

'She now further saith,' wrote the scribe, his hand thereafter caught in a blur of speed,

that Lucy Thompson, of Mickley, widdow, upon Thursday in the evening, being the 3rd of Aprill, att the house of John Newton off the Riding, swinging upon a rope which went crosse the balkes, she –

'To be clear,' interrupted Sir Richard, 'she, this Lucy Thompson, this is the same Lucy Thompson you told me about on the fourth of April, the one you met at the, where was it –' scanning the pages of depositions on the desk '– at the Riding House, after you were ridden there by Anne Dryden or Anne Forster?'

Anne Armstrong nodded firmly. 'And there she stands,' she added, pointing to a face at the front of the press of people on the courtroom floor.

Lucy Thompson threw up an arm, gesticulated. 'Your Worship,' she called, face florid, eyes blazing, hair awry, 'she lies, I have never –'

Sir Richard cut her short. 'Lucy Thompson, you have not as yet been indicted and are not required to speak in your defence. You, and many another in this court today who will be named, will not be bound over or committed to prison unless we –' he took in the bench of Justices with a wave '– feel the evidence given by the deponent, this girl here in the dock, is sufficient to merit a trial.'

Lucy Thompson, far from satisfied, fell back into a knot of people who comforted her with pats and hugs, listening to the ongoing rush of words the Justice would not hear. Fingers were pointed and fists shaken at Anne Armstrong and a general hubbub began to spread outwards from the group until the clerk called out, demanding silence. When order was resumed, he nodded at the deponent.

'... the said Lucy,' wrote the scribe, having taken the respite this disruption allowed to write the woman's name in the broad margin he had kept to the left of his script. A presumption, perhaps, as there had been no call for the names of those the court would wish to arraign, but the girl's confidence made him certain he would be carrying out this responsibility when she was done.

The said Lucy wished that a boyl'd capon with silver scrues might come down to her and the rest, which were five coveys consisting of thirteen person in every covey; and that the said Lucy did swing twice, and then the said capon with silver scrues did come downe –

'Came down, how "came down"? Slid along the rope, dropped from the roof, appeared from nowhere?' This time it was Sir Thomas Horsley who spoke. Descendent of a Lord Mayor of Newcastle-upon-Tyne who had been not only a magistrate but also the founder of the Free Grammar School – now the Royal Grammar School – in the town, he felt obliged to lend a stringent tone to the proceedings, an appearance of scholarly exactitude, however fantastic the evidence being given.

The girl turned to him with a waspish look. It was as if for an instant the pose she was determined to hold, that of dutiful reporter, modest, respectful, had slipped. In that instant Sir Thomas Horsley saw a flash of his own girls at around that age, the manners of youth gone, those of maturity not yet attained, the wild years between.

And then the witness, the deposer, the evidence-giver was back. All reason and good sense, Anne was prepared to concede a minor deficiency that underlined rather than undercut the accuracy of what she had to report. She shrugged, let the question slide, said this is what *she thought* she had seen, gave the impression that this detail was unimportant, and she should be allowed to get on with those that were.

'... and then the said capon with silverscrues did, as she thinketh,' wrote the scribe, 'come downe, which capon the said Lucy sett before the rest of the company, whereof the divell, which they called their protector –'

Sir Thomas was about to interrupt again when Sir Richard raised his hand to stop him. 'I've gone into this "protector" business,' he said, 'and there is no political significance to it that I can see.

'The rector at Edmundbyers is determined to ramble on about that Dissenting business up around Muggleswick, but even he does not claim that the Puritans are behind all this...' He waved a hand airily. 'I imagine her use of the word is some diabolic inversion of our Lord as the protector of virtuous souls.'

Sir Richard indicated that she should continue. Anne seemed barely to have noticed that she had been interrupted. She was finding her stride now, relishing the audience she had longed for, enjoying being at the centre of the ceremony called into being by what she had to say, all ears open to her, that white, spidery hand moving across the paper with her every breath, its every motion impelled by the words that came out of her mouth, at the whim of whatever thought crossed her brain, every memory, every hurt, every hope.

'... which they called their protector, and sometimes their blessed saviour, was their chief, sitting in a chair.' She must be careful, she could not swear that what she saw was so, for this detail too was not important, the nature of the material from which the chair was made not at issue, only its shining, its glistening in the weirdly lit gloom of the room.

... a chair like unto bright gold. And the said Lucy further did swing, and demanded the plum-broth which the capon was boyled in, and thereupon it did immediately come down in a dish, and likewise a bottle of wine which came down upon the first swing.

'Plum broth, no less,' harrumphed Humphrey Mitford, but Anne did not, could not, stop for this, and the rest of her audience too ignored the interjection. 'She further saith,' wrote the scribe, 'that Ann, the wife of Richard Forster off Stocksfield' – again, her finger pointed out a woman in the crowd, close by in the group surrounding Lucy Thompson –

did swing upon the rope, and, upon the first swing, she gott a cheese, and upon the second she got a beakment of wheat flower, and upon the third swing she gott about halfe a quarter of butter to knead the said flower withall, they haveing noe power to gett water.

'A beakment, now how much is that?' asked Sir Thomas, looking about at his fellow Justices.

'A measure containing about a quarter of a peck,' said the long-suffering Clerk of the Peace.

Dutifully the scribe, who had taken the opportunity to write in the margin 'Ann and Richard Forster', indicated the break in the flow of the evidence with the usual marker; 'She further saith,' he wrote, then sped up to catch the rush of words getting away from him:

... Ann Drydon, of Pruddow, widdow, did swing thrice; and, att the first swing, she gott a pound of curraines to putt in the flower for bread; and, att the second swing, she got a quarter of mutton to sett before their protector; and, at the third swing, she got a bottle of sacke.

She pointed out an older woman on the courtroom floor, glancing at the Justices as the packed audience boiled around an outraged Anne Drydon. Again, Sir Richard indicated that she should go on: 'She further saith,' the scribe took down as Anne's finger shot out, 'that Margret, the wife of Michaell Aynsley of Riding did swing, and she gott a flackett of ale –' she looked directly at Sir Thomas, ignoring the steely stare Margaret Aynsley locked on her '– containing, as she thought, about three quarts, a kening of wheat flowers for pyes, and a peice of beife.'

The challenge was not beneath Sir Thomas: 'A flackett?' he asked; barely pausing for the clerk's 'a wood-bottle, I believe' before asking again, 'A kening?'

'Half a bushel,' said the clerk, this time with the merest hint of condescension as Anne continued, her words spinning out in ink across the paper,

... that every person had their swings in the said rope, and did gett several dishes of provision upon their severall swings according as they did desire; which this informant cannot repeat or remember, there beinge soe many persons and such variety of meat; and those that come last att the said meeting did carry away the remainder of the meat.

'Ah, yes,' said Sir Richard, 'this business of the rope and the food is a fuller account of the same thing she told me, and gave in evidence to Jenison; but there's a detail here, now where was it?'

He paged through the documents on the desk, his finger moving down one of them until he found what he wanted, and then read out: '"and when they had eaten, she that was last drew the table and kept the reversions."'

'Has she not just repeated this? Something about the last served carrying away the remainders? Now, who would make up a minor point such as this?'

Sir Richard looked down the desk at the Justices. 'I find more truth in such a tiny scrap than all the descriptions of ropes pulled and food descending. Details, details and consistency, this is what we must listen for. This is what will establish the truth or otherwise in this tale of – what shall we call it – witches gathering together in, what does the deponent call it, read that back to me, Clerk.'

The Clerk of the Peace leaned over the scribe's shoulder, his eyes skimming the fresh ink. '"Which were five coveys,"' he read out, '"consisting of thirteen persons in every covey;" that is the word I believe you want, Your Worship, "covey."'

'Covey, now there is a word,' said Sir Richard. 'My groundsmen will use it for a pair of partridge or quail with a brood of young, but I have not heard it before for a group or company of persons. So, a covey, and of thirteen …'

Unobserved by his fellow Justices, Humphrey Mitford had grown increasingly agitated as Sir Richard went on. Suddenly and uncharacteristically he burst out in the middle of his legal senior's ruminations: 'Thirteen, as at the Last Supper. Indeed! This is the sort of nonsense you hear all over Europe. Pure products of the Catholic imagination!'

Mitford stopped, looked around at his fellow Justices, then down again, wondering if he had gone too far. To serve here today, each of the Justices had had to swear an oath to the king and the Protestant English Church and sign a declaration denying the Catholic doctrine of transubstantiation. But regardless of what faith they professed in public, it was a common assumption among the burghers of Newcastle – zealous Protestants now, if no longer of the Puritan type – that the gentry of Northumberland were, to a man, Catholics, along with their tenants and dependants.

Being removed from the bench would be the least of the civil disabilities imposed upon them if this were to be proved and, as Mitford was himself now so painfully and publically aware, the severe penalties pronounced against Catholics took on a particular sensitivity when it came to a case of the type they were deliberating today. The long title appearing at the head of the new statute, the print hardly dry on the recently circulated document, was 'An act for preventing dangers which may happen from popish recusants'. Pressing his point about the religious superstition associated with Catholicism – superstition that included a belief in witchcraft – was a dangerous business, as the uncomfortable silence and sidelong glances along the bench reminded him.

'Come, come, let's not be coy about this! Scratch a little deeper into these accusations and I guarantee we will find a seminary priest behind them!'

It was John Salkeld who could not contain himself this time, John Salkeld, Esquire, or Lieutenant-Colonel Salkeld, as he still preferred to be addressed. He had sat silent and glowering at the bench until now, and the other Justices had good reason to leave him to whatever passions were simmering inside his muscular frame and military bearing. Hot-headed and impetuous, he had proved himself ready to venture anything and everything for the cause of his royal master. By his account, all the more colourful if there was drink enough to hand, it was he who had taken Berwick singlehandedly in 1648, and if there was no doubt he'd played an active part in the loose warfare along the Borders which followed, he was known for throwing himself into the killing with an unrestrained enthusiasm that was not limited to the battlefield.

Well to the fore in the minds of his fellow Justices was the fact that a year into the war, the choleric colonel killed a Swinburne of Capheaton at the gates of his great house, running him through the body with his rapier for trying to leave some merriment too early. The jury had had no hesitation in returning a verdict of murder, but John Salkeld mysteriously escaped hanging; those who dared question him about this would get a mumbled and rambling story having something to do with his sword being exacted from him as a deodand – 'a rapier sword, of the value of five shillings sterling,' he'd say, still outraged – but the penalty he paid was never quite clear.

No one this morning was going to test the colonel's notoriety, however, especially as he was clearly spoiling for a fight. 'I know there are those among you,' he spluttered, 'more than ready to claim that the king's laudable attempt to extend religious liberty is evidence of both his sympathy for Catholicism – come on, out with it! – and his preference for absolutist rule. Well, I have served him with what I think I may call a constant –' he slapped the bench '– dangerous –' another slap '– and expensive –' another '– loyalty!' A resounding bang.

The thump of John Salkeld's hand on the bench shook Humphrey Mitford, made him realise how much his intervention was sending this examination in entirely the wrong direction.

'I hope you are not suggesting, Sir,' he felt confident enough to interject, 'that my family has been in any way remiss in serving the monarchy?'

'Well, I'll grant your father has done good service, and I'll do you the courtesy of extending those good offices to you,' said Salkeld, 'but as for others here ...'

'And I, as you well know,' said Sir Thomas Horsley, rising to his feet, 'had the honour to entertain General Monck at the Royal

Grammar School on his way south to effect the Restoration of Charles II.'

He did not add that the tower at the school on occasion served as a Roman Catholic chapel, nor that his name was to be included in the forthcoming list of Northumbrian recusants. Instead, he turned on someone whose position as regards such things was more vulnerable than his own.

'Yes, but what of Jenison here? The king's man now, I'm told, but only too happy as sheriff to welcome Cromwell to the town. And who, I wonder,' he went on, looking directly at Ralph Jenison, who sat rigid in his seat, 'organised the festivities for that occasion, that's what I'd like to know!'

'I meant only,' Mitford said, gently pressing Sir Thomas back into his seat and trying, with a hint of desperation, to come back to his point, 'that we should not be convinced by the more fantastical elements of the girl's accusations.'

He cast about, trying to think of something less contentious in her evidence that demonstrated how ridiculous her charges were. Food, the food she returned to so insistently: here was something more tangible and less controversial to illustrate his point, and Humphrey Mitford clutched at it gratefully.

'Capon in plum broth, beef, mutton, cheese, butter, wine and ale! The limits of what a country girl can imagine as fine food, but scarcely a feast set out by Satan. I pretend to no especially grand table myself,' he bumbled on, hoping that a touch of humour might deflect the more serious implications of his original point, 'yet this would embarrass it before any guests I should entertain.'

'Well, we should be grateful there are no cannibalistic feasts or licentious couplings,' said Mr Salkeld. He'd heard quite enough in Europe, where he'd been forced to flee after that ridiculous Swinburne affair. He'd heard first hand the tales of human flesh, preferably children's flesh, being eaten during Sabbats; of human bones being stewed in a special way to make delicious dishes; of salt, bread and oil being prohibited because the devil hated them;

heard quite enough of that popish nonsense in degenerate popish countries.

'Why, the girl talks only of country dancing,' he said, 'and gorging on the best food a servant girl can think up; let's not get waylaid by lawyer's nit-picking or trying to second-guess the devil's taste in food. And I see no need to dismiss an accusation of witchcraft because it is a little too close to what His Majesty wrote about in his *Daemonologie!*'

The umbrage Sir Richard took at the reprimand was clear on his face, but before he could respond, a low, lazy drawl drifted into the exchange.

'Let us also not forget, Sirs, that whatever satisfaction the return of King Charles II might have afforded to the younger females in his dominions, it has brought nothing save torture to the unfortunate old women.'

James Howard arched himself upright out of the chair into which he had reclined so comfortably that he'd almost vanished from the proceedings. However delayed his interjection, it did not disappoint the bench, his reputation as a wit generally off-setting the increasing tendency to add the appellation 'unfortunate' to the heirs of Redesdale Hall. All present knew that, having inherited only three years ago, he was already forced to break up the estate in an ongoing attempt to repair the family's finances. It was equally well known that he was failing, and it would not be long before the Howards were reduced to owning a single farm.

Genial to a fault in the face of such adversity, James Howard leaned forward in his chair as he went on. 'But then again, no matter how old and – with the exception, no doubt,' he said, nodding at those crowding up towards the bench for justice, 'of the accused here today – ugly, England is still England. Where have you heard, recently, of the *conviction* of a reputed witch?'

James Howard turned back to his fellow Justices with a wan smile. 'No matter how much the inhabitants of the wilder parts of the north are known for clinging to their beliefs in possession and evil influences, we, Sirs, are accountable to another world. While those who prosecuted witches in King James's first years on the throne had to prepare themselves to meet opposition, these days they must fortify themselves to meet ridicule – a far more insidious opponent, harder to defeat, and impossible to shake off once infected with its taint.

'Now I am sure you are all more generously placed, but it is common knowledge that I have little enough to preserve my rank and dignity ...'

Murmurs of commiseration and polite contradiction ran up and down the line of Justices, but James Howard lifted a limp hand. '... and I would prefer not to squander either on the tales of this girl.

'Perhaps, however,' he ended, a smile playing around a handsome face just beginning to show the effects of the ruin of his family, 'it is simply the case that men in this age are grown so wicked that they are apt to believe there are no greater devils than themselves.'

Chapter 12

Apr. 9, 1673. At the Sessions at Morpeth, as aforesaid.

It was the deponent now who could no longer keep patience. Anne Armstrong had stood silent, seemingly forgotten through the self-serving deliberations of the Justices. Now she burst out with a flurry of names. 'Michael Aynsley of the Riding,' she said, 'Mary Hunter of Birkenside, Dorothy Green of Edmundbyers ...'

The Justices turned to her, surprised, and quite unbidden the scribe began dashing down her words as Anne Armstrong's right hand became a blur, its index finger stabbing at face after face floating pale in the depths of the crowd.

And she further saith that she particularly knew at the said meeting one Michael Aynsly of the Rideing, Mary Hunter of Birkenside, widdow, Dorothy Green of Edmondsbyers in the county of Durham, widdow, Anne Usher of Fairlymay, widdow, Eliz. Pickering of Whittingeslaw, widdow, Jane wife of Wm. Makepeace of New Ridley, yeo., Anthony Hunter of Birken side, yeo., John Whitfield of Edmondbyers, Anne Whitfield of the same, spinster, Chr. Dixon of Muglesworth Park and Alice his wife ...

A new litany, a recitation of names old and new with accused after accused outraged, terrified, as their names joined the ever-lengthening enumeration

... Catherine Eliot of Ebchester, Elsabeth Atchinson of Ebchester widdow, and Issabell Andrew of Crooked-oake, widow ...

until even Anne Armstrong's knowledge, or imagination, began to fail.

With many others, both in Morpeth and other places, whose faces this informer knowes but cannot tell their names.

The flow of names may have begun to dry up, but Anne was determined not to lose the gaping, gawping faces turned to her. The power that their awe gave her coursed through her body, lifted her up, held her above the crowd, and she went on.

All which persons met upon Collup Monday last at Allensford, where this informant was ridden upon by an inchanted bridle by Michael Aynsly and Margaret his wife.

Whatever the scribe was writing, she could feel the leather being pulled off her forehead, catching at her hair, burning her ears. As it came free of her head she stood up, 'in her owne proper person', as the scribe scribbled down, then corrected and rewrote at more leisure, raising her eyes to see

the said persons before mentioned dancing, some in the likenesse of hares, some in the likenesse of catts, others in the likenesse of bees, and some in their owne likenesse.

I should have known they would choose the end of the Shrovetide to come for me. I had heard they always gathered on a Good Friday to feast upon a fast day, reversing the shriving Christians did to receive absolution in time for Lent, mocking the penance they asked for good deeds and their confession of their sins in expectation of reward.

But for once I hadn't been hungry when Anne Dryden appeared, peering from behind the barn, bridle in hand, whistling low and winking, chucking and clucking until I went over to her. A week before I had been ordered to kill the pig carefully fattened up for this day, and Dame Fouler, being the good housewife she was whatever else she may be, had spent the time since salting the flitches and hams to hang until Lent was over, cutting off and setting aside the fattest parts of the animal for collops.

Those that had more fat than meat she'd baked in a pot, pouring the melted fat into a bladder as it ran off. This hog's-lard she'd keep aside for future use, but the remains in the pot were given to me and the other workers for breakfast on this last day we were allowed to eat flesh before Lent.

For dinner, Dame Fouler made a pig-fry, broiling the fattest parts of the entrails of the animal in the oven with numerous herbs and spices added to it. This she would eat with potatoes, setting a small amount aside for her one house servant. I would also be treated with 'a drop of something good' and my antici-pation was made the more pleasurable by my mistress allowing me to spend the afternoon in conviviality. I was enjoying the company of the farm's men when Anne Dryden appeared at the side of the barn, whispering my name in the early darkening of the day.

The thought of the food I would miss made me even more reluctant to give in to her enticements, but my mistake was in going over to her. The moment I was out of the sight of the men, the bridle was slipped over my head and pulled tight, and I no longer had a choice. Quickly, silently, I was led away through the undergrowth behind the barn, tugged down to the road where to my surprise – surprise and mute acceptance, for what else can a dumb beast do? – it was Michael Aynsly who mounted me, Michael Aynsly and then his wife Margaret who leapt astride me behind him, her scrawny legs tucked into my flanks, his heels digging into me as I was ridden hard towards the Riding.

When we came to the pack bridge that would carry us over into the clearing, we did not cross: instead, my head was yanked to the left a few yards before the burn. Then I was driven south in the dark, up and out of the steep side of the Tyne's valley, then over one rise and down the next, feeling as if I were flying now, up and down again, until down, down we went, down to the deep cut of the Derwent.

There was a bridge over the river, which I was relieved we did not attempt to cross. Instead, Michael Aynsly pulled my head sharply with the enchanted bridle, driving me into the grounds of an ancient inn that looked more like a bastle than a public house. It hung above the Derwent, its outbuildings leaning over the steep bank with the river washing swiftly over the ford below. Even in my present state I shivered at the thought that this may be the place where my Mr Boyer continued with his illicit preaching, shivered as Michael and Margaret Aynsly dismounted. And then Anne Dryden appeared beside me, clapping and laughing as I took back my human shape.

Bog Wood closed in around us, out of which Mary Hunter and Dorothy Green appeared. I stared at them as bravely as I dared, and then others began slithering out of the blackness a few at a time, but soon enough making up a crowd of them. I looked about wildly, recognising every face, though there were more, more and more again, than I could ever name.

Mary Hunter and Dorothy Green began to prod me, first in the ribs and then in more sensitive places, hissing all the time, 'Sing, Anne, sing.' I could hardly get my breath, panting white clouds of air into the night. 'Sing, Anne, sing,' they went on, the others joining in now, a host cackling out that I should raise my reedy voice, my shrill whine, my squeaky throat. 'The Chase Song,' said one, the others joining in, setting up a chant, 'The Chase Song. The Chase Song!'

'I shall go into a bee,' I began, and straight away they began to swirl, in and out of each other, snaking away into groups, thirteen in every group, weaving around with each other. At first they would mimic the gait and cry of creatures as they danced, but as they spun their shapes began to dissolve away, and then reform out of the mist into hares, and cats, and bees, and other shapes I could hardly tell. 'I shall go into a bee,' I sang,

With mickle horror and dread of thee,
And flit to hive in the Devil's name
Ere that I be fetchèd hame.

I saw to my horror that every thirteen of them had a devil before which they danced, each devil in a different shape, but always black in colour, a black that was part of the night and the trees and the river and yet also that shone in the dark. Despite my terror I could not help but sing, afraid of more pokes, blows even, now that they were ducking and stretching, thirteen at a time each before their devil.

'Bee, take heed of a swallow hen,' I sang, my throat so tight I thought I would strangle,

... a swallow hen
Will harry thee close, both butt and ben,
For here I come in Our Protector's name
All but for to fetch thee hame.

'Cunning and art she did not lack,' they joined in, clapping as they swayed and shivered into one shape and then another, 'But aye his whistle would fetch her back.'

And as they sang this, the devils joined in, each with his group, entwining himself with their circle, twisting after one or another of the dancers.

Yet I shall go into a mouse
And haste me unto the miller's house,
There in his corn to have good game
Ere that I be fetchèd hame.

And then I began to see as I sang that whatever shape they took on, their devil would adapt his changes to theirs, pursuing them in the form of the animal that naturally hunted them.

Mouse, take heed of a white tib-cat
That never was balked of mouse or rat,
For I'll crack thy bones in Our Protector's name;
Thus shalt thou be fetchèd hame.

And that is when they took on their own likeness, whenever they joined in on 'fetchèd hame'. Returned to their human shape, home again, each time I was made to sing, to sing again and again this same song.

I had heard this song before, sung as a ballad between lovers, a tale of teasing with the girl fleeing in different shapes and the boy pursuing in matching forms. I had heard it, too, sung about a blacksmith threatening to deflower a lady, but now, as the witches sang their horrible chorus, they looked back to their pursuers, clearly wanting to be caught, caught and overwhelmed. For this song was nothing less than a magic spell for turning themselves into the shapes in which they did their wicked deeds.

And back: for when they were themselves again, I was silenced with a shake of the terrible claw of the devil in the group nearest me. Then the devil in each group called the dancers to an account one by one, and when each of them had confessed the evil they had done, their devil pointed at me again to make me sing. As I did, he danced first with the one who had done the most evil, making much of her in front of the others before they all danced together again,

For here I come in Our Protector's name
All but for to fetch thee hame.

London

A well-modulated voice announced that the Archives would be closing in half an hour, and that all documents should be returned to the distribution desk.

I wasn't pleased to break off at this point, but I was tired. The air felt strange as I walked back to the underground station, as if I'd re-entered another world. I enjoyed these fancies that archival work provoked, indulged them, treating them as a measure of how good the day's work had been. Apart from checking that I got on the right train, I didn't take in much of the ride back to King's Cross, the short walk to the hotel, signing in, finding my room.

It was only once I'd inserted my key card into the slot activating the light switch that I disentangled my thoughts from Anne's story. Story? A beginning and middle and end, then, but why was the beginning not at the beginning, filed away in the simple order the dates would suggest?

The more immediate problem was what to do with the night ahead. I connected my laptop to the hotel's free Wi-Fi and googled *Time Out*, where my eye was caught by an entry in the music section: at a small club, close by and starting late enough to allow for both a cleanup and a light meal somewhere, was a performance by, as the blurb would have it, 'the ultimate contemporary real folk combination.'

'In a world awash with twee fops playing queasily winsome acoustic music alleged to be folk,' continued the gig-guide listing, 'it's good to know there are still artists out there with full working knowledge of folk tales and traditions and songs of loves lost, lust, death, and witches who have not been wicca-ed into submission.'

Alastair Hyde and the Commonwealth sounded like a suitable evening's soundtrack to my day's labour, and 9 p.m. found me resting my beer on the apron of an impossibly small stage in the back room of a pub off Grays Inn Road. It took a while for the standing-only floor space to begin filling up, but people were pressing in behind me by the time Alastair Hyde and the Commonwealth took to the stage. The group consisted of Alastair himself, I assumed, seated centre with a guitar, a woman casually referred to as Kate some way through the performance standing to his right at a vocal mic, and an unnamed man, squat, balding, lurking in the background and clutching a fiddle.

Despite the billing suggested by the group's name, the show opened with Kate singing unaccompanied. I recognised a version of 'Queen Sally', sung in a voice like rich earth and setting a tone of deep seriousness only strengthened by the addition of guitar, fiddle, and haunting harmonies contributed by the two men some verses in.

The set remained tortuously sparse, more so whenever Alastair Hyde took the lead. Tall, thin, all angles and sweat, he seemed to be from another time. Kate honed in on searing harmonies, the two singers linked by the curl of their mouths as they both sang determinedly out of only the right side. But whereas Kate was big, solid, legs planted on the floor in high cherry Docs, reddened eyelids tightly closed, Alastair was remarkably light and jerky, his knees spread and swaying in front of him as he dug into his chair, his voice thin and keening, his guitar driving, taking off regularly into extended instrumental flights followed by the bare-bones scraping of the fiddle stabbing out from the rear of the stage.

I registered among a number of songs I did not know maniacally focused versions of 'The Cruel Mother', 'Lord Ronald' and 'A Lyke Wake Dirge'. Occasionally Alastair spoke about some of the songs in a distracted way, his eyes roving the far corners of the ceiling as he did so.

'This is sometimes called "The Beltane Chase Song,"' he started saying at one point. 'It's a modern thing, not traditional at all. But based loosely on Robert Graves's imaginative reconstruction of a snatch of a song quoted at Isobel Gowdie's trial for witchcraft in 1662.'

I leaned in, listening as closely as I could. Pushed up against the stage, I could see the stitching in Alastair's worn boots, and the scribbled, indecipherable set list which lay on the floor directly in front of me.

'The single authentic verse Graves quotes goes like this,' Alastair said, lifting his voice into a high-pitched chant rather than a tune as such:

I shall go into a hare
With sorrow and sighing and mickle care
And I shall go in the Devil's name
Aye, till I come home again.

'More likely that he took it from the "The Twa Magicians,"' a voice wheezed from the back of the tiny stage. 'The version Buchan collected in his *Ballads of the North*. For "imaginative reconstruction" read sloppy scholarship, the usual wild invention. Good enough for folk music, I suppose.'

Kate gave a rare smile, half turned towards the fiddle player. 'Well, we've taken our version from the singing – recording really – of the great song collector A. L. Lloyd,' she said. 'He sang it on an album with one of my favourite titles, *The Bird in the Bush: Traditional Songs of Love and Lust*, accompanied by Dave Swarbrick on fiddle. The ballad had dwindled away, he said, but in his view it was too good a song to remain unused, so he brushed it up and fitted a tune.'

'As Vaughan Williams said,' Alastair added, stern, straight faced, '"The practice of re-writing a folk song is abominable, and I wouldn't trust anyone to do it except myself."'

He hit a powerful, open-tuned chord, and launched himself into the song:

The lady stood at her own front door
As straight as a willow wand,
And along there come a husky smith
With a hammer in his hand.

The two other members of the Commonwealth joined in on the chorus, the fiddler sawing away as he sang:

And he said, 'Bide lady, bide,
There's nowhere you can hide.
The husky smith will be your love
And that'll pull down your pride.'

Kate then picked up the reply of the traditional call and response:

'Away, away, you coal blacksmith,
Would you do me this wrong?
To think to have my maidenhead
That I have kept so long.'

Soon enough, the chase had begun,

Then she became a turtle dove
And flew up in the air,
And he became an old cock pigeon
And they flew pair and pair,

'Bide lady, bide' interspersing their transformations into duck and drake, hare and dog, ewe and ram, fly and spider, young mare and golden saddle, I was especially intrigued to hear a fated spiral of hunted and hunter in which 'every change that poor girl made, The blacksmith was her mate.' Finally:

... the lady ran in her own bedroom
And changed into a bed,

And he became a green coverlet
And gained her maidenhead.

There was something about the harmony of the three singers, guitar and fiddle silent now, that gave the final chorus, in a strange counterpoint to the bawdy tone of the song and its bouncy, sing-along tune, a deep, strange pathos:

And was she woe, he held her so,
And still he bad her bide,
And the husky smith became her love
And that pulled down her pride.

There was complete silence in the small, packed room as the last line hung in the air. The applause that followed some beats later was muted, as if the audience had been moved in some way they didn't exactly understand.

Other songs followed, the instrumental 'The Wind That Shakes the Barley', the wonderful 'Castle by the Sea', with its oddly upbeat melody to an exceptionally black story, and more, but I was trying to hold on to the experience of the Beltane Chase or whatever it was called. 1662 was close enough, for folk music and the events Anne Armstrong reported being caught up in. Had the witches not made her sing while they danced in their changing shapes? I made a mental note to look up what Robert Graves had made of the song, despite the fiddle player's dismissive comments.

Every guitar stroke Alastair played sounded as if it was to be the last ever, even when it was the opening of a song, but finally one chord rang out, seemingly endlessly. When it died away the three musicians unfroze, and then melted into whatever passed for the wings of this cramped venue.

I eased myself slowly out into the London night with the rest of the audience, feeling as if I'd hardly left my solitary preoccupations in The National Archives. It was clear that Anne had followed me out into the night, and would be staying with me as I made my way back to the welcome blankness of my hotel room.

I could not sleep. Another day's work in the Archives behind me, and here I was at 3 a.m., wide awake on my last night in London. Only one day ahead of me in the Archives before I was due to return to Riding Mill.

I reached up to the switches on the headboard of the bed. Hopefully the clean, even light that brought my room into such clear focus would help clear my thoughts. The reading light was not enough, and I put on the main lights, the desk lights too. Then I got up and switched on the bathroom lights, ignoring the whirring of the extractor fan that came on with the illumination.

I stood and looked around the room. A sterile space, some would say, although I preferred to think of it as neutral, level ground on which to wrestle with the figures that wouldn't leave me alone simply because I had put down the pages they inhabited. For all the artificial brightness, the dimensions of the room refused to settle, the clarity of the lights throwing their own shadows in odd corners and angles.

Perhaps I'd stood up too quickly. The lights appeared to dim, flare up again, and in the instant in between it seemed to me that a faint outline passed between where I was standing at the door to the bathroom and the bed. It was gone in a moment and was nothing threatening, the kind of shadow I would have cast when coming out of the bathroom after brushing my teeth maybe, the ordinary effects of the most mundane activities on the light we pass through.

I rubbed my eyes, cleared them, saw nothing more and stood listening to the hum of the extractor fan: mere white noise, I thought, steady, monotonous, tuneless, but it was odd the tricks that hearing played. As I concentrated on the sound of the fan it occurred to me how easily, if I did not know what it was, I could have imagined it to be distant radio, someone listening to music in the dead of night in another room.

I walked back to the bed, got in under the covers. The hotel sheets were crisp, hard from the strangers being constantly washed out of them. I was aware then, suddenly aware, of the parade of people who'd passed through this room, and those to come, going about their solitary affairs, a distorted cavalcade, a series of spectres superimposed on each other in a composite haze, myself among them, one more temporary occupant making this space my own for the period paid for. And yes, I was certain now that that was me coming out of the brightly lit bathroom, ablutions done, humming the tune I could not help but hear now in the low noise of the extractor fan.

Turning off all the lights except the reading light, I reached for the book I'd been paging through before I fell asleep, a second-hand copy of Graves's *The White Goddess* which I'd managed to find in an antiquarian bookshop in the thoroughfare linking Charing Cross Road and St Martin's Lane after getting back from the Archives.

I continued skimming quickly, with little interest in Graves's claims of the links between ancient runic alphabets, mysterious drudic and bardic poetry, and the Celtic lunar year. I was still paging on rapidly when a footnote buried in his discussion of the *Romance of Pwyll, Prince of Dyfed* stopped me.

In the poem, Rhiannon is falsely accused of having devoured her son, and is forced as a penance to stand at a horse block outside Pwyll's palace, 'like a mare, ready to carry guests on her back'. To this Graves had appended the note:

This magical tradition survived in the Northern witch-cult. In 1673 Anne Armstrong the Northumbrian witch confessed at her trial to having been temporarily transformed into a mare by her mistress Ann Forster of Stocksfield, who threw a bridle over her head and rode her to a meeting of five witch-covens at Riding Bridge End.

I stopped, re-read: Graves was familiar then with the actual case, even if he had many of its details wrong (it wasn't Anne's trial, nor was Ann Forster her mistress); I began to read more carefully, alert for any other references to Anne while looking for Graves's account of the song I'd heard earlier that night.

Fifteen pages later the two came together in a way that grabbed my full attention: 'In European folk-lore there are scores of variants on the "Two Magicians" theme,' I read, 'in which the male magician, after a hot chase, out-magics the female and gains her maidenhead.'

Graves concentrated on a version called 'The Coal Black Smith' in which 'she becomes a fish, he an otter; she a hare, he a greyhound; she becomes a fly, he a spider and pulls her to his lair; finally she becomes a quilt on his bed, he a coverlet and the game is won,' but it was the context in which it was sung that had me wide awake, reaching for my notebook.

This English ballad, Graves claimed,

is likely to have been the song sung at a dramatic performance of the chase at a witches' Sabbath; ... Anne Armstrong, the Northumbrian witch already mentioned, testified in 1673 that, at a well-attended Sabbath held at Allensford, one of her companions, Ann Baites of Morpeth, successively transformed herself into cat, hare, greyhound and bee, to let the Devil – 'a long black man, their protector, whom they call their God' – admire her facility in changes.

Was this what Anne was singing, those tortured notes wrung out of her as the witches made her sing to them while they danced?

'At first I thought,' Graves wrote,

that the Devil chased Ann Baites, who was apparently the Maiden, or female leader of the coven, around the ring of witches, and that she mimicked the gait and cry of these various creatures in turn while he pursued her, adapting his changes to hers – for it is clear from her subsequent account that there was no change of outward shape, but only of behaviour, and the verse suggests a dramatic dance. But I see now that Ann Baites gave a solo performance, alternately mimicking the pursued and the pursuer, and that the Devil was content merely to applaud her.

On her own, acting out hare and greyhound, trout and otter, bee and swallow, mouse and cat, or one of a crowd of figures in a swirl of shapes dissolving and reforming into a tangled mist of ever-shifting change – this is what, in the early hours in a hotel room where the industrial hum of the concrete capital was awakening just beyond my island of anonymity, I felt coming off the pages awaiting me in the perfectly preserved silence of the empty Archives, shimmering in their acid-free boxes, waiting for me, the words twisting and curling on the linen pages, the black ink beginning to whirl away, ribbons leading back to mouths once open, unleashing them upon a world not, no never, wholly gone.

'The whole song is easy to restore in its original version,' concluded Graves:

The formula in 'The Coal Black Smith' is 'he became a greyhound dog', or 'he became an otter brown', 'and fetched her home again'. 'Home again' is used here in the technical sense of 'to her own shape', as Isobel Gowdie of Auldearne tells us at her trial, when she sang the witch formula for turning oneself into a hare:

I shall go into a hare
With sorrow and sighing and mickle care,
And I shall go in the Devil's name Aye,
Till I come home again.

Chapter 13

Apr. 9, 1673. At the Sessions at Morpeth, as aforesaid.

Anne's eyes glazed into a blind stare, the bench and the court riveted by her performance. The words trailed away now into a tuneless humming, a cracked and broken echo of the song she reported singing.

As the ghost of the song faded away, Sir Richard sat blinking and looking about the courtroom before he was able to ask, 'Well then, what evil had they done, these dancing witches?'

Lucy Thompson of Mickly confessed to the divell that she had wronged Edward Lumly of Mickly goods by witcheing them; and in particular one horse by pincing to death, and one ox which suddainly dyed in the draught, and the devill incouraged her for it.

'Lucy Thompson,' written hastily into the left margin.

Ann Drydon of Pruddoe confessed to the devill that, on the Thursday night after Fasten's even last, when they were drinking wine in Franck Pye's seller in Morpeth, that shee witched suddenly to death her neighbor's horse in Pruddoe.

'More about Morpeth,' James Howard began, giving just time enough for 'Ann Drydon' to go in the margin, but Anne was not to be drawn into expanding on what she had to say. The urgency of her voice carried over the interjection, the scene before the mind's eye of her audience remaining Allensford, by the bridge in the pitch black, shapes swirling around, a faint tune hanging in the air, a scared girl hearing evil pour forth from mouth after mouth.

Anne wife of Richard Forster of Stocksfield confessed that she bewitched Robert Newton's horses of Stocksfield, and that there was one of them that had but one shew on, which she took and presented with the foot and all to the divell at next meeting. And she further confessed to her protector that she had power of a childe of the said Robert Newton's called Issabell, ever since she was four yeare olde, and she is now about eight yeares old, and she is now pined to nothing, and continues soe.

Moreover Michael Ainsly and Anne Drydon confessed to the divell that they had power of Mr Thomas Errington's horse, of Rideing mill, and they ridd behinde his man upon the said horse from Newcastle like two bees, and the horse immediately after he came home, dyed; and this was but about a moneth since.

The said Anne Forster, Michaell Ainsly, and Lucy Thompson confessed to the divell, and the said Michaell told the divell that he called severall times at Mr Errington's kitchen dore, and made a noise like an host of men. And that night, the divell asking them how they sped, they answered nothing, for they had not got power of the miller, but they got the shirt of his bak, as he was lyeing betwixt women, and laid it under his head and stroke him dead another time, in revenge he was an instrument to save Raiph Elrington's draught from goeing downe the water and drowneing, as they intended to have done. And that they confessed to the divell that they made all the gear goe of the mill, and that they intended to have made the stones all grinde till they had flowne all in peeces.

'Mary Hunter confessed –'
'Ah, now listen to this, listen to this,' said Sir Richard, looking up and down at the other members of the bench, 'here is something I can tell you more about.'

– to the divill that she had wronged George Taylor of Edgebrigg's goods, and told her protector that she had gotten the power of a fole of his soe that it pined away to death.

About Michaelmas last she did come to one John March, of Edgebrigg, when he and his wife was rideing from Bywell, and flew sometimes under his mare's belly and sometimes before its breast, in the likenesse of a swallow, untill she got the power of it, and it dyed within a week after. And she and Dorothy Green confessed to the divill that they got power of the said John Marche's oxe's far hinder legg. And this is all within the space of a year halfe or thereabouts.

'Right,' said Sir Richard, 'this picks up on what she reported to me last Wednesday. *Maleficium* enough for you here, I presume, Sirs? It was there, in Edmundbyers, that she identified Dorothy Green, and that we received some confirmation from these men as regards the accusations made against Mary Hunter.'

Sir Richard turned to the assembly.

'At this point witnesses wishing to prosecute a case may testify. But not –' he added hastily, as he saw the beginnings of a scurry among those on the courtroom floor '– those in support of defendants. Now, where are Taylor and March, Bailiff? Bound over and here, I am sure, so bring them forward, bring them forward.'

Some shuffling behind the screen produced the two men, who were marched forward between the bailiff's men. Anne watched them each step their way towards the front of the bench and listened intently as they were sworn in by the Clerk of the Peace.

Neither man returned her look.

'George Taylor,' said the clerk, 'we have here your sworn statement. Repeat on oath the information you gave before Sir Richard Stote and Sir James Clavering.'

Geo. Tayler, of Edgebridge, yeoman.

Nervous as he was, George Taylor managed to give an accurate account, restating each significant detail. He used much the same wording, eliciting nods of approval from the clerk each time he did so. He told how his foal had not been well since Michaelmas, swelling up in various parts of its body, its head and lips too, and died a month before he met with Anne Armstrong. He could find no sign of a disease, and whenever he had tried to bleed the animal to heal it, he was unable to get blood from it. After its death too, he said, he opened the animal, but could find little blood. And then Anne Armstrong told him that she heard Mary Hunter and Dorothy Green confess to the devil that they had power over his animals, and since then the dam of the foal that had died pined away too, and no matter what he did, his animals never did as well as his neighbours,' and looked like *anatomyes*, he said. The clerk asked him if by that he meant skeletons, looking satisfied when he answered yes, he did.

'Precisely,' said Sir Richard to the bench, 'exactly as he told us in Edmundbyers, so proof enough. Now, John March, tell the court what you reported to us on the same day.'

At Morpeth Sessions, as aforesaid.
John March, of Edgebrigg, yeoman.

John March, yeoman, did an equally credible job. Thin, wiry, comparatively better dressed, his manner of speech was more fluent, words coming to him more easily.

He told how he too had gone to Birches Nooke, where Anne Armstrong, upon hearing his name, asked if he had an ox with the power of one of his limbs taken from him. Saying he had, he asked how she knew, and she told him that she heard Mary Hunter and another confess to the devil that they had taken the power of his beast. And Anne Armstrong said Mary Hunter and Dorothy Green had also confessed to the devil that they had bewitched his grey mare.

He then repeated his account of his ride home from Bywell with his wife two weeks before last Michaelmas, when a swallow flew over forty times under the grey mare's belly and across her breast, no matter how many times he struck at it with his rod. Two days later the mare went mad, then blind, and then died.

The clerk gave a contented nod and Sir Richard was about to repeat his approval when John March raised his hand in an awkward fashion.

'What is it, man? Have you more information?' asked Sir Richard, and John March nodded vigorously.

The clerk signalled to the scribe, and indicated that he could continue.

Mary Hunter, John March said, swallowing hard, came down to his house on Monday last –

'Last Monday?' asked Sir Richard; 'after you gave your evidence at Edmundbyers?'

Yes, answered John March; on Monday last, to his house where – he looked about, clearly concerned about what he had to say next – he had Anne Armstrong –

'Anne Armstrong?' said Sir Richard, incredulous. 'This girl here, standing before us?'

Shifty-eyed, John March said yes, the woman standing before the court.

'Well, you never mentioned before that you knew the girl. Is that anywhere in the deposition, Clerk?'

The Clerk of the Peace began to scan the document he had followed while John March repeated the information given in Edmundbyers on Friday, Friday last.

No, he hadn't, said John March. And that was because he did not know of her, until that is, last Sunday, after Your Worships had been in Edmundbyers. Anne Armstrong came back to his house that afternoon, exhausted with walking and asking if she could go to a room to sleep.

And it was the next day that Mary Hunter came down to his house, asking for Anne Armstrong. When she came out, Mary Hunter asked her what she had to say to her.

Anne Armstrong told Mary Hunter that she was a witch, and that she had seen her at the devil's meetings. Mary Hunter asked her where, and she answered, 'In this same house, last night, being Sunday, among all the company of witches.'

'What, man, were you doing when the whole company of witches was loose in your house?' It was Sir Thomas Horsely who had decided it was time to come in on examining the evidence.

John March looked at Anne Armstrong. His hair was receding, and he wiped the bald area with a handkerchief before continuing. That self-same night, he said, he was, for reasons he could not say, so afraid that he was in a manner, you might say dead. And afterward, coming to himself again he heard a great thundering, and saw a great lightning in the house, and to the number of twenty creatures in the resemblances of cats and other shapes, lying on the floor and creeping upon the walls.

And immediately after, he said, with the terror of that night still clearly upon him, he heard the girl –

'This girl?'

– yes, this girl, singing to them.

'But where was she, this girl?' Humphrey Mitford this time, concerned at how convincing this was beginning to sound.

In bed, where he had put her, with his servants. But his servants were awoken, by the sounds, he thought, and they came down out of the room where the girl lay, and said, 'Alas! the witches were gone with the girl.'

And he went up and found her body lying in the bed, as if she were dead, neither breath nor life being discernible in her. And she continued so for the most part of an hour, till he fetched in two or three neighbours to see her in that condition.

When presently after they came in she began to stir and open her eyes, and looked on them all for about an hour before she spoke anything.

'Yes, man, yes, and what did she say?'

When she spoke, she said that all the companies of witches were there, and were endeavouring to get her away, but were prevented by something.

'Something? By what?' With this interjection John Howard clearly felt he had shown too much interest, for he sat back for some time after this, saying nothing. His eyes, however, kept drifting over to the Armstrong woman.

She did not say, said John March; instead Anne Armstrong suddenly enquired of Mary Hunter if her son Anthony was there.

'There being one of her sons called Cuthbert in the house, we told her that he was the man she asked for. This she denied, Your Worships, and said that it was not the man, for she knew him well, and had seen him several times at their meetings.

'And she desired Mary Hunter to send him down from her house in Birkenside, and said also she should send a lass that she, she, Mary Hunter, had several times ridden upon and made sing to them, and this lass would resolve the matter of whether it was they, Mary Hunter and Anthony Hunter, who she had seen at the witches' meetings.'

'But she herself – Anne Armstrong – was the lass, was she not?' asked Sir Richard.

John March shrugged, going on: whereupon Anthony afterwards came down, he said, and asked Anne Armstrong what she had to say to his face, he being before her now.

She said she would let him know at the Sessions, hearing he was to be there; and because he had threatened her, she would say no more.

'But she told me after he was gone that Anthony Hunter had confessed before the devil that he had taken the power of Thomas Richardson's wife's limbs from her, and had likewise bewitched several cattle to death.'

'And do you know if Thomas Richardson's wife shows signs of such bewitchment?' asked the clerk.

Anne Richardson is in a bad condition, said John March, being sometimes able to go about, and other times unable to go without help.

With this, John March stopped and stared into the middle distance as if waiting to see what would happen to him.

'Now, let us be clear,' said Sir Richard. 'Did you know Anne Armstrong before going to Birches Nooke?'

He had never seen the said Anne in his life before, responded John March, still staring into the distance, and neither, to his knowledge, was she ever where he was, nor never saw none of his beasts, but first told him of such things when he went to see her in Birches Nooke.

Sir Richard glanced up and down the bench, each of the Justices meeting his eye.

'And further this witness saith, etc.,' he said to the clerk, who called John March to make his mark on the deposition. John March stepped forward to the scribe's desk and signed his name in full in a careful, neat script.

The clerk countersigned beneath *Capt. & Jurat in plena curia* with his large and elaborate signature, long strokes and curlicues aplenty.

'It is good to see someone who we must call a yeoman – for he is clearly no simple labourer – who is in fact a yeoman,' said the clerk to no one in particular.

'A yeoman, certainly, it would appear,' said Sir Richard. 'Tell me, John March, do you hold that land we saw in Derwent Vale freehold?'

'I do, Your Worship, as does George Taylor his.'

'And how much free land do you possess? What is it, a hundred acres or more?'

'A little more, Your Worship, of forty shillings annual value.'

'So tell us, have you voted for the knights of the shire?'

'Yes, Your Worship, for Henry Cavendish, Viscount Mansfield and Earl of Ogle, as knight of the shire of Northumberland, although I believe his office is to end soon.'

Sir Richard turned to the bench: 'A good man,' he said while the clerk dismissed John March as he had George Taylor, 'of good quality, and knowledgeable. A trustworthy witness then, I would say, and Taylor too.

'So, Sirs, what do you say of Anne Armstrong's accusations? A "true bill", is it, *billa vera*? One that must be passed on to the Summer Assize in Newcastle-upon-Tyne?'

The Justices did not confer in the seconds that ticked by after the question: each seemed wrapped up in himself, reflecting no doubt how their names would look appended to such a document.

It was Sir Thomas who, eventually, carefully, spoke. 'Given what we have heard,' he said, 'could we not deal with the matter ourselves in these Sessions?'

The Clerk of the Peace stiffened, this being the only indication that he could barely believe his ears. 'The statutes demand that the accused are to be indicted only under a commission granted to –' here the clerk could barely restrain a long sigh '– the Assize judges.'

'As I have attempted to make clear before,' said Sir Richard, 'the statutes do in fact leave Justices of the Peace in full theoretical possession of the trial powers we once held. To wit, Lambard, *Eirenarcha: or of the Office of the Justices of the Peace*: "Nevertheless their power is no whit restrained, to proceed before the coming of those Justices" – of the Assize, he means.'

'With respect,' ventured the clerk, his voice steady, 'William Lambard writes in 1599, Your Worship, before the transfer of the Justices' criminal powers to Assize. Justices of the Peace may conduct *preliminary* examinations in felony cases, as we –' he paused, then slid over the word '– are doing now, with the information of the witnesses being taken down and those accused bound over or held in gaol –'

'Ah, but Lambard is still honoured in the practices followed today; it is not entirely uncommon for Justices to instead send the documentation to be certified *after* having tried the case at Quarter Sessions.'

'It is also not uncommon ...' The entire bench and all the clerks turned to look at Ralph Jenison, who up to now had said not a word in the day's proceedings. '... for judges at gaol delivery to delegate cases to Quarter Sessions to avoid their having more felony cases than they can deal with at the Assizes.'

'Yes, yes indeed,' jumped in Sir Richard; 'the judges can and do. These days, there is many a judge who would not thank us for taking up his time with the business of witchcraft, especially a case so extravagant in its claims.'

The clerk chose not to respond on this point. Instead he said, 'We have not, in any event, completed the preliminary proceedings for this case, Your Worship.'

'Is that so,' said Sir Richard. He then called to the bailiff: 'Are there any other witness in support of these accusations?'

Chapter 14

At Morpeth Sessions, as aforesaid.
  Robert Johnson, of Ryde-ing Mill.

A large man forced his way through the press of people on the fore. 'I have evidence,' he said. On reaching the bailiff, he engaged in a low, brief exchange.

'Robert Johnson,' the bailiff fairly shouted when they were done. 'Robert Johnson of the mill at Riding.'

'Well, someone from that place we have heard so much about,' Sir Richard said. 'Swear him in, Clerk, swear him in.'

Robert Johnson squared his broad chest and shoulders and began talking as if already midway through what he had to tell:

About the latter end of August last, late at night, lying in bed at the Riding betwixt two of his fellow-servants, he heard a man, as he thought, call at the door, and ask who was within. Upon which he rose, and went to the front of the house, and laid his head against the chamber window and he heard a great noise of horse feet, as though it had been an army of men. Whereupon he called, but none would answer.

So he returned to his bed, and the next morning, rising out of his bed, he wanted his shirt –

'Ah,' said Sir Richard, 'are you then the man at Mr Errington's? Pass me today's papers, Clerk. Let's see, yes here: "the said Michaell" – that's Michael Aynsley, who Anne Forster and Lucy Thompson said "called three several times at Mr Errington's kitchen door and made a noise like an host of men."'

'I am, Your Worship, Robert Johnson, Mr Errington's miller.' A worried look crossed his face as if he would lose the thread of his story in stopping to tell this.

... rising out of his bed, he went on, he wanted his shirt which seeking after he accused his two fellow-servants, which were amazed at the thing and denied that ever they knew of it, which he further searching after, found it under his pillow at his bed head, he said, still looking puzzled at this.

'Well, Robert Johnson, it seems to me you had a lucky escape: see what Anne Armstrong tells us these others – Aynsley, Forster and Thompson – said when the devil asked them how they sped with you. Nothing, they answered, "for they had not got power of the miller, but they got the shirt off his back, as he was lying betwixt women" – were these women you were lying between, two of them, lying with you for your carnal use?'

'Fellow servants, Your Worship,' said Robert Johnson, looking shocked and pulling at the uncomfortable doublet he had felt obliged to wear for the day. 'Men and fellow servants, for this is how they must sleep at Mr Errington's, though Mr Errington and his wife are away so often to his great house in Newcastle that he supposed they could sleep otherwise. Though only by going against their master's wishes, which they – he, Your Worships, definitely he – would not think to do.'

'Errington? Thomas Errington, Ironside Errington?' John Salkeld snorted. 'Our esteemed postmaster under the Commonwealth? Is this where he squirrels himself away now that the atmosphere is a bit chilly for Roundheads? Nothing less than he deserves, to be shut away up there with this ...' he waved expansively at Robert Johnson.

'She is mistaken, then, about the women?' Sir Richard was suddenly as concerned as the witness to keep to the business of the court.

Misheard or misunderstood, Robert Johnson said, moving on rapidly, too rapidly for his tongue almost, for he could see Anne Armstrong raising her hand, mouthing silent words. But he was too quick for her.

'And the informant further saith,' wrote the scribe, chasing after Robert Johnson's voice, 'that Mr Errington's draught, and Ralph Elrington's, being away at Styford, leading tithe corn there ...'

'Slow down, man,' said Sir Richard. 'Do you mean Mr Ralph *Elrington* was at Styford collecting the tithe due to Mr *Errington* as landholder, having with him both his own and Mr Errington's draught horses?'

'No small tithe there,' said James Howard, a wishful overtone to his voice.

'Yes, Your Worship,' he said ...

and their being late in coming home, this informer could not rest satisfied, but went to seek the draughts, and to find out what was become of them ...

Splashing through the ford across the Tyne, Robert Johnson was concerned at the strength of the current. He had stood on the south bank for some time trying to gauge the situation. The single street running through Brookford led directly into the water, but none of the inhabitants of the hamlet – who made their living, after all, from their position on this major ford – was willing to risk an opinion today.

The river, broad as it was, was not particularly deep, but when rain fell it responded rapidly and unpredictably. Flooding was common, and the problem was that such dangers could not be judged by the rainfall at the ford. If there was rain in the hills, the water would rush down to Warden Rock and surge over the crossing at Styford with nothing to hinder it. There was no way Robert Johnson could know what was happening further up the valley, but it did seem to him, in the sullen drizzle, that a rapid rise in water level was likely. The bed of the ford was, like the rest of the Tyne, stony and slippery – which is what made it a dangerous spate river – so he felt carefully with his bare feet for purchase.

He kept his eyes on the north bank, hoping to see Ralph Elrington appear with the heavy work horses and the carts they would be pulling. Through the mist he could scarcely make out the grassy hump that marked the smaller hamlet of Styford, invisible otherwise on its low-lying land. He was over half way across when Elrington came into view, only now leaving Styford town end.

Robert Johnson paused, the water encircling his legs more strongly. He didn't know whether he should wait, return to the south bank, or go ahead to meet Elrington. Taking comfort in the tall stature and muscular build of the horses, he forged on, his breeches dripping as he climbed up the north bank to find Elrington looking dubiously at the water.

No time to wait, he said; if we are to cross today we must do it now. He took hold of a draught horse and began pulling it to the ford, not even looking to see if Elrington was following. The horse was a good eighteen hands and the cart properly harnessed, but he was concerned at how quickly the water was surging around the feathering on its lower legs. He heard the second horse plashing in behind him and moved forward as fast as he was able in the strong pull of the current. When the water became too much he fell back, walking next to the horse instead of ahead. Its upright shoulder was well above his head, but he was just able to get his arm on to the leather attached to its broad, short back, putting its powerful hindquarters between him and the torrent of the river.

A small crowd had gathered now on the south bank. He hung on to the dray as it breasted the water. He had no sense of how much time passed before the horse began rising with the lift of the bed, but he staggered up the bank to a few cheers. It was then he noticed the crowd was looking beyond him, back into the river.

He turned to see the second horse struggling and Elrington crying out that he was going down. He pulled Mr Errington's draught to a safe spot, and then called for another horse. Someone brought a strong enough-looking animal and he leaped on, bare-back, and urged it into the river. The water washed over the horse, up to his waist in moments and well up the horse's neck, its eyes wild and nostrils flaring. He drove the animal on, three score yards or thereabouts, reaching Elrington as he and his horse were about to be swept into a deep, swirling pool. He knew that if he could not help them before they entered that they would be lost; man, beast and cart.

It was the horse that saved them. Once he had a hand on its bridle he could feel the strength in its heavy bones. It was a matter of turning that power in the right direction, finding again the submerged stones of the ford. He pulled and pulled, registering the strength of the animal once its hooves had purchase. Strung between his horse and the draught, half off the animal he was meant to be riding, he was still able to use his heels to kick it in the right direction, keeping the strong, straight profile of Mr Elrington's draught headed towards the point where the ford rose up out of the water.

There was some more desultory cheering as he brought the second draught up to where the first stood. Now was not the time to check how the loads in the carts had fared. Drenched in heavily falling rain, he guided the soggy procession back to the Riding and the mill. He and Elrington entered Mr Errington's property together, the other servants pleased enough to see them.

Elrington collapsed inside immediately, leaving someone else to take his draught and cart, but Robert Johnson unharnessed his master's draught and made sure it was bedded down warmly and comfortably in the stable. After that, his exhaustion caught up with him and he headed to his bed.

'So,' Sir Richard said, 'all this you say in support of Anne Armstrong's accusation that the witches struck you dead in revenge for saving Ralph Elrington's draught – and Thomas Errington's, you add – from going down in the water and drowning – as, she says, "they intended to have done".'

Robert Johnson drew himself back into his not inconsiderable bulk. He stood silent for a moment, an uncomfortably long moment, and then looked directly at Sir Richard. 'I report, Your

Worship, as I did in the matter of my shirt, simply the events that occurred. Whether the witches had aught to do with this or no, it is not for me to say.'

There was a stirring among the Justices at the bench, and then some low exchanges. Heads huddled together, Sir Richard joining one group as the Clerk of the Peace stood aside, impassive.

'So,' Sir Richard began again, pulling himself upright from his consultation with Sir Thomas Horsely, who had been in whispered discussion with James Howard, 'while you have a very full account to give of the events reported by Anne Armstrong, as to the intentions she claims informed those events, the intention of those she accuses here, you have nothing to say?'

'Nothing to say either way, Your Worship. I can only speak plainly as to what I saw, and what befell me.'

Several of the Justices turned now to Anne Armstrong, almost dancing in the dock, calling out despite the bailiff's best efforts, 'Anne Forster, Michael Aynsley, Lucy Thompson!'

John Salkeld, who had been in animated discussion with Humphrey Mitford, leaned forward over the bench. 'But do you admit, Johnson, that as Anne Armstrong claims, you were, after this "struck dead"?'

Robert Johnson felt his way into the hall of the Riding House. He had crossed the road from his cottage next to the mill in the dark of the night, but the darkness of the high, echoing hall was of another quality altogether, a blackness that the last embers in the fireplace only intensified. He had no idea what time it was, but his limbs were heavy with the day's exertions. The rain, the mist, the water reaching up to wrap itself around him and pull him down, the feel of horseflesh shifting massively under him, Elrington's flailing arms and thin cries, the lurch of the carts as they emerged drunkenly from the river behind the straining work horses, all took on the fug of a dream he struggled to wake from, as difficult to pull himself out of as the dark river had been. He felt his way around the large table that filled the centre of the hall, reading the walls too with his hands as he made his way to the kitchen. Finding the doorway on his left, he could see the dull glow of a fire. This was not in the kitchen itself, as he first thought: that room with its low roof and heavy beams had its warmth still, the rising warmth that gave the bedchamber above it the most comfort, at least during winter, but the flickering light came from beyond, in the scullery. He walked across the flagstones of the kitchen to the door leading into the back room, his eyes struggling to adjust to the reddish-yellow glow filling the space beyond. As he tried to focus, he saw a servant – a fellow servant, surely, for who else would be in the scullery in the dead of night? She seemed to be swaying from side to side, arms to her sides, a trick of the light making it appear as if her feet were not touching the floor. He wanted to call out, but at that instant he felt himself being pulled down, down into the river, but deeper than the impermeable bed of the Tyne would allow. This time he could not resist, and let himself sink …

'Aye,' he said, 'struck dead, if this is what my fellow servant reports that she saw, for all I can report is dropping. I do not even remember hitting the floor.'

'It was the witches, the Riding witches,' cried out Anne Armstrong. 'I was there –' she stopped, looked about the court-room wild-eyed, '– I heard them, they told him, their protector, 'twas in revenge –'

'Enough, girl,' snapped Sir Richard, 'we have your evidence already.'

John Salkeld tapped the pages before him. 'If this is every-thing you have to report of that occurrence, Johnson, what do you have to say about the girl's account of events at the mill?'

He picked up the page to read out: 'And that they confessed to the devil that they made all the gear go of the mill, and that they intended to have made the stones grind till they had flown all in pieces.'

Anne Armstrong was nodding her head up and down, smacking her fist in her palm.

'Surely you have more to tell us?' said John Salkeld, to a suppressed chorus of 'yes, yes, yes,' from the girl. The bailiff's rock of a hand clamped on her shoulder.

Robert Johnson cleared his throat. 'He further saith that,' the scribe wrote, and then stopped to look up at the witness.

Robert Johnson appeared from the noiseless movement of his lips to be, of all things, counting. About some sixteen days before Christmas last, he began, he could not by any means get the mill properly set and, about the hinder end of Christmas holidays, being sheeling some oats, about two hours before the sun-setting …

The hoist had worked properly, tightening around the neck of each sack of grain as it should when he pulled on the hoist rope. This was just as well, as he was mildly irritated at having to miss such merriment as there was in the Riding at this season. He understood why Mr Errington frowned upon the waste and extravagance – disorder, sin and immorality, his master called it – of the ongoing celebrations, but out here in the country there was hardly any of the eating and drinking, the dancing and singing, the gambling and gaming that his master would be resenting in the town. Granted, Mr Errington only expected the mill to operate intermittently and for shorter hours than normal in the eleven days after Christmas, but nonetheless, the amount of stored grain coming in meant that his miller enjoyed none of the leisure time given to the servants, missing even the extra church services in Bywell.

Robert Johnson had spent much of the morning raising sack after sack through the trapdoors from the ground to the third floor of the mill and then emptying them into the storage bins. He was in a hurry to get as much of the grinding done before the light of the short day was gone, climbing briskly down to the second floor and winding the stone nut with the jack ring so that it meshed with the great spur wheel below. Next he opened the penstock to start the waterwheel turning and began lowering the runner stone to set the gap between it and the bed stone as accurately as he could. He prided himself on setting the nip correctly, giving the farmers precisely the fineness of meal they requested.

Today, however, the nut on the threaded rod that was meant to raise or lower the adjustable beam supporting the stone spindle would not move. Worse yet, the grain was feeding into the mill gear while he was struggling to set it. To save time, he had pulled out the slide in the chute that let the oats fall into the hopper on the floor above, so a brown torrent poured down as he worked, the dust rising off it blinding him and filling his nostrils and mouth.

At least the mill stones were rotating freely, which meant he'd be getting meal of some kind, he thought. But while he was rubbing his eyes, his ears registered another problem. Where was the incessant chattering that gave 'the damsel' its name? He peered up and saw that the arms on the iron bar protruding out of the eye of the runner stone were not striking against the shoe. The oats then were not being jogged through the eye and instead begun spilling everywhere, over the mill stones, into the stone case, on to the floor in a wild rattle.

He grabbed the crook, but the string that was meant to adjust the shoe controlling the amount of grain falling was not responding. He raced up the stairs to close it off manually, the bell fixed on the wooden frame supporting the hopper ringing loudly and unnecessarily as he did so. He knew that the hopper would be close to empty by now, the oats having poured down in an uncontrolled flood.

He poked his head into the bin floor and saw the chute from the bin dancing about violently, smacking into the hopper with each mad gyration. Dented and buckled already, the metal hopper was beginning to tear loose. He slid back down the stairs, covering his head with his arms. He hit the floor of the next level hard, terrified to find what was happening on the stone floor.

He didn't dare climb back up to close the penstock, and it wasn't possible to shut the flume gate from inside the mill building. What with all the rain, the bypass channel leading off the March Burn was pouring water into the millrace, flooding the wheelrace and slamming up against the waterwheel with tremendous force. Without any gears to control it, the massive runner stone was spinning crazily over the bed stone, and with no grist to work, the grinding surfaces of both stones were shearing against each other. At least the wooden enclosure around the pair of millstones was holding, but even as he took some desperate relief from this, the hoops encircling the stone case began to vibrate violently. He hurled himself down the next set of steps, an instant before the rivets began popping and thumping into metal and wood with the force of musket shots.

Praying the casing would not disintegrate completely, Robert Johnson pulled himself upright to find that he was not out of danger. The crown wheel at the top of the main shaft was spinning violently too, so much so that as he looked at it in disbelief its mechanism collapsed in a spray of wooden cogs. Expecting the pulleys and iron gearwheel to follow at any moment, he threw himself out of the main door, hearing as he did so a thunderous hammering. He lay on his stomach and looked back into the mill. A rain of everything from bits of disintegrating hopper to broken beams and bent metal was spraying down the stairs and a hail of unrecognisable fragments of machinery shot around in the space where the meal was meant to be delivered from the millstones in a soft, tawny waterfall, collecting in a steady stream into the meal bins, ready to be bagged and collected.

Robert Johnson stood up. He walked up the stone-lined flume and closed the head gate, watching as the water drained out of the flume. The wheel slowly came to a standstill. The last of the water ran into the millpond, losing its force in a slow, wide swirl before flowing into the tailrace and then re-joining the March Burn. Too much, to say all this, too much; enough to say ...

'The gear, hopper and hoops, and all other things but the stones,' the scribe wrote,

flew down and were cast off, and he himself almost killed with them, they coming against him with such force and violence.

'You see,' cried out Anne Armstrong, 'this they confessed, the witches. They made the mill gear go run mad and break up, and they intended to kill him, Robert Johnson!'

She pointed both hands at him, index fingers quivering. 'Do you not see it, to kill you with stones after they could not drown you!'

Robert Johnson kept his eyes on the bench, impassive.

'So, what say you, Robert Johnson?' asked Sir Richard.

'Rivers flood, Your Worships,' he said. 'And mill gear gives trouble.'

Anne Armstrong emitted a mad cry: frustration, fury, disbelief, all packed into a single exhalation.

'A Philosopher, by God!' James Howard hit the bench with his fist, laughing. 'A Philosopher who understands that we live amid uncertainties and among mysteries! Not everything can be explained –' he heard the wind gusting over the high ground above Redesdale, saw Catcleugh, Spithope, Babswood, Chattlehope, pastures once owned by the Howards now divided into farms and sold off piecemeal, blowing like dust out of the palm of his hand '– and we cannot always blame unexplainable occurrences on witches and the devil.'

'But we are lawyers, Sir, or dispenses of justice at least,' said Sir Richard, 'and our work is not to philosophise, but to establish blame when blame there is, and punish it accordingly.'

'Yes,' said Anne Armstrong, unable to contain herself; 'oh yes, yes.'

Humphrey Mitford was feeling comfortable enough by now to risk an opinion. 'Fear and imagination make many witches among country people,' he said.

'Enough, enough.' Sir Richard turned to the clerk. 'Has this witness anything further to add?'

'No, Your Worships,' answered Robert Johnson, before the clerk could frame a suitably judicial question.

Chapter 15

At Morpeth Sessions, as aforesaid.
Ann Armstrong, of Birkes-Nuke, spinster.

With Robert Johnson dismissed, Sir Richard took in the mood of his Justices. The shift was palpable, if not in accord with the atmosphere in the courtroom.

'Harm,' said Sir Richard; 'harm then we have evidence for, but cause, cause for that harm, now that, it would appear, is in question. It would appear, Sirs, as if we are slipping from *Billa vera* to *Ignoramus* –'

'No Sirs, Sirs, Your Worships!' The bailiff's heavy hand shaken off, Anne was leaning forward, arms extended, her whole body reaching out to the bench. 'This is not the whole of it, oh, the witches, the witches, these devil's pawns who do the devil's bidding! Good comes from God, but the evil, oh the evil among us at the Riding, at Edmundbyers, at Birches Nooke, only they can tell us why. Robert Johnson does not understand, and never will. John March, George Taylor, these people here ...' Before they knew it, she was underway again, the scribe without instruction having dipped his pen and begun writing, writing ...

Ann Usher of Fairly May confessed that she and Jane Makepeace of New Ridley had trailed a horse of this George Stobbart down a great scar, and that they have now power of a cow of George Stobbart's, which now pines away.

At a flick of Sir Richard's hand, the bailiff called, 'George Stobbart, if George Stobbart is present, step forward –'

'George Stobbart is not here,' said Anne, 'and neither is Elizabeth Pickering of Whittonstall, for they fear the justice of the court. But Elizabeth Pickering of Whittonstall, a widow, confessed to the devil that she had killed a child of her neighbour's. And more, Your Worships, more still! Anthony Hunter, of Birkenside –'

'Birkenside,' said Sir Richard, seeing in the haze of accusations the small, dank clearing, the musty tumble of houses, 'Anthony Hunter, a relation I presume of Mary –'

'– son, as John March has testified, this Anthony Hunter who I would accuse no further to his face when he threatened me at the house of John March, Anthony Hunter confessed he had power over Anne, wife of Thomas Richardson, of Crooked Oak –'

'Yes, this we have already, girl,' said the clerk, paging back through the pile of depositions, 'he took the power of her limbs from her –'

'Took away the power of her limbs, Sir, as I said, but asked the devil's assistance to take away her life too. And Jane Makepeace was at all the meetings among the witches, and helped to destroy the goods of George Stobbart –'

'This too you have said before, girl,' said John Salkeld. 'You begin to repeat yourself, and I fear your powers of invention are running thin.'

'Running out, rather,' muttered Humphrey Mitford.

John Salkeld clapped Humphrey Mitford on the shoulder and said, 'How much more of this do we need to hear, Gentlemen? How much longer does this list of names need to be before we turn them over to the gaol for the Summer Assizes?'

Sir Richard held his hand up to the girl, joined in on the bustle of consultation taking place at the bench. She stared at this, her restless hands plucking at her clothes, her shoulders raised, her mouth quivering in an agony of suspense. Around her the floor of the courtroom surged and hummed.

Eventually Sir Richard pulled himself upright from the huddle. 'Do you, Anne Armstrong, have any further specific evidence to add – evidence, mark you, with witnesses, no more of these wilder and ever wilder accusations?'

The girl made a clear effort at composing herself. She smoothed down the front of the thin grey dress she had been crumpling in her hands, dropped her arms to her sides, lifted her chin.

'This informer,' she said, sounding as if she were reciting the evidence in the exact form the scribe would have taken it down, 'deposeth that Ann Dryden had a lease for fifty years of the devil, whereof ten are expired.'

Specifics, this is what they wanted. Well, she could be specific, exact, precise.

'Ann Forster had a lease of her life for forty-seven years, whereof seven are yet to come. Lucy Thompson had a lease of two and forty, whereof two are yet to come. And, her lease being near out, they would have persuaded this informer –'

'This informer,' said Sir Richard, incredulous. 'This informer, meaning by this, you, you yourself?'

'You had a lease, nearly up at this time?' chimed in Sir Thomas. 'Why have you not confessed this before, girl?'

'But I did, Your Worship. The cheese –'

'What *cheese*, Anne Armstrong, what is this talk of cheese!'

The Clerk of the Peace stood, and took a step forward. 'If I may, Your Worships. In the evidence given before Mr Jenison on the fifth of February, the girl reported that it was after eating a piece of cheese that she first "disclosed everything which she formerly kept secret".'

The Justices looked at the clerk, expecting more, but Armstrong burst out again: 'They would have persuaded me to have taken a lease of three score years or upwards, and told me I should never want gold or money. Or,' she said, casting about now as she took in the various expressions crossing the faces of the Justices, 'if I had but one cow, they should let me know a way to get as much milk as them that had ten.'

'Thinner and thinner the charges, the more she stretches them, I would say.' Humphrey Mitford smiled dourly.

'We have, I think, heard enough,' said Sir Richard. 'Clerk, have the scribe append the usual "And further this informant saith not", "Taken and Sworn", etc.'

'Are we sure she has no more to say, Your Worship?'

'I'm sure she would have more to say, much, much more to say, given the chance,' said Sir Richard sharply. 'But "and further this informer cannot as yet well remember" will do for us, I think.'

Chapter 16

Sir Richard stood, acknowledged the bows of the clerks and bailiff's men, and led the Justices towards the rear of the large room. They drew themselves up as close as possible to the blaze in the large fireplace which was kept well fed during the proceedings.

'Well,' said Sir Richard, 'here we have, what, twenty or more accused?'

The Clerk of the Peace had followed the procession of Justices at a discreet distance. 'Lucy Thompson,' he began, 'Ann Forster, Anne Dryden, Margaret Aynsley, Michael Aynsley, Mary Hunter, Dorothy Green, Anne Usher, Elizabeth Pickering, Jane Makepeace, Anthony Hunter, John Whitfield, Anne Whitfield, Christopher Dixon, Alice Dixon, Catherine Elliott, Elisabeth Atchison and Isabelle Andrew, thus far in today's deposition.

'Ah, and possibly John Newton, whose house in the Riding was used for a meeting, though the scribe has not listed his name. To which we must add from the previous depositions,' he said, paging back and picking through the names, 'allowing for repetition, John Crawforth, William Wright,' and paging again, 'Anne Baites and Frances Pye.'

'Sixteen women and six or seven men, mostly husbands of the accused women,' he concluded.

'– and Armstrong herself,' added Sir Richard. 'Let us not forget Armstrong herself, who confesses to being present at these witch meetings, which brings us near to the number of suspected witches found in our town by that Scottish witch-pricker the last time a case like this got out of hand. And what came of that? Twenty-seven found guilty! Fourteen witches and one wizard executed on the Town Moor! All buried in St Andrews churchyard with nails driven through their legs to prevent their ghosts returning, only for the witch-pricker –'

'Cuthbert Nicholson,' said James Howard.

'John Kincaid,' said Sir Thomas.

'His name is not recorded,' said the clerk.

'– later to be exposed as a fraud using a retractable pin to pierce skin without drawing blood, a supposed test of a witch to which I hope we will not stoop. He confessed upon the gallows that he had been the death of above two hundred and twenty women, all for the gain of twenty shillings apiece.'

'At least this Armstrong girl has not got round to asking a fee for her services,' said James Howard. 'Well, not yet.'

'There may be more than money at stake for Armstrong.' Sir Thomas ignored James Howard's self-deprecating smile. 'A smooth-tongued woman using a shrewd method of turning away charges against herself, if you ask me.'

Sir Richard stood up. 'Now, Gentlemen, let us not forget that we have heard witnesses who support her claims, one way or another, two seeing clearly the witchcraft in them and one other reporting that the events were accurate as described, if not prepared to go into the causes behind them.'

'But what claims has she actually made?' Sir Thomas asked. 'The only evidence put forward is her eyewitness accounts of the boasts of the accused at these, these – I shall use your word, Sir Richard – these "conventicles," and yet the source of these fantasies is odd even by her own account. She tells us plainly that she is subject to swoons and fits, and is in these states when she is taken away to the witches' diabolic activities. Yet she is able to produce entirely coherent accounts of them. Moreover, she has not just watched and reported, but taken part in the wickedness of which she accuses these others.'

'Ah, but only because pressed to do so, forced, and forced most unwillingly,' said Sir Richard.

'That's as may be,' said Sir Thomas. He paused, and then shifted on his feet. 'I feel obliged, Gentlemen, to add a point of more practical consideration.' Hands to the fire, the Justices stepped back slightly as a servant brought more logs to the blaze, staring into the flurry of sparks as he continued. 'That is, the cost to the good ratepayers of our county for the arrest, examination, imprisonment and burial of those we find worthy of trial and prosecution. What is it, four shillings to the constables, for carrying the witches to gaol? Trying the witches, at least another fifteen shillings, I would say. And then let us not forget a grave for a witch – each witch will have to be buried at a charge of sixpence per grave, and committed to the earth in a parish coffin. Not a cheap business for the county, you will agree –'

'God damn it, Gentlemen, pounds, shillings, and pence!' Everyone turned in surprise to Humphrey Mitford, taken aback by an outburst that was entirely uncharacteristic.

'Pounds, shillings and pence, when giving in to this girl means we may as well go back to the days when the sergeants paraded the witchfinder on horseback through the town, a bellman ringing and crying out that any woman thought a witch be brought and tried. Then let's take them to the town hall where they can be stripped, shaved of all their bodily hair, probed, prodded and pricked before a jeering crowd of onlookers, neighbours and friends, and – most of them, you can be sure – found guilty and hanged. Barbarism, that is the real cost! So don't pounds, shillings and pence me!'

'Now, we have come some way from those times, Mr Mitford –' began Sir Richard, but Humphrey Mitford, having found his voice, did not give it up easily.

'Twenty-odd souls then, to be cast into gaol until the Summer Assizes, months hence! And how many will die in that time, given the state of our prisons? I, for one, before condemning a single one of those named here to such a fate, would want more by way of evidence than the tales of a country girl of either the lowest intelligence or the meanest of minds.'

Humphrey Mitford's knees buckled as his outburst ended, his body teetering towards the wall. He kept himself upright by resting his elbow on the edge of the finely moulded fireplace, seeming to seek out the heat, although he was sweating profusely.

His fellow Justices shuffled or shifted, their eyes fixed on the fire.

Humphrey Mitford could be forgiven a moment of despair. What difference would his speaking out make? Why should he care? His mother not dead a year, his son John dead also. His daughter Barbara, only four years old, now sick and he felt sure they would bury her within a month.

And he now ill as well, his eyes blurring as he stared into the fire. All he wanted to do was go home, follow the Wanney back home.

Sir Richard placed a concerned hand on his arm. 'The state of our prisons, Mr Mitford, is not a consideration for our sentencing. Neither is it our business here today to debate the possibility or the actual existence of witchcraft and sorcery,' he went on, addressing now the whole group gathered around the fire, faces glowing in the darkness moving in from the more distant corners of the large room; 'to deny it is at once flatly to contradict the revealed word of God in various passages both of the Old and New Testament and, in terms of the law, the acts against it that are in our statutes.

'When I consider whether there are such persons as witches, I am not alone in finding my mind divided. I am prepared to believe, in general, in witchcraft, but I have as yet been unable to give credit to any particular instance of it.'

'We are agreed, are we not, Gentlemen –' all turned with some surprise again, this time to attend to Ralph Jenison, emerging from both his silence and one of the darker corners to the side of the fireplace, '– that the claims we have heard of these gatherings of witches, coveys, is it, conventicles, what you will, are unusual in an English court. Yet here we have such claims in great and surprising detail, given their source in this young girl's experience – or so she claims.'

Ralph Jenison paused, looking around at his fellow Justices. No one spoke, and he extracted what appeared to be some kind of publication from deep in his gown.

'Would you then give me the liberty to read something to you, something which may throw some light on this case, and help us in making our decision with regard to Anne Armstrong's accusations?'

Leaning in towards the light from the fire, without any further comment, he began.

He read what must have been one or two pages, then stopped and stepped back. For several long seconds, his fellow Justices kept to the positions they had adopted and then frozen into as he read.

A log cracked, broke, flared and tumbled down into ash.

'There is more, but I trust this may suffice.'

'It is,' said Sir Richard, 'remarkable ...' He coughed, cleared his throat.

Ralph Jenison withdrew from the firelight.

Eventually Sir Richard harrumphed again and waved to the clerk, who passed him the pile of papers, sheet after sheet filled with the information given by Anne Armstrong. He paged through them fitfully, scanning lines here and there, stopping at one or two passages. 'I see,' he said, coming to the final page, 'that the deponent has made her mark with some force. Look,' he said, holding up the document to his fellow Justices, 'the pen has cut right into the paper, digging a hole in the centre and tearing the line of the ring she has drawn around it.'

Each of them could see how the thick pupil-like dot in the centre of the roughly scored circle was etched deep into the paper, giving the impression of a malevolent eye staring out of the page.

'I trust,' said Sir Richard, 'that the scribe is happy with the condition of the nib of his pen after this.'

He turned away from the fire reluctantly, cocking his head to the wind beating about the walls of the gatehouse on its high promontory with renewed vigour. 'I suppose it is time for us to return to the bench, and let her know if we believe there is a case for those she accuses to answer.'

High Riggs, Riding Mill

And what did Ralph Jenison read to the assembled Justices?

I was back home when I reached the final scene of Anne's coming before the Justices at the Morpeth Quarter Sessions. A new development at the Archives was the option of taking high-resolution colour photographs of the material one was working with and then emailing them to oneself. The files, when I opened them on my computer, were startling. Whatever was lost by way of tactile sensation, the feel of the paper, the scorings of the ink, yes, even the dust, was offset by a new dimension: there was something about the shimmer of electricity in the digitised images that gave them an unusual clarity and depth, a very different kind of presence. Called up on the screen, they had a freshness and immediacy that made them seem more authentic than the rather dingy originals lurking in their acid-free cardboard boxes. It was as if Anne herself was coming alive in some new way in this different medium.

If so, it was only to be cut short. The flood of Anne's accusations, increasingly wild and darting desperately about, is brought to an abrupt end with the formulaic 'and further this informer cannot as yet well remember.'

What came after this legal full stop penned in by the scribe we cannot know. The deposition, even in its new shimmering, bright form, floating up from the past through my screen, is all we have to go by. In all likelihood, however, Anne's accusations were dismissed yet again.

And it is not too far a stretch to assume that Ralph Jenison had a significant part to play in this. In one way or another he is implicated from the first in the waylaying of Anne Armstrong's mission or scheme or whatever else you may think it was; where, after all, did that deposition of 5 February go, prior to its being returned, out of order, to the sequence of depositions in which, between its transcription and archiving, it sits so oddly?

Who is to say it wasn't deliberately misassigned, mislaid, misdirected, before Sir Richard Stote instituted a search resulting in its discovery after the evidence he had taken? And who else could have done this but someone in the offices of Ralph Jenison, Esq., perhaps the cautious, oh so cautious, Mr Ralph Jenison himself, constantly under suspicion as to his real allegiances in so politically and theologically volatile a time?

His appearances as a character in Anne's story are of someone constantly on the edges, yet always hovering behind the most crucial twists and turns that trip Anne up, bring her down, block her out and ultimately silence her.

And what better way to have that story thoroughly discredited before the law than to find a precedent, a precedent that would not only solve the problem of how she, a poor, illiterate young countrywoman, could know of such things, but also demonstrate that this was all hearsay, a tale with no basis in anything like fact, told to her by someone else.

What were the pages he read, then, when he stepped into the firelight? A little digging around and we, like Jenison's clerk, could come up with the 'chapter and verse': 'whereupon', the Justice read,

she put her hand into her pocket again, and pulled out a thing like unto a bridle that jingled, which she put on the little boy's head; which said boy stood up in the likeness of a white horse and in the brown greyhound's stead. Then immediately Dickenson's wife took this informer before her upon the said horse and carried him to a new house called Hoarstones, being about a quarter of a mile off.

Whither when they were come, there were divers persons about the door, and he saw divers others riding on horses of several colours towards the said house, who tied their horses to a hedge near to the said house.

Which persons went into the said house, and presently after, seeing divers of the said company going into a barn near adjoining, he followed after them, and there he saw six of them kneeling, and pulling all six of them six several ropes, which were fastened or tied to the top of the barn. Presently after which pulling, there came into this informer's sight flesh smoking, butter in lumps, and milk as it were flying from the said ropes. All which fell into basins which were placed under the said ropes. And after that these six had done, there came other six which did so likewise.

And when his fellow Justices looked at him, a little unsteady still at having the basis for this elaborate case in which they had invested so much of their time, their care, their concern for their self-preservation, pulled from under it, he would have dropped into the hush that followed, 'It is from the examination of Edmund Robinson, eleven years of age, taken at Padiham, within the county of Lancaster, before two Justices. The jury returned guilty verdicts on nineteen of the sixty-odd persons put under suspicion as a result of this evidence, but the Assize set aside the decision, remanded those convicted, and consulted the Bishop of Chester.'

'And what, Mr Jenison, did the bishop conclude?' It was Sir Thomas this time.

'The bishop re-examined Edmund Robinson, and then sent him to London for interrogation, where he finally retracted his story, but not before four of the accused died in gaol. The boy stated that "the tale is false and feigned, and has no truth at all, but only as he has heard tales and reports made by women, so he framed the tale out of his own invention".'

Chapter 17

Leaving through the massive doors, Anne Armstrong was met with gusts of wet wind, and found herself only half-heartedly protected by the bailiff's men from a surging crowd of hissing, spitting people. Those from the villages nearest hers were to the fore, mouthing threats, raising fists, making cutting gestures across their throats. She huddled into herself, knees near bent as she took step after trembling step, head deep down in her hunched shoulders, not looking up and out over the rushing Wanney and the rain-swept town that would no longer have anything to do with her.

If those swarming around her could have seen the face hidden in her hands, they would have drawn back, stepped into and over each other in their attempts to get away from such darkness.

She was a strong walker: her thin dress flapped against her legs as she strode briskly through the dull drizzle, up between the grand houses lining the road to the West Gate of the town and then out through the miserable mine workings on either side of the Tyne until the road to Carlisle freed itself from the clutter of its eastern end in the town and made its muddy way across open countryside.

A cart driver passing through Morpeth had given her a lift to Newcastle last night, but she was glad to be walking again. The anger stored up in her body needed the release of her pumping legs, and she cleared mile after mile without thinking about the distance.

She cut down towards the ford. She could feel the pressure building up in her legs now, and then rising through her whole body to her head until her eyes clouded and her skull hummed. *Robert Johnson – so much for your saving of Mr Errington and Mr*

Elrington's draughts, your surviving the mill stones; I pray that such a flood will come that every ford, every bridge, will be washed away, swept away as you and your horses were not. The cold of the water, swift but shallow enough today for her bare feet to clasp the slippery stepping stones, brought her back to where she was; *as if dead*, she thought – not the way to say it, she had never found the right way to say how it felt, but today at least the fit had been slight and passing, as it sometimes was, and she could continue as if it were merely a mist she was feeling her way through.

She dried her feet once she'd safely reached the higher ground, putting her clogs on as she walked up the main street of Brookford. She wished the fading light of the afternoon were dimmer yet, and she kept her face well down.

Styford Street brought her quickly to a road, but she did not turn east to Birches Nooke or west to Corbridge. She crossed the road instead, and followed a track heading south.

Anybody knowing her – anybody knowing her who did not wish her ill, that is – would be wondering at her choice of direction. She was, despite the fury she'd brought upon herself at the Sessions, still a servant in Birches Nooke, and her father lived in Corbridge. It was understandable that she would be uncertain of what awaited her in Mable Fouler's house, and any thought of her father's house as a home had been torn apart by the ferocity that had developed between them as she approached womanhood. She bore marks of this on her body, and worse, in her memory. Occasionally, though, a flash of the closeness they'd shared when she was growing up would break through. The warmth of his large gut when she hugged it, the grizzle of his chin and cheek against her forehead when he bent down to her, even his ale-raddled breath smothering her as he folded her into his softening bulk.

But south it was, skirting the edge of the Riding, shuddering at the sight of the pack bridge over the burn, avoiding even looking at the mill. Following the track, bending into it as it climbed up the steep bank of the Tyne.

From there it was a steady rise and fall, her breath harsh, as, with fifteen or more miles behind her, she threw herself into the last miles she had to cover tonight. Leaving the track for a small path vanishing into the now thickening darkness, her feet felt their way as the night took over her other senses. Entering Crooked Oak, she knew she was both lost and precisely where she needed to be.

She walked as far from the first cottage as she dared, its walls sheltering a witch she had denounced. If Widow Andrew had any idea she was here, there was no telling what she would do in revenge. The cottage was in complete darkness, as was the larger house that came next. Thomas Richardson's weeping could not be heard tonight, and no light was refracted in the mullions of his windows either. Had the witches finally taken the life of his wife?

She moved on a few yards further, coming up against the rough walls of the outshut before realising she was upon it. For the first time there was no dull glow to tell her she had reached her destination.

She felt her way round to find that the doorway's rough planks lay fallen to the ground. Her hands were now the only means of exploring the blackness to discover what, if anything, remained of the old man.

She spent longer than was necessary in the hole of a room checking and rechecking the darkness, verifying only what her first instinct had told her. Thomas Boyer was not here, not only away from his hovel, but gone altogether. The small space, poor, broken, barely shelter for a human body, had always seemed packed, pulsing, alive to the edge of every corner with his presence; now its foul emptiness filled her with despair.

One thought, one idea, swam up through the emptiness: she did not need him any more, the old man – not his revelations to her on the path that early morning a lifetime ago, not the speeches since, the sermons, the readings, the lessons. What he had said to her, she had suffered through; what he had studied, learned, taught, she had lived. She now understood fully what she'd begun to glimpse before; she was free of him, her own witness.

She stepped out of the thick darkness of his outshut into a darkness she could understand, the darkness of the nights that had pressed in on her from her earliest memories. She walked blindly, barely thinking, back up the path, not caring for Isabelle Andrew or anyone else she might meet. The whole world might have been emptied of human life for all she could tell. She noticed nothing of the turns of the track, the direction she was taking, the mounting up of the miles as she retraced her steps.

This time she crossed the old pack bridge, numb, impervious to anything the witches could try tonight. She walked blindly passed the mill cottage and on to the road that ran between the mill and Riding House. No light came from their windows; empty too, she thought, the sleep of the innocent not the likely explanation.

Two miles, she allowed herself to register, two miles to the town of Corbridge.

Dawn was beginning to force its way into the sky behind her as she neared her destination. The river was wide at this point, dangerously swift and strewn with rocks, if not particularly deep. Along with the town, the old bridge had been allowed to fall into a state of sad disrepair. As she looked at the swaying, drooping wooden structure before her, she was sorry that she had decided not to risk the ancient ford about a quarter of a mile back, where the glassy, smooth rush of the water had looked too dangerous. There was no choice now but to take what appeared the greater danger, the bridge that fewer and fewer people entrusted themselves to these days.

Risking splinters and rogue nails, Anne carried her clogs in one hand while feeling her way for the strongest planks, her other hand taking hold of whatever support she could find. The wood creaked and shifted like a living thing beneath her as she looked at nothing else but one foot following the other, trying to avoid glimpses of the surge of water beneath them.

Her relief at stepping off the bridge on the other side was short-lived, the town giving her little sense of comfort. She picked her way through middens and pigsties, fenced off, if at all, with railings made of old, split, disintegrating boards. As she did so, she caught a glimpse of herself as a child, scrabbling in the dumps behind the houses, sorting through bones, rotting vegetables, broken pottery, human excrement, laughing and swatting aside the vermin she and the other children competed with in trying to pick out anything that could be used, played with, eaten.

People were emerging as she made her way towards her father's house. The women were sallow and thin armed, the men flabby, potbellied and 'tender footed', as her father called them, cautious, timid, tip-toeing into the streets.

When she reached her father's door, it was closed, but a shove was enough to open it. There was nothing inside worth locking away, only the usual scatter of leftover scraps in dirty utensils and rough-hewn furniture. Most importantly a bed, its heavy wood frame and odorous blanket being all she could ask for.

She next opened her eyes to find the evening closing in. By the time she was close to awake, darkness had settled over Corbridge. It took her some time to register where she was. Her father had not, to her knowledge, returned while she slept. Such work as he did was 'seasonal', as he called it – occasional or a random stroke of luck would be more like it. He regularly stayed out overnight, days sometimes. She assumed he simply hung about wherever he finally dropped during whatever drinking or whoring he was still up to.

The ashes in the hearth were completely cold, and he'd been reduced to rushlights since she was last here. A few dried piths lay on the table, but she could find no fat or grease to soak them in, nor any kind of flint. This bothered her. It had been a long time since she'd lived outside Dame Fouler's regimented household which, for all its oppressive habits, was secure and reassuring in its way, even in the dark. It wasn't possible, surely, that she could be longing for Birches Nooke and Burtree House?

She pulled aside the piece of linen tacked over the window. The linseed oil was dried out of it, so the thin material was almost no barrier between Archibald Armstrong's single room and the street immediately outside. A figure took shape in the gloom, and she thought at first it was her father. But the breeches and boots and shirt she first imagined she saw gave way to the bodice and skirts of a woman as the form became clearer – a better class of woman, given that the upper skirt was gathered up to reveal an underskirt. Then that too shimmered and lost its shape, began to resolve itself into a cat, the form of a grey cat. Before it did so, however, her mind registered the flickering, shifting shape as that of Jane Baites, Jane Baites of Corbridge.

The Wellington Inn

Based on an interview carried out in the Parish Hall, Riding Mill,
19 August 2015

Maureen Turner started working at the Wellington Inn when she was only a girl, right after she left school. And it turned out that working at the Wellington was what she'd be doing right up until she retired.

Not that she'd planned it that way, even if it hadn't been so bad, not when she was young. There were other youngsters there then, and they'd worked hard but they'd had fun together too – at the inn or up at the village shop, or in the Long Room, as it was called, between the inn and the station, completely run down now, but once the place where the villagers held their dances and leek club shows and all sorts of other social gatherings, all stopped years ago.

It was different when she got old and the only work she did was cleaning. When she'd been younger they'd ask her to do every sort of work, including being a barmaid if someone didn't show up; she'd tell herself then that she had a real future in the inn. But as the years went by she found herself with a mop in her hand more and more of the time, and for the last fifteen years or so that's all she'd been doing. By then it was too late to change, to find work anywhere else.

She'd seen a lot at the Wellington, and not just the goings-on of the villagers or, worse still, those staying over a night or two. There'd been times even then, when she was young, that she had wanted to leave, but you couldn't give up your job over something like that, some girl's nonsense. That was what her Da had said the one time she tried to talk to him about it; her Mam had died by then. They'd only been able to hold on to that house with everyone doing the best they could, and that didn't include saying you were frightened by a waff – that's what her Da would call it, a waff, a spirit or a ghost.

And she hadn't seen that much of it – *her*: but it wasn't so much *seeing* her – things would feel strange, and you'd know she was about. Especially in certain places. She couldn't say she felt it as much down by the bar, for instance. Well, that was new, the long front section where the entrance was now, with the pub counter running down it. She remembered when that had been an old outbuilding, before they started changing the place. There was an alleyway between it and Alex Bell's garage – you could fill up with petrol in Riding Mill in those days, and get repairs done to your car. But they'd knocked the garage down when they built the new bar and a car park for the Sunday lunch crowd.

The Little Back Room was the worst. Not only inside it, the room nearest to it as well. She'd noticed how few people sat up at the top of the long dining area; even when it was cold, they'd avoid choosing a table by the big fireplace at the end of the room. If the place wasn't crowded, you'd always find that part empty – nice tables, a bit far from the bar, but the waitresses would serve you up there the same as anywhere else. Still, hardly anyone ever sat there if there was room anywhere else in the Wellington, and the other staff would talk about it, make jokes, nervously, think up reasons for why people didn't like to sit there. Well, they could have as many notions as they liked, but all she knew was that none of the men ever liked to take their beer up there, and the one thing she trusted about a man was where he'd drink his pint.

She was probably the only person now who'd known the Wellington when that part of the dining area was a room on its own, before the company turned the whole front section of the ground floor into one large dining room. And that room was right next to the Little Back Room.

The Little Back Room. Everyone thought it was the nicest room in the pub back in the day, small and comfortable, a really good snug. Best bentwood chairs, red carpet with yellow designs, pretty curtains on the window. Lovely fireplace. You could drink like a lady in there. And it wasn't only the well-off visitors who'd use that room – so would any patron who preferred not to be seen in the public bar. Women would often enjoy a drink in the snug back in the day when it was frowned upon for ladies to be in a pub. She'd seen the local police officer nip in for a quiet pint, a vicar or two taking their evening whisky – not to mention a good few people using it for a rendezvous they didn't want too many others to know about.

But even then, she'd never taken to the place. She'd stop, often, when she was emptying out ashtrays and picking up the glasses after everyone had gone, and look about. She especially hated the feeling when her back was exposed, open to the room while she was down on her hands and knees cleaning the carpet.

Once, she did think she'd actually seen something in the Little Back Room. It was after it had become more of a pool room than a snug. They'd kept calling it the snug, although the tone of the place had come down a few notches when they took out most of the nice chairs and tables – lovely round tables and chairs, that bentwood worth a fortune today – and squeezed in a billiard table. That was when Mr and Mrs Eakins ran the place. They had a son, Stan, and she was just old enough to worry about him, a lad growing up in a pub, often on his own simply hanging about. He'd spend hours and hours in the Little Back Room, playing snooker. She'd see him leaning over the table for a difficult shot, and she'd think, mind your back, boy, but nothing ever seemed to trouble him in that room.

Then one day Mrs Eakins sent her to take a lemonade in to him while he was playing. She came in while he was really quiet, concentrating on a tricky shot he'd set up for himself. And there it was: she'd always say 'she' when she thought about it, but she couldn't see any features, no face or anything. She just knew for certain it was looking at him, hard. She froze, the glass on the tray, but Stan just stood up and smiled, this thing behind him. He took the lemonade and thanked her, and then he bent back down to his shot.

She didn't dare tell him what she could see, simply stepped out the door. But there was a frosted glass window between the corridor and the room, the same corridor as now, leading to the toilets. And when she looked through that glass, there were two shapes there, blurred by the frosting, but two shapes, each as solid as the other.

She never told anyone else, either. Not one of that whole run of landlords who would take over and then leave, soon after. It wasn't her place to say anything, even if the company couldn't get managers to stay on at the pub. The regulars would complain that the gov'nors came and went so fast you never got a chance to know them.

They could come and go, but she stayed. She had to stay, no matter what she saw or felt in the Wellington. The Little Back Room.

Even after the chain took over and they turned the Little Back Room into the beer cellar, she still disliked the place. All bright lights, white walls and silver kegs now, but she didn't care, it felt as strange as ever. And then one day something happened that finally made her hand in her notice, the notice she should have given years ago.

She'd left the door open between the corridor and the beer cellar. It was even more stifling since they'd blocked off the windows, filled them in with bricks. The door that led outside to the back of the building was always locked now too, what with all the beer in there. But she still had to clean, and it was trickier than ever, mopping between the big metal kegs, the stored ones and the ones connected to the plastic pipes that led through to the pub. There were so many, and packed so close together, and she mustn't bump the ones lying flat on the racks: the manager, whoever it was, was always after her if she did, shouting at her and saying she was shaking up the sediment, and then the barman couldn't pull the beer at the hand pumps.

If she didn't like the cellar, the rest of the staff were even worse. They never said anything, but they wouldn't go in alone to get ice or fetch bottled drinks off the shelves. If they did come in, it was only when she was there, and then she'd be as bad as them, trying to start up a chat, keep them talking so they'd wait a bit, give her some company. But no one had the time to stay with her, certainly not for the hour or more it took to clean the room, three times a week.

And that's how it was that day, when she was alone and struggling to get her mop between the kegs and under the racks. She felt someone looking, more strongly than ever, someone staring at her from behind, eyes boring into her back.

She turned around and there was this girl, or someone smallish who could've been almost any age.

In a dress. A Victorian dress – well, she couldn't say 'Victorian' for sure, but old-fashioned, down to the ankles. More like a petti-coat, but not fancy. Sort of off-white, very off – a kind of grey, or beige. But the girl herself was grey: that was her colour. Not misty, like that time when Stan Eakins was playing pool, although she did appear to have a sort of mist around her, or to be made of mist – solid mist: she knew that didn't make sense, but she didn't know how else to think of it.

And no shoes. That was the other odd thing, the girl was bare-foot, and her feet were very muddy. In a pub, where they serve food and everything. It was summer, but still, it was a dull day, raining, not that warm.

Somehow, she found her voice. Asked the girl if she was lost, said the toilets were out and that way, but the girl said nothing, nothing at all. She didn't move much either, only lifted her hand up to her mouth, once. And kept staring. First at her, and then it was as if the girl was trying to look around her, past her, as if she was trying to see someone behind her.

She turned quickly and looked, but there was no one. It was bright in the cellar, what with those big tube lights, three, maybe four of them. And the ceiling was white clapboard, reflecting the light off everything. You used to be able to see the roof beams in there, when it was the snug, and there were only side lights. But now it was bright, and the girl was standing in the doorway, in the full glare of the light.

She was staring at the girl, right at her, she couldn't tear her eyes away, and then – she had never been able to put this into words, struggled now, as if for once she had to get it out, get it out of her, once and for all – the next moment she *was* her. There wasn't her and the girl staring at each other any more, just the girl, looking. She was seeing through her eyes, seeing the cellar, the Little Back Room, seeing it as the girl did. Not just from where the girl was standing, though that was part of it. She was seeing the room as she'd never seen it, not through its many changes over the years while she had worked at the Wellington.

She was in a dark, smoky room, with bare stone walls and those big beams, the same beams she knew from the snug. And she could see, clear as anything even in the haze, a large wooden table in the centre of the room, and there was a big fire somewhere to the back. It was no beer cellar or snug; it was more like a kitchen, but it had the strangest smell: not a cooking smell, or dirty dishes, more like … candles, that was it, though there were no candles burning in the room that she could see – or that the girl could see, was how she should put it.

She was terrified: more scared than she had ever been. She wanted to get out, out of the room, out of *her*, but suddenly she wasn't alone; there were things moving about her, shadows, shapes, touching her, prodding at her, pushing. And then they closed in on her, and she wanted to scream. But as she opened her mouth it burst into flame, a white heat that turned her stomach to fire, melting her from the inside out …

And then she was herself again: standing with her mop in the cellar, shivering, shaking, crying, but quietly, big sobs from deep inside moving up and through her whole body. She looked at the door, and saw the girl again, only for an instant. And then the girl left. She didn't see her turn to go or walk out; the girl – disappeared wasn't exactly right, not vanished either. One second the girl was there, right before her eyes again. And then she wasn't.

Chapter 18

Ralph Jenison knew he should be surprised when he heard the constable call out the name 'Anne Armstrong' at the door of his chambers in Trinity House, but somehow he wasn't.

It had been a quiet morning so far, this Wednesday when he was available for the hours specified at the rotation office he kept as Justice of the Peace. Anne Armstrong's accusations had been resoundingly dismissed at the Morpeth Quarter Sessions, so what she was doing here again was beyond him.

It was this sort of thing that made him contemplate if the time had come for him to withdraw from public life. Like his father and grandfather before him, he'd combined success as a merchant adventurer and coal-owner with high civic duty, following his forebears in serving as both Sheriff and Mayor of Newcastle. He'd been admitted to the freedom of the town, chosen as an Alderman by the Municipal Assembly, and appointed Governor of the Hostmen's Company. He was at the very heart of the monopoly controlling the export of coal from the River Tyne and had a senior position among the leading overseas merchants making up the Merchant Adventurer's Company of Newcastle. He was, therefore, a member of the inner elite that effectively governed the town and county of Newcastle.

And yet how was he repaid his service and enterprise? Constant criticisms of the way he conducted his business and maligned regularly for the way he conducted the offices he held. The apparently endless business of Bishop Cosin complaining that he was not enforcing the Conventicle Act as he ought, for example. What did his lordship expect him to do? He knew full well that Dr Robert Jenison, his uncle, a preacher of remarkable ability, managed not only to survive but thrive in the town despite his Puritan sympathies. Was it his fault if the Puritans then assumed that he, Ralph Jenison, had leanings towards Parliament, and elected him to the Shrievalty of Newcastle? And again, was it his fault that after the Restoration the Royalist leaders elected him Mayor of Newcastle, supposing he took their part when all he had done was accept the monarchy as he had accepted the Commonwealth?

As if it was not difficult enough for him to refute being a secret Puritan, he also had to bear the suspicions that he was a closet Catholic, purely because his cousin, another Robert Jenison in fact, in irony compounded upon irony, was a Jesuit priest.

If it weren't for the possibility of a knighthood that was in the offing, he'd happily admit that he'd had enough of municipal matters – this Justice of the Peace business for a start, with Anne Armstrong standing again outside the door to his chambers.

And why him? Why not Sir Richard Stote, Sir Thomas Horsley, James Howard, John Salkeld? Humphrey Mitford, understandably not, but still, why him?

For a moment he felt her eyes on him again, that feeling of being watched which he could not shake as he slipped like a criminal through his own chambers in the dead of night to find that deposition, the one he was determined would not make its way through the processes and procedures of the law. Why, he was never exactly sure, would never be able to say. He knew only that here he was, trembling, yes, his hands actually trembling, in the very building where he should feel most feted and secure.

A few more years – a few more years without the potentially explosive accusations of the Anne Armstrongs of this world, that is – should see him called down to Whitehall, and after he was knighted he'd be able to withdraw completely from public life. But Anne Armstrong was waiting, and with a sigh Ralph Jenison signalled to the constable that she should be shown in.

The girl had a particularly sullen, obstreperous look about her as she stood directly in front of the large desk Ralph Jenison made sure was between them. He glanced at the constable, checking he was at the ready.

'Well, girl, what is it now?'

'Jane Baites,' she said, and before she could get another word out, Ralph Jenison flung up his hands.

'Baites!' he said. 'This is where it all began! This business is done with, do you understand –'

The girl had the effrontery to interrupt him: '*Jane* Baites,' she called out, 'Jane, not *Anne*! Jane Baites of Corbridge, not Anne Baites of Morpeth.'

'What? Another Baites?'

'Yes, Your Worship, sister to Thomas Baites, also once of Corbridge, where he learned his trade of –'

'Stop, stop, girl! I have no interest in this family, other than to know one thing. Is this a new accusation you wish to bring before me?'

'Oh, yes, Your Worship! Jane Baites came to me on Monday last, after the Sessions. It was in my father's house in Corbridge. I saw her walking up to the door and called out, but when I opened it, she was there in the form of a cat, holding out a bridle on her forepaw.'

'The enchanted bridle again,' said Ralph Jenison; 'come, girl, you must accept that I and the other Justices have heard all this –'

'The cat brushed against my legs, Your Worship, and then rose up and filled the room! Oh please, Sir, you must hear me! She breathed upon me and I was struck dead, and fell to the floor ...'

Through his irritation at the repetition, the same scenes, the same words, Ralph Jenison was surprised to find himself catching what appeared to be heartfelt terror breaking through in the girl's voice. All signs of impudence dissolved in the rush of panic propelling her words:

'Lying there I felt Jane Baites put a bridle upon me, again, Sir, again, I was bridled and pulled to my feet, and then ridden upon in the name of the devil –'

'Stop!' The sharpness was deserved, of this he was sure, but again, as he sometimes felt in the Sessions, a genuine note was struck. A smell of fear came off the girl, palpable, crossing the distance between them in a powerful emanation. He found himself looking at his scribe, the constable too, to see if they were registering this, but they stood, as stolid as always, awaiting instruction before they did anything.

Sir James Clavering's face floated up into his thoughts; Sir James, a close political associate when he was aligned with the Puritans and, like himself, a former mayor, forever exposed to ridicule after having a compelling witchcraft case accusation summarily rejected by a grand jury. If he suspected for a moment that somewhere in the girl's outpourings there was a truth, the merest glimmer of a truth, a truth with evidence to support it ... he thought of Sir James. The very detail, the compelling specificities of the information he'd forwarded as the basis for an indictment had been held against him, evidence only of the deponent's delusion and his lack of judgement.

The girl was still speaking, the flood of words apparently endless.

'Be quiet, Anne Armstrong. I will record no information at this time! However ...'

He could barely believe what he heard his own voice saying next, distant, committing him to a course that felt inevitable, unavoidable, inescapable.

'Today is the sixteenth of April. If you return here in five days, on Monday, the twenty-first of April, with – and this I stress as strongly as I can – the people you wish to accuse with you, so that they may hear what you have to say, and answer you. If you do this, I shall constitute a special Session of the Peace.

'But I warn you,' he said, watching her disbelief give way to slow understanding, 'this will be under my own auspices, and

I shall deal with your case summarily. You will have to confront those you accuse, and I will be examining the defendants and victims, giving them every chance to explain.'

Ralph Jenison took some satisfaction in her confusion. She spun around to leave, barely waiting for formal permission to do so, as if fearing he'd change his mind if she delayed for an instant. Her avowals that she would do what he had told her filled the air as she disappeared, the constable still looking at the space she'd occupied a good few moments after she'd gone.

When he raised his eyes it was, noted Ralph Jenison, with a studied effort at avoiding any contact with his; his scribe too, had suddenly found much to write down.

For once he didn't care. He regretted only that he had not used more of his own discretion when the Armstrong woman first came before him. He should have nipped the whole thing in the bud before it was able to flower into this potentially noxious .... Come now, he thought, no need for such florid flights of fancy; this was never his usual habit, but there was something about this girl, already, no doubt, nurturing a garden of trouble.

'Northumberland,' the scribe wrote, 'The Information of Anne Armstrong of Birchesnooke in aforesaid County taken upon Oath 21st day of April 1673.'

He scanned this quickly, noted that he had forgotten to add the deponent's title, and inserted 'Spinster' in the line below. In the instant it took to do this, Justice Jenison indicated to the girl that she could begin speaking. This gave the scribe no time to add who she was appearing before, a definite procedural irregularity, but the Justice seemed happy to proceed with the odd – very odd – omission of his name from the heading given to the deposition.

There was another legal formality the scribe could not, however, ignore. 'The said witness,' he said, 'deposes further ...?'

The questioning look at the Justice provoked an emphatic response. 'No! "Informant sayeth"; that's all we need. I'm assured by this –' he looked at the girl, her mouth still open '– deponent that she brings new charges before us today, and I will treat her evidence in this way, entirely on its own merits. What was rejected in Morpeth at the Quarter Sessions was rejected, and will remain so: new evidence only, girl, new evidence.'

He turned to the clerk. 'I want nothing in these proceedings to connect us to any past appearance; please ensure that this is the case. "Informant sayeth",' taking in the scribe now too, '"Informant sayeth".'

Anne Armstrong began by telling what happened to her in Corbridge, in her father's house on Monday, a week previously. The matter of her evidence being new evidence now settled, the atmosphere in the Justice's chamber took on a perfunctory air.

'Jane Baites came to me on Monday last, after the Sessions,' she said, careful to repeat herself as accurately as she could despite the Justice's attitude. 'It was in my father's house in Corbridge, where the witches have never come to me before. I saw her walking up to the door and called out, but when I opened it, she was there in the form of a cat, holding out a bridle on her forepaw.'

As she spoke, she could not help but be disappointed at how little this special session resembled the grand affair of the Quarter Sessions. Yes, there was the Justice on a slightly raised platform, the clerk, the scribe, the constable ranged about him, but just one of each, pressed in together at the front of a room so much smaller than the castle that it seemed to press in on her.

'The cat brushed against my legs, Your Worship, and then rose up and filled the room ...'

And no crowd, no audience other than those she accused, standing to the side and impatient to be called forward to contradict her. Oh yes, they'd come, as the old man had said they would, forced to clear their names when they'd seen she would not give up, would not go away. It was her word against theirs.

'She breathed upon me and I was struck dead, and fell to the floor. And yet lying there as if dead I felt Jane Baites put a bridle upon me. I was bridled and pulled to my feet, and then ridden upon in the name of the devil, southward ...'

Jane Baites was not among them. The whole affair was nearly abandoned when the others reported that they could not find her. But so eager were they to see off the girl and her accusations that Ralph Jenison decided to go ahead. A message was sent to the bailiff telling him to track down and bring in 'one Jane Baites, of Corbridge', and the business of the day begun.

Anne knew now what to avoid: the riding in wooden dishes and eggshells, the pulling on ropes for food as well, too many accounts of the dancing and singing. These things had become less important to her as well, scarcely more than what the old man called them, tricks to allure her. Since then she'd been wrenched into a hidden world that lurked behind this ordinary existence, where the witches passed among their neighbours under the cover of the mundane things they did, each commonplace another device in the vast deception.

The clerk fussed, the scribe scribbled, the constable all but yawned, and the Justice stared down impassively. She tried to call up her terror, make it real for them, knowing how it would be reduced to a passage or two on the page. The horror of that figure taking shape, the cat brushing past her legs and then rearing up, filling the room, and breathing on her like the breath of God that waited out in the woods, waited behind the stillness that fell upon you, where not a leaf, a twig, a branch moved, until the wave of air came rolling through the forest and everything was bewitched into movement, falling still again as the wind passed, as unconcerned with your terror as it was with the least piece of foliage it had shaken to its core.

She wanted to fall upon her knees, press her face into her apron, hide herself from everything. Instead she did what she had to do: listen to her voice saying one thing, wait to hear another thing altogether read back to her, try to correct what was written down so that it bore some resemblance to what she'd come to tell.

Apr. 21, 1673. Informant sayeth that on Monday last, at night, she, being in her father's house, see one Jane Baites, of Corbridge, come in the forme of a gray catt with a bridle hanging on her foote, and breath'd upon her and struck her dead, and bridled her, and rid upon her in the name of the devill, southward, but the name of the place she does not now remember.

Had she said that, had she said that she did not remember the name of the place? Why could she not remember the name of the place? This is what they wanted, names, places, people.

She had taken a breath then, after saying she was ridden southward. Taken a breath, that she did remember, and then said, more or less as the clerk read back to her, and to all those assembled: 'And after the said Jane allighted and pulled the bridle off her head, and she and the rest had drawne their compass nigh to a bridg end ...'

Justice Jenison's posture did not change, his expression too remained blank, impassive. There was no sudden sitting up, no exchange of looks with the clerk, no raising of a questioning eye-brow. He simply let the scribe write on just as she was left to talk on – 'they sett themselves downe, and bending towards the stone, repeated the Lord's prayer backwards ...'

And talk on she did, although anyone paying close attention would have seen that she looked more and more surprised that no one was stopping her, asking what it was now that she was reporting.

'And the devil placed a stone in the middle of the compasse,' the clerk read back to her, to her and all those gathered before the Justice.

And, when they had done, the devill, in the forme of a little black man and black cloaths, calld of one Isabell Thompson, of Slealy, widdow, by name, and required of her what service she had done him. She replyd she had gott power of the body of one Margarett Teasdale. And after he had danced with her he dismissed her, and call'd of one Thomasine, wife of Edward

Watson, of Slealy, who confessed to the devill that she had likwise power of the body of the said Margaret Teasdale, and would keepe power of her till she gott her life.

Isabell Thompson, of Slaley, and Thomasine, wife of Edward Watson, of Slaley.

Slaley, of course, Slaley, that was the name of the place to which she was ridden, the name she could not remember at first, remembered now as she said the names of the witches. South of Corbridge as a bird would fly, but not stopping there at Slaley set high on a ridge, no, following the road as it went past the village, down the bank to the small bridge over Reaston Burn – small, yes, but it served well enough for the witches to gather at and cast their circle, watching the devil place a stone at its centre, bending towards the stone, repeating the Lord's Prayer backwards. And then dancing, one by one, with the little black man in black clothes, confessing as they did so the services they had done for him.

Slaley, yes Slaley, from where they would fly to Muggleswick, then on to Edmundbyers, and Eddysbridge, and on around to Stocksfield and Prudhoe, then to the Riding and then back again to Slaley, the villages themselves making up something of a rough circle. A circle of villages connected by the gatherings of the witches, a circle like the one she had drawn for her mark writ large upon the countryside. 'The "Compasse Round", as she'd been told, 'which awakens the powers in the land itself.'

He would not be drawn, he would not.

This was, Ralph Jenison realised, nothing like anything Anne Armstrong had reported before, this talk of compass and stone and profane prayers. He caught her looking at him too, as if willing him to stop her, ask her questions, make her clarify, explain, spell it all out.

No, he would not.

Why, though, he wondered, did the girl suddenly introduce this kind of demonology into her testimony? There was no previous indication that she'd been aware of these more learned levels of magic, a realm not even dealt with by leading witch-hunting demonologists in England. The Scottish King James himself, in his *Daemonologie*, called the circles and triangles and other shapes used in witchcraft curious but 'altogether unprofitable.'

Jenison did not give in to these musings, was determined not to. The records need only show that what the deponent said had been duly taken down. Those she accused were, in any event, clamouring for their turn.

'And further she saith not,' he said to the scribe, gesturing for the page to be passed to Anne for her mark.

Ralph Jenison was about to append his own signature when he noticed the mark Anne Armstrong had put next to her name.

There, instead of the circle with its heavy dot in the centre that the girl had used to identify herself, between the 'Anne' and the 'Armstrong' written by the scribe, was instead a squiggle, a shaky line.

He was surprised enough to look more closely. At first he could make nothing of it, but then he thought of the way the clerk passed the document to the deponent. He turned the page sideways, and the unsteady line appeared as two conjoined arches, two arches approximating the letter M?

This made no sense. The girl had clearly gone out of her way to change her mark, but to what effect? He looked harder, squinting at the page. Whatever the mark was, it was too crudely written for him to make out.

He hoped the girl was not trying to get above her station in life. In his experience a smattering of learning, a little reading and writing, made the poor self-conceited and difficult to govern, apt to embrace every new doctrine, heresy, schism, sect and faction. 'Our late unhappy troubles' – the term he used, hopefully inoffensive to all sides, when required to refer to the Civil Wars in public – had raised the spectre of a world turned upside down. Educating the poor, not to mention poor women, was a risky, dangerous matter that could only add to the undoing of the natural order of things.

And then he remembered: the devil, he had read, always asks if you wish to become his servant, and if you do, demands your signature on a contract signed with free consent. If the prospective witch cannot write she may sign, just as she would before a Justice, with a cross or circle or any other mark – unless the devil puts his hand on hers and guides her hand in signing her name ...

He turned to the deponent, who stared back, blank, implacable. He looked down again to the page, the mark. Was it a sign of the devil himself, steering her hand across the page? Or was it merely an inked line, ill drawn through haste?

High Riggs, Riding Mill

Did Ralph Jenison suddenly sit up? Did he exchange looks with the clerk, raise a questioning eyebrow? Did he halt the proceedings, start asking Anne questions? Or did he let the scribe write on as Anne Armstrong talked on – 'they sett themselves downe, and bending towards the stone, repeated the Lord's prayer backwards'. And did Anne look more and more surprised that no one was stopping her or taking notice of what she was saying?

The records – transcription and original alike – show only that what she said was duly taken down, with no break or querying, as if it is yet more of the same information she has given before. The deposition could not have been taken down in a more perfunctory manner. It was brief, almost dismissive. The scribe, possibly the same man Jenison had employed in February – the handwriting, though in the generic secretary script, was similar enough – was probably as bored as the Justice, hearing the opening lines of Anne's information: the bridle, being breathed upon, struck dead, ridden to a distant destination, usually somewhere with a bridge-end, the bridle being removed, the gathering of witches ...

But then I leaned in towards the screen, checked what came next in what was reproduced there against the photocopies I had made at the Archives as a back-up, and then sat back.

This was, I realised, nothing like anything Anne had reported before.

I needed someone to share this with, check if I was correct. I'd seen no one since I returned from London, and the only person who sprang to mind now was Mrs Kerr, my neighbour Mable Kerr, who I'd heard about but not, as yet, met. I picked up my photocopies of the deposition given on 21 April and its transcription and walked out on to High Riggs.

Three doors down, I rang the doorbell at Anchusa – the ten houses with their well-groomed gardens making up the street where I live all have names rather than numbers. Mrs Lumley greeted me cheerfully enough, but seemed a little thrown when I asked if Mrs Kerr was in.

'Mrs Kerr? You mean my mother? Yes, she's here; not many people ask after her, nearly all her friends have passed on. She tends to keep to herself these days. But do come in, I'll go and check on her, see if she's up to chat. No, no trouble, she lives in the back part of the house, her own flat really.'

Mrs Lumley's voice disappeared down a passageway and she was still talking when she reappeared.

'Come through this way,' she was saying, 'mother's happy to see you, and it'd be better if you two chatted in her living room. It's small but very nice with glass doors into the garden.'

Mrs Kerr was perched on the edge of a hardback chair, impeccably turned out in a smart, well-cut blue two-piece suit, stockings, sensible yet not unattractive shoes, her white hair full-bodied but pulled back into a precise bun, her hands neatly folded in her lap. She was trim rather than thin, had been a handsome woman in her day, still was really. A stark contrast to her daughter, larger, spectacles awry, bustling about in her around-the-house clothes.

Silence settled on the room in the wake of Mrs Lumley's leaving. I became aware of the sound of the birds and the breeze moving through the big trees at the end of the garden.

Mrs Kerr spoke first. 'You enjoy living in Mountain Ash.'

It was a statement – I could tell immediately that she was a person who tended to talk in statements. Her voice was thin but clear, fluted; given her trim form, tiny hands and sharp, bright eyes, the term birdlike had never seemed more appropriate.

'Black-luggie, lammer-bead,' she said, startling me. 'Rowan tree, and reed thread, put the witches to their speed.

'You know the mountain ash is also known as the rowan? It's an old superstition that rowan trees ward off witches. A twig of the rowan carried in the hand preserves the bearer from witchcraft, or a bunch of ash keys, you'll also hear it said.

'*Sorbus aucuparia Asplenifolia* – one of our more beautiful cut-leaved native British trees, especially in autumn: stunning colours, all that purple red and orange; and the clusters of bright red berries make excellent food for the birds.

'I see the rowan next to your house is gone. It's a pity to have a house called Mountain Ash without a mountain ash in the yard. But I know the winds that blow straight up High Riggs can be exceptionally strong, so no doubt it was blown down before you came.

'But what was it you wanted to know?'

I wasn't sure how to begin, and Mrs Kerr filled the silence.

'You've been sent to me because I am the last surviving oracle on the history of the village,' she said, cutting through my awkwardness. 'It's true that years back I did write one, but it wasn't all my work, you know, *Riding Mill: The History of a Village*. Abigail Allen, she was the one who had it all in her head. It's Abigail you should be speaking to, but she's dead now. So are most of the others. We were members of the Riding Mill Women's Institute, you see, a busy branch with our monthly meetings of talks and demonstrations, drama, craft, cooking, community projects.'

Mrs Kerr stopped, looking out intently into the garden. 'That, I think, is a nuthatch at our birdfeeder. We're lucky to see that around here, they're usually further south: a lovely flash of yellow and grey, aren't they?'

I took the chance and jumped in: had they looked into the case of Anne Armstrong and the Riding witches in their history of the village?

'Oh yes, only in passing in our little publication though. That story has been told so often that no one takes it seriously now, and it was well documented elsewhere. Anne was, I've always thought, treated exceptionally badly.'

'Why do you say that?'

'Well, you have to look at the evidence, and not all of it is in the records.' She pointed to the copies of the documents in my hand.

I passed her a copy of the transcription of the deposition taken on 21 April, trying to give her a few moments to read but barely able to wait before saying, 'Do you see, there's the usual business about the bridle, being ridden somewhere, the witches gathering. But then,' I said – Mrs Kerr seemingly having no trouble with the context for all of this – 'instead of flying animal, swinging on ropes, food appearing, and witches dancing to the girl's singing, Anne Armstrong says, "she and the rest had drawne their compasse nigh to a bridg end" –'

'... and the devil placed a stone in the middle of the compasse,' read Mrs Kerr, her voice chiming with mine.

Mable Kerr turned her gaze to the garden.

'This isn't just some country girl imagining –' I began, but Mrs Kerr cut me short.

'I would agree, but let me look at this more carefully. And what else have you got there?' she asked, holding out a hand for my copy of the original document.

She read over it for some minutes, and then looked at me directly, steadily. 'How clever of you to track these down. I've only seen the transcriptions before, but they were enough for me to realise that what we have here is a glimpse into the sophisticated magic of the Renaissance magus.'

She smiled at my surprise. 'Oh, we were rather interested, our little group at the WI, in country lore, spell craft, folk wisdom. We dedicated a good number of our sessions to this, with quite a bit of reading and lively discussion.'

Again, that disconcerting wandering of her eyes out into the dappled green of her garden, her gaze taking in too the heavy shade within the stand of, what was it, hazel, birch, elder – was there a rowan among them? – just beyond the lawn?

She came back to the papers in her hand and read on for some time.

When she looked up again, I dared to speak. 'So why did Anne, in her increasingly canny awareness of what the Justices counted as evidence, suddenly introduce this kind of demonological activity into her testimony? There is no indication in the previous depositions that she'd been aware of these more learned levels of magic, and yet here in these three or four lines we suddenly get a hint, a tantalising glimpse, that she is aware of a whole other realm of witchcraft.'

'I can only presume,' said Mrs Kerr, 'that someone thought it important that Anne know about these things; someone who would have told her about, or possibly read to her from *The Key of Solomon*, or *The Lesser Key of Solomon*. These were popular seventeenth-century grimoires containing conjurations and invocations to summon up demons, including instructions on how to draw the Magical Circle.'

I had difficulty hiding my amazement. Mrs Kerr was smiling slightly as she went on, eyes still fixed on me.

'Nine feet across, with the Divine Names written on its circumference, the "Compasse Round" that Jane and the others drew would have been. Now, do you think this included Anne? It is unclear to me from the text if the "she" in "she and the rest" is Jane Baites or Anne herself. Even if she did not help draw the circle, was she standing within it? This would have been, you see, the working site marked out for the unhallowed practices of the witches.'

Mrs Kerr's eyes were drifting towards the garden again. 'The Compass is a tool for awakening the powers and forces of a place, and for creating a conduit between what is Seen and what is Unseen ...

'Or so the textbooks would tell us,' she said, abruptly bringing her attention back to the room, and me. 'Why don't you take that one up there, on the bookshelf behind you: no, the one to the left of that, *English Folkloric Witchcraft*, that will be enough for you to be getting on with, if you want some idea about Anne's circles and stones.'

I picked out the book from a small selection, mostly local history as far as I could see, although I did notice a copy of Sir Walter Scott's *Letters on Demonology and Witchcraft*.

'You're welcome to borrow that as well,' said Mrs Kerr. 'But what is it that you want out of this? What is it that you really want to know?'

I turned to her, found I had nothing to say. Before I could formulate some kind of bland response, she spoke again.

'Forgive me, that is an intrusion, and I'm satisfied to know I've been some help.'

There was nothing obvious, only a slight slackening in her figure that told me it was time to go. Picking up my photocopies and the books, I made as short a leave-taking as was polite, seeing my own way out and back on to High Riggs.

That evening, Kate Lumley was closing the door to her mother's room: have you got everything you need, she was asking, are you sure you don't need any help undressing, your nightdress is right there, on the bed. Well, goodnight, are you sure? I don't want to come in one morning and find you lying on the floor, stiff as a board. No, I know you don't want to be any trouble. Of course, change into your nightdress, tuck yourself in and sleep well now, Mother, I'll be in bright and early with your tea ...

She pulled the door closed. Mable Kerr sat bolt upright on her hard-backed chair, as she had sat through all of last night, and the night before, dead still, neat as a pin and straight as an arrow in the clothes that her daughter had not yet noticed she had not changed, making no effort to move towards the bed she had not slept in, reaching over only towards her reading lamp and clicking off the switch.

She sat there, the pale light of the night coming in through the double glass doors opening into the garden, locked into the position that would see her through this night too, her feet in their sturdy shoes placed precisely together, her hands folded in her lap, her head held up straight.

She stared out into the garden, the well-trimmed lawn shimmering slightly in the faint glow of a quarter moon, the line of shrubs marking the point at which the grass disappeared down into the darkness of the thick overhang of trees. It was another of those deliciously quiet nights on High Riggs, and she had the glass doors open, enjoying the edge on the air and the call of the owls in the woods beyond the fields.

Her daughter would find her the next morning fully dressed, back straight, feet together, hands in her lap, sitting on her chair arranged precisely as she had left her the night before. My, you're up early, she'd say, ready for the day already. And Mable would give a small smile, nod as her daughter unclasped the hands so neatly folded in her lap, and took them in hers as she helped her mother up. People presume stiffness at her age, the audible crackle of locked joints, dried-out bones, papery skin as one changes position.

But that would be tomorrow. For now, she was reasonably comfortable, hearing her daughter settling down to watch the television in the living room. She looked out into the dark, expectantly.

Come in, my dear, come in out of the garden, she said; there's no need to be scared – they've gone now, they are long, long gone. Sit there, take the comfy chair. Are you hungry? There's the tea and biscuits Kate puts on my bedside table every night. I don't seem to have any interest in eating and drinking any more, or sleeping. Help yourself, Anne, we've a long night ahead of us.

Chapter 19

Apr. 21, 1673, before Ralph Jenison. Esq.

Isabell Thompson and Thomasine Watson, furious and backed up by equally furious family and friends, were more than ready to let loose a tirade of denials. But the constable held them back, not your turn yet, he said, the witnesses first, if you don't mind, he said as the clerk called for 'Mark Humble, of Slaley, Tailor.'

And what information did Mark Humble, of Slaley, Tailor, have to give?

Informeing saith that betwixt 7 and 8 yeares agoe, walking towards the high end of that town called Slealy, Mett one Isabell Thompson walking downward, and when she was gone past him, she being formerly suspected of Witchcraft, he lookt back over his shoulder, and did see the said Isable Thompson hould up her hands towards his back. And when he came [two words scribbled out] home, he grew very sick, and tould the people in the house that he was afraid Isabell Thompson had done him Wrong, and for some 3 or 4 yeares continued very ill by fitts in a most violent manner, to the sight and Admiration of all neighbours, and whilst he continued in this distemper, the said Isabell Thompson after she heard of this [report?] came to his house, and said it was reported she had bewitchd him, she tould him if it were so, it would soone be knowne and further saith that his mother [Margaret Humble inserted above line] then lyeing not [several words scribbled out] well [inserted] said Isabell Thompson tooke some of her haire [several words scribbled out] to Medicine her and further saith not.

Thus taken on oath by the scribe. This deposition would need considerable tidying up, Ralph Jenison observed as he looked over the document with all its crossings out, insertions, and smudges.

He was bemused. He'd expected more from the witness she'd called, Mark Humble, tailor. A strange look, given seven or eight years before?

He wished Margaret Humble were present, and wondered why she wasn't. From her son's evidence, she was no longer ill, the unspoken reason being Thompson's taking some of her hair to medicine her: Mark Humble came close to saying as much. Jenison was sure it was the girl's presence that stopped him confirming this. She had probably also made sure his mother was not present to bear this out.

Not much of a witness on Armstrong's behalf, but there was another, Margaret Teasdale herself, the alleged victim.

The clerk put her under oath, and she blinked up at the Justice, twisting one of the ties from her bodice in her gnarled hands. There was something childlike in her brown, lined face, the eyes unnaturally bright, and Ralph Jenison wondered if she were quite sane.

'Well?'

'I've been sick,' she said.

'Yes, and what has this –'

'Since Michaelmas last, very sick.'

'And?'

Margaret Teasdale looked around, blinking.

'Very sick,' she said, 'but since Christmas in a more violent manner than before.'

Ralph Jenison's impatience must have been evident.

'And on Saturday I was advised to get blood from Isabell Thompson –'

He could see where this was going now: drawing blood was a much-used method of breaking witches' spells.

'The Isabell Thompson here present?'

'Yes,' said Margaret Teasdale, pausing. And then adding suddenly, 'and Thomasine Watson. *That* Thomasine Watson.' She pointed a steady finger.

'You were "advised",' said Ralph Jenison. 'You were advised by whom?'

'The girl, Anne Armstrong,' said Margaret Teasdale, bright-eyed and blinking.

'Where?'

'In Slaley,' said Margaret Teasdale, as if surprised she should be anywhere else.

'And how far is it from ...' Ralph Jenison looked at the papers on his desk, 'Corbridge to Slaley?'

'Six or seven miles,' said Margaret Teasdale as Anne Armstrong called out, 'Two hours, Your Worship.'

Ralph Jenison gave a warning look.

'And what did you do upon this advice?' he asked Margaret Teasdale.

'The advice was to get blood of Isabell Thompson and Thomasine Watson, and I did.'

Something in her tone and demeanour made Ralph Jenison look again at Margaret Teasdale. She was no longer twisting the cloth in her hands, and small, fragile as she was, he saw a firmness, a strength in her that he'd entirely missed.

'You were advised and you did?'

'Did so accordingly,' she responded.

'You did so accordingly,' he said, 'and what transpired thereafter?'

Margaret Teasdale again looked mildly surprised.

'Since that time I have been much better,' she said, as if thanking him for having the courtesy to ask, 'and more able to get about.'

She gave a satisfied look, her recovery being enough to serve as good evidence of bewitchment.

'And further saith not,' said Ralph Jenison to the scribe, indicating that the page should be passed to the witness for her mark and then brought to him.

He was taken aback to see, instead of the usual shape of some kind, the signature of 'margaret tesdall' written firmly and in a good if basic hand on the right side of the page. Not as he would have spelled her name, and no capitals, but clear, firm letters.

He looked up at Margaret Teasdale, standing before him with a pleased expression on that face it was so difficult to assign an age to, with its sharp eyes and deeply scored lines.

He waved her away, and turned, reluctantly, to the two accused.

Their long-suppressed outrage filled the chamber in a double cacophony backed by a discordant chorus of supporters and detractors. Constable and clerk weighed into the tussling group, extracting the two accused and laying about them as they demanded silence and order. The scribe was forced to join them in their efforts, with Ralph Jenison issuing loud threats of expulsion to any who did not control themselves.

When order of some sort was achieved, Isabell Thompson and Thomasine Watson stood before his raised desk. It was established that a constable had been dispatched to find Jane Baites, but that in the meantime the two defendants present would be examined. The clerk indicated that Isabell Thompson should step forward first, and the instant she did so she began shouting.

Jenison was forced to raise his voice but it was an unequal contest, and the constable achieved more effect with a few swift blows.

'Now,' said Jenison, every inch the most dignified of Justices once he was able to stop shouting, 'you have heard the accusation of witchcraft and the witnesses who have testified under oath against you. You are now to state your case.

'You will give evidence unsworn: if you are innocent, you ought to be able to prove it, and an oath will only put you under compulsion. And if you are guilty, you will take perjury with you to your execution.

'But I tell you now that when those who are guilty speak for themselves, their speech, their gestures, their countenance, the whole manner of their defence, discloses their guilt.'

The two women stood sullenly, wanting only leave to rage against Anne Armstrong. 'So, I exhort you to stand in fear of God and tell the truth.'

The clerk read the charge. Without waiting for an opening question from the Justice, Isabell Thompson launched a withering attack. Thomasine Watson was unable to restrain herself from joining in, sometimes in support of her neighbour, but more often throwing in any line of assault that occurred to her.

For her part, Anne Armstrong at first stood back, remote in an air of quiet superiority. The same could not be said of Mark Humble, incensed by the idea of his absent mother being found guilty of trafficking in witchcraft. Margaret Teasdale took to an insistent cooing about the state of her health, fluttering her eyes and hands all the while. The girl gave in too, soon enough, dropping her haughtiness to begin giving every bit as good as she got.

Ralph Jenison sat back and watched his special session dissolve into a frenzied altercation. Clerk and scribe stood motionless too, quills unmoving.

On the page, the scribe had written 'Northumberland' in the top left-hand corner, and added the briefest of headings while the Justice was introducing the proceedings. 'The Examination of Isabell Thompson of Slealy', he'd written, 'taken this 21st day of April 1673'. He'd drawn a short line to mark off the heading from the body of the examination, and was taking a moment to squeeze in the omitted 'widow' after Thompson's name when the scene erupted.

Bridge, blood, devil, power, service, body, danced, confessed, life, endless liar, truth, dids and didn'ts, insults, aspersions, vulgarities and obscenities enough to bind over a whole village or several villages … it blurred into mayhem, escalating by the minute until Ralph Jenison looked at his officials and indicated they should do something. At first their efforts simply contributed to the chaos, but when other members of the Trinity House staff were brought in as reinforcements, order of a sort began to emerge.

The echoes of abuse were still fading when Ralph Jenison called out, 'Isabell Thompson!'

The constable pushed a florid-faced woman forward.

'Where were you on Monday night last?' Jenison asked.

'In bed, Your Worship, and –'

'Enough,' said Ralph Jenison. 'And on the Friday night after?'

'In bed –'

'Enough. And do you deny you were in the company with the devil on both those nights?'

'She who says so is a liar and –'

'And do you deny you practised witchcraft upon the body of this woman, Margaret Teasdale?'

'Lies and slander, I never did Margaret Teasdale any harm, nor did I confess to the devil or dance with him –'

'Scribe, write this: "Being asked where she was on Monday last being the fourteenth instant and upon the Friday after says she was in bed both nights and denies she was in company with the devil or" –'

'A moment, Your Worship,' said the scribe, trying to keep up.

'Come on, man: "or practised any witchcraft upon the body of Margaret Teasdale, and further denies all" –'

'The hair, Your Worship, I neither took not touched a hair of the head of this man's mother,' Isabell Thompson burst out, 'nor did I –'

'– or that she had any hair of Margaret Humble, you can put that in,' said Ralph Jenison, pausing a moment to compose what was to follow.

'Let's see, "and further denies all and every one of the circumstances mentioned in two" – no, there'll be more, "*several* Informations Exhibited upon Oath by Anne Armstrong of Birches Nooke spinster and Mark Humble" – where is this place, yes, Slaley "and further" –' he ignored Isabell Thompson's furious waving and attempts to speak '– "and further saith not. *Capt coram* etc."

'Pass it to me, scribe,' he said, signing rapidly and handing the document to the clerk. 'You've heard what went into your deposition, woman, so make your mark, let's be done with it, quickly now.

'Step back, woman, you've had your say.

'Clerk, give the page to the scribe. Get along, hurry. Now scribe, "The examination of Thomasine Watson, wife of Edward Watson, of Slaley, taken upon etc.", put that down.

'Clerk, bring forward Thomasine Watson.'

Ralph Jenison did the same with Thomasine Watson, asking in rapid succession where she was on the night in question, if she'd been with the devil, and if she'd bewitched the victim. He cut short her numerous attempts to expand upon her answers as well as the persistent interventions of her husband and then asked the clerk to read out what the scribe had taken down.

'The information of Thomasine Watson,' began the clerk, catching the mistake at the same moment the Justice did. 'The *examination*, man, not information – go on, correct it, correct it,' said an irritated Ralph Jenison. 'I want no mistakes; this is a statement given by someone accused of a crime, testimony given under oath, so *examination*, not a charge or complaint, which is "information".'

Stung, the scribe scribbled out the offending word and wrote the correct one above it, then handed the document back to the clerk.

'The *examination* of Thomasine Watson, etc.,' the clerk read out.

'Being asked where she was on Monday last being the fourteenth instant says she was at home in her bed, denies that ever she was in the devil's company or ever put or practised any witchcraft upon the body of Margaret Teasdale and further denies all and every, what is this?, every *one of* the circumstances mentioned in an – get along, man, you can do better – information – good, correct here at least – exhibited upon oath by Anne Armstrong and further saith not.'

'Right, good enough, *Capt Coram* me and pass it to me, there we are, signed, and now to the defendant for her mark ...'

Thomasine Watson was still trying to speak as the clerk's finger guided the quill held clumsily in her hand to the bottom right of the page, her attempt at a circle doubling over itself messily as the page was taken away.

Three bad attempts at circles today, thought Ralph Jenison, as he looked over the finalised deposition.

Witnesses and accused done, he turned back to the deponent.

'Anne Armstrong,' he said, 'what have you to say to what you have heard?'

How could she respond? These perfunctory denials were trivialising her accusations, making nonsense of them, of her.

In her pause it was evident to Ralph Jenison that she was casting about, looking for something more solid.

At several of the witches' meetings, she began, she had seen –

'This is new information?' asked Ralph Jenison.

When she nodded, he gestured to the scribe, who picked up a new piece of paper and began again, 'Northumberland' in the top left, and then rapidly, 'The Information of Anne Armstrong of Birches Nooke in the aforesaid County Spinster taken upon Oath on 21st April 1673,' a sweep of the pen, then 'Informant saith that' ...

'– at several of their meetings I have seen Michael Aynsley and Margaret his wife,' said Anne.

'Michael Aynsley of the Riding and his wife Margaret? But we have heard of them before, several times, if I am not mistaken.'

'In the house of John Newton of the Riding and at Allensford too, Your Worship,' said the girl, 'but now prisoners in His Majesty's gaol.'

'Prisoners in His Majesty's gaol? We jailed no one to await trial for witchcraft at the Sessions.'

The girl stared back at him, her face a perfect blank. There are other things a person might be accused of, other people to report to, it seemed to say.

Jenison knew that Sheriff Morton delighted in levying fines upon dissenters and binding them over to the Assizes, so if the Aynsleys had been caught up with the nonconformists while in Newcastle, they could expect to stay in the gaol in the castle until the summer when the circuit judges came through.

'Well,' he said, more to his officials than the girl, 'we will not be expecting them to come forward for cross examination for witchcraft or anything else, will we.

'Michael and Margaret Aynsley, then. And,' he asked, knowing from experience by now that it was unlikely the list would stop there, 'who else?'

Anne Armstrong gave him an odd look. 'And Jane Baites, of Corbridge,' she said.

'Of course,' said Ralph Jenison, 'Jane Baites of Corbridge, who has also not been able to grace us with her presence as yet.'

'I saw Michael Aynsley and Margaret his wife and Jane Baites ride upon James Anderson of Corbridge – a chapman, Your Worship, a chapman – to their meetings, and hank him to the stump of a tree while they were at their sports. And when they had done, they rode him homeward.'

'And this James Anderson, this chapman, this merchant of Corbridge, is also not among us today, is he, constable?

'Well, no further cross-examinations today then. "And further saith not," scribe. Clerk, have the deposer make her mark and then pass the deposition to me.'

And there it was again, that squiggle, that shaky line. Or could it be two letters run together?

Ralph Jenison raised his eyes from those two letters, possible to guess at if you knew what you were looking for, this girl growing into her own self, given form and shape by the devil himself: 'A. A.'

'Anne Armstrong,' he said, speaking more firmly than he felt, 'are you done with your accusations?'

Chapter 20

He had forgotten about Jane Baites. It was only because he had to sort out some problem with the transfer of Trinity House to his ownership that he was in his chambers when she was announced.

He could, he supposed, have simply sent her way, but he did not want any unfinished business lingering on from this case. Besides, this was not a woman to be dismissed lightly. She spoke politely but firmly of the time she was investing in this litigation process and the cost of being called to the Justice's chambers in the town. It's not as if she was going to be given anything for her labour, she said, and it takes up days of my time going up and down from Corbridge.

Ralph Jenison was so thrown by her attitude that he almost neglected to remind her that she had been accused of witchcraft, a felony which carried a sentence of death. Jane Baites simply smiled and said that she'd heard the outcome of all that Armstrong girl's nonsense. She did wish to clarify the issue, understanding it was so serious a matter to *some*, and here she was.

Jenison did not have the room arranged for a session, petty, special or otherwise, and she had taken a chair opposite his usual working desk. He wondered who the *some* were and why she felt she was not to be included among them, but he had the odd feeling that he should not cause Jane Baites any further loss of her valuable time.

Ralph Jenison called for his scribe and clerk, and when they were settled in, began with his standard opening question.

Before he'd finished, Jane Baites was speaking: 'On Monday, "the fourteenth instant", as you put it, Your Worship, I was in bed, as all honest women should be. And, while I'm at it, I deny that I was in the company of the devil at that or any other time, and

I deny everything else that wicked young girl has said about me. Other than that, I have nothing further to add.'

It was clear that Jane Baites had heard from the other accused how their testimony was handled and, with a hint of mockery so faint she could not be reproached for it, delivered hers in the same fashion. It suited Ralph Jenison, so he asked nothing further, and it took a matter of moments for the scribe to get the examination down in the required formulation. He looked over the document quickly and then gave it to the clerk, who read it out to Jane Baites and then passed it to her for her mark.

When the document was given back to him for his signature, Ralph Jenison was surprised again in what was turning out to be a morning of surprises.

Jane Baites had signed for herself, and not with some clumsy attempt at writing her name in basic print. She had appended only her initials, an elegant intertwining of J and B beautifully executed, the pen handled with ease and mastery as she wrote the letters with grace and the lightest of touches.

He was irritated that such a pleasing piece of writing was smeared by the clerk as he passed the page back before the ink was quite dry. He looked at Jane Baites with increased respect. Such a signature spoke of someone who could read and write with great facility, able to bring an aesthetic touch to her script. He was impressed, despite himself. 'A learned woman is like a comet,' he'd been heard to quote, 'that bodes mischief when it appears.'

As for Jane Baites, she sat, hands crossed in her lap, with every appearance of self-satisfaction. Was that an almost cat-like ease in the way she held herself?

And then, before he quite knew it, Jane Baites had dismissed herself. Ralph Jenison sat back in his chair, looking at the place she'd just vacated. He was lost in thought for some time. Had he made a misjudgement somewhere in this case?

If there was any single person who'd come before his bench whom he suspected could throw some light on the girl's testimony, it was Jane Baites. No other deponent had given their initials as a signature – only the Armstrong girl, who was clearly trying to mimic something she had seen elsewhere.

He sat for a while longer meditating on the morning, despite his best intentions. And then somewhere in his musings, a picture began to take shape in his mind, nothing clear, a hazy picture at best, but a picture of a door being opened, opened to reveal a woman with a feline smile, purring a greeting in a self-assured, contented way.

In the woman's hands was not a bridle, but a book, a large, impressive-looking book. And then he could see the girl being pressed back on a rude bed in a corner of the room, with the woman leaning over her. She wasn't breathing on her, as the girl had reported; she had the book open at her chest, and was reading to her.

Close, very close, her breath indeed to be felt upon the girl's face, the words she read those from some ancient grimoire, perhaps. He had heard of such books, even been shown a copy of *The Lesser Key of Solomon* once. He recalled the frisson with which he glanced at its elaborate illustrations of pentacles, magic circles, and triangles, the conjurations, invocations, and curses to summon and constrain spirits of the dead and demons and compel them to do the one's will, its descriptions of how to find stolen items, become invisible, gain favour and love, and so on.

Would the woman bending over the girl have told her of, read to her, the elaborate preparations necessary for working with such things, the numerous items used in the ceremonies, the appropriate materials marked with a specific set of magical symbols, and blessed with specific words? Of which, of course, the girl could only remember the compass and the stone, and the hoary old belief in the Lord's Prayer being recited backwards.

Did the woman say, Come, Anne, they have dismissed you now, they did not believe you. So is this not the time to be gathered up into the community proper? Come in from the outer circle; it has not been a year and a day, but our protector feels that you are ready. Come with us tonight, let me ride you one last time to your initiation. Hereafter, we can ride James Anderson, that upstanding merchant who wishes to join our circle, and when we are done with our sports, imagine, we can ride him home again after ...

Ralph Jenison would not see Anne Armstrong again. He would not speak of her either, although if the truth were told he never felt entirely free of her. For the rest of his term as a Justice of the Peace, he half-expected that a constable would arrive at the door to his chambers and announce her name.

It was with a sense of inevitability that, some months later, he did hear her name. His clerk was placing a rough-looking page before him; it had turned up in one of the piles of paperwork that the law seemed to generate in endless quantities. Unattached to any particular case, undated and poorly written, with no heading either, there was no indication it had ever been included in court proceedings of any kind.

'Worship full Sur,' it began, the next few words faded and inde-cipherable. Straining hard, Ralph Jenison picked up the sentence at '... to satisfie you that hir Dame Mabell fular sent Anarms trong to Stocksfield to seek eggs whereas Cuthbert Newton and' – the next word was illegible – 'will witness that she was there at Stocks field seeking egs whereas it was denied by An foster that Ever she came theare ...'

The eggs, back to those damned eggs. A witness, or witnesses, confirming the egg story, at least as far as Anne Armstrong having been sent to buy them. Nothing of disagreeing about the price or her head being read, however.

'... wereas she did affirm to our hearing,' the sentence rambled on, heedless of syntax,

that theare was a box stud betwixt[t] the Cubbort and the bed that she kept wine in and other things that she gote at theare meatings she hir selfe kould not denie but the box stud theare and the rest of hir nighbours did acknowledge it was as the wensch had saide whitch we can all witness to be truth so attest your humble serva[n]t.

The letter was signed by a William Armstrong, and two Newtons, along with a Selby and a Browne.

None of Anne Armstrong's family, paternal or maternal, had turned up at any of her appearances to support her. Had this letter been sent in lieu of their attendance? Was William a brother, cousin, or uncle to Archibald Armstrong? How were Cuthbert and Hilbert Newton related to each other and, for that matter, to John Newton, whose house in the Riding, Jenison remembered, had served as a venue for one of the witches' feasts? Was John Newton there or was he, like Thomas Errington, away from his home when it was put to these purposes?

And whoever they were, what had they seen? A phrase, a phrase like many others that continued to float up unbidden into his mind out of the girl's testimony, drifted now into his conscious-ness: 'When they had eaten,' Anne had said, 'she that was last drew the table and kept the reversions.'

'She that was last.' And then, abruptly, at last, Ralph Jenison understood: Anne was saying that from the first she had *joined* the others in touching the rope and feasting on what appeared on the table; it was *she* who was last in doing this. It was Anne herself then who had taken the 'reversions' – 'wine and other things' – home, home to Dame Fouler's, where she'd hidden them in the one small private place belonging to herself, a box 'stood' between a cup-board and her bed, a hidden box it seemed that all the neighbours knew about.

This, then, was the evidence of her relations. None of the grand events she'd claimed to have witnessed, just leftover food. Here was solid evidence – a partially eaten leg of a capon with its plum broth, a gnawed piece of beef, broken bits of cheese, partially drunk bottles of sack and ale to go along with the wine, bearing out that 'it was as the wench had said.'

What had Thomas Potts said of the Lancashire trials? 'Who but witches can be proofes, and so witnesses of the doings of witches.'

All that business of the ceremony, the compass and stone, taking part in the bowing and blasphemy. And now the leftover food and drink – evidence of the truly appalling thought: that she *was* one of them, one of the witches, the Riding witches. Betraying them, she had been, all along, accusing, betraying herself.

And he, finding the accused innocent, had found Anne Armstrong innocent. What he had listened to, rejected as a 'true bill', declared 'not found', stamped '*Ignoramus*', was not simply a denunciation. It was also a confession.

Chapter 21

There was no way back. Accusations like these could not be withdrawn, and would not be forgotten or forgiven. Less than three weeks later Anne Armstrong appeared before another Justice.

She had to continue; moving on was her only option. She couldn't return to Dame Fouler's. She couldn't go to any of her family, the family she had had little to do with for years; they lived in any event in Stocksfield, close neighbours to many of those she had accused. The old man was gone from Crooked Oak, who knew where, and she was clearly no longer safe in Corbridge.

Exhausted as she was now, sick to the core of the whole business, she had to carry on, could not stay where she was, could not turn back.

She left early, trusting herself to the rickety bridge while the mist steamed off the water. Once across, she walked away from the Riding, Stocksfield, Birches Nooke. She took the road that followed the Tyne westward, keeping her head as low as possible, glancing furtively every time a person emerged from the grey haze of the breaking day. She walked fast until she reached Hexham, where she merged into the morning bustle of the cattle market on Priestpopple. The warm, rank fug of the animals enveloped her, almost masking the stink of the tanners that hung over the whole town. She took comfort in the invisibility the growing crowd of farmers and traders gave her, passing through the narrowing end of the market on to the long, handsome street running towards Carlisle.

Once out of Hexham, she took the road to Allendale. At Lowgate she branched off, seeing below her the broad sweep of the Tyne Valley. In the middle distance she could make out her destination, snuggled into a bend of the river. Five or six miles, she thought, glad of the long, steady descent down into the valley.

The road brought her quickly to Haydon Bridge. Most of the town lay on the north bank, but after crossing the river at Corbridge she had little appetite for another old, weak, wooden bridge, visibly shaking in the pull of the current.

As she approached the bridge, she saw that one of the few buildings on the south bank was a hotel, marked with the sign of an anchor. She was as likely, she thought, to find the information she needed here as anywhere in the town. A door at the rear opened on to the bridge-end. As she did not dare walk around to the entrance, let alone go inside, she waited beside it, watching the river as it churned between its banks and around the sandy islands it threw up in ever-changing patterns.

She huddled into herself, looking small and vulnerable, and soon enough one of the locals was moved to speak to her. I'd be careful standing there, he said; this hotel was once the courthouse, and they hanged people not far from where you're standing. His rough attempt at humour provoked more compassion in a woman standing not far off who'd been looking at her suspiciously. She walked up to Anne and asked her what she was doing waiting at the inn door.

Looking for the Justice, Anne replied, for there are people who trouble and torment me, and I wish to report them.

The woman's face relaxed. She understood such things, she said, for wasn't she in trouble herself with many who had begun tormenting her in this town. Her name was Anne too, Anne Parteis of the farm Hollisfield, a short way out of town, and it was there she was returning as quickly as she could. And all for wanting to do some good, she said, trying to help the wife of John Maughan, who lived in Chesterwood, a hamlet on the other side of town. Her name was Anne too – oh, we three Annes! she said, clapping her hands – and she had been sick for some time, and unable to do her work, so that when one day not long before Christmas she had gone in to visit, and not found her at her spinning which was left lying on the table, she had picked it up and done some of her work for her.

John Maughan had understood her kindness, and thanked her, and asked her to stay through the night to help, and this she had done, as a good Christian. He lived in a fine house, a bastle house, once well-fortified against the Scots, but part of a row of such houses. His wife, though, she was told, had complained about her doing what was her work, and hers alone to do, and her neighbours had begun to say that she would never get well if another woman was doing her work, and gaining her husband's admiration for doing that work. This had been going on for months and the situation was now so bad that she found it difficult to come into town, as she had told her husband. But Thomas was a hard man, not kind and understanding like John Maughan. He insisted she had to come in to get things they needed, as she had today, but she was leaving as quickly as she could, walking back to Holliesfield, and would not even stop for a glass on the way. But look at you, she said, so small and shivering, and she put her head in the door of the Anchor Hotel and asked the man who had joked about the hanging to bring out some small beer for the girl.

This he did, and told her when she asked about the Justice of the Peace, that that would be Mr Ridley of the Ridleys of Willimoteswick.

He could see the girl was looking up at him blankly, so the man told her that Justice John Ridley would be found at his hall, a mile or so further on. She was to take this road along the bank – to the west, said Anne Parteis of Hollisfield, adding a goodbye as well as she headed off to the east – and follow it until she came to Morralee Wood. She'd come to a river after that, the Alwent, which should be easy to ford. After that she should see the road leading to Ridley's grand home.

Anne barely paused to thank him before setting off, calling out a farewell to the diminishing figure of Anne Parteis. The road was well kept, as the road to a great hall should be, and in less than an hour she'd crossed the Alwent. Soon enough, misty in the steady drizzle that had begun falling, she saw a stern-looking fortified building, surely the castle, Willimoteswick Castle, balefully filling the route ahead.

She walked on, feeling less and less confident as the lane narrowed between heavy, low-slung stone walls. It carried her reluctantly but inexorably up to the maw of a great gatehouse that reared up before her, its sightless windows holding her in their empty glare. When she could tear her eyes away from this forbidding entrance she saw that what was left of the rest of the castle was run down. The massive wooden doors were partially open, and she stepped up cautiously. Peering into the stone throat of the deserted gatehouse, she could see a farm, a large wealthy farm.

A man appeared at the far end of the courtyard, shouting as he shooed her away. She found the courage to stand her ground until he could hear her, and told him that she was looking for the Justice, his worship Mr Ridley.

The man started laughing, and not a kind laugh, either: You're late, he said; a little. A mere hundred years or so, I'd say.

Did she really not know that the Ridley family had decamped from the castle a long time ago? They've moved to a fine hall they've built for themselves. Where was she from and what did she want? Hearing only that she'd been troubled and tormented and had come through Haydon Bridge looking for a Justice, he asked if she hadn't seen Ridley Hall.

She must have passed right by it to get to Willimoteswick, the man was saying, the thought provoking another outburst of ugly laughter. Then he told her to be off, and stood staring after her with his hands on his hips. He was still there when she dared look back just before she was swallowed up by the trees, thick and dark already this early in the year thanks to the constant rain.

She came back to a junction, and saw how she'd made a wrong choice earlier. Looking more carefully she could see that the wall of trees here was carefully cultivated, tall but younger than the woods, and designed to keep the world away from whatever lay behind it. From this angle she could see a heavy metal gate set in stone posts some yards down a carriageway. She took a few tentative steps and saw a substantial guardhouse set in the thick foliage under the trees.

She was surprised at how quickly, once she'd explained herself, she was escorted by a well-dressed man up the long, curving driveway. After some minutes they burst out of the trees into the spectacular presence of the hall itself. Anne had no words for its multiple floors and extensions, its filigree of castellations and elegant chimneys, knew only the awe that this was intended to provoke.

She stood as told outside a minor door into the grand edifice. She waited some time, but was finally ushered into a room that blinded her on all sides with its grandeur. She was only able to focus on the floor in front of the large and ornate table at which a man was seated, the backlit silhouette of his head and shoulders just within her peripheral vision. Somewhere beyond her focus was the scribe she'd glimpsed as she came in, seated at a far end of the table; she was aware too of the continued presence of the man who'd brought her in, standing behind her.

Mr Ridley, one of His Majesty's Justices of the Peace for the county of Northumberland, she was told during the course of being put upon oath. He must have then asked something like what was she doing here, what did she have to say, but before she knew it her story was pouring out.

May 12, 1673. Before Justice Ridley, Ridley Hall, Willimoteswick.

Telling how she had been sore troubled and tormented for months – she'd practised and memorised the phrases, to have them ready for this moment – and many times taken away by wicked people called witches (careful now, careful; she must learn to be very careful) up to their meetings at several places where there were several companies of them and in every company thirteen witches and every company had their devil.

She stopped, breathless. Was this too much by rote, she worried in the silence of the grand room, a heavy ticking coming from somewhere in the shadows criss-crossed by thick slants of light, late afternoon now hovering outside the large windows behind the Justice. Was she saying too much? Or was she leaving out the most convincing details?

And some of the witches she knows, and others she knows not, but she thinks she can know their faces when she sees them ...

Did she dare list any of the names she'd given in Morpeth and Newcastle? Would Justice Ridley know of her appearances before the Sessions?

Careful, guarded at first, she soon gathered that John Ridley had heard nothing of her previous accusations, knew nothing of what the other Justices had dismissed.

Sensing this, she relaxed, calling upon accusations she'd used before:

The last meeting she was all amongst the witches was upon the second day of May laste, at nighte, the witches carried her to Berwicke bridge end (as they called it), where she saw a greate number of them.

Back to Berwick-upon-Tweed, the site of her first allegations. She was testing her ground, wondering just how far back she could go, but even as she spoke she felt a slackening of the Justice's attention: too far, too far from home for John Ridley. In a swift, daring dash, she switched tack, pulling her accusations as close to the area for which he was Justice as she could, reaching for the most vivid splash of local colour she had to hand.

And amongste the reste she see one Anne Parteis, of Hollisfeild, and heard her –

Anne had to close her eyes now, her whole body rising up against the lie she told, a lie only for the greater truth, a lie to convince this Justice of the evil that circled in from that ring of villages drawing her in. Like that circle on the paper, lifting off the page to spin itself around her neck, tighter and tighter, until her breath, her voice, choked off in a dying fall.

– make her confession and declare to the devill that she did enter into the house of one John Maughan of the pareshe of Haydon in Northumberland. And she found the same John Maughan's wife's work lyinge upon the table –

'And her name was Anne,' she felt compelled to add, remembering as she did so the woman clapping her hands, singing out 'oh, we three Annes!'

And she tooke up the work to spinne of it, and by spineing of the work she had gotten the power of the said Anne –

'Anne Maughan, that Anne,'

– that she should never spinne more, and would still torment her till she had her life.

One of Ridley's men had been dispatched to find Anne Parteis, wife of Thomas Parteis of Hollisfield in the Parish of Hexham, directly after Anne had made her allegations. Anne herself was taken off to a small room, not exactly gaoled, but the door closed, a man posted outside.

It was early evening when the Justice took his place at the desk again. Both women were ushered in, Anne Armstrong told to repeat what she had said, every word checked carefully by the scribe against what he'd taken down earlier.

This she did, adding only, at the Justice's prompting,

And this woman standing before her at the time of giving this Information is the same woman she had confessed to the Devil she had bewitched Anne Maughan wife to John Maughan.

'This woman,' Anne Parteis: furious, fuming; betrayed, her kindliness abused. Forced to remain silent as the girl repeated the accusations, the utterly false accusations worked up from what other people said about her. Repeated them now in her presence, apparently immune to a glare that would have withered a lesser soul, a less desperate one at least.

John Ridley listened, glancing between the two women, his face impassive. As Anne fell silent he stared at his desktop for some time. Then he raised his head and told his men the women would be held overnight – separately would be best, he thought – and he would hear the accused tomorrow.

Anne Armstrong could still hear Anne Parteis's objections ringing out behind her as she was led back to the small room, the door closed with a hard slam, finally cutting off Anne Parteis's voice. A thin soup and some water were brought to her and she swallowed them down before falling into a heavy, haunted sleep. They danced in her head again, through the night, those figures swirling at the bridge-end. They drew their circles on the ground, invoked their devils, evil spilling from their gleaming, fat-smeared lips.

She was jolted awake by the sound of the door being pulled open, hustled outside before she was fully awake. She shivered in the dull light, her feet dampening in their clogs from the heavy dew as she waited with her guard outside the back door into the main house, watching a mist beginning to rise from the perfectly kept grass.

Anne Parteis was already standing before the desk, not turning to look at her as she was led in.

'Now, Anne Parteis, wife of Thomas Parteis of Hollisfield, have you ever made any contracts or covenants with the devil to kill, waste, or consume the body of any man, woman, or child?'

'No, Your Worship,' answered Anne Parteis, composed, dignified now.

'Or to do harm or damage to the goods or chattels of any person whatsoever?'

'No, Your Worship.'

'Or use any charming or medicining of any man's goods or chattels?'

'I deny all such accusations.'

'Well, let us see. What occurred when you were at the house of –' Justice Ridley consulted the papers on his desk '– John Maughan of Chesterwood? What were your actions there?'

'Shortly before Christmas last, Your Worship, I was at the house of John Maughan of Chesterwood, and stayed there all night. And I took up the work of John Maughan's wife and spun it for some hours, but I deny that I did John Maughan's wife any harm by any diabolical ways or means.'

'And were you at Berwick bridge-end upon the second day of May late at night either in form or spirit among the company there?'

'I deny it,' said Anne Parteis. 'I deny that I was ever there at Berwick.'

Even Anne Armstrong could see how convincing she was. It was all in the way she said it, a steady, quiet confidence that emanated from her. Standing there on that thick carpet, the richly hung walls about her, Anne could already feel the mud of a slippery path skidding under her feet, her clogs caked and clumsy with sludge, nettles stinging her exposed calves as her dress swung with each stride, brambles cutting into her bare arms and face, insects swarming up into her eyes and nostrils. For that is the path she would have to take now, from Birches Nooke to the Riding, where they would be waiting, all of them.

She was vaguely aware that the Justice asked neither herself nor the accused for their mark upon the papers on which their words were recorded, the woman flouncing free out of the room while she stood, dazed but not entirely surprised. The documents were simply shuffled into a meagre pile and swept up to be sent somewhere – where, she wondered, in her suspended state, where would they be kept? Where would her words finally come to rest? Then she too was hustled out, out of the room, out into the now glorious green of the gardens of Ridley Hall, back on to the carriageway. Anne Parteis had disappeared already, and the men on each side of her were speaking, to each other or to her she was not sure, did not care; she had nothing else to say.

They were waiting at the gates, a small gaggle of people she did not know. She pulled back in fear, but the men took her arms firmly and carried her forward, delivering her on to the road, that intersection of the ways to the hall, the ruin of Willimoteswick Castle, the town of Haydon Bridge.

Chapter 22

The pack of men and women gathered outside the entrance to Ridley Hall fell upon me as soon as I was pushed beyond the gates. To my bewilderment no one struck me. Instead they were talking, eager pleas blurring at first on my ears. And then I began to understand that they were appealing to me, asking me to come to their town, to seek out the witches there that were plaguing them. They had heard what I had told the Justice last night. One of their own worked in his hall, and knew that he would not believe me, would dismiss my accusations. But this is all the Justices do these days, they said. You knew better, they said. And we want you to point out the witches among us. So they went on as they hustled me down the road which tunnelled its way first through thick woods, and then began to rise up, and up, the valley of the Tyne behind me as we climbed. I was being taken south again, the direction in which the witches had so often ridden me, but I could not find it in myself to be concerned. Those pressed in about me supported me so fervently that I could lift my feet off the ground and float among them to their destination.

We rose higher and higher, the air clear and thin as we reached the highlands. What trees there were were bent, twisted, blown so fiercely by the wind that they were frozen into their blasted shapes even when the air hung, as it did now, dead still.

We came upon a small village – a tiny church thronged with graves that suggested the unseen houses and farms spread out about it. The falling away was rapid after this, as we approached a river. We forded without pausing, the splash of water not enough to wake me from the trance that had taken over once I left the gates of the hall. I had been thrown back into the world to fend for myself against the horrors that lurked about me night and day, the whispering death that assailed my ears, the shapes forming in the darkness to consume me.

Across the river we climbed again, my breath rasping in my throat, my chest rattling. Those about me did not give way for a moment, hugging me to their heaving hearts.

As I thought I could take no more, the track levelled slightly, weaved down through some rumpled fields and delivered the group with me at their centre into a market square lined with the usual shops and public houses.

The band around me pulled back for the first time since leaving Ridley Hall, leaving me stark, solitary, alone in a world all the stranger for its similarity to the everyday things that now seemed only a distant memory.

Another knot of people congregated around me, all talking to me at once in words I knew but could not understand. They parted, throwing out a woman from among them on to the ground before me. They looked at me expectantly.

Slowly a word took shape. Witch, I heard. A name too, hanging in the air, Isabell Johnson.

The woman lay prostrate. I looked at her, feeling nothing. Then Isabell Johnson began to draw herself up, first to her knees, and then to her full height. She was taller than me, clearly no girl but a woman, handsome in her way.

Here it was, the moment I had both dreamed of and feared from the first. These people would believe me. All around me, they were watching me, rapt, enthralled.

I concentrated on the woman before me, standing before me as I had stood before all those Justices. I did not look around, knew without having to see it the naked hunger in the shining eyes.

I may have denied them this, knowing nothing of the villagers here, caring less. Perhaps I should just give up now, take the money they would offer if I said what they wanted, accept their offer of more to discover more witches; I could give up the vain hope of ever being able to go home, just wander on from here to the next village, taking in farms and hamlets on the way, eventually entering villages, maybe the town of Newcastle itself, my reputation going before me, growing stronger with every gibbet raised in my trail.

If this was a surrender, a betrayal of all I had said, again and again, before those men who would not hear, I was now too tired to care.

I did not care either if they turned on me in turn, called me a witch for not being willing to expose this witch, knowing somewhere within myself that I and Isabell Johnson were sisters, sisters and strangers, that saving and condemning were much the same thing. That no one was innocent in any event.

It was too late. There was no way back. I'd known that since I left Corbridge yesterday morning. The waking dream gripped me, the endless frantic, sweating, panting run, trapped for ever on the path between Birches Nooke and the Riding House where my neighbours waited, waited with an end to all this, a searing, burning end.

There was no way forward, either. This was where it all ran out, here, here in this square in a village I did not know. This was the place where I would find I had no more words, nothing more to tell.

So yes, I may well have denied them. But then Isabell Johnson, standing straight and tall and looking directly at me, opened her mouth, and breathed upon me.

The square had fallen completely silent, but in that instant I realised that it had not been motionless. It was gathering itself – only a thought at first, then an intimation, and then a rush of air pouring over me like the world exhaling. A single breath straight from the mouth of God, the great sweep of a sigh washing over me, then passing on, leaving me in the choking stillness of its wake.

I could feel myself falling then, only the falling, no crash to the ground, no jarring of flesh and bone against the stones of the square, only the falling, slowly, endlessly.

And then the surfacing, fighting my way back to a consciousness I did not want, struggling only as one must for air after being suffocated, instinctively, involuntarily, obeying the body that would not be denied despite my having no wish to re-emerge in the world. I tried to fall back into the blackness even as the sharp light of the stone square reclaimed me, nearly weeping when those crowded in around me told me that I had fallen down as if suddenly in a sound sleep. Not as if dead, that they did not say, as if dead; as if in a sound sleep.

And when I was fully awake, and saw Isabell Johnson, still standing there before me, I looked at her and said, 'If there are any witches in England, Isabell Johnson is one.'

Chapter 23

May 14, 1673. Before Justice Whitfield, Esquire, of Whitfield.

'And further saith not.'

Further saith not, indeed. The last words ever recorded concerning Anne Armstrong. A requirement attributed to, but never spoken by her, the formal end to the deposition headed *The Information of Anne Armstrong spinster taken before me on the 14th day of May Anno Domino 1673.*

The 'me' in question was Utrick Whitfield, a Justice of the Peace for the County of Northumberland. The witch discovered, Anne was taken to Whitfield Hall, the villagers retracing their steps until they came to the small church surrounded by gravestones which they had passed through as they carried her along from Ridley Hall to Allendale. They then made their way to the house of the Justice, prodding and pushing Isabell Johnson before them, pulling Anne Armstrong along behind.

The customary formalities taken care of, Justice Whitfield's clerk or scribe took down:

That on Friday being the fourteenth of that instant May the above named Anne Armstrong being brought into Allandaile in the county aforesaid by the parishiners for the discovery of witches Isabell Johnson being under suspition was brought before her; and shee breathing uppon the said Anne immediately the aforesaid Anne Armstrong did fall downe in a sound and laid three quarters of an houre and after her recovery she said if there were any witches in England, Isabell Johnson was one and further saith not.

The usual *Capt & Jurat coram me* was appended, with Utrick Whitfield's clear and neat signature underneath.

Justice Whitfield then insisted on Anne confirming both who she was and what she had said with her mark.

What she inscribed was not the circle with its dot that she had laboured so hard at in the earlier depositions, or the scrawled lines approximating letters that she progressed to; on this, the last of her documented statements, she wrote for the first time a clear and perfectly formed single character, 'A'.

Seeing this, the clerk validating the proceedings did not write next to it, as he would have expected to do, 'Anne Armstrong's mark'; now, unprompted, unbidden, not knowing of the journey towards this single letter, he wrote, 'Signed, Anne Armstrong'.

And that was that. Signed.

No 'Examination of Isabell Johnson' is in the records, archived or transcribed. The deposition of 14 May 1673 is the very last bearing Anne Armstrong's name. After this, as far as the legal record is concerned, Anne Armstrong vanishes.

It is possible, given how much is missing in the records, that we have it all wrong. Who knows, perhaps some of those men and women accused of witchcraft by Anne Armstrong, approaching thirty by the end, were imprisoned, along with Michael Aynsley and his wife Margaret who we know – well, only from Anne's evidence – were 'prisoners in His Majesty's gaol'. Did Jane Makepeace, buried in Morpeth two weeks after the Sessions, die while waiting in the town's cramped, dark, fever-ridden, Wanny-flooded gaol to be called before the Summer Assizes? And were there others – Dorothy Green, say, if she was the Dorothy Green the people of Ebchester claim in the history of their village also died in prison – who lay in the stinking dungeons of the castle in the town, exposed to the elements and tormented by a gaoler who was a law unto himself for the three or four long months before the judges of the King's Bench came riding in, hearing through the thick walls the fanfare and celebrations that probably heralded their execution?

There are no records, though, of anyone connected with Anne Armstrong's accusations being executed. None, either, of the accused being acquitted. Can we assume then that Ralph Jenison's strategy, despite his failed effort at losing what Anne first came to tell him in the arcane processes of the legal system, managed to contain Anne Armstrong and her accusations after all, thereby saving his reputation and career as well as heading off another witch craze that could have equalled or exceeded the Great North East Witch Hunt of 1649–1650 in which thirty-nine were accused, of whom eighteen were hanged?

With the court records exhausted, the archives at an end, you could turn to the parish registers, any parish within the probable reach of a seventeenth-century Northumbrian serving girl, around fourteen years of age.

Of course, if Anne Armstrong had walked back to the Riding and, as local lore to this day would have it, hanged herself, a Christian burial and a place in the church records would have been forbidden. Hopefully there were no adherents of Minister Samuel Bird in the area, demanding that her body be dragged face down through the streets as a deterrent, a spectacle gruesome enough to dissuade others of a self-murdering mind; at best, Anne would have been buried at night, no mourners or clergy present, the location of her grave kept a secret.

There are hints in the registers that could suggest a happier end. A number of Anne Armstrongs are recorded as being buried at the time: is she perhaps the Anne Armstrong buried in Lanercost, Cumberland, in September 1674? If so, she would have married one Richard Bell before dying, possibly in childbirth. And if she'd headed east instead of west, she could be one of the three Anne Armstrongs buried in Newcastle, one in May 1686, another in July 1687, yet another April 1689. If she'd walked away to the south, she could be the Anne Armstrong buried in 1680 in the village of Hart, County Durham.

Even if she had been found hanging from a beam in the scullery of the Riding House, perhaps her father was able to call upon the good will of a churchman who, possibly familiar with *The Anatomy of Melancholy*, shared Burton's sympathy for those who took their own lives: 'Who knows how he may be tempted? It is his case; it may be thine. We should ought not to be so rash and rigorous in our censures as some are, charity will judge.' It would, however, have taken a generous soul indeed to extend such sympathy to a girl of the coarse and insensitive lower classes. Still, there is a record of one 'unknown female' buried on 9 December 1673 in Corbridge and, stripped of her name, Anne could have found a place in consecrated earth.

There's no way to settle this, of course, no conclusive evidence: as far as the records go, she may have achieved what you choose to believe she so earnestly wanted – an end to a story that, despite her youth (and we have been guessing her age throughout), had gone on too long.

To make this an end would be to ignore, however, another kind of record-keeping – those tales that live on after us, keep us alive no matter how fervently we may wish to fade away.

Anne Armstrong's story is still regularly retold in the area where she once lived. Reproduced in ever-shifting and often highly inaccurate versions, it is particularly associated with the Wellington Inn in Riding Mill. This was once the Riding House which features in much of Armstrong's evidence.

A warm, slightly sour smell greets you as you enter the inn, something that can't be got rid of even if 'the Wellie' is no longer the country pub it must once have been. Most of it is dedicated to dining now, part of the new fashion for gastro pubs, with only a small local clientele gathered at the bar for a convivial drink and the odd packet of crisps. Behind the counter, not a pickled egg in sight.

You will, however, be able to order a fairly good hand-drawn ale and take it to one of the tables tucked away in the haphazard layout of the low, heavy-beamed room – once clearly many rooms – making up the Wellington's bar area. Here a long history of alterations has taken on an architectural logic of its own, with odd nooks huddling between old doorways and narrow throughways. Identically framed photographs are mounted on the walls, local historical or architectural features captured in artful black and white.

Anne Armstrong is the subject of another decorative touch, a wall hanging done up, for some reason, in an approximation of the chalk board once favoured by pubs for announcing the specials of the day. A couple of feet across and set in an incongruous gilt-edged frame, a coat of arms and a fleur-de-lis tipped cross had been added to give a faux historical effect.

The Wellington History

The Wellington Inn was formerly known as Riding House and built as a residence for the Postmaster of Newcastle, Thomas Errington.

But in Errington's day the inn was not just a refuge for a swift drink at the end of the day. It became notorious as the claimed meeting place of covens of witches.

Anne Armstrong of Birches Nook, Stocksfield, was a self-appointed witchfinder. Anne announced her discovery of three local witches – her own neighbour Anne Foster of Stocksfield, Anne Dryden of Prudhoe and Lucy Thompson of Mickley.

She declared they had all danced with the Devil at Riding House and one night she found herself saddled and bridled by her neighbour Anne Foster, who then rode her cross-legged to the pack horse bridge. The witches of Riding were duly hauled up before the assizes at Morpeth in 1673.

In the witness box, Anne the witchfinder said that the witches turned into cats, horses, greyhounds and bees, rode on wooden dishes and spoons and danced with a man they called god while swinging on a rope from the ceiling.

She saw them feast on boiled capon, cheeses, butter, beef, plum broth, bottles of wine and 'humming ale' – which all sounds like a good advert for signing-up to the Riding coven!

Anne's eye-popping stories failed to swing the judges at Morpeth Quarter Sessions, who found her tales a bit too tall, and the case was thrown out.

The recorded punishment for snitching on a witch was to be stripped and drizzled all over with hot wax. When the wax hardened, the witches would re-melt it and pour it into the tell-tale's mouth, stopping her tongue for ever.

But Anne the witchfinder met a swifter doom. Soon after the trial she was found hanging from a beam in the Riding House scullery. Suicide ...

... or the coven's revenge?

So there it is, Anne's one public memorial, and the source of various suggestions regarding her end that are to be found nowhere in the documented facts, such as they are.

There are other contemporary references to her. 'Anne Armstrong's cringing little ghost,' you'll read time and again in the local Tynedale newspapers, in tourist material, walking guides, rail information, even in colourful adverts for residential properties in the area, 'was said for many years to haunt the scullery where her body was found.'

The scullery of the Riding House, later to become the Little Back Room, a snug in the Wellington Inn since converted into the pub's beer cellar – a place you'll be told, strictly off the record, that the staff hate going into, always avoid going into alone if they have to change a keg, clean the lines, get ice or fetch bottled drinks off the shelves.

The management may choose to play down, even suppress, spectral events associated with the Wellington, but they have been, after a fashion, documented. You will find evidence of a sort in the archives of the local newspaper, the *Hexham Courant*, held in the town's library. Should you wish to check these, you'll be directed to the numbered drawers of two unpropitious-looking grey steel cabinets where the microfilm is stored. Neither the newspaper nor the county archives have the resources to digitise back issues or put them online, so you'll have to put up with sitting in front of a metal box with a translucent screen, turning a knob on the side to advance through the pages displayed in its weak glow. No indexing or search functions of course, so eyestrain and headaches will no doubt follow on hours of scanning through the 800 or so reduced images of broadsheet newspaper on each roll of 35 mm film that you load.

If you're patient and committed enough, somewhere in the mid-1970s you'll find, emerging from the ghostly bi-tonal blur of the surrounding columns of newsprint, a headline that reads:

Smoke from the Witches' Revel.

Page 6 of the *Courant* from Wednesday 5 February 1975.

When the juke box started playing, Keith Rawson sat up and took notice.

It wasn't even playing his favourite tune. What was more, it was long after closing time at the Wellington Hotel, Riding Mill, and Keith, and his wife, Sue, were settling down for the night.

There was, they knew, no one else in the building.

By the time Keith had got up from his third-floor manager's flat to the Little Back Room in which the juke box stood, the record had finished and the machine was silent once more.

The same thing happened again – but at different times of the day.

'For no reason it just started playing a record. I slung it out at the finish. I don't think it had anything to do with spooks,' he said.

Now Keith is a level-headed type of licensed victualler, not prone to beliefs in the supernatural. But when smoke began pouring from the chimney of the Wellington he was not so sure.

It was a summer's night – and there was no fire in the grate.

Keith is one of the lengthy line of managers that have been in and out the Wellington in the past 14 years. All of them knew of the Riding Witches who danced with the devil and swung from a rope in what is now known as the Little Back Room.

They paid no heed to suggestions that modern-day eerie 'incidents' were in any way linked with the revels of 300 years ago. Yet strange, unexplained things continued to happen to managers – and still do today.

Keith is now landlord of the Coach and Horses in Gilesgate, Durham. Of his time at the Wellington, he said. 'I knew all about the place and the strangeness hits you as soon as you walk in.'

You'll turn the film back up, looking for the by-line below the subheading: 'The second part of the story of the strange happenings at the Riding Mill hotel, by Jack Watkins.'

You'll spin the knob, scanning the film as it whirs between its spools. The month before, in one of his regular Wednesday columns, Jack Watkins had written a feature on the Wellington, 'Pub Where the Devil Pulls a Pint,' retelling the story of Anne Armstrong and the witches, but adding some extra, pretty random, detail: where were these bits and pieces being raided from?

There is even a picture of the Little Back Room in its glory days as a snug. Photographic illustrations don't reproduce well in microform format and much of the nuance of the grey shade photograph, no doubt pretty poorly replicated in the newspaper in the first place, is lost with the inability of microfilm to capture halftones. Still, here it is, evidence that it existed, the Little Back Room that everyone hates, the one blocked off from the public now and used as a beer cellar, even though it's on ground level.

The next instalment of the strange happenings in the Wellington appears on 5 March, again on a Wednesday:

Another landlord who witnessed strange goings-on at the Wellington was Cyril Leeson, whose reign at the Wellington lasted only a year.

'The mystery of the beer pump which served up a half-a-pint without being touched was never satisfactorily explained to me,' he said. 'It was in the bar nearest the Little Back Room and was of the push button type. The pump used to pull half-a-pint morning, afternoon and night all on its own. We thought it was faulty electrics but nothing was ever traced.'

And Watkins is at it again on Wednesday 26 March 1975: another former Wellington manager was interviewed, 'Mrs Joey Cooper, now wife of the manager of the King's Arms, Morpeth.'

'I was glad to get out,' she said.

'I was there 15 months and in all that time I felt most uncomfortable in the place. There was an undercurrent of evil at the Wellington.

'It pervaded the place. I never went into the Little Back Room at night.

'Doors closed, or opened for no reason. Once, when I'd locked up for the night and was going upstairs to the flat I simply felt that I couldn't go on. Some force was stopping me.

'I tried to rationalise this by making an excuse to go downstairs again to check the lights. The next time I went up there was nothing. At the time you tend to think it's you, that you're being hypersensitive, but I'm not so sure,' she said.

Gordon and Edith Campbell, now at the Errington Inn, Whittonstall, were also glad to get away from the Wellington.

'There was something wrong about the place,' said Gordon: 'Shortly after moving in we were lying in bed when we heard somebody walking along the corridor outside the flat. We knew there was no one else in the place yet the footsteps went from one side of the building to the other.

'On another occasion I woke up early one morning and saw this clothed figure standing at the bedroom washbasin washing his hands. I slung my underpants at him but there was nothing there. You can laugh about it now but I wasn't then.'

'Weird incidents surrounding the "Wellie" are legion,' begins Watkin in the next in his series:

On Good Friday, 1966, Henry Sanders, another former manager now at The Crow and Gate, Bellingham, reported 'lying in bed listening to the sound of glasses tinkling as if a party were in full swing downstairs – except that on investigation there was no one there.'

This is the penultimate article. Jack Watkins turns up again, for the last time, on Wednesday 7 May 1975, when he rounds off his series by contacting the chain that owned the Wellington. The response from one of the marketing directors was brief and to the point:

'I don't think there is anything sinister about the number of managers that have been at The Wellington. We started a food operation there some years ago and managers were put in to get catering experience before being promoted and moved on.'

You can work on, skimming forwards through roll after roll of microfilm, but that will be the last of it. There is no more recent mention of the ghost at the pub. Either the management's policy on underplaying the haunting – the witches being enough of an old world touch for the high-end, gastro pub image they wished to promote under the corporate plan of the chain – or Anne's 'cringing little ghost' has, too, chosen to disappear.

It is easy enough on the basis of these sorts of tales to dismiss her, as it appears the courts did in her time. Easy to laugh off the ghost, almost as easy as explaining away the long-dead woman: a victim of the ignorance, superstition and barbarity of her age, you could say, her accusations motivated by jealousy, spite, a need for attention. Or she was affected by ergot poisoning after eating bread that had been made from rye grain infected by a fungus, or suffering from encephalitis, Lyme disease, post-traumatic stress, hysteria, psychosomatic disorders, psychological projection, teenage hormones, whatever other theory we can reduce her evidence, her visions, her terror, her actions to. So easy to let her voice be lost again. Harder to remember that she did, as far as we can tell from the evidence available, stand by her accusations despite their being continuously, persistently dismissed; stuck to her story even though, one way or another, she died for it.

Chapter 24

Anne turns from the huddle of Isabell Johnson, not bothering to wait this time to hear if she is believed. The parishioners of Allendale part before her as she passes calmly, steadily through their shouting and gesticulating, and steps outside. Then she walks away, the hubbub in Whitfield Hall falling further and further behind her.

She walks purposefully, cutting down towards the river. When she reaches the West Allen, Anne turns north, making her way back to the Tyne Valley. At some point she crosses the river and finds her way to the Allendale road. This she follows back towards Hexham, retracing in reverse the route she took only days before. A lifetime ago, it seems.

She manages the first section of the road through Hexham, but by the time Hencotes becomes Battle Hill, her exhaustion has caught up with her. She sinks to the ground with her back against the walls of the priory gardens. Ahead of her is the busy cattle market in Priestpopple, and beyond that the last four miles to Corbridge.

No one takes any notice of the small, grey, damp bundle of a girl. Still, it is not safe to linger. Stiff and sore, in the grip of the daze that has beset her ever since being dismissed from Ridley Hall, she draws herself up from the hard stone and sets off again.

Since leaving Whitfield – no, earlier than that, surely – she's had the impression that she is being watched. Walking away from the Justice's house, she assumed that this was the bailiff or one or more of the Allendale villagers who'd followed her out. She'd not turned to confirm this, only walked faster, expecting at any moment to hear a shout, feel someone running after her to pull her back, but no one came.

As she dropped down the hill and out of sight, the sensation persisted. She had stopped briefly, glanced back, looked around, but no one was pursuing her. No figure emerged out of the landscape to wonder at this girl striding steadily away from events already rippling out from Allendale and Whitfield, the news flying from mouth to mouth, growing, changing, taking on new forms as it rode the air on wave after wave of breath.

The countryside she walks through gives her no evidence of this, lets her pass unhindered, but watches, watches. She has not let herself think about this. Even now, standing up to walk on, the thought does not take hold, only the way ahead, not yet settled, still uncertain. It is her body that is carrying her onwards, her feet finding a way she has not mapped. The impression that she is being watched is merely another of the sensations she ignores.

She gives herself over again to the blind, steady strides that direct her. She takes no comfort in the warmth of the animals crammed into Priestpopple, the noise and the smell. She does not breathe more easily after emerging from the narrowing of the street where the market ends. On the open road out in the countryside again, she simply persists in putting one foot in front of the other on the road leading – well, not home. There is no longer a home to go to, not her father's house in Corbridge nor the small space with her bed at Dame Fouler's, even if she did walk the extra miles to Birches Nooke. There is hardly a neighbour or acquaintance she has not threatened or offended with her accusations. So now she simply walks, not noticing as the road leaves the banks of the Tyne or crosses the ford over Devil's Water, the small but treacherous river pouring down through the wet rocks below the brooding shape of Dilston Castle.

She does not look at the bridge crossing over the Tyne to Corbridge, walks straight on towards the Riding. Another two miles and the road begins its incline down Hollin Hill. Anne barely noticing the relief this gives to her legs – she's been walking for six or seven hours now – and hardly registers where she is. It is only when she reaches the low brow before the final descent towards Thomas Errington's house that she understands where she is going.

She stands for a moment at the top of the slope down towards the March Burn. Are Thomas Errington or his wife at the Riding House, their hideaway of a home? More often than not they are daring to stay again at their great house in Newcastle, comfortable in the grand thoroughfare of Westgate and warmed by their seventeen chimneys. Robert Johnson may well still be in the mill over the road, but he sleeps in the Riding House. Would he be there now?

She looks at the sky, not having noticed it at all since leaving Whitfield. It is an hour or more before sunset, dusk another hour after that and nightfall yet another. The grey weather will bring retiring time forward for those in the house, Mr Errington being strict about the use of candles.

Anne walks slowly down the curve of the hill, keeping an eye on the two buildings flanking the road. No one appears, and at the foot of the bank she turns in towards the burn. She makes her way carefully across the low flat meadow behind the mill to the thick growth edging the water. Here she settles herself into the foliage, watching the house.

She has a clear view, too, of the pack bridge with the trackway leading out of the clearing and up the bank. Her eyes flicker constantly between the Riding House and the bridge-end, and she finds herself drawn more and more towards watching the bridge as the darkness closes in. Exhaustion comes with full nightfall, and her back aches. She gives up on trying to tell when she is asleep, when awake, both conditions having the same nightmarish quality. With no sense of how much time has passed, she is jerked into full consciousness by the distinct sensation of some burden lifting itself off her back. Huddling deeper into the undergrowth, she peers through damp wood and leaf to see figures gathering at the bridge-end. Strangely familiar figures, the more familiar for her not being able to tell what they are: human, animal, they blur into one shape and then another. At times she thinks she can make out faces, faces that turn to where she is hiding, looking at her in the thickening blackness while their bodies swirl, their eyes a dull shine, their moistened mouths glistening, their sharp yellow teeth gleaming.

Is that Anne Forster, and Anne Dryden, and Lucy Thompson, among the ten or so others she cannot make out? And is that a tall black man, a condensation of the night rather than a corporeal being, floating above the steaming contours of a horse?

Involuntarily, she finds her lips opening, the air passing between them in barely more than a sighing sound, enough however to be called singing:

O, I shall go into a hare
With sorrow and sighing and mickle care,
And I shall go in the Devil's name
Aye, till I be fetchèd hame.

Beautiful, Anne, oh your singing is so beautiful. And then they spin away laughing, she not able to stop singing in her cracked, keening, broken voice.

Cunning and art she did not lack,

she sings,

But aye his whistle would fetch her back.

She lies there in the dark, her face pressing into the bitter damp green on the edge of the burn, the splashing of the water singing along with her, her mouth sore, so sore, and tears – yes, at last, tears – running down into the moist earth,

Yet I shall go into a mouse,

she sings on into the crook of her arm,

And haste me unto the miller's house,
There in his corn to have good game
Ere that I be fetchèd hame.

She shudders, lifts her head, looks around. Where were they, animal, bird, human – man and woman, hound and bitch, cat and mouse, hare and fox, the other shapes so terrible she dared not give a name to their form? Gone, the bridge-end empty and quiet.

And then she feels that stare again: eyes upon her, the eyes that followed her from Whitfield, no, earlier she was sure: Corbridge? Birches Nooke? Crooked Oak? Here in the Riding, when she was first ridden to the bridge-end? In the rooms were she gave evidence? She stands, raises herself off this bank as she must, because no matter how much she hides in the mud, in the dark, in these bushes, she is being watched, has been watched all along.

She is gibbering now, her jaw shaking, her whole body shuddering. She looks up, looks around before pulling herself upright, and it is then she sees a form delineated against those masses of darkness she knows are not there. She drops quickly again to the mud, but someone has seen her, and their eyes are fixed on her.

A lone figure, standing in the middle of the pack bridge, looking directly at her in the darkness where she is hidden. An outlandish figure, unfamiliar in some way she cannot tell in the thick night. But not from the Riding or any of the villages she knows. This she is sure of, even if she cannot say how; knows in the way one knows when one feels a prickling at the back of the neck, the hair moving on the scalp.

Where was it from, this figure that never danced or rode or flew, but stands more still than the devil seated on his Galloway, watching, waiting for her confession?

And then there is a voice right in her ear, sudden, sharp, in a stab of breath:

I'll crack thy bones in Our Protector's name;
Thus shalt thou be fetchèd hame.

She looks around wildly, seeing nothing. Looks back at the bridge, empty now, that figure gone.

Yes, walk away. You didn't think, did you, in your hubris and (despite yourself) enormous condescension, that you could save Anne Armstrong? Save her from the law, or history, or herself? And how? By stalking her through the records, calling her up from the traces others have made of her, reading between the lines, filling in the gaps, inserting your voice in the places where she is silent? Is this how you thought you could conjure her up?

She is here, now, way ahead of you, knowing the full cost of being found.

And how can your voice do anything but erase hers yet again, as you join the long succession of scribes and clerks and Justices who wrote her out of her own story.

A shimmer of light catches the corner of her eye, turns her head back towards the Riding House: there, silhouetted against the sheen of the whitewashed building glimmering in the dark, she sees them, all there where no one was before: Anne Forster of Stocksfield, Anne Dryden of Prudhoe, Lucy Thompson of Mickley, congregated at the door of the Riding House along with the rest, Margaret and Michael Aynsley of Riding, Mary and Anthony Hunter of Birkenside, Dorothy Green of Edmundbyers, Anne Usher of Fairlymay, Elizabeth Pickering of Whittingeslaw, Jane Makepeace of New Ridley, John and Anne Whitfield of Edmundbyers, Christopher and Alice Dixon of Muggleswick Park, Catherine Elliott of Ebchester, Elisabeth Atchinson of Ebchester, Isabel

Andrew of Crooked Oak, Isabell Thompson of Slaley, Thomasine Watson of Slaley, Anne Parteis of Hollisfield, Isabell Johnson of Allendale. Anne Baites from Morpeth too, and all the others from Morpeth and from Berwick and the other places where she has travelled in these last months, more places in England than she has ever seen before.

And Jane Baites of Corbridge, of course, in the front of this crowd, smiling, like all of them, she cat-like, purring.

Yes, she knows how this must end.

Slowly, with no volition of her own, she will drift towards the gathering. They will part as she approaches, opening up a passage towards the door. She will walk as slowly as she can, but all too soon she will feel herself disappearing into the cool gloom of the house.

The assembly will press in behind her, twittering and squeaking, writhing like a tumble of small animals. In the front room they will crowd in around her, propelling her towards the kitchen with soft, feathery touches. These become more insistent as she enters the kitchen, and when she reaches the door to the little room behind the kitchen, she will be prodded, pushed, bundled in.

She will stumble into the centre of the room. Those at the front of the press will draw back, blocking those behind them as they stretch and strain to see her. Anne stands as if before the Justices again, alone this time in the middle of the scullery. At Burtree House this is her world, the place where the messiest parts of keeping a home are done, the chopping, the hacking, the gutting and tearing, the peeling and sluicing, out of sight even of the kitchen. She is used to greasy dishes, caked and burned pots, dirty water, blood seeping into the wood of the table amid piles of offal and bone. The sight and smell of refuse would have been reassuring, but now her vague, wandering hands will feel nothing on the table. Her muddy feet in their rough clogs are out of place on a floor recently washed down. Instead of waste she will smell wax, though no candle burns in this little room at the very back of the house.

Names will be whispered, and Anne Forster, Anne Dryden and Lucy Thompson ushered through the pack at the door. They will close in around her and then lightly, gently even, their hands will begin to move, fluttering about her as they lift off her cap and her scarf. They will remove her coat and unpin her kerchief, and Anne will feel the chill on her neck and the cleft of her breast as they are exposed. She will not be able to help the tightening, the stiffening of her skin as her apron is removed. Her dress, a hand-down from her mistress, is low-cut and flimsy. When they, much taller than she, raise it over her head, a long shiver will run through her. She will look down as Lucy Thompson lifts her foot, slipping off one backless shoe with its wooden sole, and then the other, careful all the time for her balance. Then Lucy Thompson will peel off her stockings as Anne Dryden pulls up her shift in one long movement, and drops it on the floor among the poor muddle of her other clothes.

All three, more firmly now, will press Anne backwards, over the table. As they lift her legs and stretch her out full length she will smell the warmth of her body from its hurrying to get here, feel it rising from her and being drawn away into the dark corners of the scullery. The crowd at the door will begin to move into the room, Anne Baites leading the way. She will lean over her and raise her hand, holding it before her eyes as she brings together thumb and middle finger and then flicks Anne on the nose. 'Snitch,' she will say, 'can you hear it? Snitch –' she flicks again, '– snitch, a fillip on the nose.' And then once more, 'Snitch, a fillip on the nose for those who would intrude their noses into the business of others.'

Oh yes, Anne knows what will come next. The punishment for snitching in the Riding is set down, recorded. With the Psalmist she must learn to sing, 'I am poured out like water, and my bones are out of joint: my heart is like wax; it is melted in the midst of my bowels.'

They will tie her to the table now, a limb to each table leg. Then the large pot of wax will be lifted off the ingle, bubbling slowly. She will be able to smell that it is beeswax, which needs the most heat of any wax to melt. She will smell, too, the resin that has been mixed in with it, to help it run.

They will gather in closely around her now, and she will be able to feel their breath on her nakedness. Then, taking turns, they will dip a wooden ladle into the wax, scooping it up to drizzle it over her exposed body. The slight stings will increase, and then they will begin dripping larger drops on her. If she calls out or writhes, they will shush her, mothering her into silence and stillness. Slowly, steadily, they will continue, next beginning to pour the viscous, glutinous substance over her whole body. Hungry for her secrets, the wax will slide and run, sticky, inevitable, finding out her most hidden places, gathering in dips and folds. She will feel the increased intensity of the heat where the wax pools.

The tenderest parts will be saved for last, her nipples, her cunny, the soft expanse between breast and armpit. Mercifully, she will think, not yet knowing any better, her face will be kept free of the single, deep burn that her body will become.

And then they will watch as the wax cools and hardens, and once it has, they will light tapers and run their flames over her body, melting the wax again and catching it in the metal pot. Where it does not yield easily, they will pull it off, hair and pieces of skin coming away with it. They will spread each crease, explore every angle, find where the wax has buried itself and then probe it out, rolling pieces between their fingers before dropping them in the pot. She will be so sensitive that inside, in depths she never knew she had, again and again, her quaking body will erupt.

As her trunk and limbs emerge, glowing, throbbing, tender to the rough touch of the air, one of the women will place the pot back on the fire while the others will stare and sear her with their breathing. Bubbling again, the pot will be lifted off the ingle, the heat of it when they place it beside her feeling like the sun leaving its place in the midday sky and moving closer, ever closer. On each side of her, the women will press her jaw where it hinges with her skull, opening her mouth.

And as, finally, she tries to scream and scream, the pot will be lifted and the boiling wax will be poured, filling her mouth to overflowing, stopping her tongue forever.

That is the way it should end, must end.

So much still to say, and no voice with which to say it.

Knowing only that she had to tell it, if only to find out for herself if it were true.

Slowly she stands, feeling herself drawn away from the burn, across the meadow and past the mill towards the Riding House. The whole assembly gathered at its door parts as she approaches, opening up a path, the only path she is able to take, then presses in behind her, twittering and squeaking and writhing like a tumble of small animals.

As she steps inside, their shadowy presence disappears, melts away. The heavy door swings slowly into its frame behind her, sealing her into the darkness, alone. This is the place she has called up so many times for the Justices and clerks and scribes, a place that now feels impossibly strange, as if it is the first time she has ever been here.

Yet she knows that across the room there is another door, a door she must feel her way towards. Arms out ahead of her, fingers grasping at handfuls of the night, she is guided by their finding nothing until her hands touch wood.

This is the door to the scullery, a place where she might have some hope of being herself again, the old Anne Armstrong, fourteen years old, a servant girl among the dirty pots, the comfort of grease and offal and bone.

She tests her voice: I am poured out like water, she says – aloud? She tries again: My bones are out of joint, she says, my heart is melted in the midst of my bowels.

She hears her voice, hard, scratchy, dropping into the darkness.

She smells no wax. Yet she knows the way this has to end, the way it has to end if everything she has had to tell over these last months is true.

'Snitch, a fillip on the nose.' She waits for the flick of a finger, the slap of a hand, she waits for Anne Baites to speak, remind her that she, so often 'the informant' on document after document, must expect the punishment due to any informer.

She steps into the little back room, certain that this must be where they all are now. She senses all about her a crowd straining to get at her, but silent, horribly silent. She expects that at any moment the walls will dissolve into a swirl of wraithlike shapes that will pour in around her, squeaking, twittering, yowling, barking; shapes no longer chasing after each other but swarming in on her, just her, alone at the centre of a vortex of swiping claws and snapping teeth.

Now, though, nothing moves, there is no sound. She feels her way across the floor with her feet – her bare feet, slipped out of their clogs the better to feel her way, one foot sliding after the other in a blind shuffle. But the thing they find is not what she expects. A coil of rope, laid on the floor, the hemp rough against the soles of her feet.

She waits. Will Jane Baites pick up the rope, tie the hang knot while Anne Forster and Anne Dryden flutter about her, counting aloud the coils of the rope over itself, counting to thirteen before they snicker and hoot and clap, point to the beam above them, close in on her with the noose at the ready?

Is that then to be the end? Well, rather that, she thinks, rather that than telling a Justice again of the times she joined in with them, pulled on the rope that now would pull upon her, give her as she swung what it was she knew now she truly desired.

She waits, head lifted, neck exposed. She waits, certain at first, then uncertainly raising her chin, stretching her throat. She waits, the silence growing more terrible with every beat.

She waits until her body can wait no more, a tremble working through it that brings her to the floor in a long shudder, collapsing onto the cold flagstones. But not dead, not even as if dead, no, alive and awake enough to feel beneath her the coil of rope, still neatly arranged, waiting for her.

And knowing now the true horror: the horror that there is no one else. That they were not there outside the entrance to the Riding House, nor are they here in this room pressed into the walls, only just being held back by the power of something that does not want her to know, at the end, the truth of it.

She is crying now with her whole body, wet and shuddering, her hands shaking so much as to be almost useless.

Almost, but not too useless to make the knot, yes, to fold the rope and coil it around the fold, thirteen times – why shouldn't she? – and then passing the end of the rope through the bottom loop of the noose.

This work calms her, and she feels about in the dark until she finds the table, the table she remembers or dreams she remembers the three of them, Anne Forster, Anne Dryden, Lucy Thompson, pushing her backwards over; pushing her backwards gently, like lovers hovering over her nakedness.

But she is left alone now to tug its weight into the centre of the room as best she can judge it in the dark, to climb up upon the table and feel for a beam above, throwing the rope over the beam and making it fast, her mouth working soundlessly as she performs all this with a practised air that amazes her.

And as it is she that must put the noose over her own head she does so, unable not to think of other hands doing this with the bridle, its head and cheek pieces, the brow and nose bands, the bit rings and the bit itself, all scratching and digging and hurting and yet feeling now like caresses she must learn to do without.

She thinks too of Justice Jenison, the disbelief in his voice as he asked if she really believed that she became this animal, this horse, when the bridle was put upon her; and her answer, the only answer she had for him then and the only answer she has now for anyone who might ask her as she stands upright and alone upon that table, the noose settling around her neck, if she believed anything of what she had said, what they had put down on paper: 'When you are ridden you are a horse,' she had wanted to say to him then, and she says it now, out loud. And then she steps off the table, a small, grey shape of a girl falling, her last words rising up just before her jaw is jerked shut, her mouth slammed closed while all about her the figures peel away from the walls, flooding into the room dancing and saying sing for us, Anne, sing us the song, sing, sing.

END

Appendices

I. On Reflection: *The Ghosting of Anne Armstrong* as Practice Research

1. The Question

When I left the pack bridge on that autumn night in 20-,[1] I gave up. Not so much on Anne Armstrong as on myself. Staring down into the rush and swirl of the March Burn, I became certain that the water would give nothing away, nothing at least that I didn't know already – which was quite clearly not enough. I had long overrun the historical record, certainly ever since Anne walked away (did she?) after giving her last testimony at Whitfield Hall. All I had left to go on was anecdote, rumour and village lore, condemning her to one of two possible ends.

Writing these up, however, was still part of the job. The research and writing of *The Ghosting of Anne Armstrong* was made possible by the award of a UK Arts and Humanities Research Council Fellowship, 'Ghosting Through: Ficto-Critical Translation as a Means of Resisting the Appropriations of History and Place'. My application was for a practice-led project, in that the activity of creating would be the primary research method, with critical understanding being drawn from investigating that practice.[2] Having some understanding of Anne's death was necessary for the story, and an important part of the creative interventions that allowed me to engage with her as a historical subject and, where necessary, go beyond the archival evidence as such. As Mrs Kerr says in the fiction, 'You have to look at the evidence, and not all of it is in the records.'

At the time of my application, the AHRC had discontinued its 'practice-led and applied route'[3] (although I found its informing principles useful in preparing a bid in this area),[4] and practice-led applications, while still welcome, needed to demonstrate that as research projects they met the same criteria as set out in the AHRC's Definition of Research: 'Our primary concern is to ensure that the research we fund addresses clearly-articulated research questions, issues or problems, set in a clear context of other research in that area, and using appropriate research methods and/or approaches.'[5]

The broad research question driving the 'Ghosting Through' project is an ambitious one, but one I had already spent a number of years exploring; building upon my efforts in other critical and creative texts,[6] I wanted to engage in a new way with the fundamental problem of historicism: how does one represent the past without simply appropriating it to one's own position?

The specific context within which I engage with this question, as both a critic and a writer,[7] is that of historical fiction. I wanted to continue challenging the conventional definitions of the historical novel that still hold sway in the market place, the popular idea of a genre made up of invented stories set in the past, possibly based on real historical events but often with fictionalised protagonists and entirely fictional plots. In these, the past tends to be used simply as a distant, exotic location for superficially historicised figures very much of the present.

There is already, of course, a well-established tradition (one might say) of historical fiction that engages critically with the conventions of the genre: a list of some of those important to my work ranges from work in the UK by John Fowles, Hillary Mantel, W. G. Sebald, Ian McEwan, Iain Pears, Barry Unsworth, George Garrett, Rose Tremain, Jeanette Winterson and Graeme Macrae Burnet; in South Africa (my PhD and initial research into uses of history in fiction is South African in focus) J. M. Coetzee, André Brink, Zoe Wicomb, Marlene van Niekerk, Etienne van Heerden, Ivan Valdislavić, Elleke Boehmer and Anne Landsman; in the US (my MA is in American studies) William Faulkner, E. L. Doctorow, Don de Lillo and Michael Chabon; and among postcolonial writers (my theoretical paradigms as an academic are essentially postcolonial) Peter Carey, Salman Rushdie, Catherine Lim, Amitav Gosh, Michael Ondaatje and Margaret Atwood.

Works of historical fiction by all of these writers may more properly be designated as works of 'historiographical' fiction in that they display, even flaunt, their concern with how history is constructed rather than simply deployed in literary form.

My particular interest in this area, as indicated in my research question, is in challenging the tendency within history writing to become a means of controlling and domesticating the past in the process of 'knowing', 'understanding' and 'recreating' it. Engaging with the aims of 'neo-historical' fiction, which stress the relationship of historical fiction with the preoccupations of our current age, I ask if the real relevance of the past lies in finding the resistance it presents to directly instrumental uses of historical knowledge. I wanted, in 'Ghosting Through', to seek out in a context very different from my previous concentration on southern African fiction, the ways in which the radical 'otherness' of the past can challenge the present, and so provoke a deeper understanding of past, present and future. Seen in this light, historical fiction can be an important medium for invoking an awareness of just how strange and foreign history grasped in all its fullness is to our contemporary understanding.

With the 'research question' and 'context of other research in the area' more or less in hand, this left the matter of specifying 'the appropriate research methods and/or approaches' I would use. Included in my application to the AHRC was the question of whether the issues I was concerned with could be explored meaningfully in a practice-led creative project and, if so, what the appropriate fictional modes might be. The relevant methodology for addressing this research question within its proper context was a creative one, the writing of a work of fiction that stages or embodies its answer to the issues or problems identified.

The Ghosting of Anne Armstrong is then, a 'ficto-critical' combination of experimental fictional techniques, archival and field research, and investigations into relevant areas of cultural theory. Ultimately, though, these theoretical concerns are 'buried' within the narrative, the work being first and foremost literary.[8] As Simon During comments,

Poems and novels do not make arguments, nor do they develop and examine concepts logically, nor do they invent or deploy analytic methods, which are the kinds of things that most texts in the intellectual historian's archive do do. This remains true, however much literary texts may be shaped by the concepts around them, however much they may adhere to idea-driven programs (2018, 233).

Some of the 'idea-driven program' informing the work of fiction is to be considered here (more may be mapped in the Bibliography given below), but as both a research methodology and an 'answer' in itself to my research question, *The Ghosting of Anne Armstrong* was to be fundamentally novelistic in form. While the narrative may be considered the outcome of a ficto-critical writing process, I would argue against its being a work of 'fictocriticism' or, for that matter, 'creative non-fiction': it does indeed use creative strategies to engage with a nonfiction subject, but it does not use these fictional techniques primarily to nonfictional effect (see Brien, 2000). It was then as a novel that I would present my findings to the Research Council.

2. On Reflection

While there is increasing recognition across the academy that the processes of producing creative artefacts may serve as a vital contribution to knowledge, there is less agreement as to how creative practice can be defined as 'research'. One commonly agreed criterion, however, is the inclusion of some form of critical self-reflection as an integral part of the creative project.[9]

I have written several scholarly papers[10] reflecting on the writing of *The Ghosting of Anne Armstrong,* and in its own way, this addendum to the novel makes a similar self-reflective contribution. That said, the apparently easy distinction between the creative and reflective modes (separation from the creative work, where they are published, under what auspices, and so on) avoids a crucial issue foregrounded by practice research: that of voice.

This reflective essay opened with the confident use of the first person, the 'I' who initially walks away from Anne Armstrong when the historical record dries up. But that 'I' of course appears in the story, and is as such a part of the story: in appearing on stage as it were with Anne, 'he' (for it is a *he,* this character in the story, the tracker, the hunter, with his desire to own, possess, *know* his subject) blurs the line between narrative and reflection more so than the other reflective figures who form part of the story: the 'researcher' who appears intermittently, or more overtly, the user of the second person in Chapter 23 who breaks entirely with the fiction to address – who? Himself, the reader, a general unspecified audience?

These devices frame Anne's narrative within a self-reflective account of the process of recreating historical events. The intermittent metafictional interventions positioning the researcher/ writer and aspects of the research process within the story bring to the fore the often suppressed elements of subjectivity, reflexivity, and historicity in research. The inclusion of the researcher in the text as something of an impressionistic presence illustrates the ways in which the research process is always provisional, indeterminate and contestable.

Framing Anne's narrative within a variety of metafictional interventions is one thing, but carrying over a voice from within that frame into a formal self-reflection on the text is something to be handled more warily, primarily for the conventions associated with voice involved.

In reflecting on his or her work in some sort of accompanying or supplementary statement (be that an essay, academic paper, conference address, commentary, exegesis, or for that matter, an appendix to a creative work), a practitioner in the academy must adopt at least two distinct voices:[11] that of a creative practitioner working to varying degrees intuitively in or against the conventions of a particular creative mode, and that of a scholarly informed commentator reflecting through the academic conventions defining research – conventions that include, as noted above, a research question informing the project, a statement as to what is significant and innovative about the creative work, how it relates to an appropriate literature review, etc. The assumption that the academic mode gives some sort of transparent or unmediated access to whatever it is in the creative work that makes it an original contribution to knowledge is, however, problematic.

It is a commonplace today to acknowledge that the orthodox scholarly voice is not neutral, that the conventions of academic expression do not effectively erase the person or the positioning of the one using those conventions. And much the same applies to any comment by a writer about his or her creative work; at the very least we need to remember, as Philip Gross points out, 'Every writer's memoir is part of their *oeuvre* ... a calculated performance of their chosen sense of self' (2011, 52).

Introducing a fictionalised figure into what is in many ways an account of the actual writing and research process draws attention to the fact that the 'author' – both within and beyond the text in this case – is equally a construct, a device, a medium for a particular form of writing. Gross again: 'There is always an identity, a presence performed for others, at stake when a writer speaks about their work' (2011, 51).

As the novel progresses, the researcher/writer begins to infiltrate the text in various ways, his presence and mode of address finally quite close to that of an authorial figure ghosting through the work. I worked through a number of different stylistic choices in trying to find the most effective way of positioning this ficto-reflexive figure. Experiments of this sort are a given in the fiction-writing process, speaking to the overtly constructed nature of the writer as a device; as an element of the creative project focused upon the research informing that project, however, the question of the appropriate voice for the researcher/writer draws attention to the fact that in a discrete reflective commentary too, the 'author' is equally a device, a medium for a particular form of discourse.

Whether the 'self-reflection' accompanying a practice research project is in a supplementary form or integral to the creative work, practical decisions as to its rhetorical positioning will always apply. One of the advantages of embedding the reflective voice within the fiction is that it is then, explicitly or implicitly, presented not only as a discursive construct, but as an embodying of the way the creative work has come into being – a lived enactment, if you will, of the research process and the questions driving it.

3. Voice

The primary rationale behind researching and writing *The Ghosting of Anne Armstrong* was to access imaginatively the voice of a historical subject marginalised by her class, gender, age and location. It is this voice, currently lost to history now as it was to the courts at the time, that the novel tries to conjure up. It is important, however, to recognise the potentially romantic and even patronising impulse informing attempts at recovering 'lost' historical voices; as Anshuman A. Mondal asks, 'Is it acceptable to fill in the gaps through speculation – to insert one's own voice in place of the silence?' (2013, 424).

In response I can only argue that hearing Anne's voice in these pages must remain a figure (*of speech*, as one might say), a metaphorical auditory exercise. I have strictly avoided trying to achieve faux historical accuracy through some attempt at representing an 'authentic' voice; this could only be a clumsy pastiche, cobbled together from unreliable, mutated sources, the worst kind of imposition of historicity. We only have, after all, the depositions, filtered as they are through so many layers and angles that we catch at best a distant, distorted echo of the sound of Anne's speaking. I have therefore used instead multiple modes and a wide range of different fictional devices to *present*, as it were, Anne's voice, bringing it out in different ways at different points in the narrative, as appropriately as possible for the effect needed. This results in us hearing Anne from any number of perspectives, seeing her if not quite in a hall of discursive mirrors, then never through one, dominant, controlling image.

And at the very least, in following the depositions so closely, *The Ghosting of Anne Armstrong* brings her words literally again before us – words possibly distorted or betrayed every bit in the fiction as much as they were by the clerks who inscribed them into the depositions, but words which otherwise would have remained hidden in the archive, words[12] which are still all we have to go by.

And it is those words that count. What does come through in the records, and any attempt at reimagining those records, is Anne's refusal to be silenced. The growing sense of identity she finds in her appearances before the Justices (that mark, that signature) is expressed in a voice that is utterly compelling, if increasingly fraught. Her evident desperation demands that we do our best to hear her, and hear her as far as possible on her terms.

What ultimately happened to Anne is a mystery. But she leaves behind her the enigma of what could have driven her to risk her life to tell so strange a story.

4. Sources

The work of fiction developed out of the 'Ghosting Through' research project is driven by a close, imaginative reading of a complex seventeenth-century courtroom drama. As is recreated in the text, Anne Armstrong, a fourteen-year-old servant, appeared before a number of Justices of the Peace in Northumberland in 1673 to accuse various residents of several remote villages of holding witches' meetings.

Armstrong's initial accusations appear to have been dismissed at a Petty Session in Newcastle and the Morpeth Quarter Sessions, but she testifies again and again in other locations before other officials, expanding on her evidence and shaping it for each successive audience as she gathers what the courts expect of testimonies against witchcraft.

This 'highly personalised and extremely elaborate account of the witches' sabbat' (Sharpe 2013, 161) that she gives is unique in witchcraft historiography, given the apparent absence of a developed concept of the sabbat in England. This is more a feature of 'continental' witchcraft, and how a young, poor, illiterate woman from a remote part of the Tyne Valley came to have a relatively sophisticated grasp of practices and concepts that even learned English demonological works paid little attention to is one of the many puzzling features of Armstrong's accusations with which this work attempts to engage.

Anne's story begins, as she testifies before Ralph Jenison in February 1673, with her meeting 'an old man with ragged clothes' who foretells much of what is to come. Divination is in itself a defining feature of witchcraft, but he seems to be both alerting her to and warning her against the local witches. In perhaps the longest creative leap in the novel, I try to identify this figure and came upon a possible candidate in the historical records: Thomas Boyer, the 'intruder'. Boyer did in fact displace John Dury, rector of the parish of Edmundbyers and Muggleswick, during the period of the Commonwealth, and was in turn removed when Dury was reinstated with the Restoration. Recreated from a number of sources, but principally *The History and Antiquities of the County Palatine of Durham: Volume 2, Chester Ward*, the contest between these two allows me to make a case for someone with a vested interest in convincing Anne of the reality of witchcraft,[13] a reality that, once it has taken hold, leads her ever further into her own experience of witchcraft.

In this, and in the deepening of Anne's knowledge of demonological practice at the hands of Jane Baites of Corbridge, *The Ghosting of Anne Armstrong* could be said to fall back upon the standard licence historical fiction uses to deal with such lacunae. I would, however, argue that the fiction reconstructs the gaps in the evidence and problems of interpretation with a particular end in view.

While gaps in the record may be the very stuff of the historical imagination, what is known and can be established is often treated as an impediment to its creative reworking. Any number of writers of historical fiction tell us that research undertaken as part of the fiction-writing process should be put out of mind in order for it to become a vivid, convincing part of the fiction. Information, they say, is the enemy of story, and they specifically invoke forgetting research as a necessary part of the process of writing historical fiction.

'Historical' fiction, perhaps, but the historiographical mode with which I align myself is often one in which the research material – or, more properly, the practical and theoretical archival processes by which that material is accessed – is explicitly 'remembered': presented upfront, reflected upon, introduced reflexively in and as a part of the narrative structure. This is fiction in which the coming into being of history is a process that drives, even makes, the story itself.

Creative remembering of this sort is therefore important for this kind of practice research, a point worth stressing as research into the 'contextual' material one uses in one's creative practice is generally discounted in definitions of research in the practice mode.

The UK's Arts and Humanities Research Council, for example, explicitly dismisses 'content research' from the kind or work it would consider for the 'practice-led and applied route'. 'This route excludes research to provide content,' the now discontinued but still informative guidelines states. 'For example, if you wished to write a novel about refugees, the research questions should be about the process of writing the novel, not about the experience of the refugees.'

This attitude is echoed and repeated in any number of practice research guides and is good enough advice in itself, keeping as it does the creative process at the centre of practice-led research. It does, however, risk underplaying the ways in which 'content research' can act back upon the creative process. If one wishes to take seriously the ethics of otherness and recognise the materiality of the 'content' informing a creative project, this means not making that 'content' secondary to the 'process of writing the novel' – allowing it instead to resist, as best as one can, the imposition of narrative structure or 'theme', or any other fictional devices that tend towards, even encourage, the appropriation of a historical subject's story. Research here is meaningful to the degree that the 'background' material for the fiction forces writers to enter another place, one in which they are strangers, with their initial ideas and concerns tested against, altered by, and dis-located in the imaginative experience of that world of otherness.

It is for this reason that I chose to use constantly varying forms of focalisation, point of view, person, tense and pretty much every other fictionalising device in representing the depositions that make up the fundamental source material for *The Ghosting of Anne Armstrong*. The destabilising effect this has on any one controlling subjectivity, that of the writer as much as any of the characters, is a crucial part of the narrative, allowing no one discursive mode to dominate Anne's story. The overall intention of using these multiple modes is to work against the common explaining away of women like Anne Armstrong, allowing us to experience her evidence, her visions, her terror, her strange actions, from a number of shifting perspectives, each one bringing out different facets of her testimony. Self-interpretation and self-evaluation should not form part of the self-reflective component of practice research, and I must leave it to the reader to decide if this does help to draw us into the world which Anne's voice summons up, a world in which her accusations make terrifying sense.

5. Archive

The historian J. A. Sharpe considers Armstrong's depositions 'among the most remarkable texts in the history of English witchcraft' ([1996]1997, 279). For all their compelling detail, however, Armstrong's accounts fall short of full historical contextualisation. No records of a trial following on from her depositions have been found, which leaves us unsure as to whether her accusations ever came to trial, or whether they did and the trial records have been lost. As the researcher who becomes increasingly obsessed with Anne's story in the novel discovers, there is a gap in the *Vetera Indictamenta* (the Quarter Sessions records for Morpeth) between 1630 and 1680 and there is no relevant evidence in the Northern Circuit Indictment Files for 1673 and 1674 (TNA, ASSI 44/21, 22). As far as we know, then, none of those named by Anne as being present at the 'sabbat' or questioned in the wake of her statements were formally prosecuted. And as far as the historical record is concerned, after her vivid, powerful pre-trial statements before the Northumberland Justices, Anne Armstrong simply disappears.

Armstrong's case is thus a combination of specific detail and tantalising openness, both in terms of its truth status – as a case of witchcraft or, as we shall consider later, a ghost story – and its historical contextualisation. While this does make her story an attractive subject for a creative engagement with history, part of that creative engagement in *The Ghosting of Anne Armstrong* is to approach the archive as an actively produced site rather than a passive source of information.

The researcher's address to dust in one of the key passages set in The National Archives is a deliberate invocation of the geographer Hayden Lorimer's account of dust in what he calls a 'new wave of creative historical research'; 'dust,' he writes, 'is no longer to be regarded as simply a distraction from the work-at-hand, or at best an ambient side-effect to be enjoyed in wistful moments before attentions return to the proper matters of scholarship. Of late,' writes Lorimer, 'dust has become noteworthy in and of itself, substantially present, and symbolic of the greater ecologies, social conditions, transformative processes and physical textures of historical research practice.' Dust, he claims,

represents an invitation to speak up imaginatively for the archive's existence as site as much as source .... To do so, is to assert a version of archival hermeneutics extending beyond print culture and the written word, to include the context, encounters and events that constitute research practice. By implication, it is to seek out possible methodological means to evoke more of archival life: as a particular kind of place where complex subjectivities, and working relations, are created through the act of researching the past (2009, 249).

This is in line with Lorimer's '"more-than-representational"' methodology, a modification of non-representational theory which shares an interest in challenging researchers to go beyond representation and focus on 'embodied' experience. It is, says Lorimer, 'multifarious, open encounters in the realm of practice that matter most,' even when

the phenomena in question may seem remarkable only by their apparent insignificance. The focus falls on how life takes shape and gains expression in shared experiences, everyday routines, fleeting encounters, embodied movements, precognitive triggers, practical skills, affective intensities, enduring urges, unexceptional interactions and sensuous dispositions (2005, 84).

The researcher in the novel is all too conscious of the low hum in the Document Reading Room of The National Archives, the white noise informing the obligatory silence, the scuffling and page-turning, the pencil-scribbling, the suppressed coughs, the padded footfalls, the rub of clothing against desks and chairs. Such an alertness to the sensory experience of his research extends to his awareness of the three hundred and forty-odd years of grime that rubs against his fingertips as he handles the depositions, lets him feel that grime working its way into their lines and swirls, its slight moistness telling him someone else has also been handling these documents; it is the worn, uneven, ragged edges of the paper, not just the words inscribed on it, that draw him to the names scrawled in the margins (nowhere to be found, of course, in the easier textual neutrality of the printed transcriptions), lets him hear in the squeak of the quill, see in the inked names trailing behind the progress of its sharp-cut point, how much horror there can be in the act of writing.

Following developments in cultural and historical geography has been particularly useful as an informing theoretical dimension for these aspects of *The Ghosting of Anne Armstrong*, encouraging its coming to terms not only with the "'archive-as-source,'" but just as importantly, the "'archive-as-subject,'" in which 'the *practices* of collecting, classifying, ordering, display and reuse' (Ashmore et al. 2012, 82, my emphasis) become as important as what one wants to find in the historical record.

A practice-based approach to the archive seeks 'to bring the material and documentary properties of archives into play' (Dwyer and Davies 2010, 89), a process which will, for example, not only acknowledge but embrace, as Sarah Mills puts it, 'the fragmentary and disordered nature of archives' (2013, 5); Mills gives as an example Caitlin DeSilvey's work on a Montana homestead where she 'salvages meaning from incomplete sources': 'the salvage of memory makes do with materials at hand,' DeSilvey writes, 'and uses this material to craft stories about people and place that might otherwise go untold' (2007, 421–422).

Anne Armstrong's story has gone untold in anything other than minor references in historical texts precisely because of the fragmentary nature of the evidence available, and part of the crafting of her story involves the researcher in the text coming up against the problems this poses. He is reminded of them when he tracks down, in one of the 'working relations' Lorimer wants to see foregrounded in archival work, the other researcher whose presence he has sensed in the grime covering the documents he is consulting in The National Archives. This encounter brings to the fore not just the positive aspects of a deep commitment to tracking a subject through the archive, but its obsessiveness too, and its less savoury aspects of coveting, desiring, wanting, wanting to possess, and possess exclusively.

This darker side of archival exploration, this sense of ownership, personal ownership, is not exclusive to the mechanisms of research, but takes its more insidious form in the very mode with which it seeks to reconstruct the lost subject, the lost voice: the appropriating nature of the story one tries to tell.

In *Exploring Archives*, Verne Harris explicitly compares the work of archiving and interpreting archives with the writing of fiction, but he does so in a way that identifies the potentially distorting or erasing effect of the narrative mode on archival understanding. 'Archivists tell stories about stories, they tell stories with stories,' he writes, but it is for this reason that it is essential that the archivist acknowledges 'the reality of storytelling' in his or her work:

This might sound like a case of catch 22, an impassable pass, an aporia. We cannot construct meaning without narrative; the same narrative poses a threat to meaning construction. But it also sounds a call to creative engagement. To know always that we are telling a story – not detaining 'reality' or 'the truth' – and to make this plain to our readers and listeners. To trouble the narrative form, pushing its capacity to accommodate confusion, contradiction, shapelessness and partial or multiple closure. To remain open always to other tellings of the story, to retellings and to the holding of competing stories. As the receivers of story, the aporia calls us to be ever vigilant. To cherish what it gives us, but always to probe its telling, explore other tellings and other stories (2000, 87–88).

Archivists, then, in explicitly recognising their use of narratological devices, should use this recognition to ensure that the stories they construct around archival material do not occlude the latent potential of that material to generate other valid, even competing, stories, or erase the fundamental strangeness that confronts them. Like the more reflexive of novelists, they need to recognise the potential of experimental narrative forms to foreground and even destabilise the ways in which stories are constructed, the ways in which they are used both to give meaning and close down other possible meanings.

The Ghosting of Anne Armstrong is an attempt at bringing creative practice into play with other modes of inquiry concerned with 'archive' and 'field' as spaces of knowledge, and then using the cross-disciplinary site it creates to resist its own appropriations, to call up its subject – the story of that lost, fierce, defeated, determined, perhaps even manipulative, misleading, fourteen-year-old girl – as the open-ended, ongoing product of embodied acts, performances and practices.

Historians will no doubt continue to be drawn to Anne Armstrong's story, and it is not the aim of this project to contest the disciplinary specificity of such work. Rather, *The Ghosting of Anne Armstrong* develops complementary modes of understanding in which a detailed cultural analysis of the archival material is played off against contemporary research and retellings. This is not an exercise in corrective or counterfactual intervention, but an exploration of the complex ways in which a specific place constructs its past – or, in this case, is haunted by it.

6. Ghost

The official record, the archive as a formal, accredited, nationally and internationally sanctioned source is not, of course, the only site in which the construction of historical meaning takes place. Anne's story, as the novel presents it, is still regularly retold in the area where she once lived. As the researcher in the fiction discovers, it is reproduced in ever-shifting and often highly inaccurate versions in everything from tour guides and local newspaper articles to advertisements for residential properties in the area. And it is particularly associated with the building she is said to haunt, the Wellington Inn in Riding Mill. Once the home of Thomas Errington, Postmaster General of Newcastle under the Commonwealth, it was here that some of the more bizarre incidents Armstrong reported took place. When her accusations were dismissed, local lore has it that she was found hanged in its scullery, either a suicide or murdered by those she accused.

And it is the case that while the Wellington is willing to advertise its witches on its walls, to announce to its clientele that Anne Armstrong, the self-appointed witch finder, was found hanged from a beam in the scullery, it does seem reluctant to make any mention of a ghost story linked to her. There is certainly no mention of Anne's 'cringing little ghost' in the pub's promotional material, which does seem odd given that a 'Haunted Pub' is pretty much a national tautology.

It is difficult to explain the Wellington's coyness in this regard (although it does raise certain suspicions), but the newspaper articles the researcher discovers are based on actual accounts of hauntings at the pub.[14] And if the material one is investigating includes a ghost, one can't simply dismiss spectral evidence out of hand. Including the ghost in the narrative is, in its own way, another aspect of taking Anne Armstrong seriously on her own terms, as much as challenging research as a purely empirical practice.

It is for this reason that, structurally, the researcher and the ghost appear in very similar ways in relation to the main narrative, Anne's story. They both appear out of nowhere, then turn up again at irregular intervals – perhaps inexplicably at first for the reader, although certain conjunctions between the point we are at in the unfolding of the historical events in which Anne is caught up and the spectral appearances in the present of the village and the pub should begin to emerge as the narrative develops.

But the presence of the person tracking Anne down in the story also has something spectral about it. The usual authority accorded to the researcher discovering and giving meaning to his research material gives way to his taking shape in relation to that material; his repeated but largely uncontextualised appearances make him something of a revenant, a constantly returning presence as ghostly in its way as Anne's spectral intrusions into the present. The textual strategies deployed take their logic from this being ultimately a ghost story of some kind, with the haunting of the Wellington Inn serving as a centre of absence which holds at bay any authoritative control over the story or the forms in which it is told.

Placed in various conjunctions with the deposition records, the ghostly tales that circulate in the wake of the events connected with Anne lead us towards what John Wylie, in his study of W. G. Sebald, calls a 'spectral geography'. 'Spectrality' he defines, in terms that inform this project, as 'the unsettling of self, the haunting taking-place of place, the unhinging of past and present'; it is 'an irreducible condition that demands new, themselves haunted ways of writing about place, memory and self' (2007, 172–173).

Determining success on these terms brings us back to the crucial issue of voice: not the writerly voice in the fiction or the reflective one in this commentary, but the voice of Anne Armstrong and whether, in the end, it is she herself who has the last word.

II. Selected Key Depositions: 1673 Originals Followed by 1861 Transcriptions

The original depositions from 1673 are to be found in The National Archives, filed under ASSI 45/10/3/34–ASSI 45/10/55. For the interested reader, there is a good deal of information in the 'non-textual' aspects of this documentation: the legal rubric prefacing the evidence, the clerical shorthand, erasures and corrections, names listed in the margins for possible prosecution, the differing styles and even handwriting of the scribes taking down the evidence, the marks used as identification by those deposers who were illiterate (including in Anne's case a fascinating development of a simple circle in the earliest documents to increasingly accurate attempts at 'signing' with her initials). None of this is caught by the transcripts, and little of its significance has appeared in the few historical readings of Anne's case available thus far. Much of my representation of Anne's case is informed by clues found in this 'beyond the text' material.

The 1861 transcriptions of the depositions taken down from Anne's evidence, edited by James Raine and published in *Depositions in the Castle of York Relating to Offences Committed in the Northern Counties in the Seventeenth Century* (Surtees Society Volume XL, 1861), are of course much easier to read. That said, the transcriptions are sometimes inaccurate and incomplete. Where and why this is the case is at times significant to the telling of Anne's story (as indicated in the fiction), and reading the transcripts and the original documents in relation to their fictionalised recreation could be an informative exercise in demonstrating the nature of archival work and using it to inform a creative project, as well as giving some insight into the creative process and uses of history in fiction.

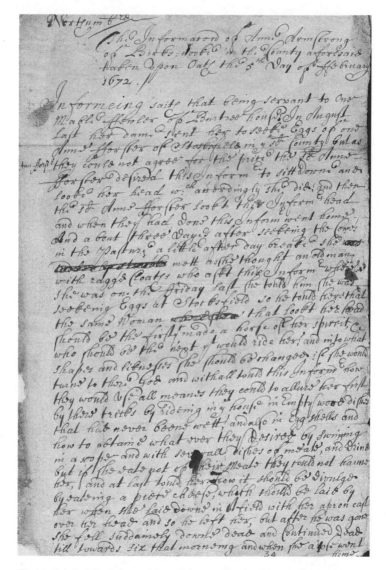

Figure 2   Original deposition: Feb. 5, 1672–3. Newcastle-on-Tyne, before Ralph Jenison. (The National Archives, ref. ASSI45/10/3/34)

but kept all these things secrett and since that time
for y[e] most parte every day and sometimes Two or three
times in the day she has taken of these fitts and
continued as aboved often from Evening till fore noon
and whilst she was lyeing in that condition which happened
on fright a little before Chrismas about y[e] change of the
Moone this Inform[er] see the s[ai]d Anne Forster come w[th]
a bridle and bridled her and ridd vpon this Inform[er]
crosse-legg'd til they came to rest of her Companie
at Riding Millne Bridgend where they vsually mett
and when she light of her back pulled the bridle of
this Inform[er] head now in the likenesse of a horse, but
when the bridle was taken she stood vp in her owne
shape; and then she see the s[ai]d Anne Forster Anne
Drydon of Prudhoe and Lucie: Thompson of Mirkley
and Jan[e]: Mould vnknowne to this Inform[er] and a long
blackman rideing on a Bay Gallaway as she thought
which they calld their protecto[r]
and when they had hand't their horses, they
stood all vpon a bare spott of ground and did
this Inform[er] sing whilst they danced in severall -
shapes first of a haire then in their owne
and then in a catt sometimes in a Mouse and in -
severall other shapes and when they had done, bridled
this Inform[er] and the rest of the horses and did ride home
with their protecto first. and for six or seaven nights
together they did the same and the last night this
Inform[er] was with them they mett all at a house
calld y[e] Ridinghouse where she saw Forster Drydon
and Thompson and y[e] rest and their protecto w[ch]
they call their God sitting at y[e] head of y[e] Table in
a gold chaire as she thought and a rope hanging over the roome w[ch] every one tou[ch]d three severall
times and what every one was desired was gott vpon the
Table of severall kind of meate and drinke and when
they had eaten she that was last drew the Table & kept
the reversions, this was their Custome w[ch] they vsually
did.

Figure 2 (continued)

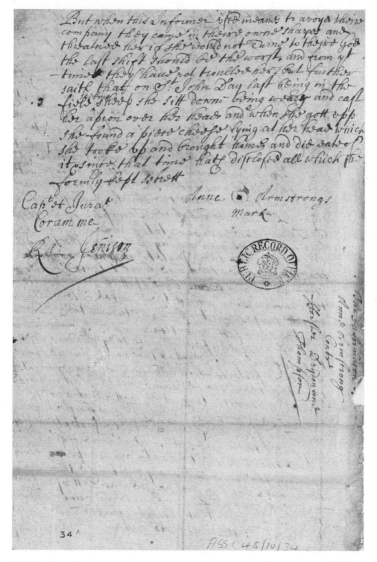

But when this Informer vsed meanes to avoyd theire
company they came in theire owne shapes and
threatned her if she would not turne to theire God
the last shift should be the worst and from yt
time they should not trouble her. but further
saith that on St John Day last being in the
fields sheep she sitt downe being weary and cast
her apron over her head and when she gott vpp
she found a peice cheese lying at her head which
she tooke vp and brought home and did eate of
itpsinto that time hath disclosed all which she
formely kept secrett

Capt et Jurat.   Anne   Armstrongs
Coram me   marke

Ri. Jenison

ASSI 45/10/34

Transcription: Feb. 5, 1672–3. Newcastle-on-Tyne. James Raine, ed. *Depositions in the Castle of York Relating to Offences Committed in the Northern Counties in the Seventeenth Century* (Surtees Society Volume XL, 1861): 192–193.

Feb. 5, 1672–3. Newcastle-on-Tyne, before Ralph Jenison. *Anne Armstrong, of Birks-nooke*, saith, that, being servant to one Mable Fouler, of Burtree house, in August last, her dame sent her to seeke eggs of one Anne Forster, of Stocksfield; but as they could not agree for the price, the said Anne desired her to sitt downe and looke her head, which, accordingly, she did. And then the said Anne lookt this informant's head. And, when they had done, she went home. And, about three dayes after, seekeing the cowes in the pasture, a little after day-breake, she mett, as she thought, an old man with ragg'd cloaths, who askt this informant where she was on the Friday last. She tould him she was seekeing eggs at Stocksfield. So he tould her that the same woman that lookt her head should be the first that made a horse of her spirrit, and who should be the next that would ride her; and into what shape and liknesses she should be changed, if she would turne to there God. And withall tould this informer how they would use all meanes they could to allure her: first, by there tricks, by rideing in the house in empty wood dishes that had never beene wett, and also in egg shells; and how to obtaine whatever they desired by swinging in a rope; and with severall dishes of meate and drinke. But, if she eate not of their meate, they could not harme her. And, at last, tould her how it should be divulgd by eateing a piece of cheese, which should be laid by her when she laie downe in a field with her apron cast over her head, and so left her. But after he was gone she fell suddainely downe dead and continued dead till towards six that morneing. And, when she arose, went home, but kept all these things secrett. And since that time, for the most parte every day, and sometimes two or three times in the day, she has taken of these fitts, and continued as dead often from evening till cockcrow. And whilst she was lying in that condition, which happend one night a little before Christmas, about the change of the moone, this informant see the said Anne Forster come with a bridle, and bridled her and ridd upon her crosse-leggd, till they came to (the) rest of her companions at Rideing millne bridg-end, where they usually mett. And when she light of her back, pulld the bridle of this informer's head, now in the likcnesse of a horse; but, when the bridle was taken of, she stood up in her owne shape, and then she see the said Anne Forster, Anne Dryden, of Prudhoe, and Luce Thompson, of Mickley, and tenne more unknowne to her, and a long black man rideing on a bay galloway, as she thought, which they calld there protector. And when they had hankt theire horses, they stood all upon a bare spott of ground, and bid this informer sing whilst they danced in severall shapes; first, of a haire, then in their owne, and then in a catt, sometimes in a mouse, and in severall other shapes. And when they had done, bridled this informer, and the rest of the horses, and rid home with their protector first. And for six or seaven nights together they did the same. And the last night this informer was with them they mett all at a house called the Rideinge house, where she saw Forster, Drydon, and Thompson, and the rest, and theire protector, which they call'd their god, sitting at the head of the table in a gold chaire, as she thought; and a rope hanging over the roome, which every one touch'd three several times, and what ever was desired was sett upon the table, of several kindes of meate and drinke; and when they had eaten, she that was last drew the table and kept the reversions. This was their custome which they usually did. But when this informer used meanes to avoyd theire company they came in theire owne shapes, and threatned her, if she would not turne to theire god, the last shift should be the worst. And from that time they have not troubled her. But further saith that, on St. John day last, being in the field, seeking sheep, she sitt downe, being weary, and cast her apron over her head. And when she gott upp she found a piece cheese lying at her head, which she tooke up and brought home, and did eate of it, and since that time hath disclosed all which she formerly kept secrett.

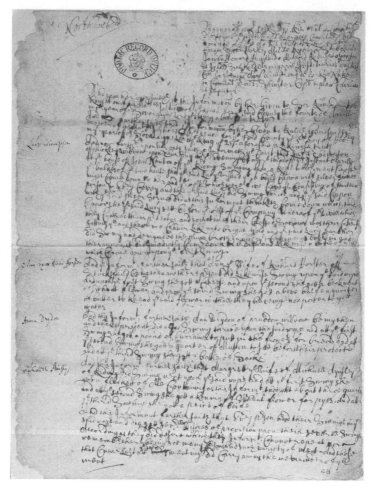

Figure 3 Original deposition: Apr. 9, 1673. At the Sessions at Morpeth before Sir Thomas Horsley and Sir Richard Stote, knights, James Howard, Humphrey Mitford, Ralph Jenison, and John Salkeld, Esqrs. (The National Archives, ref. ASSI45/10/3/48–51)

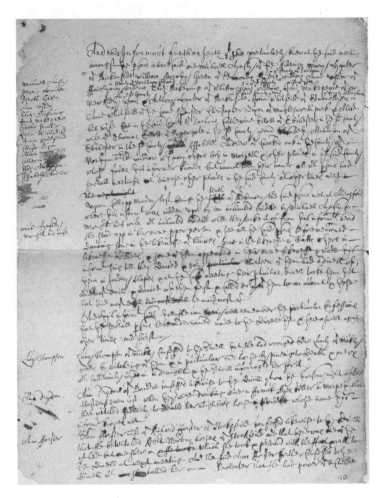

Figure 3 (continued)

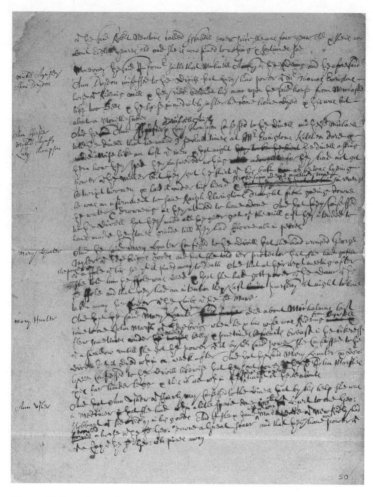

Figure 3 (continued)

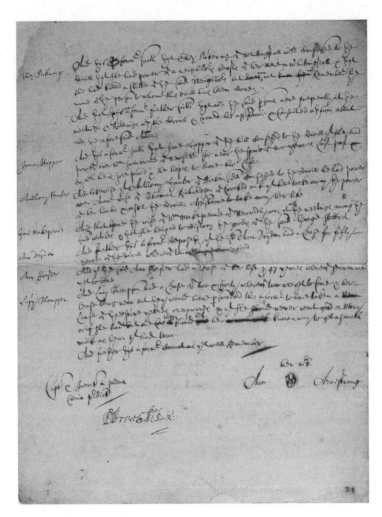

Figure 3 (continued)

Transcription: Apr. 9, 1673. At the Sessions at Morpeth. James Raine, ed. *Depositions in the Castle of York Relating to Offences Committed in the Northern Counties in the Seventeenth Century* (Surtees Society Volume XL, 1861): 193–197.

Apr. 9, 1673. At the Sessions at Morpeth before Sir Thomas Horsley and Sir Richard Stote, knights, James Howard, Humphrey Mitford, Ralph Jenison, and John Salkeld, Esqrs.

Anne Armstrong, of Birks-nuke, spinster, saith, that the information she hath already given is truth. She now further saith that Lucy Thompson of Mickley, widdow, upon Thursday in the evening, being the 3rd of Aprill, att the house of John Newton off the Riding, swinging upon a rope which went crosse the balkes, she, the said Lucy, wished that a boyl'd capon with silver scrues might come down to her and the rest, which were five coveys consisting of thirteen person in every covey; and that the said Lucy did swing thrice, and then the said capon with silver scrues did, as she thinketh, come downe, which capon the said Lucy sett before the rest off the company, whereof the divell, which they called their protector, and sometimes their blessed saviour, was their cheif, sitting in a chair like unto bright gold. And the said Lucy further did swing, and demanded the plum- broth which the capon was boy led in, and thereupon it did immediately come down in a dish, and likewise a botle of wine which came down upon the first swing.

She further saith that Ann, the wife of Richard Forster off Stocksfeild, did swing upon the rope, and, upon the first swing, she gott a cheese, and upon the second she gott a beakment of wheat flower, and upon the third swing she gott about halfe a quarter of butter to knead the said flower withall, they haveing noe power to gett water.

She further saith Ann Drydon, of Pruddow, widdow, did swing thrice; and, att the first swing, she gott a pound of curraines to putt in the flower for bread; and, att the second swing, she gott a quarter of mutton to sett before their protector; and, at the third swing, she got a bottle of sacke.

She further saith that Margrett the wife of Michaell Aynsley of Riding did swing, and she gott a flackett of ale containing, as she thought, about three quarts, a kening of wheat flower for pyes, and a peice of beife.

She further saith that every person had their swings in the said rope, and did gett severall dishes of provision upon their severall swings according as they did desire, which this informant cannot repeat or remember, there beinge soe many persons and such variety of meat; and those that came last att the said meeting did carry away the remainder of the meat.

And she further saith that she particularly knew at the said meeting one Michael Aynsly of the Rideing, Mary Hunter of Birkenside, widdow, Dorothy Green of Edmondsbyers in the county of Durham, widdow, Anne Usher of Fairlymay, widdow, Eliz. Pickering of Whittingeslaw, widdow, Jane wife of Wm. Makepeace of Kew Ridley, yeo., Anthony Hunter of Birkenside, yeo., John Whitfield of Edmondbyers, Anne Whitfeild of the same, spinster, Chr. Dixon of Muglesworth park and Alice his wife, Catherine Ellott of Ebchester, Elsabeth Atchinson of Eb- chester widdow, and Issabell Andrew of Crooked-oake widdow, with many others both in Morpeth and other places, whose faces this informer knowes, but cannot tell their names. All which persons had their severall meetings at diverse other places at other times: viz, upon Collupp Munday last, being the tenth of February, the said persons met at Allensford, where this informant was ridden upon by an inchanted bridle by Michael Aynsly and Margaret his wife. Which inchanted bridle, when they tooke it of from her head, she stood upp in her owne proper person, and see all the said persons beforemencioned danceing, some in the likenesse of haires, some in the likenesse of catts, others in likenesse of bees, and some in their owne likenesse, and made this informant sing till they danced, and every thirteen of them had a divell with them in sundry shapes. And at the said meeting their particular divell tooke them that did most evill, and danced with them first, and called every of them to an account, and those that did most evill he maid most of.

And this informant saith that she can very well remember the particular confessions that the severall persons hereunder named made to the divell then and there, as well as other times: and first

Lucy Thompson of Mickly confessed to the divell that she had wronged Edward Lumly, of Mickly, goods by witcheing them; and in particular one horse by pineing to death, and one ox which suddainly dyed in the draught, and the divell incouragcd her for it.

Ann Drydon of Pruddoe confessed to the divill that, on the Thursday night after Fasten's even last, when they were drinking wine in Franck Pye's celler in Morpeth, that shee witched suddenly to death her neighbor's horse in Pruddoe.

Anne wife of Richard Forster of Stocksfield confessed that she bewitched Robert Newton's horses of Stocksfeild, and that there was one of them that had but one shew on, which she took and presented with the foot and all to the divell at next meeting. And she further confessed to her protector that she had power of a childe of the said Robert Newton's called Issabell, ever since she was four yeare olde, and she is now about eight yeares old, and she is now pined to nothing, and continues soe.

Moreover Michaell Ainsly and Anne Drydon confessed to the divill that they had power of Mr. Thomas Errington's horse, of Rideing mill, and they ridd behinde his man upon the said horse from Newcastle like two bees, and the horse, immediately after he came home, dyed; and this was but about a moneth since.

The said Anne Forster, Michaell Ainsly, and Lucy Thompson confessed to the divill, and the said Michaell told the divell that he called 3 severall times at Mr. Errington's kitchen dore, and made a noise like an host of men. And that night, the divell asking them how they sped, they answered, nothing, for they had not got power of the miller, but they got the shirt of his bak, as he was lyeing betwixt women, and laid it under his head, and stroke him dead another time, in revenge he was an instrument to save Ralph Elrington's draught from goeing downe the water and drowneing, as they intended to have done. And that they confessed to the divell that they made all the geer goe of the mill, and that they intended to have made the stones all grinde till they had flowne all in peeces.

Mary Hunter confessed to the divill that she had wronged George Tayler of Edgebrigg's goods, and told her protector that she had gotten the power of a fole of his soe that it pined away to death. And she had gott power of the dam of the said fole, and that they had an intention, the last Thursday at night, to have taken away the power of the limbs of the said mare. About Michaelmas last she did come to one John Marsh, of Edgebrigg, when he and his wife was rideing from Bywell, and flew sometimes under his mare's belly and sometimes before its breast, in the likenesse of a swallow, untill she got the power of it, and it dyed within a week after. And she and Dorothy Green confessed to the divill that they got power of the said John Marshe's oxe's far hinder legg. And this is all within the space of a year halfe or thereabouts.

Ann Usher, of Fairly May, confessed to the divell that by his help she was a medciner, and that she had within a litle space done 100*l*. hurt to one George Stobbart, of New Ridly, in his goods. And that she and Jane Makepeace, of New Ridly, had trailed a horse of the said Geo. downe a great scarr, and that they have now power of a quye of the said Geo., which now pines away.

Elizabeth Pickering, of Whittingstall, widdow, confessed, that she had power of a neighbor's beasts of her owne in Whittingstall, and that she had killed a child of the said neighbors.

And this informer saith that all the said persons were frequently at the meetings and rideings with the divill, and craved his assistance, and consulted with him about all the aforesaid accions.

She further saith, that Jane Hopper of the Hill confessed to the divill that she had power over Wm. Swinburne, of Newfeild, for near the space of two yeares last past, by which he is sore pined, and she hopes to have his life. And Anthony Hunter, of Birkenside, confessed he had power over Anne, wife of Thomas Richardson, of Crooked oak; that he tooke away the power of her limbs, and askt the divill's assistance to take away her life. And Jane Makepeace was at all the meetings among the witches, and helped to destroy the goods of George Stobbart.

And this informer deposeth that Ann Drydon had a lease for fifty yeares of the divill, whereof ten ar expired. Ann Forster had a lease of her life for 47 yeares, whereof seaven are yet to come. Lucy Thompson had a lease of two and forty, whereof two are yet to come, and, her lease being near out, they would have perswaded this informer to have taken a lease of three score yeares or upwards, and that she should never want gold or mony, or, if she had but one cow, they should let her know a way to get as much milk as them that had tenn.

And further this informer cannot as yet well remember.

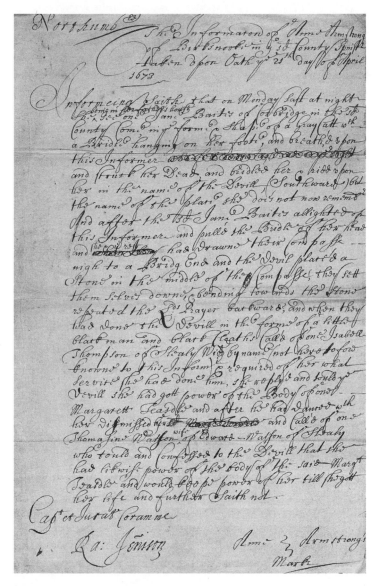

Figure 4 Original deposition: Apr. 21, 1673. Before Ralph Jenison. Esq. (The National Archives, ref. ASSI45/10/3/38)

Transcription: Apr. 21, 1673, Newcastle-on-Tyne. James Raine, ed. *Depositions in the Castle of York Relating to Offences Committed in the Northern Counties in the Seventeenth Century* (Surtees Society Volume XL, 1861): 197.

Apr. 21, 1673. The said witness, Anne Armstrong, deposes further, before Ralph Jenison, Esq.

On Monday last, at night, she, being in her father's house, see one Jane Baites, of Corbridge, come in the forme of a gray catt with a bridle hanging on her foote, and breath'd upon her and struck her dead, and bridled her, and rid upon her in the name of the devill, southward, but the name of the place she does not now remember. And after the said Jane allighted and pulld the bridle of her head, and she and the rest had drawne their compasse nigh to a bridg end, and the devil placed a stone in the middle of the compasse; they sett themselves downe, and bending towards the stone, repeated the Lord's prayer backwards. And, when they had done, the devill, in the forme of a little black man and black cloaths, calld of one Isabell Thompson, of Slealy, widdow, by name, and required of her what service she had done him. She replyd she had gott power of the body of one Margarett Teasdale. And after he had danced with her he dismissed her, and call'd of one Thomasine, wife of Edward Watson, of Slealy, who confessed to the devill that she had likwise power of the body of the said Margaret Teasdle, and would keepe power of her till she gott her life.

At severall of their meetings she has scene Michaell Aynsley and Margaret his wife, now prisoners in his Ma[ties] goale, and Jane Baites, of Corbridge, ride upon one James Anderson, of Corbridge, chapman, to their meetings, and hankt him to a stobb, whilst they were at their sports; and, when they had done, ridd upon him homeward.

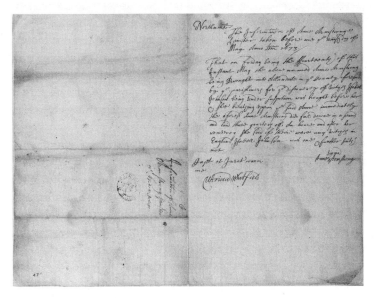

Figure 5   Original deposition: May 14, 1673. Before Justice Whitfield, Esquire, of Whitfield. (The National Archives, ref. ASSI45/10/3/47)

Transcription: May 14, 1673. Whitfield. James Raine, ed. *Depositions in the Castle of York Relating to Offences Committed in the Northern Counties in the Seventeenth Century* (Surtees Society Volume XL, 1861): 197.

May 14. She being brought into Allandaile by the parishiners, for the discovery of witches, Isabell Johnson, being under suspition, was brought before her; and shee breathing uppon the said Anne, immediately the said Anne did fall downe in a sound and laid three quarters of an houre: and after her recovery she said, if there were any witches in England, Isabell Johnson was one.

III. Author's Note

My thanks first and foremost to all at Goldsmiths Press: to Sarah Kember and Adrian Driscoll for seeing the possibilities in what Anne's story represents, and to Michelle Lo and Adriana Cloud as well as the rest of the team for doing so much to bring this into being.

Their vision for regenerating university press publishing is an inspiration in the current climate, and I can only hope that *The Ghosting of Anne Armstrong* will to some degree live up to their ideal of blurring 'the distinctions between practice and theory, experimentation and convention and the literary and artistic'.

Goldsmiths Press celebrates too the cross-disciplinary and the collaborative; without such a spirit, a novel of this sort could not have been assayed, let alone completed.

My thanks to historians James Sharpe and Peter Rushton, who were kind enough to engage with me by email about the oddities surrounding Anne Armstrong's appearance at the Morpeth Quarter Sessions. Echoes of these discussions may be heard in the novel, which also draws on Peter Rushton's 'Crazes and Quarrels: the Character of Witchcraft in the North East of England, 1649–80,' and 'Texts of Authority: Witchcraft Accusations and the Demonstration of Truth in Early Modern England,' as well as J. A. Sharpe's *Instruments of Darkness: Witchcraft in England, Crime in Early Modern England 1550–1750*, 'In Search of the English Sabbat: Popular Conceptions of Witches' Meetings,' *The Bewitching of Anne Gunter: A Horrible and True Story of Deception, Witchcraft, Murder, and the King of England*, and his public lecture, 'Thinking with Anne Armstrong: Witchcraft in the North East during the 17th century,' given at Newcastle University.

J. S. Cockburn's *A History of the English Assizes, 1558–1714* and 'The Northern Assize Circuit,' head a long list of works informing the sense of period and, in particular, the Early Modern legal environment.

Invaluable assistance in the reading of Anne Armstrong's original depositions was given by linguists Merja Kytö, Peter J. Grund and Terry Walker, both through their fine work, *Testifying to Language and Life in Early Modern England* and in email exchanges.

None of the authors of these or any of the other works acknowledged in the Bibliography are, of course, responsible for inaccuracies I may have introduced accidently or with fictionalising intent.

I would like to express my gratitude to the Arts and Humanities Research Council UK for the award of a practice-led research Fellowship in October 2012 (AH/J008192/1) that allowed me nine months in which to develop the initial ideas and draft of *Ghosting Through*.

My appreciation to Northumbria University for granting two further periods of research leave in which to work on this project.

My thanks to my colleagues in English and Creative Writing at Northumbria, especially Tony Williams, whose engagement with various versions of the texts emerging from the 'Ghosting Through' project has always been valuable and insightful.

And why else would one be a lecturer, tutor and supervisor if one could not thank one's students – undergraduate, Masters, PhD – for the lived relationship their work has with one's own.

My thanks to the staff of The National Archives for help in accessing Anne's depositions, and to Paul Johnson of the Image Library for being so proactive in having these reproduced for this book.

Thanks, too, to the staff at Hexham Library for access to the local newspaper archives, and to the Northumberland Archives for access to the original 1965 hand-made Riding Mill Women's Institute scrapbook and other assistance given throughout the research process; my thanks in particular to Archivists Michael Geary and Sarah Littlefear in the Search Room at Woodhorn for finding the 1672 map of Northumberland, and to Rob Fitzgerald for the reproduction.

Thanks must go to those whose land and property I have tramped over in the many miles covered (usually in the inspirational company of Cas, by my side in so much of the research for this book) on public rights of way, byways and bridleways trying to retrace Anne Armstrong's footsteps in a dense network of paths hundreds of years old. Nothing could have helped me more with writing my way into Northumberland than that secret and ancient history scored into hedgerows, woodlands, fields and pastures, ghosting as it does through the material realities of the modern landscape.

Thanks to Tony Liddell for the information and insights he shared on paranormal investigation by email and for material drawn from his book, *Otherworld North East: Ghosts and Hauntings Explored*, as well as the Otherworld North East website.

Thanks and apologies to my long-suffering neighbours; as presented in this work of fiction, 'Riding Mill' is no more Riding Mill than William Faulkner's Yoknapatawpha is Lafayette County. Along with the events and characters that have a basis in the historical record, the actual has been in every case, as Faulkner puts it of his own little postage stamp of native soil, sublimated into the apocryphal.

My thanks to Jenn Ashworth, who steered me initially towards Goldsmiths Press.

Special thanks go to Peter Blair for his friendship and support over many years, and bringing his creative and scholarly skills to bear on *The Ghosting of Anne Armstrong*.

My gratitude to Helena Nogueira, friend now for so many years, whose filmic belief in Anne has remained undiminished.

Before closing, I must as always acknowledge that I take my middle creative writing name from my mother: whatever it is in me that makes me write seems most closely aligned with Donnée Phelps Cawood, a loving, caring, endlessly giving parent and teacher, who died when I was ten years old. There is something unerringly fitting in the fact that the copy-editing of this manuscript was completed on what would have been her 100th birthday.

Finally, there would be no point to any of this if not for our daughters, Donnée, Maeve and Phoebe. This particular book has long been a part of your lives; thank you for bearing with this and feeding my imagination so richly with yours.

And gratitude beyond measure goes to Carole Green, co-researcher, first reader and the one who helped me carve out a story from a forest of words, images and ideas. Your editorial work, professional and incisive, has been vital to the shape this book has finally taken. Partner in all things in every sense of the word, a dedication has rarely been so appropriate or sincerely meant.

Michael Cawood Green, Riding Mill, 25 September 2018

Notes

1. We know the precise date that Anne would have returned to the Riding – if, that is, she did return – from her final deposition: 14 May 1673. The day in question for me was, as reported, sometime in the early autumn: historical and creative timelines rarely intersect. I should add too, that the whole story from first conception to completion, always had a kind of autumnal wash over it, perhaps because the year in question (as Justice Mitford experienced on his carriage ride to Morpeth) was constantly beset by bad weather; it is more likely however, that I consistently found this to be the mood and tone of Anne's story.

2. I prefer the term 'practice research', following Rachel Hann, who argues that this 'avoids the micro-politics of practice as/through/based/led' and 'focuses on the wider issues related to how researchers share, apply and critique knowledge borne of practice' (Hann 2015). The UK Arts and Humanities Research Council, however, tends to use the term 'practice-led' as a generic term for all forms of practice research; where appropriate I have followed this usage.

3. While the Research Grants Practice Led and Applied (RGPLA) scheme has been discontinued, the AHRC states that it 'remains dedicated to this area of research, and continue to provide many opportunities for researchers in the practice-led area through our established schemes.' http://www.ahrc. ac.uk/funding/opportunities/archived-opportunities/researchgrantsprac ticeledandapplied/.

4. 'Arts and Humanities Research Council: Support for Practice-led research through our Research Grants – practice-led and applied route (RGPLA)'. ND. As noted, this route has since been discontinued, but its key points on how research should relate to practice still hold. In summary:

    Practice must be an integral part of the whole research process, and not just an outcome; the project must involve a significant focus on your practice as distinct from history or theory; it must have a clear research focus (not be purely a development of your professional practice).

5. Arts and Humanities Research Council: Definition of Research. 2015. http://www.ahrc.ac.uk/funding/research/researchfundingguide/introduction/definitionofresearch/.

6. See, under the name Michael Green, *Novel Histories: Past, Present, and Future in South African Fiction* and a range of scholarly articles; under the

name Michael Cawood Green, see *For the Sake of Silence* and *Sinking: A Verse Novella*.

7 As indicated in the references to my own work, I have a distinct sense of different voices when writing in different modes, to the degree that I find it necessary to reflect this in differing, if overlapping, names. These varying identities are blurred in the self-commenting mode, a realm of shifting, intermingled creative and reflective allegiances.

8 One of the subsets to my research question asked if, as an outcome of practice research, I could create a work that was able to span both academic and popular communities of practice; could the novel find a place in the literary market, operating as both practice research and a compelling story that might appeal to a 'trade' audience of readers who enjoy literary thrillers and innovative forms of historical fiction.

9 As is stated in the now withdrawn (but as noted, still useful) guide to the practice-led and applied funding route, 'critical reflection' is a 'key criterion': 'We expect all of our research projects to have some form of documentation of the research process, which usually takes the form of textual analysis or explanation to support the research's position and to demonstrate critical reflection.'

10 'On Reflection: The Role, Mode, and Medium of the Reflective Component in Practice as Research,' a paper co-authored with Tony Williams, appears in *TEXT: Journal of Writing and Writing Courses* 22, April 2018, and a single-authored sequel to this focusing specifically on *The Ghosting of Anne Armstrong*, 'Reflection and Reflexivity: The Archive and the Creative Process,' appears in *TEXT: Journal of Writing and Writing Courses* 22 (2), November 2018. Aspects of research relevant to the novel will also appear in 'On Reflection: Coetzee, the Archive, and Practice Research' and the AHRC project featuring the work of award-holders, *Translating Cultures: a Glossary* (forthcoming).

11 Or, as reflected in my own experience of these modes, at least differing significantly, in the shifting, intermingled mode of self-reflective commentary.

12 'Words' here includes, as I've stressed in the fiction, all the 'non-textual' aspects of the documentation, the 'beyond the text' material in which the words are set, as referred to in the introduction to the appended Depositions and Transcriptions.

13 Intriguingly, this is from a Presbyterian point of view, as opposed to the usual assumption at the time that a belief in witchcraft was part of Catholic superstition. It was important, too, that I found someone in the records who could have influenced Anne from a Scottish perspective, as witchcraft

in Scotland had far closer ties to European ideas of witchcraft, including a detailed concept of the sabbat.

14 The feature articles written on the haunting of the Wellington by Trevor Atkinson in 1975 in *The Journal,* as well as the article by Angus McGill published in *The Evening Chronicle* in 1955, have been used in a modified way with the permission of NCJ Media.

Bibliography

Note: Along with the history and geography of the region in which the events covered in this story play out, all the material referred to in the texts listed finds its place in *The Ghosting of Anne Armstrong* somewhere between, in Nathaniel Hawthorne's famous distinction, the 'minute fidelity' of the novel and the 'certain latitude' of the romance.

Ashmore, P., R. Craggs and H. Neate. 2012. Working-with: talking and sorting in personal archives. *Journal of Historical Geography* 38: 81–89.

Atkinson, Trevor. 1975. Pub where the devil pulls a pint, *The Journal*, Tuesday, April 15.

———. 1975. Smoke from the witches' revels, *The Journal*, Wednesday, April 16.

Barry, Jonathan and Owen Davies, eds. 2007. *Palgrave Advances in Witchcraft Historiography*. Houndmills, New York: Palgrave Macmillan.

Bath, Jo and John Newton. 2006. 'Sensible Proof of Spirits': Ghost Belief during the Later Seventeenth Century, *Folklore* 117 (1) (April): 1–14.

Bell, Michael Mayerfeld. 1997. The Ghosts of Place. *Theory and Society* 26 (6) (December): 813–836.

Bostridge, Ian. 1997. *Witchcraft and Its Transformations, c.1650–c.1750*. Oxford: Clarendon Press.

Brien, Donna Lee. 2000. The Place Where the Real and the Imagined Coincides: An Introduction to Australian Creative Nonfiction, *Text* Special Issue Website Series No 1 (April). http://www.gu.edu.au/school/art/text/speciss (accessed 17 July 2018).

Briggs, Robin. 1996. 'Many reasons why': witchcraft and the problem of multiple explanation. In *Witchcraft in Early Modern Europe. Studies in Culture and Belief*, ed. Jonathan Barry, Marianne Hester and Gareth Roberts, 9–63. Cambridge: Cambridge University Press.

Brown, Bruce. 2015. Different Perspectives: Talk 3. The Future of Practice Research. Symposium held at Goldsmiths, University of London, hosted in partnership with HEFCE. Podcast. https://futurepracticeresearch.files.wordpress.com/2015/08/the-future-of-practice-research-bruce-brown-design-pro-vice-chancellor-for-research-university-of-brighton.wav (accessed 21 August 2017).

Clark, Stuart. 1997. *Thinking with Demons: The Idea of Witchcraft in Early Modern Europe*. Oxford: Clarendon Press.

———, ed. 2001. *Languages of Witchcraft – Narrative, Ideology and Meaning in Early Modern Culture*. New York: St. Martin's.

Cooke, Marion. 1987. *Riding Mill, a Village History*. Published privately.

Cockburn, J. S. 1968. The Northern Assize Circuit. *Northern History* 3 (1) (June): 118–130.

———. 1969. Seventeenth-Century Clerks of Assize – Some Anonymous Members of the Legal Profession. *The American Journal of Legal History* 13 (4) (October): 315–332.

———. 1972. *A History of the English Assizes, 1558–1714*. Cambridge: Cambridge University Press.

Dawson, Paul. 2008. Creative writing and postmodern interdisciplinarity. *Text* 12 (1) (April). http://www.textjournal.com.au/april08/dawson.htm (accessed 22 November 2017).

Denham, Michael Aislabie. 1895. *The Border Sketches of Folklore from the Denham Tracts*. London: David Nutt.

Derrida, Jacques. 1994. *Spectres of Marx*. London: Routledge.

DeSilvey, Caitlin. 2007. Salvage memory: constellating material histories on a hardscrablle homestead. *Cultural Geographies* 14: 401–424.

Did The Mill play witness to a coven's strange goings-on? (no by-line). 2009. *Hexham Courant,* Thursday, 19 February. http://www.hexham-courant.co.uk/business/Did-The-Mill-play-witness-to-a-covens-strange-goings-on-e3006e46-760f-4b37-a9cb-c0da89cafdf7-ds (accessed 19 February 2009).

During, Simon. 2018. Coetzee as Academic Novelist. In *The Intellectual Landscape in J. M. Coetzee*, ed. Tim Mehigan and Christian Moser, 233–254. Rochester, NY: Camden House.

Dwyer, Claire and Gail Davies. 2010. 'Qualitative methods III: animating archives, artful interventions and online environments.' *Progress in Human Geography* 34: 88–97.

Durham Federation of Women's Institutes (Author). 1992. *The Durham Village Book*, written by members of the Durham Federation of Women's Institutes. Newbury: Countryside Books.

Featherstonhaugh, Rev. Walker. 1900. VII. – Edmundbyers. In *Archaeologia Aeliana, Or, Miscellaneous Tracts Relating to Antiquity*. Published by The Society of Antiquaries of Newcastle-upon-Tyne. Volume XXII. London and Newcastle-upon-Tyne: Andrew Reid & Co.

Forster, Anne; Aynesley, Michael; Aynesley, Margaret; Makepeace, Jane; Dobson, Jane; Parteis, Ann; Thompson, Isabel; Johnson, Isabel; Baites, Jane; Watson, Thomasine; Marshall, Jane; et al. 1673. PRO, ASSI 45/10/3/34 – ASSI 45/10/55 (The National Archives, Kew, UK)

Gaskill, Malcolm. 1998. Reporting Murder: Fiction in the Archives in Early Modern England, *Social History*, 23 (1) (January): 1–30.

Gibson, Marion. 2006. *Witchcraft and Society in England and America, 1550–1750*. London: A&C Black.

Ginzburg, Carlo. 1991. *Ecstasies: Deciphering The Witches' Sabbath*. Translated by Raymond Rosenthal. Chicago: University of Chicago Press.

Gordon, Avery F. (1997) 2008. *Ghostly Matters: Haunting and the Sociological Imagination*. Minneapolis: University of Minnesota Press.

Gowing, Laura. 1996. *Domestic Dangers: Women, Words, and Sex in Early Modern London*. Oxford: Clarendon Press.

Graves, Robert. (1948) 2011. *The White Goddess: a Historical Grammar of Poetic Myth*. London: Faber & Faber; Main edition.

Green, Michael. 1997. *Novel Histories: Past, Present, and Future in South African Fiction*. Johannesburg: Witwatersrand University Press.

Green, Michael Cawood. 1997. *Sinking: A Verse Novella*. Johannesburg: Penguin.

———. 2008. *For the Sake of Silence*. Roggebaai: UMUZI (South African imprint of Random House (Pty) Ltd).

———. 2010. *For the Sake of Silence*. London: Quartet Books.

———. 2018. Reflection and Reflexivity: The Archive and The Creative Process. *Text* 22 (2) (November). http://www.textjournal.com.au/oct18/green.htm (accessed 5 November 2018).

Green, Michael Cawood and Tony Williams. 2018. On Reflection: The role, mode and medium of the reflective component in practice as research. *Text* 22 (1) (April). http://www.textjournal.com.au/april18/green_williams.htm (accessed 1 May 2018).

Gross, Philip. 2011. Then again what do I know: Reflections on reflection in creative writing. *Essays and Studies* 64: 49–70.

Hann, Rachel. 2015. Practice Matters: Arguments for a 'Second Wave' of Practice Research https://futurepracticeresearch.org/2015/07/28/practice-matters-arguments-for-a-second-wave-of-practice-research/ Posted on July 28, 2015 by goldprac. See also: Hann, Rachel. 2017. Second Wave Practice Research. http://prezi.com/i1u2ufdobaub/?utm_campaign=share&utm_medium=copy (accessed 27 September 2017).

Harris, Verne. 2000. *Exploring Archives: An Introduction to Archival Ideas and Practice in South Africa*. 2nd ed. Pretoria, National Archives of South Africa.

Handley, Sasha. 2005. Reclaiming Ghosts in 1690s England. In *Signs, Wonders, Miracles: Representations of Divine Power in the Life of the Church*, Studies in Church History 41, ed. J. Gregory and K. Cooper, 345–355. Woodbridge: Boydell & Brewer.

———. 2007. *Visions of an Unseen World: Ghost Beliefs and Ghost Stories in Eighteenth-Century England*. London: Pickering & Chatto.

Harper, Graeme, 2012. The Generations of Creative Writing Research. In *Research Methods in Creative Writing*, ed. Jeri Kroll and Graeme Harper, 133–154. Basingstoke: Palgrave Macmillan.

Hill, Bridget. 1996. *Servants: English Domestics in the Eighteenth Century*. Oxford: Clarendon Press.

'Historymick' (Michael Southwick). 2017. Riding Mill Witch-Hunt (Nz019614). *North-East History Tour: A Wander Round the Great North-East of England*. http://northeasthistorytour.blogspot.co.uk/2017/02/riding-mill-witch-hunt-nz019614.html (accessed 3 February 2018).

Hitchcock, Tim, Robert Shoemaker, Clive Emsley, Sharon Howard and Jamie McLaughlin, et al. 2012. *The Old Bailey Proceedings Online, 1674–1913*. http://www.oldbaileyonline.org version 7.0 (accessed 10 January 2009).

Hodgkin, Katharine. 2007. The Witch, the Puritan and the Prophet: Historical Novels and Seventeenth-Century History. In *Metafiction and Metahistory in Contemporary Women's Writing*, ed. A. Heilmann and M. Llewellyn, 15–29. London: Palgrave Macmillan.

Jefferies, Janis. 2012. Mangling Practices: Writing Reflections. *Journal of Writing in Creative Practice* 5 (1) (March): 73–84.

Kermode, Jenny and Garthine Walker, eds. 1994. *Women, Crime and the Courts in Early Modern England*. Chapel Hill: University of North Carolina Press.

Kors, Alan Charles and Edward Peters, eds. Revised by Edward Peters. 2001. *Witchcraft in Europe, 400–1700: A Documentary History*. Philadelphia: University of Pennsylvania Press.

Kussmaul, Ann. (1981) 2008. *Servants in Husbandry in Early Modern England*. Cambridge: Cambridge University Press.

Kytö, Merja, Peter J. Grund and Terry Walker. 2011. *Testifying to Language and Life in Early Modern England*. Amsterdam: John Benjamins Publishing Company.

Lamb, Mary Ellen and Karen Bamford. 2008. *Oral Traditions and Gender in Early Modern Literary Texts* (Women and Gender in the Early Modern World). Farnham: Ashgate.

Langbein, John H. 1978. The Criminal Trial before the Lawyers. *University of Chicago Law Review* 45 (2) (Winter): 263–269.

———. 1994. The Historical Origins of the Privilege Against Self-Incrimination at Common Law. *Faculty Scholarship Series* 550: 1047–1085.

L'Estrange Ewen, C. (1933) 2003. *Witchcraft and Demonism*. Edition reprint. Whitefish, MT: Kessinger Publishing.

Liddell, Tony. 2004. *Otherworld North East: Ghosts and Hauntings Explored*. Newcastle upon Tyne: Tyne Bridge Publishing.

Lorimer, Hayden. 2005. Cultural geography: the busyness of being 'more-than-representational'. *Progress in Human Geography* 29: 83–94.

———. 2009. Caught in the Nick of Time: Archives and Fieldwork. In *The SAGE Handbook of Qualitative Research in Human Geography*, ed. D. DeLyser, S. Aitken, M. A. Crang, S. Herbert and L. McDowell, 248–273. London: SAGE Publications.

Mantel, Hilary. 2004. Some girls want out. *London Review of Books* 26 (5) (March): 14–18.

Matless, David. 2008. A geography of ghosts: the spectral landscapes of Mary Butts. *Cultural Geographies* 15 (3) (July): 335–357.

McGill, Angus. 1955. Witches danced in the Kitchen: the Wellington at Riding Mill. *The Evening Chronicle*, Friday, 18 November.

Mills, Sarah. 2013. Cultural-historical geographies of the archive: fragments, objects and ghosts. *Geography Compass* 7 (10): 701–713.

Mondal, Anshuman A. 2013. 'Representing the very ethic he battled': secularism, Islam(ism) and self-transgression in *The Satanic Verses*. *Textual Practice* 27 (3) (May): 419–437.

Neasham, George. 1890. *North-Country Sketches: Notes, Essays and Reviews*. Durham: printed for the Author by Thos. Caldcleugh.

Northumberland – Paranormal Database Records. http://www.paranormaldatabase.com/northumberland/nhumdata.php?pageNum_paradata=3&totalRows_paradata=103 (accessed 15 December 2014).

Northumberland Quarter Sessions 1580–1971. Northumberland County Archives Service. http://discovery.nationalarchives.gov.uk/details/r/N13992687 (accessed 21 August 2014).

Otherworld North East. http://www.otherworldnortheast.org.uk/.

Poole, Robert, ed. 2002. *The Lancashire Witches: Histories and Stories*. Manchester: Manchester University Press.

Raine, James, ed. 1861. *Depositions in the Castle of York Relating to Offences Committed in the Northern Counties in the Seventeenth Century*, Surtees Society, Volume XL. Available online at: https://archive.org/details/depositionsfromc00grearich (accessed 25 September 2011).

Riding Mill Women's Institute (Author). 1965. Scrapbook prepared by the ladies of Riding Mill Women's Institute as part of their Golden Jubilee celebrations of 1965. Northumberland Archive, Woodhorn. Ref no: NRO 08547/1.

Ritson, Darren W. and Michael J. Hallowell. 2009. *Ghost Taverns of the North East*. Stroud: Amberley Publishing.

Rossiter, Anna. 2010. *Hexham in the Seventeenth Century: Economy, Society and Government in a Northern Market Town*. Hexham: Hexham Local History Society.

Rushton, Peter. 1983. Crazes and Quarrels: The Character of Witchcraft in the North East of England, 1649–80. *Durham County Local History Society Bulletin* 31: 2–40.

———. 2001. Texts of Authority: Witchcraft Accusations and the Demonstration of Truth in Early Modern England. In *Languages of Witchcraft: Narrative, Ideology and Meaning in Early Modern Culture*, ed. Stuart Clark, 21–39. Houndmills: Macmillan Press; New York: St. Martin's Press.

Scarre, Geoffrey and John Callow. 2001. *Witchcraft and Magic in Sixteenth- and Seventeenth-Century Europe*. 2nd ed. Basingstoke: Palgrave.

Sharpe, J. A. (1984) 1998. *Crime in Early Modern England 1550–1750*. 2nd ed. London: Longman.

———. (1996) 1997. *Instruments of Darkness: Witchcraft in England*. Philadelphia: University of Pennsylvania Press.

———. (1999) 2000. *The Bewitching of Anne Gunter: A Horrible and True Story of Deception, Witchcraft, Murder, and the King of England*. New York: Routledge.

———. 2013. In Search of the English Sabbat: Popular Conceptions of Witches' Meetings. *Journal of Early Modern Studies* 2 (March): 161–183.

———. 2015. Thinking with Anne Armstrong: Witchcraft in the North East during the 17th century. INSIGHTS Public Lectures, Newcastle University, 12th February. Recording of this lecture available at: https://campus.recap.ncl.ac.uk/Panopto/Pages/Embed.aspx?id=7260d846-c40a-4232-a432-5d7bbee157d4&v=1 (accessed 13 February 2015).

Spain, G. R. B. 1929. Witches of Riding Mill, 1673. *Cornhill Magazine* 66 (March): 308–315.

Styles, John. 1982. An eighteenth-century magistrate as detective: Samuel Lister of Little Horton. *The Bradford Antiquary* 2 (10) 1976–1982 (October): 98–117.

Summers, Montague. (1937) 2011. *A Popular History of Witchcraft*. Abingdon-on-Thames: Routledge Library Editions: Witchcraft.

330

Surtees, Robert, ed. 1820. *The History and Antiquities of the County Palatine of Durham: Volume 2, Chester Ward*. London: Nichols and Son.

Tapping, Colin. 2006. A real witches' brew at the Wellington. *Hexham Courant*, Friday, 15 December.

Trevor-Roper, Hugh. 1967. *The Crisis of the Seventeenth Century: Religion, the Reformation, and Social Change*. New York: Harper & Row.

Uszkalo, Kirsten C. 'Brimstone'. The Witches in Early Modern England Project. 2011. Assertions for a specific person (Anne Armstrong) http://witching.org/brimstone/detail.php?mode=assertions&pid=337 (accessed 13 September 2014).

Waite, Gary K. 2007. *Eradicating the Devil's Minions: Anabaptists and Witches in Reformation Europe, 1535–1600*. Toronto: University of Toronto Press.

Welford, Richard. 1895. *Men of Mark 'twixt Tyne and Tweed*. London and Newcastle-upon-Tyne: Walter Scott.

Welsch, J. T. 2015. 'Critical Approaches to Creative Writing': A Case Study. *Writing in Practice* Volume 1, National Association of Writers in Education, York. https://www.nawe.co.uk/DB/current-wip-edition-2/articles/critical-approaches-to-creative-writing-a-case-study.html (accessed 2 August 2015).

W.F.C. 1948. The Wellington Hotel, Riding Mill, and its History. Unpublished. Northumberland Archive, Woodhorn. Ref no: 3267/1.

Williams, Paul. 2013. Creative Praxis as a Form of Academic Discourse. *New Writing*, 10 (3) (January): 250–260.

Wylie, John. 2007. The Spectral Geographies of W. G. Sebald. *Cultural Geographies* 14 (2) (April): 171–188.

List of Figures

Figure 1: Map of Northumberland, 1672.

Figure 2: Original deposition: Feb. 5, 1672–3. Newcastle-on-Tyne, before Ralph Jenison. (The National Archives, ref. ASSI45/10/3/34)

Figure 3: Original deposition: Apr. 9, 1673. At the Sessions at Morpeth before Sir Thomas Horsley and Sir Richard Stote, knights, James Howard, Humphrey Mitford, Ralph Jenison, and John Salkeld, Esqrs. (The National Archives, ref. ASSI45/10/3/48–51)

Figure 4: Original deposition: Apr. 21, 1673. Before Ralph Jenison. Esq. (The National Archives, ref. ASSI45/10/3/38)

Figure 5: Original deposition: May 14, 1673. Before Justice Whitfield, Esquire, of Whitfield. (The National Archives, ref. ASSI45/10/3/47)

Index

337